BY SEA & SKY

THE SKY PIRATE CHRONICLES

ANTOINE BANDELE

Edited By
CALLAN BROWN

BANDELE
— BOOKS —

Interior Design: Vellum
Publisher: Bandele Books
Editors: Fiona McLaren, Callan Brown, Josiah Davis
Cover Artist: Sutthiwat Dekachamphu
Cartographer: Maria Gandolfo | RenflowerGrapx
Character Art: Sarayu Ruangvesh

ISBN: 978-1-951905-88-0

First Edition, Paperback | July 26, 2020

CONTENTS

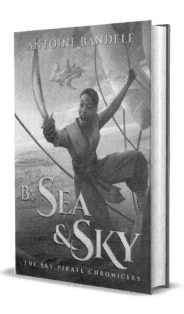

By Sea & Sky is the first book in
The Sky Pirate Chronicles, a pirate fantasy.
The series is inspired by the culture and mythos of
the West Indies, East Africa, and Arabia.

For suggested and chronological reading order visit:
antoinebandele.com/esowon-timeline

If you enjoy this story and are interested in the rest of its
world, you can join Antoine Bandele's e-mail alerts list.
He'll send you notifications for new book releases,
exclusive updates, and behind-the-page content.
antoinebandele.com/stay-in-touch

PRONUNCIATION GUIDE

Characters
Za·la - zä'la
Je·lani - je'la'nē
Fon - fän
Sho·ma·ri - shō'mä'rē
Man·tu - män'tü
Nu·bi·a - nü-bē-ə
Ka·rim El·Say·yed - kä'rēm el sā'yed
Is·sa A·kif - ə'sä ä'kēf
Ta·laat Sha·moun - ta'lät shä'mün
Has·san Ma·louf - häs'sän mä'lüf

Terms & Titles
A·zi·za - ä'zē'za
Cha·na - chä'na
Di·ka·la - dē'kä'la
Jan·bi·ya - jan'bē'ya
Kaf·fi·yeh - kaf'fē'yuh
Ki·ja·na - kē'jä'na
Pak·ka - pa'ka

Locations
Al A·nim - al ä'nēm
Al Ha·ru - al hä'rü
I·ba·bi Isles - ē'bä'bē ī(-ə)ls
Jul·ti·a - jü-əl'tē'a
Ki·do·go - kē'dō'gō
Kho·pesh - kō'pesh
Na·li·be·la - nä'lē'be'lä
Py·rus - pī'rəs

ESOWON
ESTERLANDS

The SAPPHIRE Isles

THE SAPPHIRE SEAS

SAPPHIRE SEAS

Port Zanzinala

Awassa

JULTIA

Nalibela

Dawaf

AL-ANIM

AL-ANIM
AND KIDOGO

Kidogo

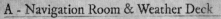

A - Navigation Room & Weather Deck
B - Captain's Quarters & Bridge
C - Crew Quarters & Engine Room
D - Supply, Brig, Communication, Infirmary, & Galley
E - Gunnery, Longboat Davits & Undercarriage

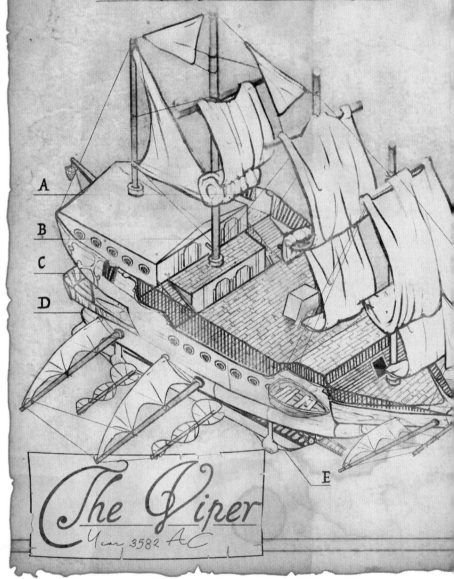

The Piper

Year 3582 AC

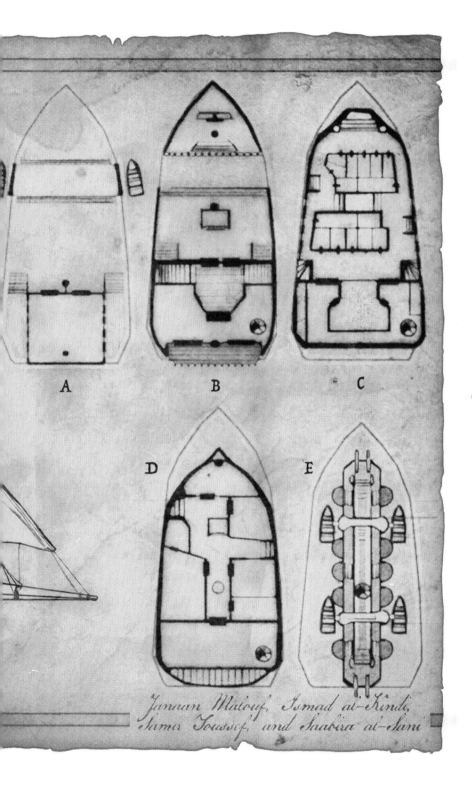

A

B

C

D

E

Jannan Malouf, Ismad al-Kindi,
Samir Youssef, and Saabira al-Sani

To my beta readers:

Carlos E. Garza Ayala,
Kristina Collins, Lukas Gibson, Seth Hansen,
Maria Ramos, and Andrea S.U.

Thank you for your time and dedication to this project.
The story wouldn't be what it is without you marvelous marauders.

———

To my editors:

Fiona for giving the characters heart,
Callan for bringing the prose and dialogue to life,
and Josiah for tying it all together.

I couldn't've picked a better
bunch of buccaneers.

You've heard the stories, I'm sure. That "sky pirate" everyone's talking about? She's no legend, no different from you and I.

Some say she led the great raid on the backs of kongamatos. *Some say she called forth the ancients from the depths of the Lost City itself.*

None of it's true. Not exactly.

Her tale is a thrilling one though. A journey that had her stumbling from the Sapphire Seas of Kidogo, to the ports of al-Anim. And now she sails the skies of Esowon.

Her story starts on the sixteenth day of the eleventh moon. Seeing as we're not going anywhere for a while, why don't I tell it to you?

CHAPTER 1
ZALA

COLD WIND WHIPPED ACROSS THE WHITE-CAPPED WAVES, wailing like a vengeful ghost. The rallying cry of the pirates who swung from precarious ropes below drowned its howl.

Neither could compete with the cannon blasts.

Zala went stiff with panic, her knees locked and elbows held tight. She always froze before the jump. It wasn't the fear of death that had the soles of her feet planted to the decking of the *Titan*'s crow's nest, it was fear that one of those death calls below might be that of her husband.

A break in the thick fog below, however, showed him engaged with a merchant, who clearly didn't know the first thing about swordplay. Zala forced a calming breath. There was nothing to fear. Jelani was doing his job; she needed to do hers. It was her fault they were out here in the first place.

It's only a merchant ship, she reminded herself.

The ominous fog, stretching wide atop the ocean's waves, didn't help her unease as it cloaked the enemy vessel in its thick, creeping cloud. If she jumped now, there'd be no telling where she'd land. Dew streamed across her skin, cold bumps rising from her bare arms and ankles.

Maybe there was a *little* fear of the jump after all.

No use standing here pondering the worst, Zala thought as she took another deep breath. Her palms clutched at the coarse rope.

"You're not gonna stand there all day, are you?" laughed a small, airy voice from within the fog. A figure appeared through the cloud, a lithe slip of a woman with the fluttering wings of a butterfly. Zala smiled at the woman—or rather, the *aziza*.

"I was waiting for you." Zala gave her a half smile.

Fon rolled her eyes. "You always say that."

"That's because I'm always waiting for you."

The two women could hardly have appeared more different. Fon barely came up to Zala's waist, with pointed ears and brown skin that seemed to glow, a tree-bough tattoo set across her forehead. Zala was short for a human woman, with skinny legs and small arms topped with subtle shoulders, all the complexion of an ebony shade. Where Fon's hair was long on one side and braided on the other, no strand out of place, Zala's was cut short, left alone to coil and tangle naturally atop her head.

"Jelani go ahead already?" Fon asked as she turned her head to the ocean mist.

Zala frowned. "On Kobi's orders, yes."

"Don't worry." Fon tapped Zala's knee with her four fingers. "Jelani's a big boy—he can take care of himself."

"So he keeps telling me," Zala said, unconvinced.

"Come on, pirate, let's get over there before those *dikala* find all the good loot." Fon put on a tough face, squinting one eye and pursing her lips like an angry scoundrel. Zala couldn't help but smile at the glint of humor in the aziza's

2

eye. The facade just didn't fit Fon. Even as she withdrew a long, sharp dagger, which looked more like a sword in her tiny hand, she could never quite shake off that disarming charm. After giving the *Titan*'s signature salute, Fon lifted from the deck and soared toward the enemy ship.

Zala's brows creased her forehead. Fon was right. The longer she waited, the less loot she'd have for herself. She couldn't afford second pickings. In an ideal world, the crew would divide the loot equally, but she knew the others were taking more than they should. It was just the way they did things around here.

Zala gathered her strength, readjusting the sword at her side and the bow on her back.

"Here we go again," she mumbled before she gripped the rope and leapt into the air.

Her heart raced as she swung the distance between the two ships, wind rushing past her ears like a kongamato's wail. But she knew as soon as she jumped that she had timed it wrong. She stuck out her feet to meet the enemy ship's platform, or a ratline, or even the side of the ship — she couldn't tell which. She found nothing but fog. Her leap hadn't been strong enough. She'd been too nervous that she might drop, too nervous about the clashing swords, too nervous that she might fail.

Look where that got you, Zala thought to herself angrily.

Berating herself with a string of swears picked up from moons spent at sea, she reoriented her body at the apex of her swing and cast her weight back toward her crow's nest where she caught her perch clumsily with one arm.

She took a moment to settle her shaken nerves and centered her mind back onto the task. She climbed back up onto the nest's ledge, and, with another deep breath, jumped once more into the unknown.

This time she listened for the sound of steel on steel, the grunts and groans of battle. When they sounded loudest beneath her, she let go of the rope, tensing her calves as she descended onto the ship. Her bare feet met damp wood with a dull thud as she landed.

Even on the ship's deck, the haze of the mist hid all. Zala could barely make out the glint of swords cutting their teeth against one another. The cry of the blades and their wielders raked against her senses.

The first figure—someone from her crew?—met an even murkier shape of a person she couldn't define at all. All around her, pirates and merchants alike traded insults between their clashes.

When would Kobi learn? Taking on ship after ship like this was taxing the crew to breaking point. They were getting sloppy, and it would only get worse.

In that moment, it didn't matter. All she needed to know right now was friend from foe.

The pirate crew wore no uniform clothing, but she could usually make out her fellow crew members by the way they fought. They had that sway about them—the "wine dance," as Jelani called it.

Zala withdrew her sword, identifying the figure ahead as an enemy, and struck the unsuspecting foe in the back. The figure let out a guttural yell—a man's yell—as he keeled over. The sound sent a shiver down Zala's spine. He was not her first, not by a long shot. But she'd never grow used to the sensation of steel cleaving through bone and sinew. Or rather, she hoped she wouldn't. It made her insides turn.

The man fell at her feet, his simple tunic soaked through with blood.

He was just a merchant... not a soldier at all.

Familiar guilt filled Zala's gut, but she shook herself of

its weight. If the man had made the choice to fight pirates, he'd brought his death upon himself. His captain should have surrendered when her's gave him the chance. It was unfortunate, but it wasn't her fault.

"Good looks, *chana*," the pirate Zala had saved said. The woman threw up a hand signal that Zala had come to learn meant "thanks" among pirates. "Didn't think you'd ever save *me*," she finished with a back-handed compliment.

Zala recognized the woman as Nabila, the gull-shifter Captain Kobi used as a scout. Zala tried her best to ignore the wound running down the pirate's arm. It looked deep. Instead of letting her eyes wander, Zala took her index finger and thumb and shaped them into a circle at her eye. If she recalled correctly, the gesture meant "I've got your back."

When the pirate smiled, Zala knew she'd gotten it right. She was barely acquainted to Nabila—though she barely knew or even recognized a lot of the crew. Kobi had taken on many new members over the past fortnight. Learning their names and faces rarely mattered when they were all dead by the week's end, whether by blade or by sea.

Zala turned to the merchant's corpse and passed her hands over his body in a quick search for loot. The merchant wore plain cream-colored robes, a checkered blue-and-white kaffiyeh atop his head, and a beard patched with white hair.

Only the Vaaji people sported those distinct headwraps with that leather cord around their heads. Zala should have known. The crew had been raiding the Vaaji for weeks. Ever since the empire had attacked their home isle of Kidogo, the crew had redoubled their efforts against Vaaji shipping while dismissing other more lucrative takes.

Zala's pat-down yielded nothing from the merchant,

save for the dagger he'd fought with and two silver coins. She pocketed the silver as nervous sweat beaded down her forehead and a tiny clink rang out from the too-light purse at her waist. That didn't matter though. She wasn't here for coin.

She needed a hatchway that led belowdecks. But each time she caught a glimpse of one leading to the ship's lower levels, a duel would block her way, fighters on both sides rushing to join bout after bout.

Her head swiveled like a hunting owl as she slipped each fight while she let her crew's wine dance flow around her. Like a vulture she scavenged the dead and dying. None had what she was looking for, and she only found bronze coins at best and soiled pants at worst. A good pirate would have helped her crewmates secure the deck *before* looting. Zala didn't consider herself a good pirate.

As she snagged a final coin purse from the latest corpse in her wake, the crash of a hatch door opening came at her side. Turning, she had to swallow a snort at the sight before her: A stout cook barreled his way out from belowdecks, stained apron and raised pan somewhat undercutting his otherwise admirable war cry. Waving his pan from left to right, the man charged the first pirate he saw.

He left the hatch behind him wide open.

It was bizarre, but Zala was never one to shunt her nose up at the rare turnings of good fortune. Cooks meant kitchens, and kitchens meant the supplies she needed.

She darted down to the lower deck, then closed the hatch after her. Her eyes adjusted from the stark white fog to the dingy shadows of a cramp storeroom. Wrinkling her nose at the stale air, her gaze fell on a set of overturned barrels. Zala sucked her teeth when she saw their contents: rich honey seeping onto the wooden floor. She quickly gathered as much as she could into a set of phials, but the sticky substance was incredibly difficult to bottle up.

A phial of honey, a bundle of dawa *root, a sliver of aloe, an eye of* tokoloshe, *and a stone's worth of* mazomba *scales*, she kept repeating to herself as she gathered up the last of the sweet nectar.

A sudden thump rumbled above Zala's head. Was it friend or foe who had fallen? She put the thought away as she searched through the rest of the stores. As much as the guilt still lingered at the back of her mind, she had to find the galley if she had any hope of scrounging up the ingredients Jelani desperately needed. Once she found what she was looking for, she would help the rest of them—not before. Besides, how difficult could defeating a group of merchants really be?

As she corked the last phial, another loud thud hit the floor behind her. Zala twisted on her heels with her sword drawn back, ready to stab. A soldier's body lay at her side with a dagger in her back. Zala relaxed her arm when she caught sight of Fon pulling her blade from the soldier's spine.

"Of course I find you in the kitchens," the aziza said with a chuckle.

Zala shook the mild shock from her face. "Aren't you aziza supposed to be light on your feet?"

"*Half*-aziza," Fon corrected her. Zala never knew how to address Fon, as she was both human and aziza—short for a standard human but tall among the diminutive forest creatures. "And we're not supposed to be on our feet at all—well, most of the time. You're thinking of *pakkami*."

"Right, right." Zala turned to the fallen soldier.

The soldier wore a green turban with red-padded armor and a tunic of white, the colors of the Vaaji Empire—the colors of their military. So, the merchants had guards after all.

"Your hands have been busy." Fon nodded to the sacks tied to Zala's belt, her already large eyes widening further. "Your mate already ran out of the stonesbane, then?"

Zala gave her a solemn nod, then sighed. "It's becoming more difficult to find what he needs on these ships."

"How long has it been since he's had some of his potion?"

"This morning," Zala said, still scanning the galley for more ingredients. "His stoneskin won't grow for a few more days, but I try to stay on top of it."

Fon pursed her lips. "What are you missing?"

"Just about everything. But it's usually easier to find aloe."

"I think I might have seen a barrel of some in the other storerooms." The aziza hooked a thumb over her shoulder.

Zala grinned, and then the pair of pirates wound their way through the narrow corridors, avoiding what soldiers they could; the ones they could not avoid were met with steel. Alone, Zala was no extraordinary swordswoman, but with Fon's flight distracting the soldiers, it made cutting down their enemies almost too easy, even in these tight spaces.

"Are none of these soldiers decent fighters?" Fon asked as Zala caught another in the back.

Zala looked down to her latest fallen foe. The Vaaji seemed young, no full beard, just the shadow of a mustache. With all these guards, the merchants were undoubtedly holding valuable cargo. It was a surprise the Vaaji were pressing so far into the Sapphire Seas at all. It shouldn't have been so shocking, however. Though the foreign nation had a reputation for being little more than poets and scholars, in recent moons they had seemed to reclaim their former titles as explorers and conquerors.

"Doesn't matter. I'll take easy targets any day." Zala patted the soldier down. "Means easier pickings."

Light feet led Zala and Fon toward the storeroom. As they continued they came across some of their own, a trio of mousey-looking men looting with eager hands.

Zala gestured their way. "You see, I'm not the only one plundering before the captain orders it."

She couldn't help pressing her nose into the other crew members' loot—despite their sour scowls—making sure none of them had taken any of the ingredients she required. Discipline was sorely lacking on the *Titan*.

Zala glanced through one of the viewports. The clouds were still thick, cloaking the waves on either side of the ship.

Well, at least Kobi is getting smarter. Using the fog for the raid is one of the better ideas he's had this week.

"How large is this ship, anyway?" Zala asked.

"Larger than Captain Kobi let on—wait just a minute, over there." Fon pointed forward, floating just above a set of crates. "The aloe should be just against that wall."

Zala started moving toward the crates, heart lifting, but she halted when two of the largest men she had seen that day stepped between her and her prize.

CHAPTER 2
ZALA

THE DIM LANTERNS ON THE WALLS THREW THE PAIR OF men into dark silhouettes that loomed over Zala. Yet neither made a move to attack. Were they so certain she was helpless? Did they think she'd simply flee? She didn't give a damn how big they were; if they got between her and Jelani's medicine, they'd be cut like all the rest.

Resolved, Zala angled her sword straight toward the dark figures, relaxing her muscles into a fight-ready stance. The larger of the shadows pushed the tip of her blade aside as though it were a feather. She swung the motion back and prepared to slash as the smaller figure dipped its head into the light. The sight of the pirate's face halted her strike.

The man was tall and lean with olive-toned skin, a close-cropped cut atop his head with a beard that had likely never known the rake of a comb.

Zala sighed with disgust. "I saw it first, Mantu. I have claim to that aloe."

"We come here before you, chana." The other man stomped into the light, his Southern Isle dialect thick in the air as he cleared his nose with a loud snort. For obvious reasons, everyone called him "Sniffs"—though only behind his back. Whenever in earshot, the crew referred to him by his given name Duma. He was one of the tallest—and largest—men Zala had ever known. Several rows of lumpy braids lined the top of his head like a weaverbird's nest. Though lit by the room's faint lanterns, the dark complexion of his face still left him in an eerie gloom.

"No, the rules are we divide our loot equally," Zala said as she tried to sidestep the pair of men. She wouldn't be able to strong-arm her way to the crates of aloe, but if she could distract them first, she might be able to swipe one and run. Fon wouldn't mind making a break for it, would she?

"Don't even front, chana. When the last time you split the loot equal?" Mantu asked, folding his arms. The man wasn't as wide as Sniffs, but he still towered over Zala. "You and the butterfly can find another barrel."

Zala bit her tongue. He wasn't exactly wrong where equal splitting was concerned.

"Fine, let's put it to a bet, then." Zala eyed the room, searching for a match she could win. If there was one thing she knew about Mantu, it was that he could never resist a good wager.

Sniffs wiped his nose with the back of his hand. "We claim this already."

"There's plenty of room in your pockets for a bet, I'm sure." Zala looked to Fon for support, but the aziza just crossed her arms and frowned.

Zala chewed on her lip as more thuds thundered above. Her crew would win soon. And the moment that happened, the looting would begin in full. She didn't have time for this. She needed that aloe now so she could continue her search.

Finding nothing in the room that favored her chances in

a wager, she directed her eyes to the bows at their backs. "Bet I can hit more Vaaji through the fog than you."

"I already killed two men," Mantu said, smirking. "Might be a challenge if them dikala could shoot back worth a damn."

"Let's see, then." Zala pulled her own bow from over her shoulder. "First to three claims the aloe."

"We was first, girl," Sniffs taunted. "We ain't need no bet, you feel me?"

Zala grinned. "Afraid I can outshoot you?"

Sniffs sucked his teeth, waving his meaty hand.

Damnit, he's not biting, she thought.

"I'll take on the pair of you," Zala added quickly. "If you two *together* can shoot down three of theirs before I do... we'll leave the crates to you."

Mantu stroked his unkempt beard in thought. Sniffs counted out "three" on his fingers as though he weren't sure of the sum.

"Three's an easy number to count, Sniffs—eh—Duma," Fon chided.

His eyes narrowed. "I weren't countin' nothin'. I was just... lookin' at my fingernails."

Zala cut into the exchange. There was no need to rile up Sniffs when he seemed to at least be humoring the terms of the bet. "So what will it be, Mantu?"

The pirate didn't budge and continued to caress his facial hair. Zala lifted a questioning eyebrow. On the *Titan*, he had always been prone to a sure gamble. *"An eff mi lose..."* She sweetened the deal with a little of Sniff's flavor of southern pirate-twang. *"Yuh kijana can tek mi share dat mi was gonna take."*

"Dat mi did ah gwine tek," Sniffs corrected her with a scoff. "Stick to the Mother Tongue, chana."

Zala felt an embarrassing heat rise up her ears. Mantu, however, didn't seem to notice—his eyes brightened as he ceased the stroking of his beard. "I'll take you on that. *When* we win, I get that fancy bow of yours. Always loved to hear them Ya-Seti strings sing."

Zala clutched at her prized possession instinctively. She could only name one other thing she owned that she truly cared for—the songstone Jelani had given her on the day they were married—but her bow was a close second. The Ya-Seti knew how to make them, recurved to perfection with a wooden finish fit for any self-respecting archer. With it, Zala was a more than decent bowwoman—without it, no better than a novice. She struggled with the thought of losing her prized weapon. Was the bet even worth it?

It's for Jelani, she reminded herself. *Anything's worth it.*

Besides, she would win.

"Agreed." She stuck out her hand. Mantu pursed his lips together as he looked at her palm, perhaps taken aback by her quick concession.

Sniffs tapped him on his shoulder. "Come on, Mantu. With the two of us that there is easy coin. Easy."

"All right, then... you got a bet." Mantu grabbed Zala's hand and shook it hard. Zala squeezed back, meeting his challenge without wincing. But when they broke away from the handshake, her hand was left red and throbbing.

Zala squatted down next to Fon as she shook life back into her fingertips. "Hey, I'm gonna need some help," she whispered, glancing across at Mantu and Sniff's retreating backs. "You can look through the fog, ya? Your kind can see the life energy of others—or something like that?"

"Or something like that..." Fon folded her arms again, her voice taking on a tone of indignation. "You could have asked me *before* you bet away your loot."

"We've got it, no problem!" Zala gave her a coy half-shrug. "There's no way I can lose with your help."

Fon sighed with a frown, and the branches of her tree-bough tattoo bristled under the crease of her forehead.

"You just have to let me know if I'm aiming the right way, okay?" Zala gave the aziza a reassuring smile—or at least she hoped it was reassuring—as she lifted herself back to her full height.

Fon let her head drop with resignation before she stamped one foot and slapped her hand to the side of her temple in an exaggerated salute. "Aye, aye, Cap'n." Her tone softened, but her eyes went downcast with disappointment. "Just don't make using me a habit."

Zala turned and followed Mantu and Sniffs down the narrow corridor. Brushing past them, she gave Mantu one last confident grin before saying, "Well, ladies first, ya?"

"Go ahead." He gestured to the ladder to the right, which led to the upper-deck hatch. "We'll take the left."

Zala climbed the ladder and pushed the underside of the hatch up slowly, using the small slit to scan what was above.

The thick cloud endured, billowing atop the deck like the cloak hem of some giant specter. The clashing of swords between the pirates and Vaaji remained. Every few moments, a figure rushed through the mist to meet another foe.

The wager had seemed so simple in the relative quiet belowdeck. Now, with the prospect of fresh battle rearing its head, Zala had to face the actual challenge before her. Even with Fon's help, it would be no easy feat.

Suppressing the thump of blood coursing through her veins, she ducked her head back under the hatch and let out short and jagged breaths. "It's still chaos out there," she told Fon.

"Yeah, the crew could probably use some help," Fon said with a sardonic eyebrow.

Despite their talk of "ladies first," Mantu and Sniffs poked their heads out of their own hatch without waiting. They each let an arrow loose at a sudden break in the fog. Any hint of a crow's nest with a bowman or a passing merchant or soldier was met with their attempts at decent archery. They both kept missing again and again. So they adjusted their tactic, waiting for a clear break in the thick mist before taking new shots.

Fon tapped Zala on her shoulder. "You gonna let them get a lead on you?"

Zala inhaled through her nose, braving another look above. The clouds never seemed to cease, nor did the battle around them. But unlike the pair of men, she didn't need to wait. She drew up her bow, and before long Fon tapped her on her right knee. Zala moved her arrow a finger-length to the right. Fon gave her another tap. She moved another touch. When Fon held Zala's knee, Zala knew she was on target.

She let her arrow fly free, but there was no satisfying thud or high scream that usually followed. She frowned. That had been as sure a shot as any.

"Archer!" an enemy cried out from the fog.

Zala quickly let the hatch fall at the sound of the shout, hiding belowdeck with more gulping breaths of air. She hadn't expected to be marked so quickly.

"How you gonna shoot what you can't see, chana?" Mantu laughed from his own ladder. He and Sniffs must have been hiding as well while they waited for the right time to spring out once more.

Zala turned wide eyes to Fon, who only shrugged.

"I told you right," Fon whispered. "I could see him glowing through the ship. You were aiming right at him."

Shoulders slumped in discouragement, Zala took another look above deck. "Not blamin' you, Fon…"

The cloud finally broke, and they all saw the enemy's crow's nests—two bowmen perched within, looming overhead. Before Zala could turn her bow on them, Mantu and Sniffs loosed their arrows. But they shot wide just as Zala had, the whistle of a gale coming overhead.

"Shit!" the men said in unison, retreating belowdeck.

"It's just the damn wind," Zala whispered to Fon. "Need to aim more to the left."

Zala peeked her head out again. The cool air brushed her face as she nocked her second arrow. Fon tapped Zala on her left knee this time. Zala adjusted. The hand held firm, confirming the shot. At the apex of her draw, Zala shifted her aim a touch more to the left, then let the arrow cut into the white wisps of fog.

The thwack and scream she had listened for before came sharp and loud, confirming her first kill.

"That's one, *kijana.*" Zala turned to the men as she ducked belowdeck again, chin held up high.

"Beginner's luck!" Sniffs pounded his thickset hand into the ladder, cracking its base into thin hairlines.

"Hah, I've been shooting since before you two knew port from starboard," Zala gloated. Sniffs tilted a puzzled expression from over Mantu's shoulder. Fon gave them a playful snort.

Mantu scowled. "She think she can sing like some famed Ya-Seti archer. That bow don't make you one of them, chana."

Zala shrugged. "All I know is that I have one and the

pair of you have nil." She took another look out of the hatch.

Sniffs furrowed his brow in confusion. "What's *nil*?"

Zala often forgot her vocabulary was a touch over the pay grade of the other pirates. She always tried her best to simplify her speech, but she couldn't help it. It was the way she was brought up. When she opened her mouth to explain the term to Sniffs, Fon tapped at her right knee.

Zala twisted her shoulders forward, her body and bow locked in a statuesque pose. But just as she was about to shoot her arrow, the deck cleared. Almost in unison, Mantu and Sniffs loosed their own arrows. This time, everyone could see where their marks landed—right in the enemy's chest.

"I got 'em!" Sniffs yelled.

"Finally got one!" Mantu threw his fist in the air. Zala hated the way he leered. His lips thinned when he did, disappearing into his forest of a beard.

"I thought you said you took down two before we got here?" she asked.

"I-I meant just now!" Mantu stuttered.

Though the cloud break allowed them to see where they were shooting, it also exposed their positions. Zala's heart raced when she saw more soldiers than merchants among the Vaaji—maybe they weren't just guards for hire after all. Her fellow crew were experienced fighters, for the most part, but the Vaaji outnumbered them. At some point, fatigue would set in for their people. It wouldn't matter how much better they were if they didn't have the energy to fight on.

"The archers!" she heard one soldier shout. "They're at the hatches."

Several soldiers turned toward the quartet and rushed

over. But they were met with another set of pirates that seemed to sprout from between a pillar of stacked crates. Both groups were more than eager to exchange steel. Before Zala could nock an arrow to help her crewmates, the fog filled the deck once more.

"All right, then, Mantu," Zala whispered to herself, focusing her attention toward the thick cloud. Fon tapped at her knees. Before Mantu or Sniffs could lift their bows, Zala had already found her second mark. She released her arrow. This time, the enemy archer fell with a splash into the ocean below.

"That's two, right?" Zala cocked her head to one side as she taunted the other pirates. She nudged the aziza with her elbow. "Am I counting that out right, Fon?"

"I think so," Fon replied brightly as she smiled in Mantu's direction. His face went beet-red and Sniffs' mouth fell open in frustration.

"How she doin' that?" Sniffs shouted. "The chana can't even see 'em when she shoot!"

"It's *her.*" Mantu pointed down to Fon. "What they say about the aziza... they can see a person's soul, or something?"

"Or something," Fon replied shrewdly.

"You cheat!" Sniffs rushed for Fon, but Mantu stopped him.

"Let them have their fun," he said. "We'll still get the win. Focus on the ones fighting our crew. There, look, help Rishaad at portside."

They could do as they pleased for all Zala cared. She knew there was no way she could be beaten when she had an aziza aiding her.

Fon tapped her again, this time higher on her knee. Zala

lifted her bow. Fon tapped her again. Zala moved up. Fon tapped once more.

"How high up do you want me to go?" Zala asked incredulously. But she didn't need Fon to answer. There was another shift in the fog, the largest one yet.

Now, Zala could see the entire ship.

Three red, white, and green flags flew high against the early-morning winds—at the center of each was an emblem sewn into the cloth: one sword with a star backing its center. The insignia was the national flag of Vaaj. But this was no ordinary trading vessel. Zala realized she had not been shooting at their crow's nest. This ship went *much* higher than that. Where their own pirate ship had a mainsail and foresail, this Vaaji one had too many sails to count in one sweep alone.

This was a warship.

Zala had been wrong. The merchants she'd thought she was fighting weren't merchants at all. They must have been lightly armored soldiers who hadn't had enough time to prepare themselves.

Mantu and Sniffs stopped to stare, but their shock wore off quicker than Zala's. Before she could shake her stupor, both men loosed their arrows at the enemies high above—in the ship's true crow's nest. But something pulled Zala's attention down to the stern.

Sniffs barked at the top of his lungs. "Yeah, man! We get two! *Big up yuh chest!*"

"Like I said... nothin' but beginner's luck," Mantu said with raised eyebrows.

"So we get all they loot, ya?" Sniffs asked as he cleared his nose again. Mantu turned to claim his prize, but Zala was already gone.

"'Ey where you goin' off to?" Sniffs bellowed in outrage. "You lose! Leave your bow with us."

Zala tossed the bow over her shoulder as she ran. She didn't turn her head to look and see if Mantu or Sniffs picked it up—she couldn't spare the two another thought.

"Zala?" Fon shouted after her, her voice almost lost in the rush of battle.

"That's right! Get to work!" Mantu shouted, his voice sounding like his hands were cupping around his mouth. "Find me somethin' nice. I'll take rum over wine if you can find it! Don't worry none, we'll cover you from right here." He and Sniffs howled all the while.

But Zala didn't care to listen. Jelani needed her help.

CHAPTER 3
ZALA

VAAJI SOLDIERS SURROUNDED ZALA'S HUSBAND LIKE A swarm of red, white, and green wasps poking at him with silver-tipped stingers. Even at her distance on the far side of the ship, Zala could see sweat soaking the bandana wrapping his shaved head. Had it not been for the captain and the other crew members who fought at his side, he'd already be dead.

Zala's feet pounded on the wood of the deck and her sword led the way as she fought soldier after soldier, each skirmish more difficult than the last. The first pair had been easy downs—they hadn't seen her coming. But even as the rest caught on to her desperate charge, they fell one by one to her steel. She cut through spine, kidney, and heart. None of them could match the determination of her blade.

But Zala couldn't keep it up.

The closer she got to the ship's stern—and the closer she got to Jelani—the thicker the Vaaji formation became. A trio of soldiers had turned on their heels and met her blade for blade. The leader edged his curved sword over his buckler, and the two at his side moved to flank with spears in hand. Pirates called it the crane formation. Zala called it cheating.

She peered over their heads. There was no way around them, and she knew Jelani wouldn't last long. Her jaw clenched around mounting nerves.

Zala wasn't the best head-to-head swordswoman. She was effective, but a true master of the blade would scoff at her form. Her swings were too wide, cutting from shoulder rather than from elbow, and her thrusts were stiff, struck from a rigid hammer's grip. Jelani had told her about proper blade grips for certain strikes and thrusts, but she had never taken his advice to heart.

"What's it matter how I hold the damn thing as long as my aim is true? A cut is a cut," Zala had said to Jelani time and time again. He would always just shake his head and laugh that laugh that could light up any room.

Zala had her own form of fighting—she knew how to cheat too. She targeted throats and groins, or gouged eyes when she could. Dirty, but effective. During her sessions with Jelani, she often used these "unorthodox" techniques. Instead of chiding her as she'd thought she would have been, Jelani adjusted her training to adopt this new "style."

"Most of your opponents gonna be bigger than you, man or woman. Your best friend gotta be distraction and—"

"A bit of scrappiness?"

Jelani had chuckled. *"And a bit of scrappiness, yes."*

Suddenly, a sharp pain bit into Zala's shoulder: a red line etched into her skin. Blood ran down her bicep in a stream, but her instincts saved her from the fatal follow-through—just barely.

Both spearmen of the trio were boxing her in, giving her no respite as they forced her to the ship's starboard edge. As she swung at their jabbing spear tips, she grunted, desperate to bat them away. A quartet of her fellow crew mates noted her peril and ran to engage the spearmen, which left Zala alone with the single swordsman.

Her cheeks flushed with a tense heat. Her mind often wandered beyond the moment, despite Jelani's constant reminders to keep her mind focused on the task at hand, lest she find herself run through with steel.

He'd told her the best way to defeat another swordsman was to identify his tells. She squinted, neck tense—though she knew it should've been loose—as she looked for an angle. Once she managed to catch the swordsman's rhythm, she could guess his attacks.

There!

The soldier kept dropping his arm before striking, and he seemed to tap his foot before every lunge.

She let the man swing his sword over his shoulder in an arc, and then parried his blade when it fell. Zala tried to gain control and slip through the soldier's guard, but he was too fast, always resetting before she could mount a proper counterattack. She grunted in frustration, spurring a second sequence.

She tagged the soldier once across his exposed hand, employing what she called the "touch and rip" approach. It took far less energy than a quick stab or a heavy cleave, but it only left her opponents with mild cuts—more annoying than lethal. They soon added up, though, and little injuries could quickly grow cumbersome in a life-and-death duel. Once she saw her opponents begin to falter was when Zala pressed her final assault.

Though her method was effective against most merchants and the light armor of novice mercenaries, it was almost entirely useless against the Vaaji soldier's padded leather.

Each time she found an arm or a leg to drag against, her blade split nothing, scuffing the soldier's leather at best. Worse, each strike taxed her smaller arms, her poor technique not helping in the least.

The soldier spun his sword beneath her guard, the sharp edge of his blade finding the underside of her wrist. He swiped the blade back, letting the edge sear through Zala's skin like a deft-handed butcher against a pig's throat. She dropped her sword and winced, biting the inside of her cheek so she wouldn't cry out in pain.

Great. Now the dikala's using my own moves against me.

Before the soldier could bring down his sword in another overhand swing, Zala took a step back to evade the strike. She ducked low to swipe up a loose piece of wood and threw it at the soldier's face. Her throw did no real damage—it wasn't meant to—but it gave her the split-second distraction she needed. The soldier hesitated, and before he could recenter, Zala seized him by his wrists.

She couldn't hold the soldier; he was too strong for that. Instead, she dug her nails into his wrist, fighting the pain in her own as blood poured down onto the deck. She dove in with her teeth for good measure, biting at his bare skin. Two knees to the groin later and the soldier dropped his sword with a guttural cry.

This is why I fight dirty.

Now disarmed, the soldier's anger redoubled. Fueled by a sudden panic, he wrenched back the freedom of his wrists and wrapped Zala in a bear hug so tight she couldn't breathe.

With each moment, the soldier squeezed tighter, his padded armor crushing against Zala's skin. Every time she thought she could find air through the hold, the soldier seemed to just tighten his lethal embrace even more. The edges of her vision darkened as she struggled for breath. She tried to free her arms to get to the soldier's face, but he pinned them into her ribs.

Then... Zala felt nothing.

At first she thought she had passed out, but then she realized the soldier had released her—and he had three arrows protruding from his back. Zala clutched at her throat while she struggled to refill her lungs with air.

"What in the Sapphire Hells are you doing?" Fon caught Zala by the arm, lifting her up as best she could. "There's too many of them. You'll get yourself killed."

"But Jelani! He'll—" Zala stopped herself. Her eyes darted across the deck, catching sight of the other soldiers engaged in savage fights of their own. She stole another glance to the stern. Through the cloud break, her husband fought like a madman just to stay alive, and she was *still* a quarter ship away.

Fon was right. There was no use attacking when so many of the Vaaji surrounded them. If she kept it up, she'd be dead before she made it halfway there.

Zala needed a plan. She scanned the deck for something, *anything* that could help, but nothing caught her eye. Then she looked above.

"What are you thinking?" Fon asked as she handed Zala her fallen sword. "Take their crow's nest? Give our crew cover?"

"No, we need to use the ratlines," Zala answered.

"How are we going to do that?"

Zala looked at Fon. "I'll need you as a distraction."

"Why me?" Fon asked with a pout, hands on her hips.

The human raised her eyebrows at the aziza. "You're the one who can fly."

CHAPTER 4
ZALA

"*THAT THING IS CLIMBING TO THE CROW'S NEST!*" ZALA shouted in the tongue of the Vaaji as she hid from the rush of battle behind a set of crates.

Fon flew up the length of the mainmast, weaving through the air to make herself a harder target. When the first soldier pointed up toward the aziza, Zala grinned. She cupped her hands around her mouth and added, "*What are you waiting for! Bring it down!*"

At the top of the stern deck a score of Vaaji soldiers surrounded Jelani. The captain stood beside Jelani, his large gut and thick, white beard drenched in sweat. Though it was hard to tell from Zala's distance, she thought she made out six other crew members besides her husband and Kobi.

"*Move your asses!*" she bellowed again.

At Zala's third cry, at least a half-dozen of the Vaaji peeled off and gave chase up the ratlines. And in the next moment, another pirate went down. Now only five remained to support Jelani and Kobi. Zala dug her nails into her palm, her nerves spiking as she watched Fon fly higher and higher.

Come on, girl, you can do it.

As Fon reached the top, she caught the two archers perched there by surprise and stabbed each through their necks before they knew what was happening to them. Zala let out a breath of relief, and her eyes darted between the crow's nest and the ship's stern. Just a few more moments and this would all work out. It had to.

Fon started work on the rope itself, cutting with her dagger as fast as her tiny arms could move. When the pursuing soldiers were halfway up the ratlines, Zala lifted herself from her hiding place. "Crew of the *Titan!*" she shouted. "On me! Support to the stern!"

A few heads looked her way, though when they saw it was Zala, their only answers were scowls.

What is wrong with these dikala?

Most of the pirates turned back to the battle amidship, dismissing her cries. At least the fight had died down in favor of the pirates. But that just meant early looting and less support.

Zala furrowed her brow in disbelief that they'd let the captain die—that they'd let Jelani fend for himself. Then she shouted a second time, saying, "Your captain—*our* captain needs us!"

One head remained turned, tall, pointed ears silhouetted against the bright of the fog and the two half-moons behind it: Shomari, the pakka. He arched his feline back, and his nose turned up to the platforms above. After a few sniffs and a slight twitch of his furry ears, he went back to his looting. But the screams of Fon brought his ears up in attention again.

The first soldier had reached the aziza up in the crow's nest. Fon tried to fly away as she wrestled the soldier, but the Vaaji held her wings pinned. Zala's heart sank in her chest as she watched her friend struggle against the much larger man. Even if Zala sprang from her position behind the crates and somehow found supernatural speed to climb up to the crow's nest herself, there was little she could do to help.

Shomari dropped his loot—a sack of Vaaji coffee beans by the looks of them—and climbed the ratlines with a balance only his cat-like agility could afford.

Thank the moons.

The pakka made his way into the crow's nest hastily, somersaulting into the small space as though he were some nimble dancer from the Big Isle. Before the arc of his gymnastics was even complete, he stabbed the soldier neatly through his padding. The whole motion looked like one unbroken movement.

Zala let out a sigh of relief as she watched Shomari pull Fon from below the dead man's body. Fon tapped at Shomari's furry shoulder and pointed her dagger at the lines. The pakka gave her an affirmative salute, and they both cut swiftly through the rope.

"Thank you, Shomari," Zala whispered to herself, not letting her mind wander to the worst-case scenario Fon had only barely avoided.

The ratline snapped free with a loud *thwack*. Fon and Shomari grabbed the end of the rope and threw it down to Zala below. The ratline mesh acted as a net, arcing over the charging soldiers' heads. Before they knew it, they were captured like fish ripe for the taking. The soldiers did their best to throw the ropes over their heads, but Zala tugged at the end of the makeshift net and drew it low to the deck.

She rolled a nearby barrel over the ends, weighing it down to prevent the Vaaji from escaping.

"Crew of the *Titan*!" Zala shouted again. "Now's our chance. Attack!"

None turned this time. Not one. Were they so foolish? Precious moments passed, and more and more of the Vaaji worked free from the net.

A second bellow came from the group at the ship's stern. Zala twisted to the sound and knew it was another pirate that had fallen. The voice was familiar, but it wasn't Jelani's. It didn't mean he was safe though. There must have been only three or four crew members left among them.

A sickening feeling churned in Zala's stomach. She was going to lose him. She should have secured the deck first, should have skipped the stupid bet with Mantu. But how could she know? The captain had said this was a merchant ship. It was supposed to be an easy take!

Then Shomari let out a roar only he could muster. "Well, what are you waiting for, dockrats? You think the Vaaji will die of natural causes? The woman said attack!"

That got their attention.

Zala pointed to the net and raised her sword menacingly. "Gut them!"

The soldiers that had escaped the netting met the approaching pirates, and the two groups clashed iron within bloody ocean mist. Zala drew back her sword and focused on those Vaaji still stuck in the net. Her blade ran slick with their blood.

"Yield and keep your life!" she shouted to the hesitant few—she gave no mercy to those with ready weapons. The crew followed suit, stabbing only those who tried to tear themselves from the mesh or those who raised up weapons in defense. Before long, those that remained gave up their efforts at escape and begrudging grunts of surrender came soon after.

Zala gave a sigh of relief. She hadn't expected that to work, but she was glad it had. Fon flew down from the crow's nest and landed next to Zala. The aziza clutched at her arm, blood streaming down her elbow. Zala's lips parted in mild shock.

"It's only a scratch," Fon reassured her.

"That was quite the performance," said a purring voice from behind Zala. She turned to meet Shomari's yellow-slitted eyes.

"Thanks." Zala nodded her head. "But we still need to save *them*." She pointed to the ship's stern, where Jelani and the captain still fought like tired dogs. The fog seeped in, cloaking the pirates under another sheet of gray-white cloud.

Zala turned to Fon. "Can you see them? Can you see *anything*?"

"They're faint," she said with a concentrated expression, two fingers at her temple. "But they're in there. The Vaaji aren't even aware that their friends here were captured."

"Fools." Shomari scowled.

Zala ignored him, asking Fon, "Is Jelani okay?"

A violent thumping came to her throat. Jelani couldn't last much longer.

Fon's gleaming white eyes narrowed in concentration. "I can't tell. There are so many of them in there. I'm just getting a big, glowing mass." Zala frowned. "But I'm sure he's okay," Fon added quickly.

Zala pressed her lips to a thin line and pointed to the short bow on Fon's back. "Can I borrow that?"

The aziza offered her the bow. Zala took it and nocked

an arrow, then began crouch-walking across the deck. "Follow me."

"You too, Shomari," Fon ordered. "Make use of that cat's balance again and cover us from above, please and thank you!"

"For you, Flutter, anything." Shomari bowed, his tail curling over his back before he jumped high onto the first strut of the mizzenmast.

Zala led the way up the stairs to the stern deck. While she could barely see a thing, the clashing of swords guided her path well enough. When the rattling of a duel grew too close, she stopped short and pulled up her bow.

"Point me," she said to Fon.

"A little to your left, just a finger or two."

Zala whipped her head to Fon. "Or two?"

"Split the difference?" Fon canted her head, the expression of her glowing eyes timid.

Zala bit her lip and moved her arrow a touch to the left before letting the shaft fly free. The short bow gave less resistance, but she made the adjustments. Her arrow cut through the air and the clanking of steel-on-steel abruptly stopped.

"Did I hit the right one?" she asked, turning worried eyes to Fon.

"I... I think so?"

"What did that?" said a familiar voice through the fog. "Whose arrow did that?"

"It was us... me and Fon," Zala said. "Don't stab us."

"Good looks. We needed the help." The voice belonged to a female pirate Zala didn't know by name. "Captain say we supposed to be attackin' a merchant boat. It look like him make a mistake."

"We know." Zala nudged her foot forward, probing for a body. "Where are you, anyway?"

"*Mi ovah yaso!*"

Zala almost tripped over the woman. She recognized her long face, the green bandana that wrapped her head, and the deep scar that ran through her left eye.

"Have you seen Jelani?" Zala asked her.

The woman thumbed farther into the thick white. "See him there. And move your asses, chana." The woman waved them off as she dragged herself between a pair of barrels.

Zala and Fon continued along the stern. "Where's Shomari?" Zala asked. "He should have made it down by now."

A corpse fell at their feet, claw wounds raked across its neck.

Fon's eyes passed over the body and back up to Zala. "I wouldn't worry about Shomari."

A familiar, guttural bellow reached them through the fog, and Zala's amusement died a quick death as her heart dropped to the pit of her stomach.

"Jelani!" Her muscles went stiff. There was no time for caution. She sprinted off into the fog.

"Wait, Zala! Wait!" Fon tugged at Zala's loose pants. "You'll give us away."

Zala pulled away from Fon's grip, but then tripped and fell over a motionless figure. She looked up from her fallen position, terrified to see the face of the man she loved. For just a moment the thought paralyzed her. When she had steeled enough courage, she turned the body over. Then she sighed with great relief to see it was just another pirate.

"Sorry, you're right." Zala said to Fon, lifting herself up. "I don't reckon they heard me."

"But I think you're right," Fon said. "Jelani's just ahead

—he's always had a different energy about him. And he's right next to the captain."

The fog thinned and Zala saw her husband clearly now, only a few strides away. A dozen Vaaji were closing in on him, the captain, and the two surviving crew members fighting with them. The rest lay dead at their feet.

Captain Kobi looked like an angry lion as he swung his sword in wild arcs. Sweat poured down from his wizened face and white beard. It was a wonder he hadn't passed out already. Each swipe or rush against the Vaaji was sloppier and slower than the last, his age clearly showing.

Jelani caught sight of Zala and his eyes brightened with a flash. One of the soldiers seized the lapse and stuck Jelani through the stomach with his spear. Zala gasped, terror and guilt spearing her own stomach in the same instant.

Yet the weapon didn't break skin and there was no blood —perhaps the soldier's thrust had not been true. Still, the strike caught Zala and Jelani off-guard. It was too close a call. The soldier, in shock, didn't even defend himself as Jelani brought his sword overhead and through the Vaaji's shoulder.

Zala rushed forward only to be halted as half of the soldiers spun to her and Fon while raising their curved swords. The others turned to another soldier wearing a green turban, who had a gold cap resting at the top of his head. Zala had come to know that only Vaaji captains and senior officers wore such a headpiece.

"You four, take them. The rest of you, finish these off with me." The man spoke with zeal, the sharpness of his voice accentuated by his severe face and pointed goatee. Four soldiers took measured steps toward Fon and Zala, brandishing their sabers in guarded positions. The rest kept their attention locked on Jelani and the others.

Zala's arrows loosed quick and true from Fon's bow, but the ready shields of the advancing Vaaji intercepted them. The shafts that did not break against a shield flew wide; Zala's hands were shaking and her nerves were getting the better of her aim.

Fon darted past the soldiers that came after her. They had no hope—she was too small and too agile. Each time they swiped at her, she floated backward just out of reach. The aziza darted swiftly down right between one of the soldier's legs, using her dagger to cut through his ankle. With a cry, the man fell to his side.

Zala wasn't doing nearly as well. With Fon preoccupied she had no way of knowing where the Vaaji were coming from through the fog. And when the first set of soldiers attacked, she had no time to loose any arrows, instead casting her short bow aside to draw her sword once more.

She tried her best at a flightless imitation of Fon's style, but she was nowhere near athletic enough. Instead of clearing a path as she'd hoped, she took shallow cuts to her shoulders, knees, and back. The wounds were superficial, but they stung something fierce—and they slowed her down.

Fear flooded her body then. If she couldn't keep her arms up in defense, if she couldn't fight back...

Fon was trying to reach Zala to help, but she had her own problems, and the Vaaji soldiers worked well together. One facing Zala turned to Fon and kicked her square in the gut, his companion switching out with him and jumping forward at Zala. Fon flew back in the air several paces before slamming into the side of the deck with a resounding thud. Zala winced, feeling the impact her friend took deep in her own chest. Aziza weren't built to take those kinds of hits. Hells, they weren't built to take hits at all.

The soldier turned back to Zala, lifting his sword over-head. She brought her arms in front of her and stopped the man's downward strike at his wrists, but the blade hovered inches from her face. Blood pounded in her ears as she fought to hold him back. The man pressed his full weight into her forearms, forcing her to fight for every breath. Another moment later, the sword pressed into her cheek, splitting skin.

Just as Zala felt the blood drip down the side of her cheek, a pair of black-furred hands wrapped around the soldier's face. The Vaaji's head jerked sideways, neck crack-ing, and his head fell face-first against Zala's shoulder, revealing Shomari from behind. The other two soldiers lay dead on the deck with necks torn and backs shredded open.

"Took you long enough, dikala," Zala spat through a strained voice.

"You didn't tell me how big this ship was!" Shomari shot back. "I had to climb all the way up the mizzen just to get back down here to you. And what in Yem's name do these Vaaji eat?" He grunted as he strained to roll the soldier's weight off her.

Zala sucked in a deep breath, her lungs free to inhale once again. "Let's go save them already, ya?"

Without another word, Shomari bounded off toward the soldiers surrounding Jelani. When he ran, he did it on all fours, *"as all pakkami should,"* he had once told her. He leapt atop one of the Vaaji's shoulders and snapped his neck as easily as he had the previous. With effortless grace, he somersaulted off the falling corpse even as he withdrew his pointed sword from another's chest, riding his momentum over the crowd in a blinding display Zala couldn't begin to follow with her human eyes.

She shook the awe from her face. *How does he do that?* The cat was never short of surprises.

The grunts and clash of swordplay turned Zala's attention back to the captain. Kobi was fighting with the last of his reserves, growing ever sluggish in his broad, sweeping strikes. Jelani defended more than attacked, and he was losing ground. Each time one of the Vaaji tried to cut or stab at the captain, Jelani had to step in front and deflect the strike away with his own sword.

The other soldiers took notice, turning to the preoccupied Jelani. Shomari spun between the few who took advantage of Jelani's defensive openings. With pointed steel, he ran his blade through the soldiers' guards, his tail maintaining his impossible acrobatics. And each time Jelani defended the captain, Kobi sprang out to cut through the soldiers one by one. Both men and pakka alike seemed to work in improvised concert.

Before Zala could properly find her feet again under her cuts and bruises, Kobi was already bellowing, "That's it! Push these dikala back! They're no match for us!"

The captain seemed to ride the high tide of a second wind, driving forward with his curved blade. Zala couldn't deny his tenacity in battle. He was relentless and his resolve never faltered. Before long, only the soldier with the golden cap and green turban remained. And the crew backed him against the bloodied stern's taffrail.

Without a second glance to the Vaaji captain, Zala ran to Jelani and leapt into a deep kiss, salt and sweat be damned. A warm heat rolled through her, melting away the cold of the moist morning air.

"Are you okay?" she asked as they finally broke away.

"*Mi all rite, Zee.*" He smirked, giving her a peck. She always preferred the way his Southern Isle Tongue,

Pakwan, sounded as opposed to Sniffs'. Jelani's was smooth and suave, not stuffy and clipped. Goosebumps crawled atop her skin as she pressed her mouth into his once more. She'd thought she'd never feel his full lips again.

"You're not even bleeding." Zala pulled at his hole-ridden shirt, checking for injuries. "After that soldier... I... I thought you would've—"

Jelani put a finger to her lips. "I'm okay, Zala. *Mi deh yah. Mi deh yah.*"

Zala took a moment to drown herself in his deep brown eyes. They were always so calm, so gentle. Jelani pressed his body into hers, his shirt damp with what, she didn't care. When she opened her eyes again, she caught sight of a tiny figure fallen against the deck.

"Fon, are you okay?" Zala pulled away from Jelani and rushed down the deck to where Fon had collapsed. "Fon, can you hear me?"

The aziza didn't move. Zala brushed stray hairs from her friend's face, tucking them behind her pointed ear. Sometimes her friend's child-like build made it hard for Zala to remember that Fon was technically the oldest person she had ever known. Even so, Fon didn't deserve to die right now. Not yet.

"Come on. You're not gonna let a little kick like that take you down, are you?" Zala traced her finger along Fon's cheek. She sprang back when the cheek started to expand. Then, a great cough came spewing from the little aziza's mouth.

"This." Another cough. "Is why." A third. "I'm the *cook*..." Fon finished through harsh, grating breaths.

Zala's lips curled into a smirk, but her whisper was sharp. "Kobi is too much. He doesn't need us all fighting like this. Each raid leaves half of the crew dead." Zala pulled Fon up to her feet.

"Please! Please, don't," a Vaaji soldier cried from somewhere behind. "I yield!"

"You must have heard of me before, kijana," Kobi said with a wide grin. "Captain Kobi! The Whitebeard! The Platinum *Kubahari*!" Zala rolled her eyes. "Am I to assume you are this ship's captain?"

"I am... I am," the Vaaji captain stammered. "I surrender my ship to you."

"Thank you for the kind offer, but we would take it either way," Kobi said with a laugh, turning to the crew that steadily gathered about them, many of them hiding loot behind their backs or in satchels bursting at the seams.

"I ask only that you spare my crew," the Vaaji said, head held low.

"I think I will. I must replace the ones we've lost today." Kobi turned on the spot, disposition shifting with his spin. "*You* should have surrendered when I gave you the chance."

Kobi ran his sword through his scabbard as he squatted on level with the cowering man. Something felt off to Zala. The Vaaji weren't known for their bravery, to be sure, but they weren't cravens either.

"Now tell me," Kobi said. "What brings the Vaaji so close to the shores of Kidogo?"

CHAPTER 5

KARIM

AN OLD SAYING HAD EMERGED DURING THE EARLIEST days of the Vaaji Empire: *Efficiency is the manifest of the Supreme One's Will.* It had been the foundation of all the empire's endeavors since it had been reformed. The saying extended to the founding of its government, the authority of its religion—even the simple customs of a greeting.

And these principles extended to the cabin space of the *Viper,* the first airship of the Vaaji Air Fleet.

Though Karim el-Sayyed was the ship's chief officer, his quarters left little space for his work. As he wrote, he was forced to keep his elbows tight to his body, his penmanship suffering for it. The empire would never accept the jagged scribbles he etched on the parchment. He crumpled up the dozenth letter, tossing it alongside the others at the edge of his desk before starting anew.

Karim had thought his position on the Vaaji's pride and joy would have been more exciting, but for the most part his time had been relegated to simple bookkeeping. Though there was not much activity on the ship itself, keeping tabs on Captain Malouf's purchases of rum and women left Karim busy enough. Often, it was nearly impossible to keep up with the captain's wild purchasing habits.

Clenching his jaw, Karim finished the manifest's last line. The captain was spending more money than he should be... again. Over the past week, Malouf had thrown no less than *three* parties in celebration of his new title and the success of their empire's invention.

It was wasteful and premature.

There had been no real success. At least not yet. The airship's sole accomplishment to date had been the simple act of flight—and the vessel wouldn't have been much of an airship without it. As a military ship ready for combat, it had yet to come even close to proving its true potential.

The *Viper* had set out on its first live mission almost a fortnight prior. Her crew had been charged with neutralizing the pirate threat sweeping the Kidogo Coast and securing an as-yet-undisclosed major target. But all Malouf had been able to manage was his slow choosing between their last purchase of palm wine or sugar rum. It was fortunate their mission was close to the homeland, or else there would hardly be enough resources for a return trip.

"Don't fret," Karim could hear Captain Malouf's grating voice in his head. *"When we find those pirates, we'll replenish what we've spent and then some."*

Karim sighed at the thought as he stroked his short beard and traced his thumb over the old scar that drew from lip to chin. For those in the military with an ounce of acumen, it was a wonder how Malouf could have been assigned to his post heading the empire's greatest technological achievement to date. But those more privy to the political machinations of the empire knew that it had always been that way with Malouf. He had a propensity for rubbing the right shoulders, and his family had *very* deep pockets.

It had been different for Karim. He did not share the same upbringing that certain other officers did. He was a grunt who had started from the bottom and worked his way up. It was his work ethic that had earned him his position, not a silver tongue or a purse full of coin.

Karim pushed his chair out, bumping into the wooden wall behind him for the fiftieth time that week. He couldn't wait until this prototype ship was signed off so they could make for better accommodations. He knew such an early version of the airship couldn't afford to spare the extra space, but he still would've allocated more to crew accommodations if he had been in charge of its constructions.

How was a man to work like this? Sighing and hunching over to avoid the low ceiling, Karim rolled up the parchment and tied it off with a bow. He'd faced worse than a cramped workspace before.

A small trill chirped outside the ship and Karim peered out his cabin's viewport. Through the morning fog, he made out the wingspan of a large seagull approaching. Its voice carried over the ocean's waves below, signaling an incoming message. Karim recognized the bird's distinct black-and-gray-patterned feathers as the shape-shifting messenger from the naval ship, *Saber's Edge*.

Hopefully she brought some good news, he thought.

But his musings were dashed when he noticed the gull-shifter's jagged flight path. She must've been wounded. That meant there had been an attack—which meant the pirates were close.

In excitement, Karim rushed to shuffle his documents in order. For the first time in a week, news of pirates had come. He composed himself before wrapping his papers in a small pouch, stilling his mounting glee—though he couldn't help the grin that creased his cheek.

When he had everything in order, logs for foodstuffs and the latest weapons cache documents in hand, he began his walk to the communications deck.

Karim strode down the corridor, some portions of the ship so small he had to walk sideways. Though the space was cramped, he admired the finish of the wood panels that lined the walls. His people's architects were nothing if not talented craftsmen.

Ducking through the crew deck—and down to the utility deck and a supply room below—he came out into a long, tight corridor which led to the communications room.

Karim struck a short knock against the door and asked, "Permission to enter?"

The wooden door swung inward to a sparse room with a simple administration desk in its middle. Shelves pressed against the walls, each carrying a cage with an assortment of hawks, gulls, and owls. A single open viewport large enough to let in the birds who carried messages to the *Viper* lined the side.

Two women stood at the room's center. The first, Officer Tahan, held the door ajar. She wore the empire's signature naval uniform: padded red armor over a white tunic, wrapped at the middle with an emerald sash, and topped with a green headwrap and black underscarf. The bronze clasp at her breast denoted her position as communications officer.

The other woman's clothing was less impressive: simple rags and no shoes with tangled dark hair. But her eyes were a particular shade of golden-brown, a signature trait for any shape-shifter. Karim was familiar—all too familiar—with the dimples that caved at her cheeks as she gave him a half-smile.

"Chief Officer el-Sayyed." Tahan saluted. "We have a message from *Saber's Edge*."

"Then you should report to Captain Malouf," he said begrudgingly.

"I did, sir, but he is—" The officer stopped herself then cast her eyes down to her boots.

Karim gave her a knowing nod. The captain was likely too drunk to be woken.

"Very well," he said, turning to the messenger. "You may convey your report to me, Runner."

Nabila, the gull-shifter, limped forward and away from a cage of mundane messenger birds. "Sorry it took me so long. Had to wait for my chance to get away from the pirates with a valid story."

"Understood, Nabila," Karim said, using her given name intentionally. "What do you have to report?"

"The pirates, sir. The ones we were looking for on Kidogo. They found *Saber's Edge* just as planned."

"As planned? Was this Malouf's doing?"

"Yes, sir. I found the mystics like he wanted. And at least two *wageni*—an aziza and a pakka."

Karim had suspicions about their undisclosed target, but he thought whoever he or she was would have done a better job of hiding themselves. Still, the question needed to be asked. "Were any of the mystics sea speakers?"

"Yes, though from what I could tell there is only one left. I identified him before the pirate captain, Kobi, set me to flight. Their last raid nearly cost me my life." Nabila withdrew her tattered blankets, showing that her arm had been skewered from shoulder to elbow. "This was done by one of our own. I didn't have time to identify myself."

44

Karim's lips parted, his voice taking on an urgent yet gentle tone. "Why have you not checked in with the surgeon?"

"I wanted to report the information as soon as possible..."

Karim slung Nabila's uninjured arm over his shoulder before she could finish. "We can walk and talk. Let's get you to Surgeon Abadi before you bleed out on us."

Nabila gave Karim a small nod and a smile that reached her eyes in all the wrong ways. Karim decided to ignore the visage for now. If her unwanted looks continued, he'd reprimand her for them when necessary.

"Thank you for processing her," Karim said to Tahan. "I'll take it from here. Try to wake the captain if you can—oh, and see to it that these documents make their way to al-Anim." Karim gave his sealed pouch to Tahan.

She inclined her head to the point of her crisp military salute, palm flat and thumb pressed to her chest in a one-handed prayer. "As Shati'ala wills it, sir."

"As Shati'ala wills it," he echoed.

Karim led the way out into the quiet corridor, hefting more of Nabila's weight onto his shoulders. Small lanterns filled with moonstones lit the red-and-black banners adorning the wall, each sewn with the star and sword of the Vaaji Empire. The walkway was too tight for the pair to walk shoulder-to-shoulder, so Karim awkwardly sidestepped with Nabila.

"So, these pirates," Karim said. "Do they believe they have the upper hand?"

"They seemed to, sir. Captain Mahmud gave up the information as commanded."

Karim pursed his lips. "What do you mean?"

"Malouf, sir. He gave him certain orders to… divulge the *Viper's* location."

Karim hummed under his lips in thought before saying, "Hopefully he did not surrender it too easily. Did you get a count on their group?"

Nabila squeezed around a bend in the hall. "They've been bleeding crew by the week. They had sixty-four when I first arrived two weeks ago. Then down to fifty-one by week two. They made another pass for Kidogo to recruit, bringing their numbers up to the seventies, maybe more. During the last raid they took heavy losses, thirty at least. Long story short, they should be an easy target."

"Good, good." Karim opened the door into the surgeon's room where a mesh of swinging rope greeted them. "Surgeon Abadi, we have someone who needs mending."

A dark lump stirred from its sleep, tousled hair hanging down from a hammock and shifting with the airship's quiet drift. Karim pulled a moonstone from a side table and flicked it like a flint against the lantern that held its twin. The room filled slowly with delicate blue light. The lantern was a unique item of Abadi's, just another piece in his collection of oddities.

As with all other areas in the ship, the old surgeon didn't have much space to work with. Abadi's room was larger than Karim's though: there was room enough for a hammock and a cot, and enough height to hang his medical instruments from the ceiling. To Karim, the tools looked like hooked talons silhouetted against the cabin's dark viewport.

"Whozzit?" Abadi slurred. "S'not the captain again, is it? I can't keep easin' erry damned hangover he—" Abadi stopped when he caught sight of Nabila leaning against Karim. "Oh, I see. All right, then. Come in, come in."

Nabila turned to Karim. "Thank you, Ka—Officer el-

Sayyed."

"Anything for a loyal servant of the empire." Karim dipped his head. "Take care of yourself. We need you back on your feet and out in the field. Or should I say wings and skies?"

Nabila rolled her eyes at the bad joke. Karim was never very good at them.

"Yes, sir," she said under a light smirk.

Karim gave her a casual hand wave and nodded to the surgeon before leaving. "Be safe, Nabila."

Abadi gave them a sidelong glance, likely because Karim used Nabila's given name instead of her family title. But Karim didn't pay it any mind as the surgeon scanned his collection of potions, an assortment of vials filled with greens, purples, and other colors Karim couldn't even begin to name or describe. Some looked as though they were trying to bubble over but couldn't quite muster the effort, while others remained as still as a placid lake—ignoring even the ebb of the airship.

"I'll get her right in no time," the wily old man said. "I have *just* the brew."

Karim saluted and took his leave.

He directed his steps back down the corridor without thought, routine leading him idly to the captain's quarters. He fought to keep his excitement contained. Finally, they'd be able to prove to everyone what the *Viper* was made of. Karim caught himself smiling, and he realized his walk was too eager to be considered a prudent military trot. If the pirates were close, he'd need to get the airship battle-ready for their arrival.

But he should have known better. There wasn't anything he could do with Nabila's report on its own, at least not without Malouf's go-ahead. His was a captain who'd sooner screw up the intel and send them on a wild kubahari chase than capitalize on securing the pirate crew.

Lost in his thoughts, Karim almost walked straight into the largest, most audacious door on the ship. He gave the overly neat and fine-crafted mahogany—the only door Malouf demanded be installed despite its expense—a swift knock. There was no answer. Karim knocked again with more vigor. Still, there was no answer. Karim looked behind to the empty and excessively wide corridor that led to the captain's quarters.

Most of the crew were on different decks and attending to their orders. The only ones he could see were the ones just outside the double-doors leading to the weather deck. With no one to stop him, he decided to let himself in.

As he pushed open the wide-set doors, the strong odor of rum and sweat wafted its way into Karim's nose. He lifted his hand over the whole of his face and tried to shield his nostrils from the stench. Captain Malouf snored loudly, flanked by a woman on either side. Fellow crew, or some of Malouf's hired women, Karim couldn't tell—nor did he care.

"Captain," Karim whispered. Malouf did not stir. Karim gave him a deft slap. Still nothing.

Karim sighed as he looked about the room. Unlike the rest of the ship's quarters, this one was nothing short of grand. Malouf had carved himself enough real estate for a king-sized bed, a large viewport that stretched from wall to wall and led to a balcony—which revealed the edges of the airship's stern and the ocean beyond—and a small study that rivaled the artistry of the private temples in al-Anim.

"Captain, can you hear me?" Karim said, slow and loud. "We've identified the pirates. You're needed on the bridge."

For a moment, Karim thought the captain might've been

dead. He put his head near the captain's face—only to be met with a large belch. Karim withdrew just as the captain heaved his supper on the floor. Specks of vomit spotted the back of one of the women, and she woke with a scream and covered herself. Now Karim recognized her as one of the working girls they had picked up back near Asiya Bay. Despite her scream, the captain still did not move and remained plastered on his back. Whatever had put him under, the second woman must have been on it too. She was just as listless as her one-time lover.

Covering his nose again before the worst of the stink could hit him, Karim waved the first woman away. She lifted her blanket around her ankles and scurried out of the room.

For a moment, the captain opened his eyes as though he could sense his girl leaving. "Who's there?"

Karim sighed, tip-toeing around the mess on the floor to lean closer to Malouf. "It's your chief officer, sir. We need to start preparations for the pirates."

"What?" Malouf's head fell back into his bed and his eyes closed again.

"Captain, you can't sleep. You have to—" Karim stopped himself. If the captain was out of commission, it was the chief officer's duty to take over his responsibilities. So, he changed tact. "Sir, permission to begin battle preparations."

Malouf lifted his hand as though to say "shoo."

"Does that mean you are giving me permission to—"

"Get out of here!" Malouf grumbled.

Karim smiled and turned on his heel. Malouf's exclamation wasn't *exactly* a confirmation but it was good enough for him. He would need to hurry before Malouf came to his senses.

For the time being, he had work to do.

CHAPTER 6
KARIM

KARIM QUICKLY WENT ABOUT WAKING THE CREW OF THE *Viper*. When he told them that they were making ready for a raid, many appeared excited to finally see action. The captain had subjected them to menial work, just as he had done to Karim. Decorated gunners had became glorified cannon cleaners, accomplished navigators spent their time studying irrelevant star charts instead of pirate shipping lanes, and—until today—the surgeon's most thrilling affair had been treating rather violent cases of alcohol poisoning.

Some crew—those in Malouf's pocket—questioned Karim's words, asking for the captain himself. When Karim told them the captain had given him permission to begin battle preparations, they scoffed in disbelief. But their objections had subsided when they found the captain asleep next to a young maiden in a tight embrace. None of them dared to wake him. The last junior officer who had tried that had been demoted on the spot.

Most of the crew, however, had heeded Karim's words and immediately set to work under his direction.

Confidence coursed in Karim's veins as each crew member carried out their orders with charged enthusiasm. They seemed more than eager to follow his lead, and he was happy to be their head. Unlike the "good captain" Malouf, he understood the importance of delegation.

First, Karim checked the engine room, which housed their fuel source. He didn't know how it worked *exactly*, but he had a reasonable enough understanding.

The skyglass was the key to the whole operation and their reason for being out here in Kidogo waters—skies—in the first place. The pirates were an obstacle before an island that held one of the largest sources of skyglass in Esowon.

Different glass types were scattered around the world. Before the empire's discovery, the glass had been used to enhance the *a'bara* of mystics, the energy force that manifested their power. But there was a rare form of the glass that floated—the largest deposit of which rested in the Holy City of Vaaj: Akeem.

The high priests had called the discovery a declaration of the Supreme One's Will. *"The people of Vaaj have uncovered this substance to lead the world into a new era,"* they said. This material, renamed skystone, was then engineered as a fuel source for the Vaaji's new fleet. And, after a long decade, their hard-fought research and development had finally culminated in the *Viper*.

Karim smiled as he thought of the progress his empire had achieved, and he thanked the stars he had been fortunate enough to be born on the right side of the Sapphire Seas. Had he had his start among the stretch of islands the pirates called home, he would never have reached the heights he'd managed.

As part of the battle preparations, it was Karim's duty to make sure the engineers had everything in order. He watched as they pulled levers and turned wheels to manipulate the skystone's movement within a labyrinth of gears and cogs.

"Everything holding steady?" Karim asked the chief engineer.

The balding man nodded, perhaps a touch too enthusiastically, as he tugged on a pulley. The airship lurched forward underfoot. "Ready to soar, sir."

"Careful there, al-Kindi," the chief's second, a lanky youth by the name of Amir, chided before pushing the lever back to center. His long neck seemed to strain between the cramped cogs and wheels of the engine room as he ducked them.

"How about the exhaust?" Karim asked with a faint grin. "Any progress?"

Amir wiped sweat from his dirty brow with a handkerchief that was a mound of black. "Nothing can be done for it, Chief. There's no way to vent the fumes."

Karim folded his hands behind his back with a frown. "Something for the yard-hands to figure out when we return to the capital, then. I'm sure you did your best, al-Kindi. Carry on."

He wasn't even halfway out the door before the pair's bickering voices had ratcheted over the engine's clunks and rattles. Before Karim shut the door he heard al-Kindi's second shouting, "I told you! Now the yardies are gonna stick their noses in and mess with what don't need fixin'. We should have just—"

With a light chuckle, Karim decided it best not to intervene. He wouldn't have been able to offer much of an educated opinion on their musings. The rivalry between the shipboard engineers and the dock workers back home was as long and storied as the imperial navy's history itself.

Karim wondered how the *Viper* would fare in the coming battle. The skystone gave them lift, but the engineers still couldn't figure out how to apply enough speed and acceleration to keep up with the pace of typical seafaring vessels. In their first attempts, even the larger warships had outstripped the airship by a fair few knots.

As Karim ascended to the top deck, he took a measure of the sails that snapped against the high winds. To let it keep up with the smaller, faster sea vessels, the boatswains had outfitted the airship with standard sails, using the natural winds to propel it forward.

From afar, the airship didn't look much different from a common sea ship, save for the gunner's deck, which protruded from the bottom in an open platform, and the bridge, which was at the airship's bow instead of its stern. Deviances aside, the chief difference between the *Viper* and her cousins in the sea was that she rode the clouds while they rode the waves.

"How are the sails looking?" Karim asked the boatswain.

"Same as the day we left, sir," he said with an air of the obvious. "Not like we've seen any combat, after all..."

"That'll change soon, I assure you." Karim nodded. He scanned the sails one last time as he made his way belowdeck again. Everything seemed to check out, and all that was left now were the gunners.

The wind tugged through Karim's turban as he descended onto the gunnery deck. The crew worked tirelessly, supplying each station with enough cannonballs to take down several pirate ships. But not every station held a cannon. Some were designated for bowmen, and others for elemental mystics.

At the end of the platform stood Issa Akif, chief gunner

and captain of the *Sindisi Bahrün*. Sindisi—known as myst-guards more colloquially—were the elites of the Vaaji military. They were regularly placed at the front of whatever force needed leading, and directly responsible for the protection of the nation's most important assets, such as mystics or airships.

Issa shouted orders at each crew member she passed. Her loose red under tunic wafted in the air against her black-padded armor, invoking the image of a blazing fire. Her thick eyebrows, deep reddish-brown eyes, and sharp tongue matched the visual. To the crew, they saw a demanding leader who expected nothing less than the best. To Karim, he could only ever see his long-time friend.

"Get those cannons cleaned," she ordered.

One gunner lifted her head from her station, grime caking her cheeks. "But we cleaned them immediately after we left port."

"Clean them again. And did we test all the starboard stations yesterday?"

"Yes, ma'am," droned a chorus of junior officers.

"Good. And less of the sass, or you'll be cleaning them twice."

"Yes, ma'am," they said again with a shade more urgency.

Karim stifled a snort, though he covered it quickly with a cough. He realized he likely hadn't fooled anyone.

"Hajjar, what are you doing on that cannon?" Issa asked sharply. "You're with the other elementals."

The young gunner named Hajjar, who had a distinct mole over his lip, stepped away from the cannon he had been cleaning and said, "But I'm the best shot."

Issa shook her head. "You know the rules, back to your station."

Every crew member had their part to play, and they had to stick to it—*especially* the mystics. The emperor always said the Supreme One made no mistakes. They had to appreciate and adhere to their natural gifts. Opposing such a thing was considered a sin against Her Will, whether one liked their gift or not.

Hajjar's eyes shifted not-so-subtly to Karim. It had always been assumed among the crew the Karim was one of the gentler officers, at least against someone as strict as Issa. But in this case, Karim sided with the chief gunner. And with a short gesture he knew he'd disappoint the young mystic as he held out a hand to the outcropping set for the elementals.

Hajjar gave a great sigh, hanging his head as he lumbered back toward his station, where his assigned myst-guard waited with impatience and a frown.

Karim returned his attention back to Issa. "How are they looking, Gunner Chief Akif?"

"All ready to see what the *Viper* is capable of, sir."

Karim nodded, smiling. "You keeping everyone in line?"

"I don't know, let's ask them… Alhazi!" she barked suddenly in a gunner's direction, startling him to attention from his post as he loaded a munitions crate nearby. "What do you think?" Her lips raised in her infamous sphinxian smile. "Am I keeping you lot in line?"

Alhazi's answering salute was as sharp as a scimitar's swing. "Yes, ma'am. Of course, ma'am."

Issa left him sweating a moment longer than necessary before saying, "Good. At ease, Junior."

He swiveled back to his crate, fingers moving noticeably faster than before as he unloaded his ammunition.

"They're good kids." Her eyes flickered back up to Karim. "Though some of them are a bit *too* keen."

"It wasn't so long ago we were just like them."

"Gods, you're right." Issa let out a breath, gazing out over the clouds wistfully.

Karim's thoughts whirled with nostalgia. "Six years in another moon."

"About that..." Issa's eyes shifted to a quieter corner of the gunnery. "Do you have a moment?"

"I do."

Issa led the way to the edge of the gunner's platform. The day had turned clear in the hours since Karim had written his first letter; the sun was just breaking out across the horizon, and the blue sky glistened in the mirrored ocean far below. Karim couldn't help but stare at the ocean's edge, hoping to see a dark dot crest it in the distance. But the pirates were at least a half-day away, even if the *Viper* was traveling at her top speed.

Karim pulled his focus back to Issa, waiting for her to speak her mind.

"I didn't think I'd see you promoted to captain so quickly. What happened to Malouf?" she asked, that familiar smile resurfacing in her eyes.

Karim leaned on the cold edge of a cannon. "A bit too much fun last night."

"Let's hope he stays knocked out long enough. We might actually see some success for once."

"I'm only preparing the ship," Karim replied bitterly. "I'm sure he'll come to with time to spare."

Issa chewed at her lip in thought. "So this is it, huh? Let's hope it goes better than last time."

"It will." Karim creased his brow, a look of determination. "We've got the *Viper* now. Those Kidogons can't touch us — not when we've got an airship."

Issa joined Karim near the platform's edge, letting the

moment pass in silence as the wind whipped through their tunics. Karim had always admired that about her. She knew how to let a quiet moment simply be.

"No word from your father?" she finally asked.

Karim thought back to the letter stored and hidden in his room, though he preferred to forget about it. Things weren't easy for his family back home and he didn't want to get into it with Issa just then. So he lied. "Nothing yet. Maybe that's good, though. Could mean things in al-Anim are getting better."

A change in Issa's eyes told him she thought otherwise. "Yeah. Let's hope as much." The expression left her face as soon as it came. "Anyway… we're ready to get this done. My gunners are ready. *I'm* ready."

"I know, Issa—Gunner Chief."

"Don't worry." Smiling, she drew her head close to Karim. "I won't tell anyone you called me out of my title, *el-Sayyed.*"

Karim returned a smirk of his own. "Back to work, Officer."

She stepped away and saluted. "Ready for orders, sir."

Karim returned her salute before ascending the ladder to the center of the airship. A single level up and a stretch of corridor opened access to the rest of the ship, the hall leading directly onto the bridge. It was the only area of the ship—besides the captain's quarters—that allowed for any semblance of breathing room. Like the captain's cabin, the viewport stretched wall to wall. At its center stood a pairing of rudder controls and a single, sidelong wheel: the helm of the *Viper.*

"Officer on deck!" one officer shouted as Karim crossed the threshold into the bridge. Every one of the eight men and women stood up from their stations to salute him.

"As you were," Karim commanded. "What's our status?"

"Skystone steady and glass ready for full burn."

"Gunners locked and loaded."

"Sails ready to release at your command."

Karim nodded. "Great. Let's get the glass working at capacity. Open up the sails as well. All ahead at full. Gunners at rest until we have first sighting."

Boots stomped hurriedly against the wooden paneling of the bridge as the crew worked hard to carry out the orders. Their steady energy seemed to charge the room. The airship shifted beneath Karim's feet as it lurched forward into the clouds.

"Can't you keep this damned thing flying straight for one minute, el-Sayyed?" Karim smiled at the familiar sound of Vice Admiral Shamoun's voice. The senior officer stumbled around the corner, his discomfort clear as he covered his mouth. His skin was dark—not from natural complex, but from a lifetime on exposed weather decks and long trips out to sea along desert ports. And though he was bald and wrinkled, his arms thin, and his knees knobby through his tunic, Karim never thought him old.

"Sorry, Vice Admiral. Perhaps you would be more comfortable down in your quarters. Surgeon Abadi can cook you up another batch of cloud flower."

Shamoun issued Karim a crooked grin as he gave the young officer's shoulder a hearty tap. "I can't very well spend the *entire* trip asleep in my quarters, el-Sayyed. I wouldn't make much of an inspector if I did, now would I?"

"No, sir." Karim's thoughts swiftly turned back to one drunken captain sleeping down below. "You'll find your sky legs soon enough."

"I'll take the sea any day."

"The way the empire is moving, our sea ships might well become obsolete."

"There will always be a place for sea vessels, mark my words... But one day at a time, el-Sayyed. Let's get the young gosling through her first trials before we get ahead of ourselves, yes?" Shamoun placed his hands behind his back, observing the deck officers' hard work.

"Everything is in working order, sir," Karim answered. "We should be meeting the pirates before the sun sets."

"What in Shati'ala's name is going on here?" Captain Malouf bellowed from the bridge's threshold, flanked by several of his closest advisors.

Every muscle in Karim's body felt numb and deflated.

CHAPTER 7
KARIM

MALOUF LOOKED LIKE SOMETHING BETWEEN A WALRUS and a wet mop, his thick mustache hanging low around his lips. Karim glared at the captain's advisors, who must have woken him.

What did they do, pour a bucket of water over him and warn him that I was trying to undermine his position?

He wasn't dressed in full uniform, just an undershirt and dirty slacks. His belt hadn't even been buckled. Karim wondered if the dark spot about his boots was more bile.

Karim slumped forward with a half-hearted salute, doing his best to hold back a frown. "Battle preparations set, Captain. We are ready to engage the pirates."

"Who ordered this?" Malouf grunted, sodden hair crawling beneath his dampened headwrap.

Karim held his face firm. "You did, sir. This morning."

"I have no recollection of giving such an order."

"Well, you were... otherwise occupied, sir. It was my understanding you wanted us to —"

"You understood *wrong*."

Karim clenched his jaw. It would do him no good to confront the captain openly on the bridge like this.

"Captain, if I may…" said Vice Admiral Shamoun. "El-Sayyed has done some good work. It's been a long while since I've seen a ship brought to action so swiftly."

"Be that as it may, there's an *order* to these things…" Malouf trailed off. The vice admiral turned a pointed stare at Malouf. The captain's mind seemed to catch up with his mouth a second too late. "Forgive me, Vice Admiral, I spoke in haste."

"The chief officer has done nothing you wouldn't do, Captain," another bridge officer named Ahmad spoke up right on cue. He had always been the branch between Malouf and el-Sayyed. The wide-nosed, thick-eyebrowed young man was a family friend of the Maloufs and had been a friend to Karim since the academy.

"His preparations were by the book," he went on. "The gunners have been checked, the sails are all at full capacity, the skystone is functioning as it should, and the crew is in good spirits. We're ready to see this mission through, sir."

Karim did his best to suppress the gratified grin that fought to crawl across his lips. Officer Ahmad had just poured salt onto Malouf's already wounded ego. The captain seemed to suppress another outburst, and a vein began to bulge in his forehead.

Malouf's brows pinched tight as he looked to each crew member on the bridge, searching for anyone who might undermine Karim's procedure. Though the crewmates remained professional, a tense energy filled the bridge.

The captain rushed over to Ahmad's station and riffled through the latest set of notes scrawled across the officer's personal logs.

"What is this?" Malouf bunched the parchment between his spidery fingers. "You're using the glass at full capacity?"

Karim took a step forward, interceding for Ahmad. "Yes, Captain. We need to catch up to the pirates quickly, after all —*before* they make it back to port."

"Why are you spending needless energy?" Malouf whipped to Karim, the ends of his mustache snapping like a cape. "We'll catch the bastards long before they reach Kidogo waters—*without* the need to burn all the glass this speed will cost us."

"I've already checked with the engineers," Karim said. "We have enough to make the trip and still get back to the capital."

Malouf's voice grew sharp. "No, this is all wrong. We need to pull back on our use of the glass. The admiralty would prefer if we came back with fuel left to spare."

Shamoun moved to interject, peering over Ahmad's documents. "I'm sure that Grand Admiral Awad would understand. I've known him many years, Captain. He is not one to disavow his officers' initiatives, so long as they yield results."

"The main objective is to test this vessel's combat ability." Karim tried his best to keep his voice professional and even. He stood still, his hands planted behind his back. "As well as to bring those pirates down in the process. Correct me if I'm wrong, Captain, but I don't recall any orders regarding fuel moderation." He knew his words would come as a challenge to Malouf, and the bridge would see it too. The captain's next response would be measured carefully by his attentive audience.

Malouf's face went flush. "There's also the case of chain of command. I am the final voice on this ship, and I say such use of the skyglass is wasteful. This airship doesn't have the resources to spend carelessly."

That wouldn't be an issue if you hadn't spent so much time flying over the Vaaji coast to 'throw off the scent from onlookers,' just so you could pick up your trusted whores, Karim thought, although he chose different words to speak aloud. "You said it yourself, Captain. We'll be able to recoup once we have the pirates under our thumb."

Malouf bared his teeth. "I never made such a claim. That is foolish."

Karim clenched a fist. Malouf would do anything in an attempt to save face.

Malouf turned to the bridge crew. "Our fuel source is finite. Tell the officers to pull back to half-sails and bring the energy on the glass down to float levels only. We'll use natural power for now."

If they pulled back to half-sails with no use of the stone's glass, it would take a full day to reach the pirates. What if the raiders caught wind of the *Viper's* approach? It would ruin *weeks* of waiting.

"Listen, Captain—" Karim blurted out, his hand raising to point between Malouf's eyes when an arm clamped at his wrist.

"You did a good job, el-Sayyed," Shamoun muttered in his ear. "Don't spoil it all now with an outburst."

"But the pirates, sir. If we—"

"The pirates aren't going anywhere, Officer."

Karim nodded in agreement and withdrew his hand. Then he directed his voice to Malouf. "Permission to leave the bridge, Captain."

"Yes, leave," Malouf said, his tone curt. He didn't even turn to look at Karim. "It'll take time to clean this mess you've made, so go think on what you've done. Perhaps you should refresh your understanding on proper protocol."

Karim took his leave from the bridge, seething internally. He had been so close. His first chance to prove himself as captain, all stripped away because Malouf had finally been woken from his drunken stupor. It didn't matter that the crew backed him. It didn't even matter that the vice admiral supported his actions. It still came down to Malouf's title, no matter how undeserved it was.

Caught up in his thoughts, Karim didn't even realize he had walked straight onto the main deck at its starboard side. He clutched the railing, gazing down at the cumulus clouds billowing below. The delicate wind and the gentle beat of the sun on his neck helped calm his rising resentment. He'd been the one who acted, and the crew had been receptive. All he could hope now was that Malouf didn't ruin what he had already done.

Out of the corner of his eye, he saw a familiar figure step up and mirror his awkward lean against the deckside.

"So… he woke up, then." It was Issa. Of course she would already know. It was probably written all over his face.

"He stopped everything. Said we were using too much of our 'finite' fuel source. As if he cares about that."

"The rest of the crew knows who got this thing up and running." She leaned in close, nudging his elbow. "If it wasn't for you we'd be losing the tail on these pirates."

Karim raised his voice. "It isn't fair, is all. Malouf is maddening."

"Keep your grievances down. Even up here your voice will carry." Issa pulled him away and to the hatch that led belowdecks. She didn't turn to him until they were well within the halls of the crew quarters' level. And she didn't speak again until she led him to his personal quarters.

Finally squeezing through the narrow corridors, Issa pushed him in, gave a kiss to the door frame, followed him in, and finally closed the door behind her. "You need to relax. That temper won't do anything for you. You can't control every situation."

Karim sat on his cot. "Maybe I should—"

"You will do *nothing*, Karim." Issa's eyes went sharp, joining him on the bedding.

"Careful not to let anyone else hear you call me that."

"Don't worry, unlike you, I know how to keep my voice down."

They traded smirks, followed by a brief silence. Issa had always been good at keeping Karim out of trouble. Her presence was soothing. She knew when to press him and when to let him be.

"Have you been praying to Deh'ala?"

Karim's neck stiffened. "The old religion is done with. It's useless. Forbidden."

"You didn't answer my question."

"I don't need to."

As always, Issa didn't press the issue. Instead, she pivoted the conversation. "Well, I have. And all my prayers have been answered. Every time I've set myself to cannon I pray to Ugara as well. And each time He has Blessed me. The Gods have brought me here, and they have brought you here as well."

"No, it's because *you* put in the work. They give nothing to us. Only Shati'ala gave us free will."

"Oh, yes, 'the Supreme One'... She's only one face of many. It's like saying there is just one star to light the whole of the night sky."

Karim stood from the cot as though to walk away from Issa's dogma. "She wanted us to achieve what we have on our own," he said. "Not because we give credit to dead spirits—we shouldn't even be having this conversation. You know how the empire feels about all this."

"Yes, I know. And I play by their rules. But when it's time for me to come through, when it's time for me to perform, I know who's there for me. And you know it too."

A swift knock against the wooden door interrupted Karim's response. Karim's thoughts froze in his mind with shock while Issa's hands clenched against the cot's sheets. How much had the person on the other side heard?

"Enter," Karim called, standing away from Issa as the door opened. But there was barely any room to put an adequate amount of distance between him and her.

Ahmad stood on the other side. Judging by his flat expression, he had heard nothing, but how sure of that could they be? Worse yet, did he think something untoward was happening between them? Karim looked back at Issa, who was sitting on the bed; it wouldn't be too difficult to jump to conclusions. Hell, their knees were still touching.

Whatever he thought, Ahmad held his fixed facade. "I heard raised voices, and I wasn't sure—"

"No, it's all right." Karim lifted open hands.

"We were just venting…" Issa gave Karim a sidelong glance. "About Malouf."

"Ah, yes." Ahmad peeked down the corridor before leaning in close. "Don't worry. He'll come around. It's best to make him feel like he's the one ordering the decisions, is all."

"Right, of course," Karim said. "Is that everything?"

"No, sir. It's the captain, in fact. He is calling a meeting of the senior officers. You are to report to the map room."

66

Issa tilted her head to Karim. "Here's your chance. Show them what's inside that head of yours. And don't let them turn you away. Just… keep your wits about you, okay?"

Karim knew he couldn't keep the promise. Even so, he replied, "I'll do my best."

CHAPTER 8
ZALA

CAPTAIN KOBI WASTED NO TIME MOVING EVERYONE OVER from the *Titan* to their latest conquest, freshly renamed from *Saber's Edge* to *Osiris*.

When the clouds revealed the morning's sky, the crew could finally take in the whole of the Vaaji ship. It was easily four times the size of their own. Zala overheard her fellow pirates grumbling to the captain how slow the ship would be, but Kobi didn't care. He said they needed a fleet, and the *Osiris* would be its flagship.

Not much of fleet with only forty of us left after that last raid, Zala thought in irritation.

"So now we'll be havin' two vessels," one pirate said as she and Jelani headed to the *Titan's* infirmary.

"Captain's gonna start himself a proper collection of ships," another pirate chuckled.

A third chimed in, *"Mi tink di hul gyal's betta. Much faster."*

"He's right, you know," Zala said to Jelani as they dropped belowdeck.

"'Bout the fleet?" Jelani asked as he ducked under a set of hanging barrels. Zala didn't need to bend at all.

"No. About the Vaaji ship. It's too big for us. Too slow. We should have sunk it like the rest."

"I don't think sinkin' the other ships was ever the plan." Jelani smiled wryly.

"Right, stab first, ask questions later." Zala crossed her arms. "Kobi is mad."

"I think the captain just wants to live out his good ol' days, is all,'" Jelani said.

"I'd have us off this ship already, but Kobi's the only pirate with enough balls to turn a profit right now. I know he used to be some naval captain but still..."

Kobi had been a decorated officer during the conflict between Aktah and Ya-Set, the War of the Red Dunes, but had been dismissed after the war's conclusion. Or maybe he left of his own accord. Zala was never sure what story to believe with Kobi. Whatever the case, without a steady income from the Aktahrian Navy, he had been forced to acquire coin in more nefarious ways.

Zala sighed. "Well, if he wants to be a proper pirate, he needs to have a proper ship. And that lumbering thing ain't gonna cut it. It'll just put a target on all our backs."

"What you know 'bout bein' a proper pirate?" Jelani asked with humor. Zala waved a dismissive hand. It was a fair question; he and Zala had only been out on the waves a few moons, enough time to get their hands dirty but not enough to be known as seasoned vets.

As they walked through the lower deck many other pirates nodded at Jelani. Being the ship's navigator, the crew respected him. He was one of their best fighters as well, and he had saved several of the men and women on the ship. Zala had her fair share of nods too. It confused her at first before she began recognizing the faces of those she had saved during the morning's raid.

When they finally arrived at the ship's infirmary it was packed wall to wall along the corridor with at least two dozen other pirates in front of them, all of them with a complaint spoken in grunts and groans. The smell of sweat stuck to the walls of the cramped cabin space.

Zala shook her head. "This is getting out of hand. We need to lie low for a bit. The loot from that Vaaji ship should buy us a week at least."

"Captain Kobi says he wants to raid again first thing in the morning," Jelani said.

Zala's eyebrows jumped. "Tomorrow? Look at the crew!" Jelani set his hands on Zala's shoulders to calm her raised voice, his eyes darting for any eavesdroppers. She continued on, undeterred, "They need rest. We're not fit to make an attack tomorrow. We've been raiding ships for the past fortnight. Besides, we don't know if that Vaaji captain was even telling the truth to begin with."

Jelani pressed his palm deeper into Zala's shoulders. His thin fingers felt warm against her skin as he said, "Look, I ain't like it neither. But what else we gonna do?"

What choice *did* they have? It was hard enough finding the ingredients for stonesbane on their own. And the potion required a brewmaster, who came with a hefty price. Even working on Kobi's ship wasn't a sure thing to make up the funds.

The life expectancy of pirates was short—even shorter on Kobi's crew. Eventually, they'd have to find a more stable source of income—perhaps with the Golden Lord's Council to the south. With enough coin or prestige, if they could somehow attain a position within the golden court, then perhaps they could stabilize Jelani's health without them putting their lives in danger every week—every day. For now, they were nobodies in the Sapphire Isles, so hard work would have to do, no matter *how* criminal their activities. Still, all the effort would be for naught if they got themselves killed on overzealous raids.

Zala shook her shoulders free of Jelani's grip. "We can't keep putting good people at risk. Fon almost died today."

Jelani frowned as he took a step away from Zala. "That ain't all, is it? I ain't never hear you talk 'bout the 'good people' of the ship before."

There was only a brief silence before Zala admitted, "*You* almost died today. I know you mean well, but there has to be a better way to earn what we need. If we keep at it, it won't be the stoneskin that will get you…"

Jelani didn't argue further, keeping his eyes locked on the line into the infirmary.

"What is it?" Zala asked quietly and with earnest.

"Maybe the tip of a blade ain't so bad for me. Would be better for you. No need to worry 'bout me no more," Jelani said grimly, almost to himself.

Zala punched him in the gut, but her tiny fist met a wall of rigid skin. Had Jelani's stomach always been so strong? They had been so busy trying to keep up with the pirating, she didn't even remember her own husband's body.

"Is it…" Zala grabbed for Jelani's shirt, but his firm hand stopped her. "It hasn't gotten worse, has it? Did it spread to your body?" She rubbed his back. "I thought we had enough of the stonesbane for at least another moon."

"Not since that last raid," Jelani said. He had a way of hiding the truth behind his dark eyes.

"You're saying we're *all* out?" Zala asked, her raised voice drawing the other pirates' heads. Jelani pulled her out of the line this time.

"Y'all talkin' for a minute or can I move forward?" one of the elder pirates asked. Old Man Ode was his name, if Zala recalled correctly, one of the few pirates who continued to survive Kobi's careless leadership. The old man looked worse than anyone else in line though, with a gash across his eye and a stream of blood soaking his trousers.

"Go on, kijana," Jelani told him. Ode limped forward in line with an appreciative nod as Jelani led Zala away from any keen ears to a set of crates filled with broken sabers.

Jelani tilted his head close to Zala, his voice low. "I drank it off before the battle. And the Vaaji ship didn't have none neither."

"You're lying. Who did you share it with this time?"

Jelani's lips parted as though to speak, but he held his tongue. Zala groaned.

"When?" Zala raised her voice an octave. Jelani put a finger to her lips.

"Two weeks ago," he confessed.

"Who?"

Jelani took a deep breath. "Tajo." His hand muffled the shout that almost slipped from Zala's mouth. "You gotta calm down. That's why I ain't never tell you, Zee."

Zala slapped his hand away, and an angry fire smoldered in her eyes. Her whisper cut sharp. "Show me."

She tugged at Jelani's hand. When he finally relented, she rubbed the back of his glove. Her eyes were serious, intent, locked on what hid beneath. Jelani pulled his glove off slowly, making sure no one else on deck saw. What had once been deep-brown skin was now a hideous ash-gray with purple veins spread out like a river delta. She drew the sleeve of his loose shirt farther up, horrified at the stony crags that were stuck to his skin. It never seemed to end.

"Jelani, it's past your shoulder now!" She lifted his shirt, then traced her hand over his stomach. "And where did this section come from? It's not even connected to the rest of the infection."

"Don't know," he said offhandedly. "The stone is spreadin' all over my body. Look, I ain't want to worry you none. I still have a good portion of the year. Thought we woulda find somethin' up on that big ol' ship. Or else I woulda tell the captain to wait to see what kind of ship we was dealin' with."

Zala pounded her fist against Jelani's chest. "So *you're* the reason you almost died today?"

"Uh, oh! Lover's quarrel?" one pirate in line jeered. Zala gave her a scowl as Jelani stepped between them. He grabbed Zala's elbow and moved them farther away to an even darker corner filled with nets and old wash rags.

"That's the life you got us in," Jelani said, clutching Zala's hand under his. "I'm just living up to it now."

The words hit hard for Zala as the tips of her mouth curled down. "*We* agreed to it. Not just me."

A pause came then, an awkward one that had become far too familiar between them in the past few moons.

In an attempt at levity, Jelani added, "We can always reach out to Majida like you said."

It worked—Zala cracked a smile. "No, I don't think I'm quite cut out for that kind of work. And neither are you." She pinched him playfully on the chest again, and almost let out a laugh she had been so used to sharing with Jelani in the past. But her fingers had found another hard spot, drawing her light laughter back into another frown.

"Pirating was the only way to keep you alive," she said softly. "This ain't the shit you play around with, you hear me? You can't let us take on ships we can't see in the fog."

"I know, Zee. I'll stay more careful."

"And what about that Vaaji captain? He shouldn't have broken that easily. Kobi had barely touched him before he told us about that 'weapon.'"

"*Captain* Kobi," Jelani corrected, looking over Zala's shoulders to the queue. "Don't let the crew hear you disrespect him like that."

"You saw it too," Zala said, ignoring the rebuke. "It was almost like he *wanted* us to know his people were coming tomorrow with some secret whatever."

Jelani pulled his glove over his fingers and ran his hand over his bare head—a tick of frustration for him. Tajo walked past with a bloody cloth held to his eye. He gave Jelani a nod of respect. Zala couldn't help noticing that his own case of stoneskin had spread halfway up his neck already, even if the man tried to hide it with a scarf. No wonder Jelani had given him his share of stonesbane. Without it, the man could have been dead in the next moon.

A pang of guilt settled in Zala's gut and her thoughts went to Tajo's little sister back home on Kidogo. The girl would be fourteen soon, nearly a woman grown. Tajo was all she had left. How could Zala fault her husband, who was at least a half year from his disease taking over, when Tajo only had weeks.

"You all right there, Taj?" she asked, hoping her tone didn't come across with too much pity.

"Doing better," he said, then turned to Jelani to speak in Pakwan. "*Wah gwaan, Jelani.*"

"*Mia a duh well. Bless up, bredda,*" Jelani replied, then switched to the Mother Tongue. "May Her waves be merciful."

Tajo nodded sagely. "May Her waves be merciful."

Zala slumped to Jelani's side as she watched Tajo walk up to the weather deck. Her shoulders were still tense. "I don't like it, any of it," she said. "The raids, this new shit with the Vaaji. We're overreaching. And I know you don't like it either."

"It don't make a difference what I like or what I want. Can't afford caution no more." Jelani gave his head a second rub. "It up to the crew for a vote and the captain to decide right now anyway."

"Maybe you should be the captain," Zala muttered. Jelani gave her a short chuckle, catching himself mid-laugh when a pirate in the line turned to look.

"I'm serious," Zala said. "You're cut out for it."

"You the one with all the plans. I'm just a decent navigator."

"More than decent. And the crew respects you." Yet another passing pirate nodded to Jelani.

"Well, right now I have to get my cuts dressed and tended to. And I don't speak the Mother Tongue good, you know that. Captains have to give them speeches all the time." Jelani waved the notion away.

Zala turned an annoyed expression to the others. "I'd do it if the crew respected me, if they even knew my name."

"I know your name," a small voice came from below.

Zala and Jelani stiffened for a moment, but relaxed when they saw Fon was the one who had spoken. Zala let out a stilted breath, then smiled. "You don't count, Fon."

Fon shuffled to a set of cannons near the wall, but tripped over a loose board in the floor.

"Ouch," the aziza squeaked, as she leaned against the cannon nearest her for support. "I'm still finding my sea legs again. The doc said I'd need a few days until the soreness wears off."

Zala gestured to Fon as she made a face at Jelani. "See? We can't keep putting our friends in needless danger."

"Sorry, Fon." Jelani knelt down to the aziza's height with a frown. "You shoulda never been out there today. I'm gonna have a chat with the captain for you."

"S'okay," Fon said. "I'll just stick to the kitchens for now. Crew's gonna be hungry."

Zala pointed to the gash across Fon's arm. "Hey, what about that? The doc couldn't mend that cut on your arm?"

Fon shook her head, loose hair drifting against her nose. "He doesn't have the supplies."

"I would have sworn you had some when we were on that ship," Zala said with a questioning look. Her expression changed the moment she realized Fon wasn't meeting her eye. "Oh, come on! You too? Who'd you give your dawa to?"

"Ajola…" Fon looked up quickly when Zala sucked at her teeth. "You saw how bad she was bleeding. She needed it."

Zala pinched the bridge of her nose. "Ugh, what am I going to do with the pair of you." She turned from Fon to Jelani. "Do you know if the Vaaji had any more dawa?"

"I only looked for the stonesbane ingredients. I haven't gone through all the inventory yet. I'll ask the quartermaster later."

Zala bit her lip as she gave Fon a sheepish side-eye. "Do you *have* to ask the quartermaster? I… might owe him my share of loot."

Jelani lifted his hands to his hips. "Mantu? Why?"

"Long story short, I lost a bet."

"Badly," Fon added.

"Shhh, you." Zala turned slitted eyes to Fon, who shrugged her shoulders. But when she saw the deep cut on the aziza's arm—a collage of purples and blues—she softened her expression again. "How are you feeling?"

"It doesn't hurt much anymore." Fon stretched her elbow. "I'm still not used to using a dagger so much. No one ever tells you how exhausting knife fighting can be."

When Zala had pledged to Kobi and the *Titan*, she and Fon had bonded over their mutual... ineptitude for fighting. Sure, they were decent at stabbing unsuspecting foes in the back, but when it came head to head they were best in support roles. Neither of them was even supposed to be a fighter. Hells, before a few moons ago Jelani hadn't known the difference between a sword and a saber. Kobi had hired Jelani as navigator, not a swordsman, Fon as a cook, not a knife fighter, and Zala wasn't sure what she was supposed to be, but it certainly wasn't an archer.

Zala knelt down to Fon alongside Jelani. "Have you been doing the exercises Jelani told you to do? You must train your arms to be stronger."

"I've been trying," Fon said. "But with all these raids—"

"I know, I know," Zala said, turning a second set of dark eyes to Jelani.

Jelani raised his hands. "It's not my fault!"

Zala slapped her knees in frustration as she stood back up. "I really don't understand it. It's monsoon season, so we should use these fogs to raid the Vaaji docks, not attack them at open sea."

"Bring it up at the next meetin'," Jelani suggested.

"You know they wouldn't hear it from me."

Jelani pressed his gloved hand into his chin. "Maybe if I tell them the plan, they'll listen."

"That might work…" Fon mused.

"I'm not asking for much," Zala said. "It's not like it's that complicated a plan. We could have the coin we need in a moon if we just run smaller raids along the coast. And, with the fogs, we might be able to carry out more hits along the way. Who knows when it'll clear up?"

"Some of the crew ain't gonna bite," Jelani said. "Captain might be crazy, but he makes things happen. We get good takes from these raids." He pointed out the gun port toward the warship drifting atop the delicate waves.

"Well, we don't need *all* of the crew for a vote," Zala said.

"We only need *most* of the crew," Fon finished for her.

CHAPTER 9
ZALA

CAPTAIN KOBI HELD THE MEETING ON THE NEWLY christened *Osiris* once most of the crew had tended to their wounds. Those with injuries too grave remained on the *Titan*, a fact Zala was not happy with. If her plan had half a chance of success, she needed those who were impaired to be there.

As she scanned the rest of the able-bodied crew—if she could even call them that with their malnourished forms—she noticed that most of them fit comfortably on the new ship's top deck, unlike the smaller *Titan*, where some crewmen were always left hanging from ratlines.

Kobi had left a skeleton crew on the *Titan*—a few of them the previous members of the Vaaji fleet. Most of the crew on the *Titan* stood at the ship's starboard railings, listening to the captain's words.

Long, dark flags drifted down the masts of the enormous warship, each written with Vaaji words. Zala could understand the Vaaji language for the most part, but she had a harder time with the written word. From what she could tell, the writing was all religious text anyway—not something she ever had much interest in.

"First order of business," Captain Kobi bellowed. "I shall be taking the helm of our new conquest, the *Osiris*. But that leaves the *Titan* without a captain. Who among you is worthy of her, I wonder?"

Zala scanned the crew. Where there had been almost a hundred of them before at their height, now there stood barely half. And those that did remain were half-broken, wearing cuts and bruises at the least, and amputated limbs and missing eyes at the worst. Their faces spelled defeat and fatigue. But a few did step forward.

The first was Mantu—with Sniffs clapping stupidly like some jester at his side.

The second was a pirate Zala didn't know the name of, a newer male recruit they had pulled in only a week ago. His thin body looked as though it could fall apart and his face was disturbingly gaunt.

The third was a woman Zala had come to know as Ajola, the same woman she and Fon had saved during the raid before reuniting with Jelani. When Ajola passed by Zala's group she gave a salute to Fon. The aziza returned the gesture with an "I got you" salute. Even Zala had to admit that Fon's charity was for the best in the long run, even if the aziza had to suffer through perpetual throbbing along her arm.

Ajola was tall, long-necked, and dark-skinned. She wore her hair short like Zala, though Ajola always covered her head in her signature flowing green bandana. Unlike the rest of the crew, her cheeks bore a healthy complexion, and she walked with a strong posture, her eyes as fierce as a hawk's. Were it not for that brutal scar running down her face, Zala would have thought her closer to a queen than a criminal, even as the woman twisted the fiercest glare in Mantu's direction while looking him up and down.

Zala felt a tug at her pant leg. "You should stand forward," Fon suggested.

"This would be the best time," Jelani agreed, placing a hand on the small of Zala's back.

Their encouragement was met with a curt shake of Zala's head. "I don't think so. None of the crew respect me enough."

"I respect you," Fon said as she looked up to the ratlines, where a certain pakka perched and watched over the assembly. "Shomari respects you—I think. You saved a few of the crew in that last raid. They should be on your side as well. You may not win the vote, but at least you'll have a start."

"This the best time to get the whole crew's attention—the only time," Jelani added.

Zala watched as the other candidates took their positions. They eyed each other like a trio of sharks in a reef. Zala's right hand started twitching of its own accord, the tell-tale sign that somewhere deep in the recesses of her mind something was egging her on. But if Zala joined them she'd look no more commanding than a guppy, and seeing how the crew watched them intently—despite how low energy they all were—she couldn't bring herself to find what it took to step up.

She stood there convincing herself that someone like Ajola wouldn't be so bad in charge of the ship—but then again having Mantu as a captain would be hell. If anything, she could oppose his claim by stating her own. Perhaps that was enough. At the very least she could lay her grievances out for all to hear.

Fon nudged Zala's knee. "Come on. The worst they can do is say no."

Zala took a large gulp of air as she looked for any others who might step forward. It seemed like only three wanted to make a claim. She turned to look up to Jelani, who gave her a warm smile, a smile that always reached those gentle brown eyes. A small tension released in her stomach. She could never live it down if she didn't at least *try.*

Zala inhaled deeply; sea mist filled her lungs, and with it, a renewed sense of courage. She stepped forward to Captain Kobi's—and her own—surprise.

"Anyone else?" The captain eyed the rest of the crew, though no one else had the backbone to meet his question. "All right, then. Each man and woman will be given one minute to make their claim. Ajola, we'll start with you."

Captain Kobi withdrew a small minute-glass from his loose shirt. He set the object on a barrel, watching the sand drift down its shaft. To Zala, it looked like the sand fell faster than normal as it careened with the ebb and flow of the ship's bounce atop the waves.

Ajola stepped forward to the middle of the deck, giving Zala a short nod. Zala returned her own. "Ahoy, crew of the *Titan.*" Ajola saluted the *Titan's* hand sign—two hands in the shape of a "T." Sounds of stiff and dirty clothing rustled as the crew mirrored the gesture.

"Me once served for the Ya-Seti Navy long, long ago. For a time, Kobi and me were enemies." Kobi looked up from the minute-glass, nodding affirmation. "Me was never captain to any of the Ya-Seti ships. But me was quarter-master to many. We pirates tend to live short lives out here at sea—a year or two is all some of us can hope for. But me have braved the Sapphires for more than ten."

Ajola made eye contact with each crew member, measuring her words. When her eyes passed over Zala it was as though Zala had been truly seen, even among the greater crowd.

How can I make the crew feel like that? Zala thought.

"Me know these waters and me know the Ya-Seti ports too," she continued. "After we take this new Vaaji invention —and earn *our* way onto Golden Lord Zuberi's Council— me gonna lead us true."

'Our' way? She's good.

"Me can get a holding on the Esterland coast. With me at your helm, on Yemàyá, we will see greatness that none since the pirate lords of legend have ever known! Mosiya and the *Marauder*." A few pirates gave respectful claps. "Lekkun and the *Sanaa*!" This time Ajola was met with grunts and a few hollers. "Zuberi and the *Do'hruba*." A wave of recognition came for the first ship still afloat today, the pride of the golden lord himself. "Let the next be Ajola and the *Titan*." The crowd roared. Zala couldn't help but find herself clapping as well, taken by the energy of the masses. Ajola bowed her head and walked back into the throng of pirates. The crew welcomed her with cheers and claps to her shoulder.

"Well said, Ajola, well said," Captain Kobi bellowed, then licked his yellowed teeth.

Zala wasn't sure how she could possibly top that. She didn't have enough experience, and her voice wasn't anywhere near as commanding.

"Rishaad." The captain turned to the newest of the pirates. "Let's hear from you next."

The young man stepped into the center. "Greetings, crew. Most of you do not know me. I am Rishaad, formerly of Vaaj. Most of you might mistrust me simply because of my nationality." One pirate spat on the ground. "I do not deny my homeland. I love it, but I do not love what it has become," Rishaad drawled as he pointed to the sky. "Ula knows what villainy has been done under Her stars. And as I've proved this past week, the empire is as much an enemy to me as they are to you, if not more. You see…"

The boy was as dry as sand. He continued listing off the places he had been and the experience he held, but he had none of the passion Ajola had put forth. Quickly, the eyes of the pirates drooped and sagged. In only thirty seconds, this Rishaad boy had bored them stiff, sapping them of all fervor they had held before.

The pounding in Zala's chest settled for a moment. Where before she had been too nervous to follow Ajola, now she was eager to speak her mind. Perhaps she could adopt a thing or two from the seasoned woman's speech. She looked across the deck to Mantu, who was whispering to Sniffs and laughing. Clearly he thought the same.

"I've known this empire my whole life," Rishaad went on. "I know how they think. Make me your captain, and I will help defeat whatever this new weapon of the empire is."

"Thank you for your words, Rishaad," Captain Kobi said with heavy eyes. Rishaad sagged back into the crowd. "All right, who's next… Zala, let's hear from you."

Zala's heart dropped to her stomach. She hadn't expected to follow Rishaad. Mantu looked so eager to say his piece, she'd assumed the captain would choose him next. Though surprised, she did not let her face fall. The crew would sense any misgivings, any weakness at all, and if she wanted to lead them, that wouldn't do. Once she finally composed herself, she stepped forward.

"Good morning to you all," Zala said, trying to put as much weight under her voice as she could. *How did Ajola do it?* "Some of you know me by name, some by face, most of you know me through Jelani, our navigator—and my husband." Jelani waved acknowledgment as the crowd's eyes followed her gesture. She heard one of the pirates call him a "decent man." That was good. She'd take any credit, even by association. "I've been on this crew a few moons now. I was one of the first to sign with Kobi—Captain Kobi —when he offered our people on Kidogo aid." Heat rose in her ears, and she fought desperately to keep it from her face. "I owe much to him, as we all do."

Zala held a hand out to Kobi, trying her best not to choke on her use of his title "captain." Kobi returned her gesture with the muted face of a grizzly statue.

"But… we've lost good men and women these last few weeks. And I think it's time we took a more cautious approach to these raids. We can't keep up with this pace!" Zala caught the eye of Old Man Ode, who looked to her as though she were mad. "I'm not saying we should stop pursuing a place on the Golden Council, far from it." Her speech grew faster and more slurred with every word. "But we need to be smarter." Zala looked up and wished she hadn't—even *Fon* was holding her head in her hands. The heat Zala repressed in her ears finally spilled across her face. Her next words came slow and on the edge of a quiver. "If I am made captain of the *Titan*, I can get us in with the golden lord and his court while still retaining our lives. I may not be as experienced, and I don't have a personal relationship with the Vaaji, but if you give me—"

"That's enough." Captain Kobi raised his hand. "You've had your minute."

"But I only have one more thing to—"

"I said that was enough," he grunted without looking at Zala. Mantu and Sniffs covered their laughter with their hands.

"Mantu. I believe you wanted to speak?"

"Yes, Captain," Mantu said as he parted through the crowd. Zala still hadn't moved from the center, her fists clenched.

Mantu leaned his head down to the side, awkwardly craning over her and obstructing her view of Kobi. He thumbed a hand over his shoulder. "Chana, the captain said you were done."

Zala looked from head to head. She found no support from the men and women about her. None of their eyes met hers, save for Shomari's yellow ones. The pakka only shook his head and sighed. She had been so sure most of the crew wanted new direction, yet they just didn't have the resolve to face Kobi. But how could they? How could she expect them to support someone like her? Zala, with her apparently meek and small voice, nothing like the assertive Ajola or the grand presence of Kobi. Zala, who was only good enough to make the crew flavorless soup in the kitchens. Zala, who couldn't even fight when it came to a straight-up bout. A nobody.

It wasn't all the crew's fault, though. She hadn't made her message clear, nor had she made her presence known on the ship. If only she'd had another moment, she could have explained what she meant to do. Her plan was sound. She knew it.

"Come on, girl," Mantu added with a sickeningly smug grin. "I think there's a crate of mazomba scales over by your man for you to loot while none of us is lookin'."

Zala might have been able to contain herself if it wasn't for the few pockets of sneers about her. Before she even realized what she was doing, her open palm was arcing straight for Mantu's cheek in a slap. But the large man had anticipated the move. Zala's hand wasn't even halfway to his face before his meaty grip was around her wrist. A few gasps released from the crowds, followed by a steady stream of instigating "ooos."

Sucking his teeth, Mantu said, "Tsk, tsk. The code says we ain't to strike another member of the crew." Zala tried to pull away, but Mantu's hold was iron tight. He pulled her in close where she could smell his rancid breath and his dirty beard. "Don't try me, chana. Me and your husband are friends, after all."

"Let go of me," Zala said through gritted teeth.

"That's enough," Jelani intoned from behind. Zala edged her eyes over her shoulder to see him parting through the crowd. The moment she felt Mantu's grip loosen, she pulled back and released herself.

Mantu held his hands to his sides in pseudo peace. "Just reminding Zala here that there's a proper way to do these things."

Despite wanting to go for a second slap, Zala reluctantly stepped back into the group. She didn't realize how bad her blood was building until Jelani gave her a gentle pat on the back while whispering in her ear, "You gotta be careful. The captain don't like talk back and you can't just go to hittin' whoever."

"But I didn't finish," Zala said with frustration. "I didn't even tell them my plan —"

"I ain't talkin' 'bout that," Jelani said. "You weren't speechin' to replace Kobi. You were supposed to be going for the *Titan*."

Zala raised her voice. "That's what I did, didn't I? I —"

"Called the captain an idiot."

"I didn't mean tha —"

Someone shushed them just as Mantu reached his stride. The man saluted the crew with a "T" symbol like Ajola had.

Damnit, Zala thought, *I forgot to do the damn hand sign, of*

87

course.

"As you lot know," he continued. "I been on this crew as long as the captain himself. We did our time in the Aktahrian Navy together. They set us up in different positions, of course—he was a commander, and I was captain to one of his ships. Both of us served under Admiral Itet. But when those dikala did what they done, I knew I had to join up with good ol' *Captain* Kobi in the free seas."

Mantu threw a glance Zala's way, brown-nosing and mocking in one fell swoop.

He's smarter than I give him credit for.

"There ain't no man or woman you can trust more on this ship. And there ain't no man or woman with more experience with the captain neither. I know the way he thinks, and I know how to work his tactics and plans, the same brand of genius that's earned us more in this past moon than many of us ever thought we'd get in our lives. The captain's done right by us." Mantu locked eyes with Ajola. "I don't give you empty words. It's my actions that do the talkin'. No one on this crew can say they've worked harder for our family. If you name me captain of the *Titan*, I promise you you'll have all the riches our captain has won us and more!"

A few of the pirates nodded in approval—not the raucous cheers that Ajola had received but the subdued silence of legitimate thought. Sniffs clapped, his hands looking as though he were beating two giant stones together. Kobi clapped as well, slow, loud, and powerful.

"That was more than a minute," Zala said, eyeing the sand timer which had long since expired. She furrowed her brow so far down it came just between her eyes. Most of Mantu's speech was unadulterated bootlicking.

Jelani placed a hand on her shoulder, halting her increasing ire. "Easy."

She hadn't even noticed the fist her hand had curled into.

"Nicely done. Thank you, Mantu," Kobi said. Mantu dipped his chin to his chest, turning his hand over in dramatic flair, and yielded the deck to the captain. "Well, with that I turn the vote to you lot, then. For those who back Ajola as the new captain of the *Titan*, show me your support."

Almost a third of the crew raised their hands.

"Good, good." Captain Kobi nodded. "Now, who backs Rishaad?"

Fewer hands rose into the air, though it was a respectable backing.

"I see, I see," Captain Kobi said. "Maybe next time, Rishaad. There's plenty more ships out there for us to plunder. All right, how many do we have to back Mantu?"

"Mantu!?" Zala shouted without thinking. Was she so forgettable that the captain could pass her over completely?

"Oh, forgive me." Kobi frowned unceremoniously, his tone unapologetic. "Who here backs Zala?"

At first, Zala thought no one voted for her. But then she saw Jelani and Fon's hands raised high. Next, she saw Tajo lift his own as he kept the scarf hiding his stoneskin taut around his neck. She heard the tightening of a ratline and turned her eyes up to the mainmast. Shomari hung from the ropes upside-down like the jungle cat that he was. He sighed a low purr before dropping a languid hand in a reluctant vote for Zala. Most times he didn't vote in meetings like this. A few whispers of surprise trickled through the crowd.

"Well, you got a vote out of the cat, ain't that something," Jelani muttered.

"Maybe next time, chana," Kobi said, regaining the

focus of the crowd and turning to the rest of the group. "As I was saying before, who here backs Mantu?"

Another third of the group rose their hands.

"This is close." Captain Kobi stroked his large white beard. "Here's what we'll do. The remaining votes will only be for Ajola and Mantu. First, who holds their support for Ajola?"

Nearly half of the group rose their hands. Zala was one of them. If anyone was going to be captain, she'd want Ajola. Mantu would just be a worse version of Kobi.

"I see," Kobi said. "I think I know how this will go. But just to be sure, who here puts their faith in Mantu?"

The majority of the group raised their hands.

"Then that's settled," Kobi said. "By the right of Yem, Mantu of Khopesh, you are now captain of the *Titan*. Congratulations, friend."

Mantu bowed. The way his thin grin disappeared into his beard sent a wave of disgust through Zala. "I'll try to lead it as well as you, Captain."

Kobi took his spot in the deck's center. "With that business out of the way… as most of you know, we have information about a secret weapon the Vaaji Navy will be sailing through here tomorrow."

"What's so secret about it?" one of the pirates asked. "Some new warship?"

"We don't know yet—not even our Vaaji friend down below in the brig knows." Kobi started to circle the center, hands behind his back and belly out. "But if it's something that needs to be kept secret from their own, it must be something good."

"How are we supposed to attack something we know nothing about?" Zala couldn't help but ask.

Kobi turned his belly to her. "A good question, Zala.

Our friend told me they've a ship. 'The deadliest the world will ever see,' I think is what he said. And on that ship is something of great value."

"They haven't seen what our captain—excuse me, commodore, is capable of," Mantu said, measuring the crowd with his eyes. Some of them approved of Kobi's new title. Zala rolled her eyes. Mantu already had the *Titan*, he didn't need to kiss ass anymore.

Kobi continued his circle. "This ship of theirs isn't complete. It's only an early build. And it's coming out here to Kidogo Sea… *without* an escort."

"So it's a trap," Zala whispered to Jelani matter-of-factly. It was beyond her how it wasn't apparent to anyone else, least of all Kobi.

Jelani rubbed the back of his head. "I'm with ya there. Somethin' fishy goin' on."

"Well, I can't say anything about it." Zala darted her eyes toward the group, nudging Jelani to get in there and fix it. "I told you: these people don't respect me, but they'll respect *you*."

"If I can have your ear, Captain," Jelani spoke up, taking a respectful step forward.

Kobi twisted on his heel, leering a yellowed grin when he saw his favorite navigator. "Ah, Jelani. Yes, of course. What say you?"

"That man." He pointed down below. "He got a big, big mouth. Too big. The Vaaji may be poets, but one of their captains should have tighter lips, ya?"

Kobi's mouth became a thin line and he lifted a single finger in the air. "A good point. But I already thought of that. You see, I sent a scout out just after our raid to verify this man's story. Nabila, step forward please."

The small, thin woman with golden-brown eyes, a

hooked nose, and coarse hair stepped to the center of the deck. She was a shape-shifter—a gull-shifter, specifically. And if Zala remembered correctly, the fastest one on the ship. She had joined the crew only a week before Rishaad did. Though she was friendly whenever Zala had spoken to her, she mostly kept to herself.

Kobi had used her several times to scout out many of the ships and seaside towns they had raided. Perhaps she had found out something useful, something that Zala could actually believe.

"The Vaaji's port-city, al-Anim, looked normal at first." Nabila's head moved on a swivel like that of a twitchy bird. "But hidden in cover was one of the strangest ships I have ever seen."

Old Man Ode spoke up. "Another one like this warship?"

"No. Different," she said. "Smaller, for one."

Zala huffed through her nose and moved her head close to Jelani. "Something's not right. There has to be more to the ship than size if it's some big secret."

"The ship only looked half built," Nabila continued. "The underside was open with cannons fitted within, and I suspect they still need to fill out the rest. But it is an interesting design, entirely new."

"Don't know about this…" Jelani shifted his shoulders to Kobi, his head held low in consideration. "We barely survived takin' on this ship. How we gonna take on another this soon? Might be better to ransack al-Anim itself if this thing will be at open sea. Let's at least head back to Kidogo to recruit more hands."

A moment of silence hung above the deck as Kobi's eyes shifted between Jelani and Zala. His next words cut deep. "Is this coming from you… or your woman?"

Zala gave him an ugly scowl, grinding at her teeth so as not to make another outburst.

"I agree with her," Jelani confessed, lowering his voice. "You and me both know we almost died this mornin'."

Kobi's ears went red—from shame or anger, Zala couldn't tell. "What are you going on about? I took out half those men myself. Not one of them knew how to wield a sword."

"Aye, Captain, you were ferocious as a cornered mazomba, but you *were* cornered. I fought with you then, and I'd do it again now, but we been testin' Yem's waters. And Her mercy is not eternal. Our luck will dry at some point, ya? Let's go back home and refill it some, I say." Kobi turned a frown to Jelani, and Jelani changed his tone. "Just want to be honest with you, Captain."

Kobi considered the words, his hands pressed behind his back. "Thank you, Jelani. But we cannot pass up this opportunity. Yem has shown us mercy. She led us to this very ship." He spread his arms out wide. "We would be going against Her Will if we turned tail now. This new invention of the Vaaji will get us a one-way trip to the golden lord's private bay, and a seat at his table."

Zala kissed her teeth, stepping in front of Jelani. "Listen, if we hit Vaaj's coastal towns we can get the coin we need—it would only take a moon, maybe two—and we'd have an audience with Lord Zuberi. We won't even need a big ship, we can invest in smaller ones at the port—"

"Enough," Kobi spat. Pockets of gasps rippled through the crowd. "You are only on this ship because Jelani asked it of me. Had he not, you would have been left behind on Kidogo."

Zala crossed her arms. "Well, fortunately, it's not up to you. This ship—and any ship in Lord Zuberi's seas—are commanded by votes. And perhaps the crew is less inclined to go on another suicide mission."

Kobi tilted his head with a mocking smirk. "Oh, you think so?"

"They may not want me as captain," Zala admitted, though it was a hard thing to say. "But I'm sure they don't want to throw their lives away either. We don't know nearly enough about this... whatever this vessel from Vaaj is."

A silence cut between the pair, filled only by the water lapping against the ship's sides. Many of the pirates whispered to one another.

"Very well then!" Kobi clapped his hands together suddenly. "Let's have the vote your heart desires. Who here wants to attack the Vaaji and acquire the riches that won't only put us *on* the Golden Lord's Council, but put us on *top* of it?"

Many of the crew gave a great cheer, though the frown on Kobi's face said he'd expected more support.

"Come on, you dikala," Mantu shouted. "You pirates or no? Do you want the riches or not?"

More of the crew roared this time.

Zala stepped up. "And who here would like the same, but without half the faces here sleeping at the bottom of the ocean?"

There were no cheers, just sad eyes. She should have expected this. The people she needed on her side were simply too hollowed out. They didn't have the energy to fight anything, even the captain. Zala couldn't blame them. Kobi was an intimidating man, and when he got in everyone's faces like this, it was easy to be bullied into backing him.

"Then it's settled," Kobi said, his smile stretching wide. "We attack at dawn."

CHAPTER 10
ZALA

ZALA AND FON RETIRED TO THE WARSHIP'S GALLEY WHILE Jelani requested a private word with Kobi in the captain's new quarters. The last thing Zala could pick up before their conversation was locked behind closed doors was Jelani trying to delay the attack by at least a day. It was a small chance, but at least he was making the effort.

Fon prepared some salted meat for the red-eyed pirates gathering to have their bellies filled. The Vaaji's galley was almost the size of a proper mess hall. On the *Titan*, however, their tables were merely barrels and hammocks.

Fon plopped a brick of dry meat onto a wooden plate and offered it to Zala. Zala declined the food in favor of the sugar rum and was on her fifth chug before Fon stopped her.

"Are you trying to kill yourself?" Fon asked.

"What's the point?" Zala said through a belch. "Looks like we're all heading to our deaths tomorrow anyway."

Fon leaned in close to Zala, looking to the others busy with their meals. "We don't have to stay here, you know."

"Desertion?" Zala raised an eyebrow. She looked over her shoulder to the pirates. Only a handful of the crew sat about, all busy chewing through plates of tough meat. Most of them were not loyal to Kobi, from what Zala could tell, but Fon knew better than to suggest such a thing. "Don't let anyone hear you saying that."

The aziza shrugged. "Well, it's better than being dead. Night will be here soon. The ship's got some longboats we can take, just the three of us. Maybe the ol' cat too."

"And where would we go? I still need the coin for Jelani." Zala reached for her sixth chug. Fon intercepted her with a deft slap to the wrist.

Zala dropped her head onto the table, groaned, then spoke through her arms. "No, this is our best chance. High risk, high reward. I knew what we were gettin' into with Kobi. I don't like it, but we don't have a better choice right now. It was hard enough convincing the captain to take us on in the first place. We're not exactly veterans at all this."

"What do you mean? Jelani's a fair navigator," Fon said.

Zala grunted. "He cheats."

"How's that?"

"He couldn't read a map if he tried. He just uses his a'bara."

"How does that work exactly?"

"Ask him. He's tried to explain the magic to me. I just call it talking to fish."

"A sea speaker..." Fon said lightly as she scooted down the bench to lean in close to Zala. "That's why his glow's different. I knew he was a mystic, but I didn't know what type. Sort of rude to ask sometimes, ya? I had heard you Kidogons had a few. There were rumors that you all summoned a..." She trailed off, then gasped. "That's why

Jelani's infected, isn't he? Was he one of the ones defending your cove?"

"We didn't want to tell anyone," Zala confessed. "We just wanted to lay low, get our coin, and be on our way."

"I still say we should be on our way. We can earn coin out in the West."

"And brave that great desert for how many moons? That's a sure way to get Jelani killed."

Fon frowned. "Right... no wings."

Zala and Fon sat in silence. Deserting wasn't an option for Zala. She and Jelani had tried to run cons on their own, but the only people they had been able to swindle were those on their home isle, people they knew. They had discussed traveling to Zanziwala once, where the golden lord and his Golden Council sat, but the towns there were too hot, too cluttered with others like them trying to turn over quick coin. They had been lucky to find a crew that would take them on at all. In the end, it was the only real option they'd had.

Fon swiped Zala's cup, taking a sip. "So, if we aren't going for the d-word, does that mean you have one of your famous plans?" Fon took another tiny sip. It was all she could manage or else she'd be swiftly drunk—aziza bodies and all that.

Zala lifted her head from her arms. "Not exactly. But I'm sure something will come up in the moment. It's gotten me this far."

"Didn't help you when Fon got kicked into the side of that deck," purred an accusing voice from behind them.

Zala and Fon's eyes went wide. A shiver ran down Zala's spine as they turned to a dark, looming figure—a grim specter of black fur, though the pair of yellow eyes were familiar. A crescent of white teeth flanked sharp fangs shooting into a leering smirk.

"What did you hear?" Zala started, fear lacing her voice. She shot a glance down to Fon. She knew the pakka better than Zala did, though Fon only gave her a vague shrug.

Shomari slid onto the bench between the pair while Fon sidled to make room. "I thought I heard nothing good. But if you were so startled by my presence, then perhaps I did miss something..." He turned his eyes to Fon as he bent low over his paw-hands, golden rings around each of his fingers. "I'm curious. Anything I should be knowing, Little Flutter?"

Fon had no word for him, her pointed ears red.

"I see." Shomari dismissed the notion with a fluttering hand. "Keep your secrets, then." He turned back to Zala, leaning an elbow on the table while his head rested at an angle on his hand. "So, that was a shit speech you gave, huh, Zala?"

Zala had no response as she dropped her head back into her arms, embarrassment claiming her thoughts again.

"Shomari!" Fon beat her hands against the cat's back. "At least she spoke up!" She stood up onto the bench to meet him eye to eye. "And what do you mean it was shit? You voted for her, didn't you?"

Shomari pawed away Fon's punches half-heartedly. "I'm not trying to offend the chana, Little Flutter. But we all need a dose of truth from time to time."

"Not right now I don't." Zala knocked her head against the table, disgruntled. "Why'd you vote for me, anyway?"

Shomari shrugged. "I've a good feeling about you. And I saw what you did on that deck. Aside from you getting poor Flutter here manhandled, it went pretty well."

Fon shoved his shoulder with both her hands, frowning.

"Zala didn't get me kicked into that deck, and you know that."

Shomari smiled at the shove, not budging an inch. It seemed to Zala as though any physical contact with the aziza was a victory in those unctuous cat eyes.

"Hmm," he said, "it was she suggesting you attack that group while so ill-equipped, was it not?"

"Neither of us knew they'd have so many soldiers." Fon thrust a finger between his eyes. "None of us did."

The pakka's gaze narrowed ominously for a moment, then he directed his voice back to Zala. "You need to start working things through. You think on your feet well enough, 'tis true, but you could stand to give yourself a running start here and there."

Zala's spirits lifted at the half-compliment for a moment, though that nagging voice telling her "she couldn't do it" lingered at the back of her mind.

"So do you agree we should ease up, then?" she asked as she rested her chin on her forearms.

"I think *you* should ease up, certainly. That slap of yours against Mantu was completely amateur, far too telegraphed."

"Oh, come off it, Shomari," Fon said. "We saw you yesterday. You're just as exhausted as the rest of us!"

"So I want a bit of a rest, and Zala is the only one offering it. That doesn't mean she cares about Kidogo's plight —"

"That's not true," Zala cut in, that voice in her head growing louder once more.

"Is it not?" Shomari raised his head, the golden band around his goatee jingling. "The way I see it, you only care for what happens to our navigator. That's what your wager with Mantu was about, yes? Oh, don't look so surprised.

Mantu and Sniffs were boasting about it the moment the raid was over. There are other people on this ship besides your life-mate. More still on Kidogo."

The lump in Zala's throat was hard to swallow. Dose of truth, indeed. *Cold hard truth.*

Shomari went on, "The pakka I traveled with suffered from the same plague as your Jelani. But those who would sympathize on this ship are too weak, and those who would not… well, they care for one thing and one thing only."

"The Golden Lord's Council," Zala finished for him.

Shomari took the forgotten cup of rum and chugged it down. "If you want to lead these people, you need to appeal to what they want... regardless of your actual intentions when all is said and done."

Zala mulled over the cat's advice, then turned to Fon with searching eyes. Were Shomari's words true? Had Zala been up her own ass? She knew Fon was too nice to tell her the truth. Maybe she should've taken the words to heart. Not that it changed anything either way—there would still be a raid the next day. Perhaps she could lead the crew to a successful victory. If this new Vaaji ship was really what it was chalked up to be, this could be their last job and an out for her and Jelani. They had managed to scrape through a fortnight of non-stop raids, after all.

What was one more?

CHAPTER 11

KARIM

BESIDES THE CAPTAIN'S QUARTERS AND THE BRIDGE, THE navigation room was the largest space on the airship. Karim sighed deeply before entering the room filled with the other senior officers of the ship: the sailing master, the purser, the priestess, and the vice admiral. Meetings like these were rarely enjoyable.

Most of the officers sat as close as they could to Captain Malouf's head chair. Karim took a seat at the far end of the meeting table, which had a multitude of scrolls and maps spread across it. He was never the type to involve himself in brown-nose conversation with his higher-ups. He preferred to let the merits of his work prove his worth to the empire, not his tongue.

There was an unwritten rule within the academies of Vaaj, though, a saying spoken in whispers amongst its students: *Like all valuable commodities, truth is often counterfeited.* Karim never found value in the saying as he listened to the chit-chat about the room, the subjects ranging from disingenuous recollections to forced banter that feigned interest.

The whole room stank of politics.

Karim kept quietly to himself as the seniors' stewards filed in. Occasionally one of the officers would turn and send a false smile his way. That kind of socialite grin sent his eyes rolling skyward, or a shiver up his spine—depending on who was doing the smiling. Karim returned their looks with as much courtesy as he could muster, which probably came off as little more than a hard grimace.

Once Malouf arrived, the senior officers jumped to give him firm handshakes and a kiss on each cheek—Karim's own handshake was half-hearted, to say the least, and he kissed air, not skin.

When they were all seated once more, Karim took notice of Sailing Master Anwar Rashid, who moved like a crab in his simple white robes. He had earned his position by funding the airship project, and his navigational skills were rudimentary at best.

Next to him was Priestess Dahlia Fahyad, a portly woman with a *tarha* tightly wound around her head. An assortment of glistening jewels bedecked the headwrap. She said they had religious significance, but Karim had always thought she was just flaunting the wealth granted to her by the empire. She had found her way onto the *Viper* through actual merit, however, after studying in the temples of Akeem. But she often spun religious text to favor Malouf's decisions. Karim had argued with her before—al-Qiba's text as his backing—but she'd simply scoffed, telling him he knew little of the "true meanings" behind the Great Book.

Then there was Purser Umar Jad, who cared nothing more than for how the *Viper* could profit the empire. With the Malouf family being one of the richest in Vaaj, his loyalty lay firmly in the captain's pocket. Unlike Fahyad, Jad's dress was sleek, a simple blue robe with no ornate design or gold trim. Karim had come to know this as a farce—the man was likely the wealthiest officer on the ship.

And then there was Vice Admiral Talaat Shamoun. He was the only one of the lot Karim truly respected. The senior officer was one of the few who had seen active combat during the Andala Inquisition. His was the last fleet to successfully hold back the Andalans in the Midland Seas, a campaign that went on for years before an eventual and forced retreat. Karim had often modeled his own approach to tactics with Shamoun's famous exploits in mind.

Lastly, there was Captain Malouf himself, whose family managed a vast portion of the lumber and metal used to build the sea ships—and now airships—for the empire.

None of the other old hats had quite been able to get the feel for the airship as Karim had. Many had built their military careers on the sea, and the airship was drastically different in a great number of ways. There were important nuances that Karim had proven himself apt in, a skill that earned the attention of Grand Admiral Awad. Despite all that, Karim sometimes felt like a glorified helmsman with only the *title* of chief officer.

He had hoped the grand admiral himself would have led the testing of the new airship, but for whatever reason, in their infinite wisdom the military council had settled with Malouf.

"Thank you all for joining us this afternoon," Malouf started, poise restored to his words now that he was once more back in control of the ship. "Earlier this morning we received word that *Saber's Edge* came into contact with the Kidogon pirates a few leagues south of Asiya Bay." He unrolled a new map across the table, which depicted the seas between Vaaj and the Sapphire Islands. "One of our spies was able to get a message to us, and the pirates have taken the bait. They believe they'll be catching us unawares tomorrow morning." He paused for effect, eyeing each smile as they lit across the room.

Karim's lips flattened and he dug his nails into his chair, yet he could not hold his tongue this time. "We used our *own* as bait?"

"Yes, that's what I said," Malouf returned flatly. Karim was quick to form the start of a retort in his throat but he kept his mouth shut. He knew it would be for naught. Now it made sense why Nabila had said what she did. How could Malouf be so daft as to think it was a good idea to let the pirates attack and take one of the empire's own ships? Had the admiralty really approved it? Did they even know?

Umar Jad sat forward, his simple robes falling over his hands. "Are we not attacking them preemptively? I heard orders that the *Viper* would press ahead today."

"I gave no such order." The finality in Malouf's tone put to rest any thoughts of Karim's previous instructions.

"So the mystics from Kidogo are among them, then?" Dahlia Fahyad asked, her headdress clinking as she moved in her seat; Karim shifted uncomfortably in his own. Did everyone in this room know more than he did? Granted, he'd expected their targets would be the sea speakers from the island, but that was only a guess. What did they think? Was he too young, too green to know what it was they were doing on this mission? Surely the chief officer of the ship should have been more well informed than the religious consult.

Karim caught the edge of Umar Jad's sidelong glance. It was like the man could read his mind, a sly tilt of his mouth betraying a wry grin.

"Indeed," Malouf said. "If we capture just one of these

sea-speaking mystics, we should be able to extract from them how to get to the island's skyglass deposit."

"Now that they've taken *Saber's Edge* as bait, will we be proceeding with our initial plan?" Talaat Shamoun asked.

Malouf's voice went soft when addressing the senior officer. "If you still think that's the best course of action for us, Vice Admiral."

"Well, it certainly demonstrates our superiority well enough," Shamoun started with a nod. "Forces them to surrender with minimal damage. With the *Saber* in their possession they'll be hamstrung in their initial retreat."

Karim would give credit where credit was due. Perhaps Malouf had set the bait so that the pirates would take the much slower ship, giving the *Viper* an even chance of keeping up. Despite the praise, Karim didn't feel any better about sacrificing their own. There had to have been a better way to entice the pirates into manning a bulkier ship.

"We'll send out another scout to confirm they haven't scuttled her, of course." Malouf gestured to one of the stewards. The young man gave a crisp bow and left, the kind of obedience attributed to those looking to raise up in the ranks. Malouf's favorite kind of underling.

"With two ships present," the vice admiral said, "it becomes a matter of which we believe the mystics will be stationed on. It may well be both." Shamoun stroked his bare chin. Unlike most of the men in Vaaj, he kept his face clean.

"I've heard their captain once served Aktah," Anwar Rashid said.

"Captain Kheti, correct?" Malouf asked.

Rashid raised a finger in the air, his hand glistening with rings of gold and silver. "That's the one. Though he goes by Captain Kobi these days. Knowing his reputation, he'd fancy the *Saber's Edge*. Not the best for pirating, but it would let him relive his glory days as a true captain of a more respectable vessel—not to mention the added firepower afforded by the warship."

"If that's the case," Shamoun intoned, "I say it's best to assume he'd keep any mystics with him, especially that sea speaker, if our spy is right in her identification." The airship jostled underfoot. Shamoun knotted his fingers, swallowing hard against what seemed to be a new fit of motion sickness. "With that said, we should attack the smaller of the ships. Sink it without delay. That way we'll both secure a quick surrender and have a comprehensive test for the *Viper*."

The information was a lot to catch up with, but Karim was unwilling to sit back and be treated like a child of war. They would hear him before this was through; he just needed the right moment to cut in and give his own input. But assessing all the new developments and forming his own plan was more than challenging. He kept going over it in his mind though. There were two ships at play—one pirate, fast and agile, the other, one of their own, big and strong. There was a sea speaker at play that needed to be taken alive at all costs. And they needed a successful run with the airship.

"But what if some mystics are left to the smaller ship?" Karim asked, addressing the vice admiral directly. At this table, there was little point aiming his question anywhere else. "Shouldn't we abstain from sinking the ship outright? We could at least give the pirates a chance to abandon the vessel. They'll likely retreat to *Saber's Edge*. That way we can kill two rocs with one stone—"

"We'll only need one to tell us where they're hiding the glass," Malouf cut in. "There's no need to leave their retreat open."

Shamoun held up a sage hand. "El-Sayyed may be right.

We should give them an opportunity for escape. The pirates of these seas are close-knit. And if they've mystics in their ranks, they'll want to save them in particular. I'm sure you remember our run-in with the Meroé Rovers and the *Redtide*."

Malouf clenched his jaw. "Very well. Does anyone have any further suggestions?" he asked the group, though none of them had anything to add.

How could a room full of senior officers have nothing more to present to such an important mission? Karim shifted in his seat before speaking again. "We should attack at night. It'd be an added advantage with our air supremacy."

"At night?" Malouf questioned, condescension coating his voice. "And how do you presume we'll be able to *see* the pirates or their ships?"

Karim gave a sidelong glance to Shamoun. "It'll be much easier for us to see them than they us. None of them expect to find enemies in the sky. The northern dragons are all but gone, and the last of our own native rocs haven't been seen for two generations. The only sighting of any flying creatures are the kongamatos, but they're far off in Kunda. Besides the average bird, the pirates have no reason to draw their attention to the clouds. With a night approach, we can assure a first strike."

The vein across Malouf's forehead looked ready to burst again. "We're assured a first strike with the sun at our backs."

"I'm confident our gunners can function at night, sir. I can speak with Gunner Chief Akif myself and—"

"No, there will be no need. We can't risk the disadvantage."

"But it wouldn't be a disadvantage. We'd—"

Malouf raised his voice. "There is no need for us to strain our gunners and use more ammunition than required shooting in the dark. Not for the sake of one or two surprise salvos."

"But even if the first shots miss, we'll still be able to follow through before they can even —"

Malouf pounded his fist into the desk, sending scrolls rolling onto the floor. "That's enough, el-Sayyed. We will not attack at night. That's my final word."

Silence fell across what now looked to be a far darker room. The black-and-red banners strung from the walls a falsehood of their true power set among such a petty debate. Only the creaking of wood and the subtle shift of the ship against the clouds split the dense quiet. Karim could only say so much, after all. He was merely the chief officer; Malouf was the captain.

Shamoun broke the silence first. "El-Sayyed's logic may have merit. Tell me, Malouf, have you spoken to our technicians in the engine room?"

Malouf shook his head. "I have not."

There was a second awkward pause, punctuated by Shamoun's raised brow; it said more in one motion than an entire tirade could have.

"I checked with them a few hours ago when prepping the ship." Karim turned his words back to Shamoun. If he could help it, he didn't want to have to speak directly to Malouf for the rest of the session. *Hang the captain and his tantrums.*

Shamoun shifted toward Karim. "Tell me, have they found a solution to the glass' cloud problem?"

"No, they have not," Karim answered, the tension in his neck relaxing now that he was speaking with the vice admiral. "They're still working on some of the chief's latest ideas.

That's partly why I brought up the notion of a night attack."

"Perhaps we can use it to our advantage," Shamoun directed his voice to the rest of the table. "El-Sayyed is right to be cautious. But instead of using the cloak of night, we could use our own exhaust—"

"As a cloud cover..." Karim said, almost to himself. "Apologies, Vice Admiral," he added as he noticed the room focusing in on him.

The others must have expected another outburst. Rashid's shoulders clenched up, stiff as a crab's. Fahyad's eyes darted between the chief officer and the admiral.

Shamoun didn't smile, but he gestured for Karim to continue. He did. "It could work in theory... we'd just need to find a way of getting the cloud to shroud us. At the moment it just trails behind."

"With you at the helm, much as I shudder to suggest it, I see no reason we cannot try a Samara's Spin," Shamoun offered. Karim clenched his jaw. It would be a difficult maneuver, but he might just manage it. When he raised his eyes to the others, they all wore faces of utter confusion.

"I'm seeing a lot of perplexed faces," Shamoun said.

"Sorry, sir... but what's a... what did you call it? A Sam—what spin?" asked Rashid.

"In the lands of Andala there is a type of fruit tree whose seeds, when they fall loose in autumn winds, spin in perfect rotation."

"You mean like hawks before they dive?"

"Somewhat... but on a shorter axis. It's almost like they are turning upon themselves. We can apply the same maneuver to the *Viper*, which will enable us to shroud ourselves effectively within the cloud."

"But what about our gunners?" Malouf asked, finally

composed, though the residual throbs of his forehead vein persisted. "All that spinning would have to affect their accuracy, not to mention the fog that would surround them."

"Not too much, sir," Karim replied, braving a response toward Malouf. "From above looking straight down, the impact on aim would be minimal."

"Hmm..." Malouf trailed off. Again, Rashid tensed, ready for a second eruption from the captain. But the blowout never came. Judging by Malouf's receding vein, it seemed like a plan he would at least consider. That was more than any of them could hope for.

Karim stroked his hand over a scroll of schematics. "We could even see if our engineers can rig the exhausts to shoot out to our bow as well. That way we'd be completely enveloped."

"That sounds like a good idea, provided the captain agrees, of course." Shamoun turned to Malouf and his cohorts. All eyes followed his gaze to the captain, sitting at the table's head.

Malouf looked embittered, but he gave a long nod. "Those pirates won't know what hit them."

CHAPTER 12
ZALA

ZALA'S HANDS CLAMPED DOWN ON THE *OSIRIS'* BOW railing, all color drained from her knuckles. For hours the ship had been drifting through gray-white mist. All that could be seen were a few tides mere feet ahead of them. Her head twitched at the sound of each wave lapping against the hull. She didn't even know what she was looking for.

Every so often she caught sight of the *Titan*, a small shadow slicing through the sheet of gray alongside them. Did Mantu and his crew feel the same as she? She looked over her shoulder. Several crewmates had gathered with her at the bow, and nearly every face mirrored her unease.

Fon looked perhaps the most fretful, but that could have just been her child-like face at play again. Jelani, of course, held as firm an expression as always, the thin line of his mouth revealing nothing.

Kobi had stationed Jelani on the *Osiris* for his navigational skills, wanting to keep the sea speaker close to his side for the upcoming raid. Jelani and Zala were a package deal though, so she had been posted along with him, much as the 'commodore' might have wished other-wise. The arrangement suited her fine—she wanted nothing to do with the *Titan* when Mantu was at her helm.

The ship's bowsprit cut between wisps of white, parting the way into a clearing in the fog. It was an eerily beautiful day—sky blue, the water an even deeper indigo. But there was no Vaaji ship, just a line of small rocky isles and harsh waves crashing against them. The rhythmic tide splashing against the rocks sounded like the beat of a war drum.

The bright sun seemed to bring an ease to the crew's tension as the *Titan* joined them in the clearing free of fog. Where before the crew of the *Titan's* movements had appeared stiff and measured when they set out, now there seemed to be an easier air among the men and women.

Whispers spread across the two decks, and nervous buzz turned into cautious chit-chat as the minutes rolled by.

Each moment that passed brought another squeeze of the railing from Zala. "We should have seen something by now, ya? Can you spot anything?"

Fon shook her head. "I sense nothing at all. Maybe we got bad information?"

Zala scanned the other platforms and crows' nests. The crew that had gathered at the bow started to turn back to their stations. Some had faces of relief, others masks of disappointment. Their location had to be right. The rocks ahead indicated the northern tip of the Ibabi Isles, sure as salt.

Zala kept her attention locked on the beat of the waves. She couldn't shake the uneasy feeling in the pit of her stom-ach. It had been too quiet, too still—like someone or some-thing was watching them from the fog, ready to strike like a sea hawk against its prey. Perhaps it would have been better if they had remained cloaked instead of exposing themselves in the clearing.

"We've some clouds coming in." Fon pointed to the sky. At the far end of the fog's clearing, just near the rising sun, a group of dark clouds rushed over the ocean.

Zala's eyes widened, her brow lifting high. Those weren't just clouds.

"A storm's brewing," she said. She tapped Fon along the shoulder, pointing up toward the crow's nest. The pair quickly climbed to get a better look. When they reached the top, there was no doubting the bruise-colored clouds.

"Full sails to port!" Captain Kobi shouted from the stern deck.

"Full sails to port!" Jelani repeated. The order echoed across the grand warship from crew member to crew member.

Zala lost her balance for a moment as the ship banked hard to portside. Her stomach tightened and she grabbed onto the foremast—what had been a small movement on the deck was a harsher thing so high up.

"Bring me that Vaaji!" Kobi shouted. "You, cat, go get him." Kobi pointed to Shomari, who was standing near the deck's starboard edge. Zala couldn't hear the pakka's response, but she saw his facetiously flamboyant salute before he scampered down belowdeck.

As the ship continued its retreat from the storm, Zala inspected the clouds again. There was something odd about that encroaching darkness. It didn't move as it should. Instead of spreading wide, it was concentrated into a single cloud bank, which rolled forward to an unnatural point, almost like the head of an arrow. The whirlwind was moving too fast as well, and it had a strange cyan hue wafting behind its barrier.

"Fon?" Zala asked. The aziza looked up at the notable fear in her companion's voice. "What do you see in that cloud?"

Fon turned her eyes to the sky, both her irises and tattoo glowing bright. Her expression changed from a focused squint to wide-eyes of shock. "Something's alive in there… a big something."

"Get Kobi," Zala said. But when she turned, the captain's attention was locked on the Vaaji prisoner being dragged up by Shomari.

"Where is it?" Kobi shouted. "Where's your secret weapon?"

The man's hair hung loosely over his eyes. He looked different without his headwrap, almost like a pirate himself. When the Vaaji stared up into the storm all it seemed he could do was laugh.

Kobi smacked him across the mouth. "What's so damn funny? Where's the bloody ship?"

The Vaaji took another moment to get out a series of guffaws before nudging his head skyward. "See for yourself, pirate."

A loud roar bellowed from within the cloud.

"It can't be," Zala said, her heart pumping suddenly in her ears. "No way."

Fon's face fell open in disbelief. "It's impossible! I haven't seen a roc since I was a child." That was saying something. Fon was nearing her one-hundred-and-fiftieth birthday.

Zala whipped her head back to the sky, breathless, expecting the thunderous wingspan of the great beast. She had heard stories about them, everyone had. It was said that the great rocs could swallow ships whole. Was that the Vaaji's new weapon? Had they summoned one of the long-dead beasts? But that Nabila woman had said it was a regular ship with a few modifications, didn't she?

"Captain, we have to move! It's a roc!" Zala called out from the crow's nest. But the captain was already directing the crew in their retreat.

"We can't go no faster while we turnin' round!" Jelani shouted to an angry Kobi.

The Vaaji captain let out another series of rough laughter. "It's not a roc, you idiots!"

The roar sounded again from within the clouds. Now that Zala was listening for something different, it didn't sound like the cry of a monstrous bird. It sounded more like a horn.

Zala squinted her eyes. "If it's not a roc, then…"

The cloud broke, and through its wake came the spear tip of a ship's prow.

A ship! Flying?

She couldn't wrap her mind around what her eyes told her, and her mouth fell agape.

Half of the ship looked normal enough: two masts atop its deck, topped with fore and mainsails, and led by a bowsprit, all built from fine wood whose polish shone bright against the morning sun. But the lower hull had sails swept back like wings, and what looked like an exposed underside deck, guns at the ready and pointed downward.

Zala snapped her mouth shut. How long had she been covering it with her hand? For a moment there was silence as the pirate crew craned their necks toward the sky as though the Gods themselves had returned to Esowon once more. Zala would have almost preferred the roc. They were dangerous, but at least they made sense.

Fon prayed into her hands and sung a quiet hymn. The other crew stood in awe, some on their knees, others with their hands in the air. Zala knew what they all thought. How would they ever fight a thing like that? How could they even survive it? The best they could do was submit.

Another thundering horn split the hush across the deck, and from the great beast that was the Vaaji's sky ship, a duet of fire and cannonballs rained down upon them.

Most of the shots fell harmlessly into the ocean behind the ships. But it was clear by the arc of fire that whoever was summoning a hellstorm on them were just measuring their aim.

The *Titan* peeled away first, crashing off toward the rocky line of isles. The crew members of the *Osiris* gaped at the flying vessel, mouths still hanging from their faces.

"What kind of magic is this?" one of them asked.

"How?" asked another.

Zala shook them from their stupor. "Get to your defensive positions, people. Staring at the thing isn't going to take it down." The other crewmates rushed to their posts, tripping over each other while their eyes refused to pull from the sky. Zala couldn't blame them; she was doing the same.

Kobi shouted at the helmsman. "Turn this ship around! Full sails. Ship to starboard."

"Full sails. Helm to starboard!" Jelani repeated the command.

What's he doing? Zala thought. *We need to* run *from that thing, not attack it.*

"We'll show those dikala what we're made of." Kobi whipped toward the Vaaji captain, who continued to laugh. His cackling echoed across the entire ship, carried by the waves that crashed against the hull. Kobi reached into his belt and withdrew a long, nasty-looking dagger stained with blood. The Vaaji eyed the knife like it was a joke, smirking in derision even as the captain brought the blade to the man's neck.

Zala shook her head in disbelief. The man had snapped. Did he really think Kobi wouldn't do it?

The captain grabbed the man by his hair and ran the blade across the front of his throat. The cackling turned into a sick gurgling, the air of laughter replaced with sprays of blood. The enemy captain fell forward with a dull thud, a smile etched across his face.

Zala waved her hands frantically at the captain. "We'll never outrun them in this thing!"

"What are you doing up there?" Kobi looked to the crow's nest. "Start shooting them down."

"How do you expect—" The ship gave a shudder, and Zala went flying against the nest's rail. A heavy creak of wood groaned from below as the mast protested the too-sharp turn.

Zala couldn't help scoffing at the helmsman's poor work as each turn seemed to lead directly into a new set of fire jets and cannonballs instead of away. "Captain! I can steer us—"

"You're not the fucking helmswoman!"

"Enough, Zala! There ain't time," Jelani shouted up, a serious edge to his voice.

Zala nodded, keeping her mouth shut. Even she could agree that only one voice should command in a time of battle, especially with things as messed up as they were.

When she and Fon turned their secondhand bows to the sky, another set of fireballs scored a direct hit. The ship's hull was mostly undamaged, but the blast caught two crew members beneath its flames. The man and woman who were now engulfed screamed a terrible cry. Their pained hollers sent the other crewmates into a panic as they tried to quell the flames with sea water.

Zala braced for another impact, but it never came. Had the first attack only been a warning, a show of force?

She looked up, using her hand to shield her eyes from the morning sun. The sky ship drifted away from the *Osiris* and made its way to the smaller *Titan*.

Were they being toyed with? The sky ship was easily quick enough to put the *Osiris* down, yet it was turning its attention to the lesser vessel.

The *Titan* broke fast from left to right, using the straits of the small isles to hide itself; it was an effective tactic against other sea ships, but against something soaring at them from above it was next to useless. The sky ship pursued it unabated like an osprey to sardines. But just when it looked as though the *Titan* would be hit on its stern, it peeled out of range, leaving empty water in its wake.

Captain Kobi shouted orders for more speed, "Catch up, catch up! We can't let them take the *Titan*." But the crew was already giving the large ship as much as she could take.

Zala loosed arrow after arrow at the flying ship, but none of them reached. The underside of their hull was open, and she could make out tiny figures manning the cannons, but hitting their gunners and elementals would only work if they managed to close the gap. So she decided to wait for the enemy crew to board. She'd just shoot them as they came down.

But they never did.

The sky ship kept pursuing the *Titan* as though it were the only vessel on the sea, yet they made no move to board. Why were they concentrating so much effort on the meeker ship?

"Why aren't they boarding?" asked Zala, voicing her thoughts to Fon.

"Why would they when they can just have their way with us from up there. They're not the only ones with wings though." Fon pointed her thumb to her back. "I could go up and take a look?"

"No," Zala said, shaking her head. "We don't know what we're dealing with. You almost died on that last raid. If you go up there alone… you might not come back."

Zala watched as Mantu's ship took a bad turn on a wave, and they were too slow to evade the next barrage. Thrice the ship was hit with fire and cannonballs. A blaze sprouted near their ship's bow. No one seemed to be putting it out.

"Didn't those elementals stick with Mantu?" Zala asked. "Can't they shield them with the ocean's water?"

"You mean Usali and Liya? Usali died last week in that raid against the Ya-Seti, and Liya was killed in yesterday's raid."

"Great." Zala drew back as full as she could and shot another arrow at the flying ship. Her arrow didn't even make it half the distance before it fell back down into the ocean.

She turned back to Fon. "This is going to be a very short raid."

CHAPTER 13
KARIM

"Sink that ship! Don't let up!" Malouf yelled at the top of his lungs.

"We are trying our best, Captain. The smaller vessel is just too fast," Deck Officer Ahmad said, his gnarled fingers working into knots around thrust controls.

The *Viper's* first real test was upon her.

The bridge crew worked double-time, anticipation manifesting in sheens of glistening sweat beads atop knitted brows. The most nervous of them seemed to be the captain himself. The man's uniform was dampened by perspiration and his turban sagged askew as he paced the bridge frantically. Each step was paired with a sidelong glance at Vice Admiral Shamoun, who sat at his station with hands clasped over crossed legs.

Malouf pointed a shaking finger down below. "I don't care how fast it is. Our gunners should be able to make their marks against the damned thing by now. We've already hit it three times."

"We're too high, Captain," Officer Ahmad said. "They have enough time to react to our fire."

"Then lower the ship!" Malouf shouted at the officer. But Ahmad was not the one steering the airship. The captain spun around toward Karim, who tugged against the controls. "Lower the ship, el-Sayyed."

Karim suppressed a groan as he focused his attention on the helm and swung around for another pass on the smaller ship. "This distance is what's keeping us out of reach, Captain."

"We should be able to take a few arrows," Malouf said.

"It's not just that, sir." Karim spun the controls to the left. "That speaker is still down there. If we get too low, their arrows will be the least of our worries."

The captain stomped across the bridge, his hands rubbing against each other without pause. Was this really their captain? Many of the crew were anxious, of course, but they kept a grip on their emotions. Had the reality of the situation finally caught up to the captain's hubris? With such an advantage, the battle should have already been won. Yet the first sign of struggle had him sweating buckets. It was bad enough he had wanted to give up their position by sounding the horn.

"Put fear in their hearts," he had said.

Get a grip on yourself, you old fool, Karim had thought.

The captain halted near the bridge's edge, tapping the glass of the large view port. "If the smaller ship won't allow us to get in another hit," he pointed below, "then we'll target *Saber's Edge.*"

Karim arched his neck to the warship below, which lumbered after the smaller vessel. It was too large to tail the pirate's little ship through the thin straits. Perhaps attacking it would be easier, but it would also risk the mission.

"Captain, you know we can't," Officer Ahmad said. "One of the targets could be on that ship."

"I don't care. Turn the *Viper* around. And you, tell those gunners to target *Saber's Edge* once more." Malouf pointed to Officer Tahan, who instinctively looked to Karim. She had dealt with the captain's drunken episodes too many times to trust his orders alone and had been one of the foremost supporters of Karim in his earlier preparations.

Internally, Karim grinned at the subtle gesture, but he quickly nodded his head. Hopefully the captain hadn't seen where her gaze had fallen.

"Right away, Captain." With a quick turn, she moved to her station, a tangle of copper pipes capped with funnel tops, and shouted the new orders down through the tube that led to gunnery.

Malouf shifted his eyes to Karim. "What are you waiting for, el-Sayyed? Turn this ship around."

"Officer Ahmad is right, Captain," Karim said. "We'd be risking the mission."

Why didn't Malouf listen to any of the recommendations given to him? It was what Karim would have done—what *any* decent captain would have done.

Malouf clenched a fist. "Our primary mission is to test the might of this ship. We are *failing* that test."

Karim risked a glance across to Shamoun as he pushed his heels into the rudders. "The council may disagree, Captain."

"Are you denying my order?" Malouf's voice went ice cold.

"Of course not, sir," Karim replied as he banked the ship's rudder to the side, forfeiting the chase of the smaller ship below and realigning with *Saber's Edge*.

The *Viper* cut through the clouds, gaining fast on the

much slower target. As they approached the hulking ship, Malouf shouted, "Fire!"

The first volleys reached the bow of *Saber's Edge*. The impact devastated the hull, obliterating their chase cannons.

Karim struck a frown and hoped the damage would satiate Malouf's fervor. None of the pirates should have died in the impact, save for those manning the guns. He wondered if the pirates would have really set their sea speaker to a cannon.

Unlikely, Karim thought as he peeled away from *Saber's Edge*.

"That's more like it!" Malouf clapped. "Next salvo! Target their sails."

Karim shot the captain a bewildered glance. Malouf met him with yet another pair of sharp eyes, daring the young officer to speak out against him.

Vice Admiral Shamoun, who had remained silent until that point while leaving Malouf to his responsibilities, threw his two coins into the ring. "I think the young officer is correct on this one, Captain."

"With all due respect." The edge to Malouf's voice did not soften as it often had before when responding to the vice admiral. "I am the captain of this ship. The success of our mission is my responsibility…" His voice softened. "Sir."

Shamoun settled back into his seat with one eyebrow quirked. "Very well, Captain."

Karim darted a quick look to the scribe at the bridge's rear. The young man scribbled across a scroll relentlessly. It was like he was a student punished with lines. But Shamoun had his objection on the record, as Karim assumed was his aim to begin with. As Malouf said, the mission was *his* responsibility.

Sighing deep from his chest, Karim shifted the ship back

in line with *Saber's Edge*. Malouf called for the starboard gunners to fire even before they were in range. Most of their shots dropped harmlessly into the ocean, to Karim's not-so-guilty satisfaction.

Once the *Viper* drifted directly over the vessel, every gunner had a line of sight. With so many shots raining down, the mainmast was soon ablaze, an inferno trailing down its shaft toward the deck like a coiling salamander. The sea ship would be dead in the water now.

Surely that will halt Malouf's fragile ego.

"Keep at it!" Malouf demanded.

Karim could no longer keep his mouth shut. "Captain, they aren't going anywhere. The smaller ship will likely try to rescue them."

"I won't leave it to chance. They're pirates. The other ship will be out of range by now, escaping to one of their islands."

Karim strafed the commandeered ship again. "These pirates are different, sir. The Kidogon factions don't leave their own behind, even in the face of a loss." Which the captain would have known had he paid attention to the council's briefing before they left the capital.

"No, we have to show them that the Vaaji Empire is not to be trifled with," Malouf rushed out, sweat reaching down to his hairy knuckles now. "Fire again!"

Karim measured the distance to the ship below before veering the *Viper* out of range. He couldn't let Malouf compromise the mission. Someone had to snatch back their victory from his conceit.

The second volley from the *Viper* missed the pirate ship's foremast by inches.

Malouf was livid, a white-knuckled grip clutching the edge of the bridge's railing. "How did we miss completely?

Someone bring me the gunner chief. I will not tolerate incompetence."

"It was the first miss since we've targeted *Saber's Edge*, Captain," Karim said, trying to keep his expression flat and respectful. He had no desire to get Issa in trouble if he could help it. It was his fault they'd missed. "Chief Akif deserves a promotion, not a reprimand."

Malouf pounded his fist in his palm. "Someone needs to answer for it. We can't let that ship get away!"

"I'll see that the gunners are kept in line, Captain," Karim said. "Ahmad can take my position at the helm. *Saber's Edge* is all but defeated."

"Yes, go put them in line, el-Sayyed. That's the first of your suggestions I've actually liked."

Karim nodded, doing his best to suppress a grimace. "Right away, Captain. Officer Ahmad, take the helm."

"Of course, sir," the young officer said as he took Karim's place.

Karim raced to the gunner's galley in a sideways hop through the compressed halls. If he could get there fast enough, maybe he could save *Saber's Edge* from being sunk entirely. Each cannon blast that shook the walls quickened his pace.

When he finally arrived at the ladder leading down to gunnery, he half-expected to find the image of smoldering remains in the deep blue sea. He was relieved to see that the enemy ship below was at least partially intact.

After jumping down onto the metal grating, he looked for Issa within the throng of soldiers. Finding her was easy. Of all the voices shouting orders and confirmations, hers always rang sharpest and loudest.

"Gunner Chief, what happened with that last volley?"

Karim asked, his voice a tone of indignation. He had to play the part in front of the others.

"Apologies, sir. We must have miscalculated the speed of the ship," she said, standing straight with a salute at her chest. She blamed only herself in situations like these, a soldier through and through. Karim smiled despite himself. Issa's honor was one of his favorite qualities about her. He almost felt bad for disrupting her work with his own steering, but it couldn't have been helped if the mission was going to be a success.

Karim pulled her away from the ears of the other gunners, whispering to her, "Don't blame yourself. It was me. I couldn't let the captain sink the ship. The target is likely on board."

Issa's eyes went bright, her expression one of concern. "The one from the skirmish at Kidogo?"

"None of us can be sure, but it's likely."

"What do you need me to do?" Issa asked, standing up straight.

Karim didn't care to hide his smile this time. *That's my girl.* "Just keep that ship afloat long enough for us to board them."

"I can buy you some time, but if the captain gives another direct order, I can't miss too many more volleys."

"Thank you, Issa."

A blast bellowed and a terrible cracking noise shot up from below like a forest being brought down by a firestorm.

"Gunner Chief, that was a direct hit!" one of her gunners shouted from the deck. The others stood around the mystic named Hajjar, giving him supportive slaps on the back. The mole above his lip rose with his wide beam.

"Where?" Issa asked.

"The foremast!" the mystic's spotter cried. "He got them! Hajjar got them!"

Karim sprinted to the railing at the edge of the gunner's platform where he looked down to the pirate ship below. His mouth fell open when he saw the damage. The foremast splintered as it split and fell back into the stern of the ship. He couldn't even see the deck through the curtain of hellfire.

The sea speaker was as good as dead.

CHAPTER 14
ZALA

THE FIREBALL RACED FOR THE FOREMAST IN A frightening blaze of vermillion. Zala could do nothing but brace for the impact.

"Fon, fly!" Zala yelled as the ball of flame snapped the foremast in half. Her feet buckled as she fell, and she didn't have time to see if the aziza got away.

Zala reached for the lines of the ship, grasping air until she felt the rough braid of a rope. She clutched hard despite the grip tearing her skin. Her arm gave a wrenching twist at the sudden change of momentum, but she clung on. Clenching her jaw and biting away the pain that rose through her, she wrapped her bicep around the ratline.

A loud *snap* curled in the air. Whether rope or bone, she couldn't tell—adrenaline masked the truth. Whichever the case, she couldn't afford to care. So long as her arm and hand could maintain a grip, that was all that mattered. The pain could be dealt with later.

But she couldn't hold.

Her grip slipped, and she fell back-first onto the deck. A sharp fire snapped through her spine as she cried out in pain. The fall wasn't as high as it could have been, but Zala was slow to rise. When she placed her hand to her back, and she realized her tunic wraps were *actually* on fire.

Quickly, she rolled atop the damp deck, but a frightening thought snaked through her veins when the flames did not immediately quell. She had seen burn victims before, heard their cries, and it wasn't hard to understand why with the heat so close. But she didn't stop rolling, just like the crew had told her on her first day on the ship.

Roll or die, they had said. *Don't stop until it's out... or you're dead*.

And she kept to her rolling as flames licked and snapped at her ankles, until finally the fire went out. Thank the stars she'd paid attention to the crew.

Zala glanced down at the hems around her trousers. They were singed off and her legs were only slightly raw with minor burns.

For a moment, she laid atop the deck, watching the sky ship above through the gaps of smoke and fireballs raining down upon them.

Had Fon made it? Had Jelani?

Flames engulfed the deck. The only thing she could hear were the sounds of cannons punching through wood and the death cries of the surrounding crew.

None of the voices belonged to her husband or friend.

She had to get up, but her body protested. Every muscle in her arms and legs fought to keep her plastered to the ground. Perhaps it was better to give in. It would be easier to just lie there and let the exhaustion take hold, let everything go to black.

Get up. You can sleep when you're dead, Zala thought as she managed to lift herself up to her elbows.

The ship had lost two of its three masts. There was no opportunity for escape now. Perhaps the Vaaji would finally board, though it seemed their only intent right now was destruction. They could burn the ship down for all Zala cared. So long as she could make her escape, she, Jelani, and Fon could find another. But they had to survive first.

Zala forced her body up, lifting herself to her knees. As flames stung her face, she watched as her fellow crew jumped overboard. She'd be right behind them once she found Jelani and Fon.

A set of sails wafted through the break of the flames, cloth falling from the mast in long drapes. She squinted her eyes and could barely make out the *Titan*, which seemed to be sailing to their rescue. Zala searched the sky for the flying ship and wondered if it had been going at full speed. It looked like a lot of weight to move around. She couldn't be sure. Who knew what it was capable of?

But it made sense. The *Titan* was too fast for it. The sky ship's captain must have grown tired of the chase, which was likely why they had turned their attention back to the slower *Osiris*. If the *Titan* came to rescue the rest of them, they'd be in range of the sky ship and then they'd all be dead.

Zala rushed to the ship's port. She waved her hands from side-to-side, but stopped when a sharp pain shot through the length of her arm. It didn't feel broken, but it hurt something fierce.

"Don't come!" she shouted. "Retreat! They'll destroy us all."

She searched for a flag to signal the ship to turn around, but she could find nothing. They would all be in flames by now. Even if she could find one the fire had spared, she wasn't sure what would be the appropriate signal.

An escape from the Vaaji may yet be possible, though not if the *Titan* was destroyed as well. Besides, could she even keep the *Osiris* alive long enough to think of something to get out of this? Zala turned her eyes sternward, yet the fires roared too high to see. Before anything, she needed to get to the helm. If there still *was* a helm.

Zala bounded forward, smoke burning her throat as she leapt over debris and ducked through flickering fire. As she approached the helm, the outlines of the sterncastle grew clearer. Two figures still stood.

As she coughed, covering her nose and mouth with her hand, she climbed around the main deck, where other crew members tried to cut a longboat from its lines.

As Zala scaled the sterncastle's side stair, the captain's voice roared over the crackling flames, "What are you dikala doing? The battle isn't lost, the *Osiris* still floats!"

"Captain!" Zala shouted as she climbed closer to the sterncastle. "Tell the helm to turn to port. We need to shake those fireballs!"

"Didn't I tell you to go to the crow's nest?"

"There are no more crow's nests, Captain." Zala swung her legs over the deck, nearly landing on the Vaaji captain Kobi had killed.

"Where's Jelani?" she asked quickly, but Kobi was somewhere else, the firelight reflecting in his old, milky eyes. Zala knew he knew it then: the reality of the situation was settling in as sure as a sunset dips at the end of a day.

"I didn't think it'd end this way." The captain turned grim eyes to her, ignoring her question. His once olive-toned skin was now a mess of soot and his white beard was gray and ashen, smattered with blood. "We'll give them a good fight, aye?"

Zala raised her voice. "Captain, where's Jelani?"

"This day has been a long time coming for me," he said darkly, ignoring her. "If we go down, then we go down."

Zala shoved Kobi's shoulder. He didn't move at all. "Where's Jelani, Kobi?"

Kobi shook himself back from the brink. "Where the hells *is* Jelani?" he asked as he turned to his helmsman.

"Still in the navigation room, I expect," the man said, spinning the helm with the fires blazing in his crazed eyes. Loyal to the end.

"Well, tell him to get out here, it's time for a proper fight," Kobi grunted.

"I'll get him," Zala offered, rushing into the navigation room before she got an answer she didn't like.

When she burst through the door, she found Jelani sitting cross-legged, his back to her. Was he meditating? At a time like this?

His torso was bare and drenched in sweat. Zala could see his ribcage under his skin. When was the last time he had eaten? How long had they been on this ship, barely surviving? Zala had almost forgotten what he looked like at full health.

"Jelani, we have to go," she said. "This ship is dead. Kobi's lost his mind."

He did not answer. Zala stomped to his side. Jelani's eyes glowed white and he mumbled under his breath. Zala scanned his body. In his left palm sat a marbled, cloudy ball: Gods' Glass, a darkstone at its center.

She slapped it out of his hand. "What in the Sapphire Hells are you doing?"

The glass clanked against the wooden floor, bouncing

against the far wall, and Jelani's eyes returned to their normal brown.

"Savin' this ship," he said through labored breaths.

Zala scowled. "With the shit that got you infected in the first place?"

"The Vaaji can't get the glass, Zala. They can't take me. They won't make me talk. Look what they done with the glass they've got now." He lifted his chin above. "How you think that thing's flyin' up there?"

"Why are we discussing this?" She pulled at Jelani, but he wouldn't budge. "They'll kill us if we stay; we need to go *now*."

"They usin' skyglass, Zala. Ula's Glass." Jelani lifted himself up, his words seeming almost dismissive as he scrambled for the Gods' Glass again. "That's what we was protectin' on the isle."

Zala took a step in front of him. "Get away from that. I swear, if you touch that thing again —"

"It's the only way. I already called one of the whales. He's real close!" Jelani knelt down near an overturned chair, but he was looking in the wrong spot. Zala saw the glass first, dashing for it and grabbing it in her uninjured hand. Then she threw it out of the window, value in gold be damned.

Jelani stumbled toward the window as another cannon blast struck the hull. Both of them stumbled into the far wall before Jelani turned and said, "Zee, what in Yem's name are you doin'!?"

"I'm saving your life," Zala said. "What are *you* doing, Jelani? How could you think of doing that? How could you think of doing that to *me*? What was I supposed to do, find you dead in this room because you wanted to talk to some fish? We did all of this so we could save *you*!"

133

"Ain't no curin' this thing, Zala. We only delayin' the—"
Jelani stopped himself short.

Zala swallowed hard, her eyes glistening. Jelani hung his head low and shifted his eyes away from her sorrowful gaze.

"Go on, say it." Zala slapped him across the chest, which was now dotted with chalky stone. "Delaying the what? Say it."

The door to the navigation room burst open, and the voice of the helmsman echoed off the wooden walls. "The captain said to get out here now."

"No... I told them to get their *asses* out here. What are they doing anyway? The *Titan* is nearly here."

"We comin' right now!" Jelani shouted over Zala's shoulder.

Zala frowned with a hand covering her leaking eyes. She didn't turn to face the helmsman, and instead fought back tears. Jelani grabbed his shirt from the desk and jogged past Zala toward the deck.

She bit her lip before she spoke again. "Wait!"

She turned on her heel. She couldn't leave it like that, not when a firestorm was crashing around them. She wasn't angry with Jelani. She knew that. Maybe he knew it too. But the situation was too much—everything was happening so fast. Why couldn't they go back to the way it was before, before the stoneskin, before the unrelenting seas, before the skies birthed flying monstrosities?

Jelani stood there hanging back for Zala as she tried to form her thoughts into words. The helmsman was just behind him waiting as well, and out the door was Kobi spinning the ship's wheel like a madman.

And then... there was nothing but a blazing light where the captain once stood.

For one silent moment, a bright luminance outlined Jelani like a halo. But the image tore away violently as a blast jerked Zala backward.

She tried to grab for Jelani, anticipated his finger hooking into hers. Fear flooded her heart when her hand missed his by a finger's length.

Then she felt nothing at all.

CHAPTER 15
KARIM

"That was our only chance."

Karim watched as *Saber's Edge* sank into the ocean, his hopes of capturing the target alive likely with it. His shoulders sagged as though weighed down by sacks of grain and his heart filled with bare disappointment.

None of the gunners seemed to catch his downcast face, too caught up in their jubilation as they watched the effects of their precision shooting.

Issa dipped her head in prayer, mumbling something to herself. From the bits and pieces of phrases Karim could make out, it was a prayer for lives lost, not the failure of their mission. Worse, she was praying to one of the Old Gods.

Karim did his best to suppress his irritation.

"The Kidogons are crafty. Our target might have survived," Issa said, though there was no confidence in her voice or eyes as she watched the ship sink beneath the waves.

Karim raised frustrated hands to his face in disbelief.

"The captain completely compromised—"

Issa laid a gentle hand on his shoulder. "Karim, you can't let this fluster you. Get up to the bridge and make the most of it."

"The most of what? There's nothing left for us to do." Karim stretched a hand down to the fire and smoke below.

Issa crossed her arms. "Is there really *nothing* else we can do?"

Karim knew that expression too well. Issa had shown it often throughout the years, a look that said, "don't give up now."

Karim shook his shoulders free of tension. "You're right. There had to be more than one mystic down there. And there's still one ship left."

"Look." Issa pointed down over the railing. The smaller ship, as Karim predicted, had abandoned the narrow island straits for the sinking ship's rescue, and was ferrying as many of their crew as they could. But to his surprise, they threw up a surrender flag as well.

"They're bluffing," he said. "They're banking that they'll be able to pull their people out and escape before we get down there. Or they want us to lower the ship so they can get a few hits in. They must know by now that we can't catch them if they slip out of range."

"Then perhaps our chief officer should stop them before they carry out whatever ruse they have planned." Issa raised her eyebrows leadingly.

Karim nodded before spinning on his heel and bounding for the bridge. Hadn't Nabila said there were wageni on board the ships as well? Though not as valuable as the sea speaker, they *might* know the secrets of Kidogo's coves. It wasn't as though he had any other options to place his hopes in.

With another side-hop through the narrow halls leading to the command deck, Karim made his way to the bridge, his spirits lifted for a moment. He could at least save the smaller ship. And if he was wrong about where they kept the mystics, perhaps the sea speaker was still alive as well.

When he reached the command deck, the crew were still congratulating one another with hollers and curled fists in the air.

"We have to stop that ship!" Karim yelled, ending the melody of cheers.

"The captain just ordered us to board," Officer Tahan said.

A good idea for once? Karim thought.

But when he looked through the bridge's viewport it appeared the airship was descending. Karim stomped toward the helmsmen. Surely they weren't going to make a direct boarding. That would completely negate their height advantage.

"What are you doing, Officer Ahmad?" Karim asked. "Why are we descending?"

"Captain's orders, sir." Ahmad kept his eyes out toward the viewport while he fumbled with the controls. Karim had to remind himself it was the young officer's first time at the helm during active combat. "He's ordered us down for boarding action."

Karim almost swore. Instead, he took a quick breath. *This* situation required delicacy. Of course Malouf was screwing it up again, but he couldn't just shout that out on the bridge. So what, then? What could he do to redirect this latest stupidity?

He twisted his head to the vice admiral. The man sat at his seat as before, watching the bridge as though he were a spectator at a bazaar. When would he step in? Surely he didn't agree with Malouf's plan. What was the point of descending on the ship just to put the *Viper* within range?

Another decry worked its way up Karim's throat. Instead of shouting, he marched to Malouf and cleared his wind pipe. "Captain, may I have a word?"

Malouf swiveled around, a grin stretched across his face, and his pointed mustache curled in what looked like an exaggerated second smile. His amusement quickly soured when he saw Karim.

"First," Karim said, "congratulations on taking down *Saber's Edge*, sir. The *Viper* has exceeded all expectations."

"Get to your point, el-Sayyed."

"Right." Karim straightened his back. "Sir, I think we should exercise caution. Boarding them is the best course of action, I agree, but we should keep our distance. We could dispatch our longboats — or even the new gliders — to meet them."

Malouf shook his head. "The gliders haven't been tested yet. Not an option."

"We don't have to use gliders necessarily, just a thought to cover all angles. The longboats would be enough for the boarding itself, and the *Viper* can remain above to deter any resistance. The pirates know if they try anything, they'll go the way of *Saber's Edge*. If you give me just a few minutes, I can gather—"

The captain lifted a hand. "That's enough. We don't have time for that. The pirates are trying to rescue their fallen crew even as we speak."

"I know, but that doesn't mean we should put the *Viper* in harm's way."

"What harm?" Malouf asked, his mustache twisting into another smile. "They've surrendered, given up."

"A white flag means nothing to pirates. I know you've

made your career facing the other Great Nations' Navies, but these scum are different. I grew up around people like them. This is just them trying to buy time."

Captain Malouf put a hand to Karim's shoulder. To the young man's surprise, he was met with a chuckle. "Persistent. I can see why Grand Admiral Awad likes you. But you don't have to worry—I have the situation under control. Helmsman, bring us down."

Karim bristled beneath the condescension of Malouf's words. What had brought this change on? Where was the spittled rage? He was a fool if he thought he had the situation in hand as he claimed. But Karim had nothing to offer in retort.

"Right away, Captain," Ahmad said. He nearly lost purchase with the floor as the airship's descent cut sharp.

Malouf gestured Karim over with a wave befitting royalty. "Come, Karim. Introduce me to these pirates. I've heard so many stories about them."

Karim placed respectful hands behind his back—*fake it until you make it*—and followed Malouf through the ship as they descended onto the gunnery deck.

"As you've said," the captain intoned, "you grew up with rats like these."

Malouf positioned himself near the edge of the starboard railing while the *Viper* drifted closer to the defeated pirate ship.

When Karim passed Issa on the gunnery platform he whispered into her ear. "Keep an eye out."

She gave a short nod before twisting her shoulders starboard.

As the distance between the ships shrank, Karim's heart pounded faster and faster, his eyes never wavering from the guns on the pirate ship. From what he could tell no one manned their cannons, but that didn't mean a few of the scum weren't hiding in the shadows of the lower decks, ready to strike. At least they still held the height advantage. If the pirates decided to attack, they'd need to angle their heavy cannons upward, which would have been a cumbersome affair. The moment Karim saw any such movement he'd order the ship back up into the clouds, Malouf be damned.

Out of the corner of his eye, Karim could see Hajjar standing atop one of the platforms. Karim dipped his head, locking eyes with the young elemental. He hoped his dark look was enough to communicate the danger they were drifting toward.

Once within earshot of the pirates, Malouf beamed, and outstretched his hands like a street merchant ready to perform. The end of his headwrap waved along the wind, adding to the showmanship. "A fine morning this is, is it not?"

Malouf's audience was less than captivated.

None of the pirates were familiar to Karim — he had seen no faces during his first attack of the island — and to his surprise, some of them looked genuinely defeated. Most nursed injuries, while others pulled their comrades who had survived the initial assault against the *Saber's Edge* into their ship. *Perhaps* the captain was right after all. Their surrender might have been an honest one.

"You may have heard of me," Malouf bellowed. "I am Captain Hassan Malouf, son of the great General Qasim Malouf of the Vaaji Empire. You will forfeit your ship and all of your possessions by right of conquest in the name of Their Majesties, Emperor and Empress al-Nasir."

Karim and Issa traded sidelong glances which were clearly intended as internal eye rolls.

No response came from the pirates, save a few groans from the wounded. Karim could only assume their true captain had perished during the battle. However, a man with a large beard and sun-baked skin stepped forward.

"You're right, Captain Marissa Kamoof. We haven't heard of you," he said in jest.

The able-bodied crew laughed. A large man next to the mouthy pirate kept sniffing and clearing his nose; he laughed the loudest. But through all the guffaws, Karim sensed a touch of unease. The pirates seemed to know they were outmatched.

Malouf, offended by the jeers and the man who led the peanut gallery, jabbed an agitated finger toward him. "Yours will be the head I take first! Crew, prepare to board."

Malouf's words were met with little enthusiasm, and the silence weighed even until...

"What are we?" The bellow from Issa whip-cracked their spines.

"We are one!" the crew drew their swords.

The *Viper* drifted closer, a mere ten strides above the pirate ship now, then descended parallel with the vessel. The defeated crew sprang to action in a flurry, and a symphony of unsheathing swords echoed across their deck. Malouf's smug grin turned into a full glower.

A terrible feeling pressed against Karim's temples as he scanned the faces of the crew. One of them, a woman, kept darting her eyes at the almost-closed gap between the ships. He had thought she'd been shamed in their defeat, but now he couldn't help thinking she was looking at something…

Malouf lifted his boot atop the railing, looking ready to lunge off the ship as soon as they were in range. Karim saw a mat of black fur clasping the platform's edge, just below the —

"Captain!" Karim shouted with an outstretched hand. Too slow.

A dark shadow sprang atop the deck, rapier point leading its stride. Malouf saw it too—not that it helped. The blade's tip pierced him through the shoulder where his padded armor was exposed.

Without a thought, Karim rushed the dark figure and rammed his shoulder into its side. The mat of black flew into the deckside, grabbing the railing and spinning overtop before sliding back beneath it in a casual display of primal grace—not unlike a cat.

Pakka! Karim thought as the feline figure led a blasé strut atop the deck's railing.

Karim waved a hand to the others. "Captain down! Captain down!"

"I got him! I got him!" Vice Admiral Shamoun came running, then dragged the captain away from the deck's edge and into a throng of soldiers, who guarded the two with shields.

Fire arrows flew past Karim's head—shots from the crowd below. The pirates sought to maximize on the crew's distraction, many arrows finding targets against unarmored tunics and setting sails quickly aflame.

Imperial professionalism seemed to keep morale in check as the crew patted the fires out and shields rushed forward in tight formations. The less fortunate among them were already hitting the floor, burning arrows protruding from throats and chests.

"Hajjar, shield!" Issa ordered from somewhere to the side.

The young elemental and his cohorts oscillated their hands, then lifted their arms above their heads. Like a mirror to their gesture, waves lifted from the ocean in a translucent blue wall between the two ships. In moments, the water solidified into cool ice, which was peppered by the orange glow of the pirate's arrows from the other side.

"We can't hold it for long, sir," Hajjar strained, sweat already dripping down from his bushy brows and gleaming around his lip mole. His comrades looked no better.

Karim turned to the pakka. The cat had either failed to notice or just didn't care that it was effectively trapped. It leapt atop the crew's heads and shoulders, never once coming close to getting hit and leaving a crimson line trailing in its wake. Its rapier jabbed, cut, and sliced, determined to reach Malouf. If only the cat knew how useless the captain actually was.

"Someone kill that damned cat!" Karim shouted, brandishing his sword. "Ahmad, get us back in the sky!"

Karim hustled after the pakka as Ahmad climbed back up to the bridge. In the brief moment the cat had been on the deck it had already felled nine soldiers. He had been wrong before. It wasn't the creature that was trapped with *them*, it was they who were trapped with *it*.

Karim vaulted off a crate, landing in front of the cat and intercepting it just three steps in front of the retreating captain. Karim stuck out his blade in a guarded position, giving parry to the cat's first attack. Its slitted yellow eyes grew wide as though surprised by Karim's ability to defend at all. The brief shock lasted only a moment though as it sprung into a new sequence of attacks.

Where the pakka kept jumping off barrels and platforms to attack, Karim stood his ground, relying entirely on defensive posturing. Most of Karim's peers in the academy used their bucklers like a standard shield, when in reality served best as a means to protect the sword hand. That meant that, by extension, binding was the key in sword and buckler combat. Karim hoped that the cat hadn't yet fought anyone competent—which was likely the case. Karim often won his bouts by duping his opponent into underestimating him. The pakka's previous duels with his comrades would feed the creature's confidence.

He hoped.

Karim closed the distance with his sword and buckler. To his surprise, he was more comfortable dealing with the dark creature's silly acrobatics than he was with its blade-to-blade strikes. And he was thankful the pakka didn't catch on.

His feral opponent lunged its blade forward and steered clear from cuts now that it recognized Karim's skill. Karim grunted against the cat's strikes, and failed every desperate attempt at a bind. Each time he tried to catch the pakka's blade, it pulled away, ready for another attack.

Stand still, cat.

Were it not for the rest of the crew poking and stabbing at the cat's side, Karim suspected he'd already be dead. Even with the help, he could not score a proper hit against the feline's acrobatics. At least now the interloper was too preoccupied to wreak further havoc as it attempted to break Karim's guard instead of wounding more of the crew.

Karim feinted, forgoing another ineffective bind, and instead smashing his buckler into the cat's furred wrist. The pakka sprang back, emitting a cry that sounded somewhere between a lion's growl and cat's mewl.

Karim didn't pause to admire his work. He lunged forward, thrusting a deft jab up at the pakka's chest. But again, his opponent recovered with preternatural speed.

Karim's heart lurched as he saw his mistake a step too late. He had left his buckler extended and now he was exposed. The cat saw it too. Karim watched helplessly as the tip of his opponent's blade found his retreating wrist.

He cried and fell to his knee.

Before the bastard cat could finish him off, though, three silhouettes pushed in front of it. A wall of water erupted from the deckside, separating Karim from the pakka's approach.

A hand clasped Karim's elbow and lifted him up. He looked up to find Issa gazing down with worried eyes and heavy breaths. He gave her a short nod while he clamped a hand to his throbbing wrist.

"You're not bad, Vaaji," the pakka said, voice muffled by the water wall. "Most would have already fallen to my blade."

"Get off that thing, Shomari," one of the pirates shouted from below. "It's flying back up!"

Had they already started ascending? Karim watched the pakka through the flowing water, a grimace on his face.

"Attack!" Karim ordered.

"Another time, Vaaji," the pakka said with a leer before backflipping over a jet of water and off the gunnery platform.

Karim followed its flight path off the ship, barely catching the image of the pakka balancing atop debris floating in the ocean, as it skipped its way back to its friends.

Karim gritted his teeth. "Target the pakka!"

The gunners quickly fired down at the creature, but none of them hit as it continued maneuvering out of harm's way.

"Damn pakkami..." Karim cursed at himself.

For the first time, he took in the maelstrom that was the cat's destruction. From what he could tell, only two of the nine injured crew had succumbed to their injuries, the rest were merely wounded. More still had acquired injuries from unlit arrows, but none of them had perished from what Karim could see. Among the wounded was Vice Admiral Shamoun, who nursed an arrow lodged in his ribs, blood streaming down his side.

Karim's body tensed as he approached the first pair of the dead. Fayez and Jinan were their names, both only a year out of the academy. He recalled the look of their bright eyes only the day before, when they all thought this mission would be nothing more than shooting practice. None of them had expected to be wounded, let alone die. And for what?

"Why'd you step in front of me? I had it fine," came the voice of Hajjar from somewhere to the side.

Sindisi Abbas, the boy's mystguard, turned to the young man. He had an arrow through his bloodied arm. "It's my job, kid. We want them shootin' at me. It means I'm doing it right."

Karim turned a dark look to the captain, who was propped up on a crate near the end of the platform with Surgeon Abadi already tending to his wounds. Karim shook the grimace from his face. This was Malouf's fault—and he'd be sure to let the admiralty know personally—but it wasn't the captain that killed the two crewmembers. Karim shifted his animosity toward the pakka and its pirate crew.

Rushing to the voice pipe on the platform, Karim bellowed an order into its funnel. "Ahmad, get us down just behind the pirates."

"But sir," the filtered voice of Ahmad said. "You said to get us in the sky. Aren't we retreating?"

"No, we're going to show those pirates who they're dealing with."

CHAPTER 16
KARIM

ONCE THE *VIPER* HAD DRAWN BACK A SAFE DISTANCE AWAY from the pirate's ship, Karim ordered them to set down in the open ocean, where they hovered just above the waves. He bolted for the single-sail longboats tied to the side of the airship. He had one of the deck hands bring him a crossbow, though he kept his saber strapped to his belt, his *janbiya* just next to it. Before he could even step into one of the boats, a hand grabbed at his elbow.

"What do you think you're doing?" Issa hissed.

"I'm leading a charge to make those pirates pay. If we let up, they'll make a break for open sea." Karim broke Issa's hold as he took up an oar.

"Don't you think that's a bit headstrong?"

"It seems like a sound decision to me," he said matter-of-factly.

"Your idea isn't bad, but why do *you* have to go, especially with *that* hand?" Issa pointed down to his wrist where blood was already seeping down to his fingers. The sea air stung the cut and somehow it felt worse now that he saw how truly deep it dug.

"Well, the captain—"

"Is nursing his wounds. And if those wounds are grave enough, you'll be captain, Karim."

"Your point?"

"We'll need you here on the *Viper*. We wouldn't be in this situation if Malouf had just listened to you."

Karim clenched his jaw and turned his head to the pirate ship breaking for the horizon. They hadn't made it far, still rescuing the rest of their crew from the wreckage. But as soon as they set their sails—tattered as they were—their ship would be a dot in the distance. "I can't order a retreat —the admiralty would have our hides."

Issa shook her head. "I'm not saying that. I'm saying let me lead the boarding party while you cover us in the air." He must not have looked convinced, because she continued, "Karim, don't be like Malouf. Be better than him. Let me and my unit do this. Our aim is even better up close." She gave him a wink.

Karim sighed. "All right, we'll do it your way. You remember your flag formations?"

"Like the back of my hand. The academy beat it into us enough. How much time do we have?"

Karim looked over his shoulder to the pirate ship. "Can you have your unit ready in five minutes?"

"We'll be ready in two."

Karim gave her a small chuckle. "Good to hear, Akif. Bring your best—and definitely don't leave any mystguards behind. We'll make do without them."

"I'm sure you will." Issa was already turning to make ready, waving a hand to draw her second's attention at one of the gunnery stations.

Karim left for the command deck, and he made good time, quickly briefing the bridge-crew. Many of them were crestfallen, with heads held low. The air in the room was stale with inaction and dampened spirits. Even Shamoun looked weathered, his arm clutching at his bloodied side.

"Sir," Karim said. "You should head down to the surgeon."

"Too full right now," he grunted. "Besides, I'm needed here."

Karim had to give them a strong face, no matter the losses taken. He stood up straight, flattening the creases in his uniform. His hand came away with a line of blood of his own. "The captain is out of commission, I have the ship."

"Aye, sir, you have the ship," Ahmad, the next senior officer present, acknowledged.

"The gunner chief is preparing her team for boarding. We're using the longboats." A few downcast eyes rose up brightly. "We'll need to replace the gunners that are leaving or have been wounded. I want everyone we have manning a gun and trained on that ship, deckhands included. Our primary concern is keeping the enemy pinned while our people make their approach. To your stations. Let's move it." Karim clapped his hands together, and the bridge crew slumped off to their stations. Karim paused, unsatisfied by the lukewarm response.

"*What* are we?" he bellowed, borrowing a page from Issa's book.

"We are one!" the crew shouted in chorus while they saluted in unison.

"Our mission is far from over." Karim strode toward Ahmad at the helm. "Thank you, Ahmad, I'll take it from here."

"Yes, sir," Ahmad nodded, smiling with vigor.

Karim took his place at the helm and shifted the airship's controls to starboard. "Full sails ahead!"

BELOW, FOUR LONGBOATS SHOT OUT ONTO THE WATER'S surface, white-capped waves trailing their rudders in a thick line. Pulled from the sea, a wave of water rose to drive the boats forward. Two elementals worked the torrent behind them into a surge, then released it just as the boats cut through the break. Momentum set, the waves, moved by mystical power, launched their boats forward with even greater speeds.

Karim pushed against the *Viper's* controls. "Where are my full sails? We can't fall behind."

"Compromised, sir," Officer Tahan informed him. "The pirates knew what they were doing with their trap. Only our foresail remains untattered, for the most part."

"Then I want full capacity on the glass—let's get that stone pushed forward!"

"Right away, sir," Officer Tahan said. She relayed Karim's message through the voice pipe as the airship lifted once more into the sky.

Almost there, Karim thought. *Almost there.*

Great columns of water burst around the longboats below as the pirate cannonades opened on them. At the speed the away crew was going, it must have been impossibly difficult to maneuver, and Karim found himself praying that no shot from the pirate scum found its mark.

As good as the elementals were at deflecting cannons with their water walls, they couldn't do it *and* keep their boats propelled at the same time. They needed support, and fast. But the *Viper* was barely in range. Had the primary gunners still been on board, Karim would've given the order to fire without a second's thought, even at this distance. But with only the secondary team manning the guns, even simple suppression would be too great a risk. They might hit their own boats.

"Tahan, Chief Akif is to hold, but stand ready to fire at a moment's notice," Karim ordered.

"Right away." Tahan nodded to her second, who grabbed at a rope near her station. The line led to a series of flags outside that hung slack along the hull.

Once the *Viper* was within a respectable range, Karim gave the order. "Now!"

The gunners fired their cannons, their blasts vibrating underfoot. Only a few of the balls impacted the pirate ship and the rest soared harmlessly to the side, but none fell near Issa's team. That was what counted right now.

As the *Viper* glided closer over the pirate ship, Karim ordered a second salvo. A streak of cannon fire shot atop ocean waves. More hits were scored on the enemy's stern, but the near misses came entirely too close to Issa and her squad, who were finally rounding the pirate's bow. The elementals pushed a series of water surges against the forward hull, impeding the momentum of the enemy ship.

"Cease fire! Watch your targeting! You'll hit our own!" Karim ordered. That was close. Suppressing the pirates was paramount as the longboats made their wide run, but with them so near to their target—and Karim's stand-in gunners so inexperienced—they'd have to make the last of the approach on their own.

Now that the elementals had the pirates slowed, it might be possible for Karim to set up a shot to disable the enemy masts.

If the green gunners can pull it off, he thought.

If they could just distract the pirates instead, perhaps the elementals would have enough breathing room to set the enemy sails aflame. But it would be impossible if the away crew concentrated their efforts on blocking the ship instead of attacking it.

"Apologies, sir," Officer Tahan said. Her loose headwrap shifted against her small shoulders. "None of the crew left over are as experienced as the gunner chief's."

Karim nodded as he pushed the controls forward again. "It's fine. I should have flown the ship farther overhead. My call came too early."

Once the *Viper* soared a few yards from the pirate ship's stern, Karim handed the controls over to Officer Ahmad. "Keep her steady above the ship, you hear me?"

Ahmad gave him a swift nod and took the helm once more.

Pressure weighed against Karim, and his chest clenched as he reviewed the officers about the bridge. He couldn't let the pirates get away, not with the ship under his command. There was too much riding on it all.

Karim rushed to Tahan at her station. "Tell the gunners they need to aim their cannons forty-degrees higher than their intended target."

Tahan relayed the message while Karim drew his nose closer to the viewport. Another streak of cannon fire raced toward the pirate ship, impacting against its stern once more.

"No. We don't want to sink them, just disable their masts," Karim said with a tight fist.

Tahan turned to him with not-my-fault eyes. "They acknowledged your instructions, sir."

"Tell them again," Karim ordered. "We can't afford another slip-up. She won't take much more down there."

Tahan brought her mouth to the tube again, repeating the previous order. When Karim heard the muffled response from the acting gunner chief, he shook his head and stepped to the station himself.

"No," Karim said, "you did not fire at forty-degrees upward distance. You're still aiming directly when you should be angling."

It was simple mathematics, new as the concept was to the younger of them. All academy students were required to commit basic geometry to memory. Many military recruits thought the discipline was only of use to the nation's architects and designers, not its military branch—and certainly not their gunners. They would soon learn. "Point and shoot" they used to say. Karim bit back a grunt.

"A-Apologies, Chief Officer," the dim voice said. Karim thought he could hear stammering in the words. "I-I thought I had it right... I-I'm just not used to... We'll get it right, sir."

Karim pinched his nose. Perhaps he should have used simpler terms. "Just aim a touch higher, yes?"

The acting gunner chief responded with an affirmation. A moment later, a new series of cannon fire strafed the mizzenmast of the pirate ship. It looked like it cracked, but it wasn't giving. One more direct hit would do it.

"Very good, Gunner Chief, keep it up," Karim said over Tahan's shoulder before moving to her second. "And get those flags flying. Let our people know they're set for boarding soon."

Karim watched the flags whip against the high winds as a fresh volley tore toward the pirate ship. But again, they shot too wide, nearly taking out the boarding crew. Karim lunged over to Tahan's station again to speak into the funnel himself. "What was that, Gunner Chief?"

"W-we held the same firing solution, sir," the muffled voice came stammering once more. "T-the *Viper's* not steady."

Karim turned to the helm with fire in his eyes. They were so close. What was the issue now? "Ahmad?"

"Apologies, sir. Still don't have quite the knack with the controls as you." Ahmad gritted his teeth with each word. "These rudder pedals aren't exactly the helms at sea, and the pirates keep sailing closer to our longboats. They must know we'll stop firing if there's a chance we might hit our crew."

Karim peered over the bridge's edge. True enough, the pirate ship steered close to Issa's unit, putting little distance between themselves and the imperial boats.

Sharp bunch, this lot.

"Don't worry," Karim said. "I'll take over."

"Chief Officer, a word?" It was Vice Admiral Shamoun, still clutching at his side.

At any other time Karim would have shown more respect, but now, amid battle and the burden of command on his shoulders, he couldn't afford to. "Sir, I don't have any time—the pirates will get away. I have their foremast nearly down. If only I can reposition the ship myself maybe I can rush down to the guns and disable their—"

Shamoun held up a sage hand, though the gesture brought a wince from his lips—his side still bleeding through. Then he pulled Karim to a quiet corner of the bridge. "Karim, lose the 'I's.' You have an entire crew at your disposal. Use them."

Karim shook himself. Was he floundering as Malouf had? He didn't think so, but then...

"'We are only as strong as the unit,'" he said, recalling the quote he knew Shamoun would recite to him.

"Right. And don't you think it might be better if you directed the crew as a captain would?"

"Yes, but the pirates—"

"Cannot be defeated by a single officer." The vice admiral cut Karim short. "No matter how talented he is." He allowed himself a smirk.

Karim sighed with a nod. "Right. Thank you, sir."

Shamoun gave him a swift pat on the shoulder, sending Karim back to his position at the center of the bridge. Had the old man suffered through his wound just to make sure Karim didn't mess up? A slight pang of embarrassment laced through him, but he heeded his senior's words.

When Karim approached Ahmad, the younger officer was already lifting himself from his chair.

"No, stay seated." Karim put his good hand to Ahmad's shoulder. "Fly her true. There's a little give to the controls when you thrust them back and forth. Work with it. You see the central strut?" He pointed to the wood panel that cut down vertically through the viewport. "Use the lower third to direct the ship."

Ahmad inclined his head. "Right where that cloud is?"

"That's the one," Karim said. "The pirate ship is shifting close to our longboats, as you said. They're smart, but the gunner chief and her crew are smarter. They're riding the waves, see there? They've let the pirate ship drift away to give us a clear shot. Once they signal with their flags you make the call. But make it *before* the gap opens. You gotta feel for it, anticipate it."

"Understood, Captain," Ahmad said, his grip on the helm white-knuckled. Karim decided he wouldn't correct him. He was an acting captain at best. Technically he was still just the chief officer.

"And Tahan." Karim turned to the communications officer. "I'll leave it to you to direct the gunners. Tell them to shoot with both eyes open, not one. If they're having trouble steadying, remind them to take their two breaths. If they're not sure, they don't take the shot at all, got it? I'd rather make another pass than hit our own."

Officer Tahan clasped her hands behind her back and swung to her station where she relayed Karim's order.

Another moment passed before Ahmad gave out his first call.

"There it is, el-Sayyed," he said, pointing. "The flags are up, sir, fire now." Ahmad glanced at Karim, waiting for an override. When it didn't come, he gave the order. "All cannons, fire!"

Karim echoed the command and Tahan shouted the order down to gunnery. The booming roar of cannon fire came an instant later. Shots smashed through the mainmast and the shaft tipped and crashed down in a storm of splinters.

The bridge celebrated with a cheer, and a number of fists were thrown into the air. Karim leaned back, letting out a long and deep breath.

Shamoun's sturdy hand came down around Karim's shoulder. "Don't forget your two breaths yourself, Karim. You did well. Now, go ahead and finish this fight." He winced. "I'll be at the infirmary like I should have been all along."

Karim nodded. "Understood, sir." He turned to Ahmad. "Bring the ship down, helmsman."

"Sir?"

"Don't worry, they're not going anywhere with their mast felled. Chief Akif will have their crew subdued and captured in short order. Without their chance for escape, they've no option but to surrender—honestly, this time. I suppose they could put up a fight if they're really in the mood to die." Karim gave him a smirk. "But we'll be ready for that."

"Right away." Ahmad pushed the elevator wheel forward and lowered the ship's tilt which tipped the *Viper's* nose down for a sharper dive.

Karim's eyes swept over the bridge; the crew's spirit was soaring from their latest victory. It was greater even than the energy that had flowed so readily the day prior, before Malouf had spoiled their inertia.

Officer Rashid, though, stood like a statue. His eyes shifted between his fellow bridge crew as though feeling a step apart. Without the comfort of Malouf's coattails, he seemed like a child lost in a crowd. Rashid might not have been Karim's favorite person, but he was still a member of his crew. And he looked like he genuinely wanted to be a part of the celebration.

"What's your assessment, Officer Rashid?" Karim asked.

Roused from his stupor, Rashid looked to Karim, taking a moment before answering. "The *Viper* has only taken minor damage. Outside of the tattered sails there's nothing we can't mend once we return home."

"And her crew?"

"The pakka did the most harm, sir. Aside from the men it wounded and killed, and those on the away crew, of course, we're still running with all hands strong."

"And Captain Malouf?"

"Surgeon Abadi is looking after him now. Do you want to wait for his orders, sir?"

Karim didn't take long to answer, "No, we'll proceed with boarding. Thank you, Officer."

Rashid gave him a satisfied nod, a newfound respect crossing the man's eyes.

Karim turned back to the helm. "Ahmad, you have the ship."

The helmsman gave a quick salute at his seat. "Aye, sir, I have the ship."

"Tahan," Karim turned to the communications officer, "Have four of our marines meet me at gunnery."

"Sir, yes, sir," she answered, then smiled. "Give them their Sapphire Hells, Captain."

CHAPTER 17
KARIM

GENTLE WINDS CUT THROUGH SEA MIST AS KARIM descended to the longboat davits, anticipation crawling through his skin. Seagulls sang faint melodies as they took refuge among the wreckage, a song for Karim's victory. Several times he caught himself smiling and then reining himself back into a good and proper military veneer.

He flexed his hand. The dawa root poultice gleaming at his wrist was already stitching the cut and impeding the bleeding there. Four soldiers, three men and a woman, came to him on the deck. Each of them approached with a sharp salute to their chests. He returned his own and set them to their disembarking duties. The marines were equipped with a saber at their hips, a bow on their backs, and a visage of grit. From memory, Karim knew they were fair fencers, but he didn't expect their skills to be put to much use today.

Karim looked to the pirate ship which was just a few strokes away. With everything set, he ordered a deckhand to lower them to the sea. Once wood met water, two of the marines rowed them in.

Karim sat back to take in the morning's carnage as they approached. Deep in the blue expanse, *Saber's Edge* smoldered atop white-capped waves while the *Viper* floated majestically overhead like a hawk after a hunt.

The pirate ship rested just before Karim, waiting to welcome him to his first active victory in the imperial navy. He could almost hear the commendations of the admiralty creeping at the edge of his mind, and he swore he could feel the weight of new medals hanging from his sash.

The pirate ship's destruction had been surgical. Besides the mishap of Malouf, the *Viper* had tested perfectly. Once the empire revealed their airship to the rest of Esowon there would be no stopping their conquest. And the council would know it was Karim who could be the one to usher in their new age.

Eager to solidify his triumph, Karim was first to board the pirate's ship with his chest out and posture straight as he stepped through the cloud of ash. When the smoke cleared, his eyes met a welcome sight: the pirate crew, broken and bound—as all pirates should be.

And there, to hand them to him with her crimson tunic flickering like the flames of the ship's wounds, stood Issa.

Those pirates left unbound by rope were held at arrow-point by sindisi. Each wore a scowl more menacing than the last as Karim walked the deck. Two at the bow threw their hands in the air at the finger-point of the elementals, Hajjar and Damji. The tips of the mystics' hands danced around balls of fire which Karim knew were ready to shoot out at a moment's notice.

Karim wondered if this band of marauders had seen better days. He had heard about the merchant kings who called themselves "golden lords," but these pirates could not have been in the same faction. Most of them were missing teeth, and blisters peppered their legs and arms. Only a few of them wore proper boots, the vast majority sporting bare feet. How they had evaded the imperial navy for so long was beyond him. But Karim reminded himself that these pirates knew their island coves better than he. If it were otherwise, he wouldn't have to question them at all.

Issa's voice followed from behind as he paced the deck. "We took as many alive as we could."

"The pakka?" Karim asked, searching the many faces. He reminded himself that the cat didn't matter now. His focus needed to be on finding the sea speaker first and foremost.

"It wasn't here when we arrived, sir. Must've snuck away."

Every shadow drew Karim's eyes as he scanned the deck for the tuft of an ear or the flash of a tail. "I'm sure we'll be seeing it again. Keep your eyes open." He cast slow-moving eyes over the crowd. "Which of you is the captain?"

None of the pirates lifted their heads, as though they had not heard him at all. Karim looked for the tanned pirate with the large beard, but the man was nowhere to be found —perhaps he had abandoned ship too. Fled to the islands. Pursuit would be possible if these pirates proved to be tight-lipped, but Karim didn't favor the notion. It would take hours to find even a single pirate hiding within the rocky expanse of tiny half-islands.

"Was your captain killed?" Karim offered. Still, no pirate spoke.

Issa stepped forward, boots echoing on the deck. "Most tried to escape when we arrived, sir. If their captain survived, he may have escaped. There was only a skeleton crew on board when we found them."

"They must've used this lot as a distraction."

Issa's hand hovered over her saber. "Should we kill these and look for the rest?"

"Yes, let's start with this one," Karim replied, playing along. He tilted his head toward the old pirate next to him.

"No, please!" a female voice cried from the crowd. "I'll tell you what you want."

Karim and Issa both turned to the cry. That familiar squawk could only have come from Nabila, their gull-shifting spy. Karim had almost forgotten she was on board.

"*Kibba yuh mout!*" another woman with a dark complexion said in Pakwan as she kicked Nabila in the gut with her free leg. A bloodied green bandana was wrapped around her head.

"He's Vaaji, Ajola," Nabila cried. "He'll kill us all."

The woman called Ajola gritted her teeth and snarled. "*Wah a yuh a tink using fi mi name?*"

"Bring that one to me." Karim pointed to Nabila, who thrashed theatrically against her captors. She knew how to put on a show. Karim almost believed her himself.

The sindisi threw her to Karim's feet. Karim leered as he said, "I don't care if your captain is dead or alive, if I'm being frank." He knelt down face-to-face, playing his role of the interrogator. Then he leaned forward, his voice barely above a whisper. "Today, we are hunting mystics. And I know Kobi was not one of them." His voice rose. "Tell me, which of you was at Kidogo that day?" Nothing. "Come now, we all know what I'm referring to. Who here stood against us?"

"I'll tell you whatever you want, just don't hurt me," Nabila pleaded, throwing her hands above her face as though she were about to be struck.

"Just point out who the mystics are on this ship."

Another pirate gestured to the cloud of smoke in the

163

distance. It was the smoldering remains of *Saber's Edge*. "They're all dead."

Karim pursed his lips in thought. Nabila sat before him with a blank stare, her eyes shifting subtly to her left. So, there was a mystic on board after all.

"Somehow I don't believe that." Karim tilted his head. "You're holding out."

"I... um..." Nabila stammered.

Karim drew his janbiya and placed it at her throat with the speed of a mantis. He pressed deep enough to draw blood; it was just a nick, but for all her tears and wailing, one would've thought he'd run her through.

"You hold your fucking tongue, Nabila," the dark woman shouted again, in accented Mother Tongue this time. "Or me cut it from your mouth!"

Karim ignored her, following Nabila's eyes to the edge of the bounded crowd. There were no cracks in the pirates' expressions, no weak links among them—save one.

He was a tall, yet thin man with ebony skin and a brown bandana wrapped around his bald head. It looked like one side of his face was healing horribly with gray welts and he seemed to twitch with small spasms. Was he... chanting to himself?

Karim rose up from his crouch, leaving Nabila to her crocodile tears, and walked toward the man, whose face scrunched up as though concentrating on something deep and profound. Perhaps he was merely praying to one of the Taboo Gods. Or perhaps...

Karim reached out a hand to the man's face, placing his fingers atop the pirate's eyelids to pull them open. But before he could pry them, there was a blood-curdling yell from his side.

"*Git aweh fram him!*" the woman named Ajola shouted as

she rushed toward Karim. Her long-flowing green bandana snapped in the air, revealing a glinting knife in her hand. The rope around her wrist was cut loose.

Karim's muscles stiffened. Naked shock tore through his body. Six years of military training took control of his arms as he instinctively dropped into a defensive posture.

It didn't matter though.

The woman made it one step before taking a bolt through the shoulder and two more arrows through her arm. As she stumbled to a halt halfway to Karim, Issa struck her in the chest with her spear, the tip driving through the woman's heart. Then, in one fluid motion, Issa slit the woman's throat open with a graceful cut. Before the body slumped forward, the gunner chief spun the pirate over one shoulder and carried her to the deckside to throw her overboard.

The affair took all of a dozen heartbeats.

Karim suppressed a shudder; he too often forgot just how lethal Issa and her sindisi could be. He turned back to the man he had been examining, but—

"Where did he go?" Karim spun on the pirates as though they were hiding him beneath their tattered clothes. "The sea speaker. Where?"

Karim turned slitted eyes to Nabila, who shrugged with a blank expression. Karim quickly scanned each crate and barrel atop the deck. He hadn't noticed how disorganized the pirates kept their loot. But the mess would not hide the man for long. It was just a matter of time.

So why did the sea speaker try to hide at all?

The pirate crew looked at him dumbfounded.

"There are plenty of men here," a small voice said. "Which one do you mean?"

Karim turned his head to what looked like something

between a child and a woman grown. Her skin was inhumanly flawless, and her eyes were twinkling emerald, like the canopy of a forest in the morning light. Half her hair was loose against her shoulder. The other half was braided, exposing a pointed ear.

Karim turned his attention to the creature. "Aziza. Powers of perception, correct?"

"Something like that," she said. Her wings were tied. Karim hadn't noticed them before. She had been just another face in the crowd with them pinned behind her.

"Perhaps you can help me then, little one. You might not know where the mystic is, but with those aziza eyes of yours, I'm sure you can find him… if properly, *motivated.*"

The diminutive creature spat on the deck. "I'll die before I tell you anything, *youngster.*"

Karim withdrew his janbiya again and brought his blade in front of the aziza's face, resting the sharp edge against her cheek and just under her overlarge eyes. Her expression was as rooted and unyielding as an ancient ebony tree.

Karim removed his dagger from her cheek and cut the arm of the pirate who sat next to her, a gaunt man already littered with old wounds. What was one more cut to his patchwork of scars? A red line poured from the man's loose and threadbare shirt near his tricep as he suppressed a whimper.

They're a strong lot, I'll give them that.

He gave the man a second cut without even looking, never taking his eyes from the aziza's glare. "I can keep this up all day—"

A wave of water threw Karim to one side, his last words drowned by the rush of an ocean jet. His head hit hard against the deck as brine slipped through the cracks. Karim spat the taste of salt from his mouth, then raised himself against the starboard deckside. He watched a huge tail fin dip back into the ocean just as he regained his balance.

Karim turned toward the deck, but his boots slipped underfoot. The wave had spread his marines across the deck, turbans damp and padded armor soaked through. The pirates were drenched too, but they seemed to have expected the wave and were already making a break for it.

Some jumped straight overboard while others made a desperate grab for weapons. Those foolish enough to challenge the sindisi were quickly taken down. Disoriented or not, the elite mystguards were quick to action.

The aziza wiggled out of her ropes, her shoulders at odd angles, as though she had dislocated them to free herself. Then, in one fluid motion, she reset her shoulders and flew out over the open sea.

A damp bow and a quiver of arrows by the deckside caught Karim's eye. He rushed for the bow, nocking an arrow in place. He aimed for the aziza's wing, then pulled back on the draw as his open wound stretched and bled again. Taking a deep breath, he let his arrow fly. Karim missed the wing—he blamed that one on his injury—but the arrow lodged into the creature's shoulder blade and the aziza spiraled into the ocean with a short cry. If she survived, he'd deal with her later.

Karim scanned the deck for the sea speaker, his breath quickening not from fear, but anticipation. The man couldn't have escaped, not after an act like that. If he *was* the mystic they were looking for, that trick with the sea creature should have exhausted him. The pirate didn't have his friends with him this time. Gritting his teeth, Karim slammed a fist into his side.

Karim pushed through his crew, who were fiercely trying to subdue the remaining pirates. A terrible thought shot through his mind as he continued his search among the soggy netting and overturned barrels covered in blood.

What if the strain of the magic had killed the man? Karim had seen it before, mystics who drained themselves until their bodies simply gave up. That whale, or whatever it was, had almost been the size of the ship itself, so death by mystical exhaustion wouldn't have been out of the question.

His thoughts calmed when he finally found the man sprawled on his back between two crates. His eyes were a normal brown now, but his chest heaved rapidly as he gasped for air.

"There you are," Karim exhaled, too bleary to flash a triumphant smile. The mystic was drained, all right, his skin already turning a pale gray. "You must be exhausted. What was that, a baleen?"

"Don't... know what... you talkin' 'bout," the man sighed, keeping his breath still in a forced manner. "Weren't me."

"Forget the rest!" Karim shouted to his crew. "We've got what we need."

CHAPTER 18
ZALA

ZALA DIDN'T STIR FOR A WHILE. A LONG WHILE.

Something wet pushed her against a hard and jagged surface, and she woke from her stupor. She coughed up a lung-full of water, then tried to get up. She could barely make out the gold blob and gray blur about her, or the green substance stuck on her arms and torso.

Her head felt like lead. She succumbed to fatigue, to pain, to injury, and let them force her head back down into the damp sands.

She closed her eyes, felt the sun crawl against her pruned skin. All she could hear at first was a ringing sound, long and monotone. Through the drone came the muted squawking of seagulls and the crashing of waves.

Then, there was the cold.

Water brought forth goosebumps, and sand stuck into the valleys of her wrinkled skin. She tried to get up again, only just craning her neck before sinking back to the sand once more.

It went on like that for another half-hour until she finally had the strength to keep her eyes open, and keep her head from lolling over.

From what she could discern, she was on a beach with great big rocks jutting from the shore. The green about her body was seaweed, salty and moist. The sun shone high in the sky and not a single cloud graced the blue. The fog had passed at last. And she was alone.

Where's Jelani? she mused weakly.

Even her thoughts seemed to come sluggish. The last thing she could remember was shouting at her husband and then just missing his grasp as she crashed into the deep sea.

Zala stretched her neck to the ocean's horizon. There was nothing to see. No smoke. No wreckage.

The ringing in her left ear wouldn't stop. She slapped it with her palm, but that only brought pain and a small cry from her mouth. As she looked down at her hand, ear still throbbing harshly, she saw blood lining the creases of her palm. Just beyond her hand laid a circular object lodged in the sand. She thought it nothing more than a rock at first, but as she brushed away the sand from its edges she saw that marbled ball with that terrible little cloud under its glass.

It was probably beautiful to most.

Zala could admit the multi-colored collage under its surface was mesmerizing. But Gods' Glass was the last thing she wanted to see right now, especially the same one Jelani had used before she chucked it off the ship. Was it following her? Did it mean to mock her? It would've been a cruel irony if she were left alone on a deserted isle with the very object that had sent her off to pirating to begin with.

She lifted the glass in hand and examined it for a moment. On instinct she drew her arm back, ready to throw the thing back into the ocean where it belonged. Then a thought struck her. If she was stuck here, this was the last item she'd have of Jelani's. Maybe it was worth keeping for now. If she got picked up, perhaps she could trade it for passage.

Sucking her teeth in frustration, she tucked the orb into the pocket of her tattered rags. Her hand brushed against something jagged and she realized, with a short gasp, that the Gods' Glass wasn't the last thing she had of Jelani's.

She pulled out the songstone that she always kept with her, its orange hue glinting against the bright of the high noon sun.

Her heart lifted for a moment, remembering that Jelani could communicate through the stone. She pressed it to her ear but heard nothing, and anticipation died in her heart when she recalled that the tiny gem could only emit a single hymn Jelani often sung to her.

What were the rules for this thing? Something about thinking of each other...

That was it!

She and Jelani were married under the Eyes of the Old Gods, the *Jo'baran* Gods. Tradition said each person entering into a life bond was to gift the other with something dear to them. When Jelani had given the songstone to her he'd said that if he was singing to her, and if Zala concentrated hard enough, she would hear his voice through the stone. But it would only work if they both were thinking of each other at the *exact* same time. With their current circumstances, that didn't seem too difficult a task. Yet the notion also brought with it a sharp spike of fear through Zala's spine. If she didn't hear Jelani's voice, that could only mean...

She didn't allow herself to go there.

Distantly, she thought she heard something, but it was

171

only a muffled whisper. Her heart raced again and she lifted the stone to her ear. It was still ghost quiet. Where was that noise coming from, then? Zala lifted her head, though she saw nothing besides beach and rock. Then there was a furry hand at her shoulder.

"What is the matter?" The voice of Shomari purred behind her. "I have been shouting over at you. Are you deaf or something?"

A rush of fear ran through Zala's chest and her lips parted in horror. "Of course not!" she blurted, but the voice from her mouth sounded distant as well, distant to her left ear. "Oh, no…"

Shomari let the weight of the situation sink in before saying, "It is all right, Zala." For once, his voice was free of his typical cavalier humor. "You have still got all of your limbs. Some of the others have not been so lucky as you."

"The others?" Zala stood up too quickly and tipped to one side, still disoriented. "Jelani? Did he make it?"

Zala grasped at Shomari's arms for balance while she gazed over his shoulders for the "others" he described. Jelani might've been all right after all. Her eyes traveled to the far off coastline as she thought of her husband. She could almost imagine, vividly, how the afternoon sun would glisten off his bald head when she saw him again. As much as it tried to, the dull pain coming from her right arm earned no attention from her.

"I do not know, I have not seen him. We are still taking count of the survivors. I came out this way to see if anyone had hit this side of the isle."

"Which isle are we on?" Zala asked, eyes darting down back and forth in thought. If they weren't far from where the Vaaji had attacked, then Jelani could have easily survived as she had.

"We're not sure exactly," Shomari answered. "Ode says the Ibabi Isles." So the old man had made it too. If *he* could do it, then Jelani… "It only takes five minutes to get to the other side." Shomari waved a dismissive paw, holding Zala's head firm to focus her flitting eyes. "We'll be figuring all that out, but let's get you looked at first."

"What about Fon? I lost her when the Vaaji took down our crow's nest." Zala shifted her weight, but her knees dipped of their own accord. Her ear, her arm, now her legs? She really was a mess.

"Haven't seen her yet, either." Shomari's eyes cast downward with a worried twitch of his whiskers. "Wait."

He pointed past Zala's shoulder. The ocean's waves curled wide and hard, and the outline of a dark figure rode with them.

Zala wobbled, surprised her legs did not give out from underneath her completely. Shomari moved to step away, then said, "I have been trying to pull anyone I find in from the waters, but I can't go that far out..."

Zala's eyes shot wide. "You mean you haven't dived in to save anyone?"

"I haven't found anyone else still alive, not in the waters at any rate. Besides, I cannot swim, Zala. You know this."

"And you're sure you're a pirate?" Zala asked indignantly as she pulled off her loose, damp trousers and stumbled to the surf.

"My accent doesn't give it away?" Shomari asked from behind. Zala rolled her eyes as she pulled off her top. "I would be no help to anyone out in the water. I'd only drown myself if I tried to save them. I prefer my lungs filled with air, not water, thank you very much."

The first rush of water hit Zala's toes, sending more shivers up her calves. She turned her head over her shoulder as she jogged farther into the waves and called out, "How did you manage to get to this isle in the first place?"

"Rode a piece of debris, used another to row," Shomari shouted back through cupped paws.

Zala snorted. "It's okay, we'll do it together."

When she was deep enough into the water she dove headfirst for the breaking waves. The ocean washed the blood from her ear and pounded against her eardrum, giving her the illusion of sound. For the first time since she'd woken up, she felt whole again, not broken or worried or useless.

Somehow it was easier to swim than to walk. She had always been a natural swimmer, one of the few qualities she felt would have made her a decent pirate, and one of the activities that had brought her close to Jelani. Whereas on the beach her legs felt like hollow things, in the water—where the current and the back waves pushed her forward—they felt solid and strong. And her arm, which had been throbbing before, seemed to quell at the ocean's caress.

It didn't take long to reach the figure in the sea. But once Zala arrived, she knew she was too late.

It was Ajola, the woman who had served the Ya-Seti. The dark skin around her neck was split open and her body was riddled with bolts and arrows. Zala swallowed down the grief threatening to take hold. It would do no good while she swam. Just as she was about to grab Ajola's shoulder, she heard a cry farther out in the ocean. It wasn't a normal cry, however. It sounded more like a…

"Just push whoever that is over to me," Shomari shouted from the beach. "The waves will bring them in."

Zala hefted Ajola's weight toward the shore as best she could, letting the ocean carry the body the rest of the way. She turned again to the small voice she heard, swimming farther into the ocean's current where the waves rested easy. As she approached the second figure, she recognized the cry. Zala choked on a splash of water as a rush of joy filled her heart.

Fon was alive!

"Help! It's my shoulder," Fon spluttered as she struggled to stay afloat on a piece of wood. "I can't move it right, and my wings are too wet."

Zala's heart plummeted. She had never heard such panic from the aziza before. With a second wind, she thrusted her hands into the waves, rushing toward her friend.

"Don't worry, I got you." Zala took one side of the wood and pushed forward, using her legs to drive them toward the beach.

"Glad to... you... made," Fon's voice came muffled and stuttered to Zala as the aziza gave her a weary half-smile. Shock turned to exhaustion on her friend's face.

"What's that?" Zala asked.

Fon spoke louder and slower. "Glad... to see... you... made it."

"Oh, yes. You too."

After a few too many hard strokes for Zala's tired arms, the pair reached the beach. Fon had a wooden shaft protruding from her back, just above her left shoulder-blade. She tried flapping her wings, but they were no use.

Despite her own injury, Fon nodded toward Zala's ear. "Does it hurt?"

"Not too much. I just have this irritating ring that won't go away."

"The damage shouldn't be too bad," Fon winced as she rolled in the sand. "If... you know, we get to a healer fast enough."

"Me?" Zala blurted. "What about you? You could bleed

out any moment. And I know that salt must be hurtin' bad." Zala brushed Fon's hair out of her large eyes—half of her braids were coming undone. "Let's just see if we even have a healer anymore…" Zala sighed as Fon kept trying to move her wings, but when they did not flutter the aziza tugged at the wooden shaft at her back. "And *don't* strain yourself."

Fon let go of the shaft, her eyes pinched in pain. "I tried to get it out myself, but it's in too deep."

"Are you trying to bleed yourself dry?" Shomari's voice purred from the side. He, unlike Zala or Fon, sauntered over without injury. "You never yank an arrow from a body. Have you never seen anyone get shot with a Ya-Seti arrow? It's worse going out than in."

"Well, this is a Vaaji arrow," Fon said defiantly. "If that makes a difference…" Her eyes curled in pain as she looked down to the sand.

"Same idea. Lucky for you, Little Flutter," Shomari wiggled his furry fingers, "*These* are surgical."

"And lucky for you, cat, aziza don't bleed like pakkami. You'd struggle to do me more harm if you tried. I can already feel my skin sealing underneath." Fon squirmed in Zala's grip. "What were you going to do, anyway?"

Zala's head swung back and forth between the two, shaking her head. For an aziza, having the arrow pulled out would be no more painful than yanking a hangnail. Zala thought of Jelani and how much he hated when she pulled his hangnails. They played a similar cutesy game of cat and mouse whenever his hand maintenance got out of control.

Shomari pinched his snout. "I was going to get that arrowhead out without you dying, of course. Does the *how* really matter, Flutter? Aziza healing or no, you can still cut yourself bad pulling it out… and unlike the merfolk, we can't just toss you in the ocean to heal if something goes wrong. No, we will have to be doing it the old fashioned way. But I have to warn you, it's going to hurt real bad."

"I can deal with the pain." Fon shrugged. The jerk of her shoulders, even as minimal as it was, brought a hiss through her teeth. "Fine. Get it over with."

She turned her belly to the sand, exposing the shaft at her back.

Shomari gaped at her. "I can't just do it here!"

Fon pushed her lips out in a pout. "I thought you said those fingers were surgical…"

"They are, but I need the proper tools. We'd have to check with the others first. Something might have washed up to help me. Unless you want me to use my rapier?"

"What do you need a sword for?"

Shomari looked up into the clouds, then began reciting the procedure like it were a quiz. "Well, I have to open the wound up a bit more, see if the arrow hit any of your bones—"

"You mean you have to hurt me more!" Fon flipped her head, her matted hair casting sand onto Shomari's shaggy legs.

The pakka put a finger to his lips. "When you put it like that it sounds worse. But it's the best way to prevent further damage."

"That's the craziest thing I've ever—"

"Okay you two, enough," Zala said with a sigh, then dropped her head into the sand. When this pair started their little flirting sessions they could go on for hours.

Zala tilted her head to Ajola, frowning when she saw the woman's lifeless eyes. Her head was bare for once—her signature green bandana must have been lost at sea. Without it, she looked as though she could have been related to Zala, a cousin or some distant aunt. Zala bit at her lip. She had never asked where Ajola was from. It was too late to know now.

"I barely knew her…" Zala mumbled.

Fon placed a hand on Ajola's chest, whispering something Zala couldn't make out. "May Yem take you into Her Ocean's Grace" was all Zala could catch. Was that a prayer of that old religion? The same one Jelani was obsessed with?

Zala shot to her feet. "Come on, I want to see the others. Jelani may be among them."

Shomari and Fon traded somber looks.

"What?" Zala looked between the two. "What happened after I got knocked out?"

Fon frowned. "I'm not exactly sure *when* everything happened."

"It all developed at once, really," Shomari added. "They got a direct hit on the captain though. There's no way he would have made it."

The image of Kobi enveloped in a brilliant light of flame sprang back to Zala's mind. "I saw it. Kobi's gone. I might not have liked the man, but that was no way to go. Jelani was there too, but I don't think… I don't want to think…"

"No, Jelani's fine…" Fon assured her, but the aziza's voice was near to a quiver. "Well…" She looked to Shomari. "Well… last time I saw him he was doing his tricks with the fish again. But when I flew away I don't know what happened after that."

"It was the best way to go, I'd say," Shomari said as he crossed Ajola's arms across her chest. "Kobi, I mean. Right in the heat of battle, right in the middle of it. Quick, too, I bet. He wasn't feeling a thing, sure as salt."

"What *was* that thing, anyway?" Zala turned from

Shomari to Fon. "That flying ship. I've never seen anything like it."

Fon shuffled next to Shomari to close Ajola's eyes. "Neither have I. Haven't seen anything that big in the sky since the kongamatos. I must have been in my second twenties then." She pursed her lips. "And back then those creatures weren't even half the size of that ship."

"Well, Kobi found his secret weapon all right." Zala turned to Shomari. "Anyway, about those survivors…"

The pakka waved a paw. "Yes, of course. Follow me."

CHAPTER 19
ZALA

WHEN SHOMARI SAID THERE WERE SURVIVORS, ZALA HAD expected there to be at least a dozen crewmates, maybe ten at the least. But when they arrived at the other end of the isle—Ajola held up between Zala and Shomari—there were only four others, and only two of them were whole.

"Good to see you among the livin'!" Mantu called out with a wide smile. Oddly, his words seemed genuine to Zala.

She should have expected him to survive. He'd probably sacrificed his own crew just to get away.

"What happened to the *Titan*?" Zala asked.

"Down at the bottom of the seas now," Sniffs voice came from somewhere down the beach. He cleared his nose like always and appeared from behind a set of crates that had washed ashore. "Good eatin' for the kubahari."

"And this is everyone?" Zala didn't want to look the other two in the eye as she set Ajola down. One was missing an arm, which was tied with a tourniquet, and she looked half dead. The other, Old Man Ode, was littered with fresh cuts along his arms.

"Is Jelani here?" Zala asked.

Mantu's eyes shifted to Sniffs. "Didn't get a good look when they attacked. Don't know where he is."

"Oh…" Zala dropped her head, her eyebrows furrowed. It didn't mean Jelani was gone—it just meant he was out there ready to be found. What would he have done if he was stranded? What would he be plotting just then to get back to her?

Mantu took a step closer to Zala. "I told the crew to scatter among the Ibabi Isles. If any of them come across Jelani, they'll take care of him—"

Sniffs lifted a finger. "What 'bout that badman Vaaji who—"

"He's fine, I'm sure of it," Mantu said.

Zala couldn't see his eyes as he turned to the large man, but she didn't like his tone or how he cut Sniffs off.

"What was that about?" she questioned.

Mantu turned to her with a half-smile, one too reassuring for any real comfort. "Nothin'. We got into it with one of the Vaaji—might've been their captain, but he was too young. The kijana cut up Ode pretty bad."

Zala tilted her head again to the old pirate. Some of his cuts were already turning color. She turned her head to Fon as well, who still had an arrow shaft sticking out from her back. The aziza was doing a good job of suppressing any discomfort, but the subtle lines through her forehead tattoo betrayed her pain.

Zala asked, "What about the healer?"

"Never made it." Mantu stroked his beard solemnly. "Tried to get him off the ship, but he got hit by one of those fireballs."

"Them damn Vaaji," the woman with the tourniquet said. She spat blood as she spoke. Zala should have known her name too. When they had the time she'd change that. "That Nabila girl was lookin' to turn traitor, curry favor with that Vaaji captain. Had to be, with how she was gettin' to talkin'."

"She was scared half-dead." Mantu shook his head. "She's a messenger, not a proper pirate."

"Well, it was that damn Vaaji captain on that warship, then. That one who couldn't stop laughin'. He wanted us there today. They knew we was comin'. Damn them to the Sapphire Hells." Spurts of blood from her mouth punctuated each of her words.

An "I told you so" ran through Zala's mind, though she did not verbalize it to the wounded woman. How could she when the pirate was on death's doorstep? What mattered now was getting off the island, getting everyone the help they needed, and finding the Vaaji who had done this, not doling out blame.

"Don't worry, we'll make them pay." Zala turned a look to Mantu. "First, though, we need to treat the injured."

"Considerin' I'm still alive," Mantu said, "I'm givin' the orders around here."

"Right, I wasn't… I was only suggesting—"

"Of course, of course," Mantu interjected, nodding. His tone was patronizing and he hadn't even tried to cloak it. Zala was reminded of the day prior and how the arrogant man had leered after her embarrassing speech.

"But yes," he went on, "We was workin' out what to do next. Ode reckons we could fashion a boat. Nothin' big, of course, just enough to get us back to Kidogo."

"We only need to hollow out one palm," Ode added as

he massaged bare skin near one of his cuts. It looked as though he'd cauterized one of the wounds. With what, Zala didn't want to know. Must have hurt like nothing else, but the old man didn't even seem to pay his wounds any real mind. She almost gagged at the sight, turning to the isle to distract herself from the gruesome image. The picture she found was perhaps even more bleak. There were no trees in sight at all, only jagged rocks.

"Make a boat from what?" Zala asked. "Even if we had the lumber to work with, we don't have the manpower or the energy right now. We need to either feed ourselves, or make a signal fire. Does anyone know where we are?"

"We can't be too far from Kidogo," Shomari said. "If these are the Ibabi Isles, then that means we're just north depending which isle this is."

Zala walked down to the waves, pointing to the western horizon. "So there should be a lot of traffic coming through this way, right? A signal fire wouldn't need to be that big."

Mantu put his hands on his hips. Zala had barely noticed he was without a shirt—she wasn't sure how, when his chest was a forest of hair.

Mantu cleared his voice before saying, "Again, it sounds like you're makin' plans that ain't yours to make."

"*Again*, I'm only making—"

Mantu raised a hand. "A suggestion, right? Just cause I'm glad to see you alive and whole don't mean I don't got the mind to cast you out for mutiny on this Godsforsaken place. And yes, before you ask about the lumber situation, there be a palm tree on the other side of them rocks."

Zala jabbed her finger out. "Listen—"

"No, not now," Shomari whispered into Zala's ear, his voice purring.

Zala mirrored Mantu, placing her hands on her hips defiantly. "Fine, what is it you propose then, *Captain*?"

"Ode's plan could work if we use the able-bodied to get a boat to sea," Mantu began.

Damnit, Shomari, I can't just sit here and listen to this. "Even if we do craft a seaworthy vessel with a single palm," she said. "There's no guarantee we'd survive out on the water."

"Ain't no guarantee a signal fire would save us, neither." Mantu gestured across the ocean's waves. "No matter how much traffic runs through these lanes."

"Well, I think we should start a fire." Zala crossed her arms as she walked to one side of the group. "Anyone who agrees can stand with me." She turned her eyes to Shomari, who stood firm. To be fair, he had told her to stand down. And he had barely voted with her on the *Titan*. So Zala turned to Fon, but she too cast her eyes down into the sands.

"Let's give the boat building a chance, Zala," Fon breathed meekly, her shoulders tense as though she were tiptoeing around Zala's reaction. "If we just burn it, then we'll have nothing to fall back on."

"I'm with Mantu," said Sniffs.

"And I," said Ode.

"Aye, aye," the woman said with an exhausted breath. Someone needed to do something about the blood spluttering up after each of her coughs. But how could that be done without medicine or a healer? Zala put the thought away as she turned to Shomari, who abstained from the vote.

"All right, how do we go about taking down this tree, then?" Zala uncrossed her arms.

Mantu smiled. "Glad you asked. Might've lost the *Titan*,

but our weapons are just fine. We'll take the steel against the palm. Shouldn't take long, ya?"

"I don't know about that. I don't see any axes, and swords are meant—" Zala started, but Shomari clutched her arm. "All right, let's give it a try..." She clenched her jaw. "Captain."

Mantu and the others gathered their preferred swords from the coastline. Zala decided to grab one of the larger ones that had drifted against a rock. Usually, she'd go for a sword with less weight, but if they would be cutting down trees, she figured a broadsword was better suited for the task.

Once she settled on her weapon of choice, she followed the group to where the single palm tree of the isle stood. Sniffs was already working the base, his large arms hacking mechanically one after the other. But even he could not make a dent. If he had the axes he usually favored, perhaps he'd make better work of it.

Mantu went next. Instead of constantly chopping at the tree's base, he took longer, heftier swings. His efforts weren't much better. The swords simply weren't cut out for the job.

The pun was not lost on Zala.

After an hour, the palm only had a small notch in it. Zala and Shomari had their own swings at it—Fon's wounded shoulder sidelined her along with the woman she now learned was named Siya and Old Man Ode—but neither of them could do much of anything.

They all took turns hacking away at the palm tree. Whenever someone tired out, another replaced them. For all their fruitless efforts, Zala didn't think it necessary for all of them to stay, so she told Shomari to tend to Fon's wound, despite Mantu's protest.

"Well, I can go in place of Shomari, if that's okay," Zala said.

Mantu grunted, "No, I say we all get this done now before our energy is spent."

After another hour, the crew had only cut the palm tree a finger's length deep.

"Well... it *can* be done," Mantu said after he took one last swing. "It just need time."

"At this rate, it'll take a whole day," Zala said while she shook life back into her arms. That was too long if Jelani was still out there somewhere. Their group needed to be found now, not later. And their wounded likely wouldn't last long either.

"Well," Mantu heaved his sword atop his shoulder, "We have the time."

"No, you don't understand. A day is too long, especially with how we're spending our energy. We're working with limited time here." She spoke fast like a merchant from the Big Isle as she walked behind the group, getting the words out before Mantu or Sniffs could interrupt her. "The *Osiris* will surely have cast smoke from the wreckage. If someone comes looking, they'll see a second plume from this isle if we burn now. Plus, we need food or water soon, otherwise we'll die of exhaustion." Zala pointed over the rock where Fon, Ode, and Siya rested. Siya in particular was weakening with every passing hour. "And the others won't make it that long. You saw the old woman. She's got a day at best."

Mantu waved Zala's complaints away, looking almost delusional. "Siya will be fine. We ain't gonna need long." Mantu walked over to a crate near the coastline and he used the tip of his boot to kick it open. From inside the box rolled tiny barrels marked as rum. "Nothing clears the head better than a good drink. It might even make you come up with

one of your 'genius' plans to get this tree down faster."
Mantu grabbed one of the barrels and threw it onto his
other shoulder. Sniffs snagged a barrel of his own. Zala
sighed.

"We *all* can think it over on a drink," Mantu said.

Sniffs smiled wide. "Or four."

CHAPTER 20
ZALA

THE CREW DRANK THEIR FILL WELL INTO THE NIGHT.

Mantu and Sniffs jumped and skipped around the beach in drunken joy, lit by the twin moons that shone bright in the cloudless sky. The wounded rocked from left to right on the sand. Even Fon took an uncharacteristic swig of rum and was drunk and stupid within a minute. She, too, danced circles around the other pirate's knees, jumping high in the sky but never taking flight. Shomari had tended to her wound with dawa root that had washed ashore, but her wings did not spread wide enough yet for flying.

Zala saw all the jubilation for what it was: drinking and dancing the sorrow away.

They had lost so many, their ship was sunk, their captain was dead, and they were stranded. In the end, Zala couldn't really blame them for prancing around. There was *some* merit to what Mantu was attempting.

Only she and Shomari abstained from the small festivities, electing instead to play audience to the performed shanties. Even though Zala couldn't hear them clearly through their slur—even if they *were* coherent—she would have been hard-pressed to hear them. Her ruined ear had yet to improve. Still, any self-respecting pirate knew the words well enough, no matter how incongruous the lyrics. The pirate's song rang out strong and clear:

> *Can you come back right now?*
> *Did you up and flee now?*
> *Are you drowned and dead now?*
> *We're not sure now.*
>
> *Lekkun, where you go now?*
> *Lekkun, where you go now?*
> *Lekkun, where you go now?*
> *Where you go now?*

Fon sung the first lines, which were meant for a solo. She had the most beautiful voice, a trait apparently shared among the aziza. The rest of the crew sang back to her in the second half of the stanza. They sounded terrible, a trait apparently shared among most pirates—especially drunk ones.

Usually Fon sang a duet with Jelani. Zala tried to imagine her husband's voice in place of the slurred words of Siya, Old Man Ode, Mantu, and Sniffs. When she closed her eyes it almost worked, but Jelani's voice was distant, as though it were drifting farther and farther out to sea.

Zala clutched the songstone at her sash belt. Throughout the day she had thought she heard him humming his favorite hymn from that old religion, but every time she lifted the stone to her ear there was nothing, and she'd wave it off as her own hopeful imagination.

Fantasy be damned, she needed the real thing.

"You know we could hang for singing this song if we were in Zanziwala," Shomari said as he clapped, encouraging Fon to keep up the beat. "The golden lord doesn't much care for Lekkun."

"Yeah, I heard they feuded," Zala said, her foot tapping along the cool sand. "I don't know all the story."

"Did I ever tell you I knew Lekkun?" Shomari asked.

Zala brushed loose sand from her knee. "I don't think you have. I've only seen him from afar. He used to bring food and supplies to Port Kidogo. I never realized it until I joined up with you lot, but he probably stole all that stuff. Jelani and I got into all this piratin' business after his time, after the golden lord took over. How did you know him?"

Shomari leaned back on shaggy elbows, and looked up into the stars in reverie. "I was in one of his crews. Just one job."

"Was he as mean as the songs say? He seemed friendly when I saw him."

"He wasn't a madman or anything. But yes, he had a temper. It was necessary though, kept us in line, not unlike our late Captain Kobi."

Zala turned back to the dancers. Mantu and Sniffs joined lips as they finished the last lines of the song. Fon perked up again, turning around in circles with perfect grace. Though the woman named Siya wore a broad smile and laughed loud, her once sun-kissed skin was paling quickly. Zala had given her a day initially—now she wasn't sure the woman would make it through the night.

Mantu seemed to know her time was short as well. He didn't even protest when Zala suggested Siya get the lion's share of the rum. If nothing could be done for her, at least she could be made comfortable.

Still, it didn't help fill the aching pit in Zala's stomach.

Though she tried to make conversation before the woman was properly drunk, she was only able to pick out superficial nuggets. All she could find out was that the woman was from the Big Isle and that she had a particular hate for the Vaaji. One just couldn't get to truly know another in the span of a few hours.

It had been Zala's own fault. She had never seen a reason to get to know a crewmate when oftentimes they died by the dozen. Usually, they perished during the raids, outside of her knowledge until someone mentioned their absence. But now, with a crew member dying right in front of her—despite how jovial Siya seemed—Zala couldn't help feeling pangs of guilt.

And Siya would only be the first if someone didn't do something fast.

"We have to get off this isle," Zala said, her tone suddenly low and serious. "Jelani needs me."

Shomari purred through his lips. "I'm sure he's doing fine. I would wager he is thinking the same about you right now. He might even be headed to this isle as we speak."

Zala closed her eyes again and focused on the songstone. There was still nothing. She rubbed her blistering hands, unconvinced. "I don't know... not against what the Vaaji had. What if they come back for us. And not just that. My husband, he..."

Shomari titled his head, causing the earrings in his pointed ear to clink. "What is it?"

Zala considered telling Shomari about Jelani's condition. It wouldn't have hurt if he knew. But many in Esowon didn't understand stoneskin. It wasn't contagious—only passed on by the touch of a Gods' Darkstone, but many still wanted nothing to do with those who were infected. It didn't matter now, however, even if Shomari knew; Jelani was nowhere near. And hadn't Shomari said the malady had affected his own clan?

"He's got the stoneskin," she finally said.

"I thought as much." Shomari shrugged with a sidelong glance, no judgment in his eyes. "Whenever we looted together, he always asked if I could save him eyes of tokoloshe and scales of mazomba. Not too many ask for these two items together unless they're trying to brew stonesbane."

Zala lifted herself, her elbows digging into the sands. "So you understand why I can't stay here."

Shomari gave her a short nod. "Yes, I understand. He's on a timeline, yes? When's the last time he is taking his potion?"

"A fortnight," Zala sighed heavily. "Probably more that that, honestly; he's always sharing."

"Yes, that sounds like him." The pakka titled his head toward Zala. "Well, in terms of getting off this desolate rock, you'll hear no talk back from me. I'd like to leave this isle too as soon as possible. I don't intend to be dying here."

"Same can't be said for Mantu."

"His plan isn't the most pragmatic," Shomari said. "The liquor is a nice distraction, but that tree isn't coming down anytime soon with just our swords."

"Then why didn't you vote with me!" Zala said, a bit too loudly. It didn't matter. The rest of the crew were too far gone to hear her properly.

"You've got to read the room—ah—the beach. We would've lost the vote, and I'm a cat, not an ass."

"You'll just let me look like a fool on my own instead." Zala shook her head. "Dikala."

Shomari returned her gesture with a shrug of his own. "So am I right in assuming you have a plan?"

"I do." She turned her head to the beach. "But it involves the rum."

"I think I know what you're getting at. But what about them?" Shomari nodded to the group.

Zala laughed. "They're already out of it as it is. It won't be long, maybe an hour until they pass out."

"I'm surprised Fon hasn't dropped already."

"Me too, actually."

Fon *did* look wobbly, though, and before long she was lying among the sand crabs. Second and third were Ode and Siya. Zala went to the pale woman's side to check her pulse, trying her best to ignore how shallow Siya's breaths came. Mantu and Sniffs were last, shuffling off deeper into the rocky isle to enjoy each other. Zala ordered Shomari to make sure they were out as well before they proceeded.

Light feet carried Zala around the sleeping figure of Fon. The aziza's body curled into a tight ball against the night winds that swept off the waves.

It'll be warm soon enough, friend, Zala thought.

When Shomari returned with news of the lovers sleeping in one another's arms, they started their work. It took a few minutes to decide how they'd move the barrels, as neither were strong enough to lift them. Zala hit herself in the head when she realized they would be easier to roll. Common sense, really. But the simple things could get very difficult when faced with nerves and tension.

So, Zala and Shomari took the barrels of rum and rolled one next to the other around the base of the inland palm. Though rolling was a much better idea, it still took most of the night to get the barrels into position. To the east, a sliver of blue-orange rose from a materializing horizon.

Morning would be upon them soon.

Zala wanted to time it just right. With the rising sun, the

rest of the crew would likely wake, but she also needed the daybreak for the signal to be seen. When the light on the horizon turned from indigo to a delicate azure, she used a piece of flint to spark a flame against one of the large rocks, keeping a husk of palm close to keep it alight.

A morning gale started up. Each howl of the wind stopped her movement short. Every little sound could have been Mantu or Sniffs shuffling through the sands.

"Don't worry, I'll smell them before they come anywhere near," Shomari assured her.

Zala took a deep breath and gave Shomari a short nod. It would be nice if her damned heart would settle down. It pulsed so hard that it was making her hands tremble.

She turned back to her work, blowing on the tree ferns between her hands. Once the husk glowed a bright orange she brought the piece over to the barrels with gentle care, as though the smoldering bark were as fragile as an *impundulu's* egg.

"I don't know about this," Shomari said. "How long do you think it will burn for?"

Zala shrugged. "I know rum burns well, but I'm not sure how long or high with just the wood of the barrels and a single palm. If this isle had at least one more tree, it would make all the difference. I've never seen a land so desolate."

"Why do you think no one has settled here?"

Zala set her kindling against the barrels and watched as the flames rose high above the rum crates, which set the palm tree into a blood-orange blaze. With a speed faster than Zala expected, the fire bounded up the tree and to its head, setting it alight with a snap and crack. It wasn't long before the branches of the palm fell down around the bleak rocks.

Zala smiled as the flames and smoke rose high. Any ship

from a league away would see it. Shit, maybe even two leagues. But her elation was dashed after a few scant minutes.

"What in the Sapphire Hells are you doing?" Mantu roared as he stumbled out from behind a set of rocks shirtless, his trousers around his knees. "That's our only way off the isle!"

Zala turned dark eyes to Shomari. "'I'll smell them before they come anywhere near,' ya?"

Shomari gave a small shrug. "The smoke masked them."

Zala inhaled deeply through her nose as she turned to Mantu. "We don't know where we are! We don't have the energy to row, and we could be sailing straight to our deaths. This way we could at least let ourselves be known."

"Oh, yes?" Mantu rushed up on her, Sniffs not far behind. "And what if it's the Vaaji who find us, huh? Or the Ya-Seti? Or any of the other nations we've robbed. Once they find a band of pirates wounded and alone on this island, what do you think they'll do?"

"I... I hadn't —"

"Right, you hadn't thought of that," Mantu finished for her, spraying her with rum-infused spittle.

All feeling drained from Zala's body, replaced with naked shame. She had been so focused on her own plan that she hadn't properly thought things through. "I—It's still a risk worth taking, though. No matter who finds us... w-we could act like merchants..." she stammered. "We could say *we* were the ones attacked by pirates, that we were stranded here. As long as we clean ourselves up, the story should sell —"

Mantu raised his hand. "No. No more of your words or your plans. Listen, you're one of the smart ones on the crew, I get that. But you need a lesson in listening." An internal smile rose within Zala. Had there really been crew members, especially someone like Mantu, who thought that highly of her? "You really think I would set a boat all the way to Kidogo? We'd island hop our way down the Ibabi straits, of course." He scoffed. "That's it though. You've had too many chances, Zala. It's time you walked the plank."

Despite her guilt, Zala fought back an eye-roll. "What plank? We aren't on a ship."

"You know what I mean!"

"Same go for Shomari," Sniffs added. "The kijana in it too."

Mantu clenched his jaw. "I don't know if I want to compromise Shomari. This is his first offense, after all. We gonna need him now if one of them nobles find us here. He's good in a fight."

Sniffs rubbed the back of his hand over his nose. "That fair."

"But I can't go back to camp lookin' lenient." Mantu stroked his beard.

The two men somehow appeared larger than they had before. But Zala convinced herself it was only the flames throwing their shadows. The dramatic lighting made them look like ghoulish specters. It was one thing when they were fighting alongside her, but with Mantu talking about the virtues of leniency, they were starting to feel like real threats for the first time. Had Sniffs always really been that large? He truly was a goliath, standing nearly half as tall as the palm tree burning behind him. At least to her eyes.

Steady. Deep breaths. Big means slow.

"What does it matter?" Zala said. "You'd only have to deal with an aziza and two crew members who are half-dead." Judging by the scowl on Mantu's face, those were the wrong choice of words. "Listen, we want the same thing.

I just don't want to see any more of the crew perish when they don't have to. We don't need another Ajola or all the rest on our hands."

"Sniffs, take her," Mantu ordered.

Zala made it three strides back before Sniffs had her pinned in a bear hug.

Yeah, real slow.

Panic shot through her limbs, fueling her thrashing against the giant man's grip. She barely moved a finger's breadth. She gave up the wrestling match for a scowl—for all the good that would do.

"Zala and Shomari, you have committed mutiny against your crew," Mantu recited the pirate's code. "By my right as the captain, I sentence you, Zala, to—"

"Wait!" Zala struggled against Sniff's thick arms. "What's the point? Give me two days, just two. We're already stranded as it is. If we're not saved—if it's the Vaaji or the Ya-Seti that finds us, then you'll need another sword hand like you say. But if we *are* saved, if we survive... then... then... you owe me..." Zala couldn't think of what at first. "Well... an apology, at least."

There was a long silence amongst the group. Sniffs still kept Zala locked in the strongest grip she had ever been wrapped in. Shomari held his yellow eyes firm, while Mantu's stare was blank and dead. But after a short moment, he let out a great guffaw.

"Ain't no one talkin' about killin', girl. Was just going to rough you and the cat up a bit—"

Shomari stifled a snicker.

Mantu whipped his head to the pakka. "You think I can't take you?"

"No comment," Shomari said, throwing up his catspaws, and clearly thinking otherwise.

Mantu let out a snort that rivaled one of Sniffs' loudest grunts. "Whatever, the girl still needs her beating…"

"*I have basked in the light of Yem, and She shall be my only judge,*" Zala recited quickly, trying to get all the words out before she forgot them. "*These words I speak are true, and by moons' light, I hold the right to be found false.*" She wasn't sure she had that first part right. Jelani had paraphrased them often enough when they argued, but religious lines had never meant anything to her. She'd have to pay more attention if—*when*—he threw it in her face again next. "Oh!" She remembered. "*And may Her waves be merciful!*"

Mantu stopped laughing after that. "You'd really try to get out of a simple beating on the back of the lawtide? You want the Mother of the Ocean, the Maiden of the Big Moon, to back you on this of all things? Them are strong words, Zala."

"That's submission of your soul, it is," Sniffs added gravely.

"You don't have to go through with that, Zee," Shomari intoned, shaking his paw cheerlessly. Zala could barely make out his silhouette against the burning tree. She only saw his reflective cat eyes and pointed ears.

It didn't matter either way. She didn't believe in any of that stuff, never had. But the gambit always held weight when used against those that did.

"When did you even have the chance to be tested by Yem?" Mantu retorted.

"I didn't drown yesterday, did I?" Zala offered. "Her Grace or whatever spared me… right?"

Mantu shook his head slowly, looking at Zala as though she had committed great heresy. Well, technically she had. But he seemed to honor it all the same.

"Come, Shomari," Mantu ordered. "We need to put out

this fire, and see if the tree can be saved." He turned to Sniffs. "Bring Zala, make sure she doesn't get loose."

Shomari nodded as he threw sand to the fire. Sniffs continued pinning Zala's arms behind her back, though his grip on her loosened slightly. Once the fire died down, Sniffs let go of her, but Shomari took her by the arm instead.

"If it it worth anything," Shomari muttered in her ear, "I thought it was a good plan. If we aren't saved, don't worry. Mantu won't be surviving, either. He will likely die shortly after you."

Zala couldn't help being taken aback. "Is that a threat?"

"No," he chuckled. "We'll all simply be dying of thirst, of course."

THAT DIDN'T GO WELL, ZALA THOUGHT AS SHE SAT BEFORE A tirade from Fon.

"*Why* would you do that?" the aziza shouted, her gaze a blazing anger.

Zala had never heard that tone aimed at her before, not from Fon, and not with such hurt in her friend's eyes. Though still tipsy from her drink, she held her pointed finger firm, striking it right at the edge of Zala's nose. The image almost reminded her of her instructors back at the Jultian Academy—small women with equally severe expressions.

Fon was more frightening than those women could have ever hoped to be. Zala actually *cared* what her diminutive friend thought, for one. Where she had tuned out her instructors, she hung on Fon's every word, every proclamation of "irrational" or "foolish" or, worst of all, "irresponsible" cutting painfully deep.

"And you went off with the *cat* instead of *me*," Fon went on. "Oh, Yem, let your waves be merciful!"

Not even Mantu and Sniffs could find the laughter that usually came so easily at Zala's expense. Secondhand embarrassment colored their ears as they headed back to try and douse the smoking ruin of the palm tree, Shomari in tow. Half of Zala would have preferred the beating if it meant avoiding the heated unease rushing from her head to the tips of her fingers.

She thought she'd done what was best for the group. But in her rush to be right, she hadn't considered the potential threat she might've called down upon them. The likelihood of the Vaaji finding them again was slim, yet in the face of Fon's anger, Zala was beginning to doubt that.

"And furthermore, how dare you do it while we were sleeping!"

Despite the trickling feelings of remorse down her spine, Zala couldn't see how her plan was any worse—how could it be?

If the Vaaji had really wanted to do the job right, they would have cleared the isles before leaving. And considering the morning blue was free of any sky ships, it would seem their small band of pirates was the least of the Vaaji Empire's worries.

It was more likely they'd get picked up by someone from Kidogo, a merchant ship or one of Golden Lord Zuberi's own.

"Even if the merchant ship hailed from Vaaj," Zala countered back to Fon. "We could claim we were attacked—which isn't entirely untrue. We'd just leave out the detail about being attacked by a Vaaji sky ship."

"Excuse *you*," Fon spat back, "I wasn't done!"

And Fon went on, but only for a minute more. After winding down her rant, out of breath and red in the face, Fon put her hands to her hips and looked into the clouds, as though taking stock on whether she had everything out of her system. Zala was confident she had received the aziza's message loud and clear. The shouting had seemed to take a toll on Fon — or perhaps the hangover was finally kicking in — and she stumbled to one side, catching on Siya's leg in the sands.

"Oh, sorry," Fon mumbled, but Siya didn't move.

Zala traded a look of horror with the aziza. "Oh, no…"

The pair rushed to the pirate's side. In her panic, Fon shook Siya by the arm vigorously, but the woman's body only slumped like a ragdoll. The infection in her shoulders had spread farther through her chest in a collage of green, purple, and red over a sheet of paled skin.

"She didn't make it," Zala said, placing a gentle hand to Siya's throat. No pulse. "How about Ode?"

Fon went to shake the old man, who swatted her away and turned to go back to sleep. The aziza rubbed her hand and gave Ode a pout he didn't see. Massage slowing to a gentle rub, she turned sadder eyes to Siya again. "What should we do with her?"

Zala didn't respond at first, taking in Siya's motionless form. She knew it had been coming, but it still hurt to see her now as merely another corpse in the sand. "We'll bury her with Ajola. We have nothing else to do, anyway. Maybe I should dig a grave of my own while I'm at it… I made a deal with Mantu."

Fon raised an eyebrow. "Another one? What did you get into this time?"

"Well, there's potentially good news."

"And you know I want the bad news first."

"Right." Zala leaned her head on her shoulder. "Well, I told him if we don't get rescued he could kill me himself for mutiny."

Fon's wings fluttered somewhere between disbelief and amusement. "And you know he'd love to."

"He was actually against killing me. At least when I said he'd need as many hands as possible if the Vaaji find us again. But yes, he probably wouldn't lose sleep over it. He wanted to beat me instead."

Fon moved Siya's arms over her chest and curled her legs into a fetal position. If Zala recalled correctly, it was the position of *Final Rest* from the Old Way.

"So, what's the good news, then?" Fon asked.

"If I'm right," Zala began. "He promises not to beat me and, well… give me an apology."

"What? And he agreed to that?"

"Yes… although, I may have used Yem again…"

Fon's hands shot straight to her hips again, that look of scorn lining her brow once more. "*Again?* You didn't! That's fine in your cutesy little squabbles with Jelani, but not with someone like Mantu. He'll hold you to that, Zala. That's sacred."

Zala threw up her hands defensively. "Well, what else was I supposed to do?"

Fon shook her head, then sighed as her attention returned to Siya's body. "So do you have a plan if no one shows up?"

"Still working on it."

"Well, you best think of something fast. Mantu doesn't make idle threats."

Zala turned her eyes down to where the rocks cut into the beach. Around the corner, Mantu, Sniffs, and Shomari must've been cupping ocean water to the still burning tree.

"I know," she said.

An hour passed and the men and pakka still had not returned from dousing the fire. And in the meantime, Fon and Zala awkwardly dug a hole with the flat of their swords. Zala let her mind wander to Siya, who laid feet away from her.

She's already gone, you can't do anything for her now except dig. And so she dug, dug until her legs, back, biceps, and shoulders were good and sore.

By the time Zala and Fon finished digging, the sun had reached its apex in the sky. And with the day's light came the figures of more dead bodies washing ashore.

Zala scanned the corpses for Jelani, her heart skipping a beat each time one of the figures showed a bald head or deep-brown skin, but none of them matched. She couldn't help thinking one of those bodies could be hers in the next few days.

Though the fire was long out, a black cloud still rose above the isle and drifted west and south. Zala held to her belief that burning the tree had been the best course of action, but that didn't mean they would be saved. She wondered what would be the worst way to go: at sea where they could drown and become food for sea monsters, or on the beach baked dry and dying of thirst instead.

Zala brushed sand from her face, and winced when her hand passed over her left ear. The ringing had stopped, but sound was still muted.

She had to admit, throughout her many weeks as a pirate, she had gotten herself into situations that had led to her own injury—or others, more often than not. But she had to get back to Jelani at all costs. In the end, it would be worth it. She glanced between the graves and the smoking tree.

No matter how many times she ran her plan through her mind, there was no other choice she could see herself making.

CHAPTER 21
KARIM

Umar Jad was one of the most orderly individuals on the *Viper*. Karim's thoughts always called back to the empire's mantra of efficiency whenever he watched the stern man's weathered fingers riffling through ship logs or personnel records.

Today it was the loot recovered from the pirate haul.

Jad's attention to detail didn't end at his desk either. He took great care to ensure that every inch of his sizeable workroom was as orderly as it could be. From loose coinage to brass lanterns, every item had its position, and any who dared to move anything out of place invited Jad's ensured wrath. Even the dim light cast through the viewport slats behind his hunched silhouette seemed to line up the room in sections, bowing to his vision.

At his side lay his only personal possessions: three leather-bound books he kept with him at all times. *The Great Book of al-Qiba*, of course, and two other tomes on arithmetic and the history of commerce. Despite the many years Karim had seen him with the books, they always looked as new as the first time he'd laid eyes on them.

Karim cleared his throat. As fascinating it was to watch Jad at work, he had his own to get on with.

"These Kidogon pirates were busy," Jad said, never lifting his head from the scratching of his ornate reed pen. "They had loot enough to—"

"Buy their way onto their Golden Lord's Council," Karim finished.

Jad's hand halted, his gaze flicking up to Karim. His long face always cast an eerie shadow when steeped over his writing desk.

"Right you are, sir. Very sharp." He dipped his pen in his inkwell before returning to his papers. "What can I do for you, Chief Officer?"

"I'd hate to disturb your work, but I was wondering if—"

Jad lifted his hand toward one of the chests before jabbing a ringed finger down at the wall. "Your share's in that one there, third from the right. Just look under 'S.'" The old man lifted his chin in thought. "You know, I never liked you 'el' types."

Karim raised an eyebrow. *What is that supposed to mean?*

Jad caught his expression and chuckled weakly in bemusement. "Can never decide if I should log you with the 'E's or the 'S's."

Jad always had a way of making idle commentary directed at Karim some sort of subtle jab. Karim could never call him out for it, because each of the old man's quips could have easily been considered innocent wisecracks, but that didn't stop the scowls that crept along Karim's lips from time to time.

Wiping the grimace from his face, Karim knelt to the

chest Jad pointed to. The lid opened to what looked like a mountain of gold, silver, and bronze. At the base of the twinkling hill, a sack with his name tied to it lay on its side. When he picked it up, the weight of the bag nearly caved his wrist. Karim's lips parted in mild shock, his breath stilling. Surely Jad had made a mistake. This loot should've been for two, skies, maybe even three crew members.

"That's a good take for your first day as captain, yes?" Jad smiled. "You've come a long way from street ratting, *el-Sayyed*. Ismail will be proud."

Karim's spine straightened at the back-handed compliment and he nearly cracked at the mention of his father's name. He had tried his best to keep his past hidden from the other members of the crew. He should've known better than to think it would have slipped past Jad.

"I'm no captain," Karim said, clutching the hefty sack's neck tightly in his hand to contain his irritation. He couldn't let Jad see the second frown escaping the edge of his mouth. "Our captain is still nursing his wounds. He'll be back soon, I'm sure."

Jad gave him another long smirk, then returned to his scroll as though Karim had never interrupted him at all. "Certainly, sir. And no one will be more pleased than you."

Karim stood still for a short moment, lines etched in his forehead and a retort at the edge of his lips. But he had never been good at off-the-cuff rebuttals, so he stayed his tongue. Whatever wordplay Jad was baiting him into wouldn't work. So Karim took his leave of the room — almost too abruptly — and without a farewell.

Each crewmate Karim passed on his way to his quarters addressed him with pointed salutes or wide smiles. He tried his best to return their earnest greetings with the same fervor, but he couldn't shake off his encounter with Jad.

Had the purser known where most of Karim's coin had been going to? The old man had said nothing telling, per se, but his words dug under Karim's skin.

Strictly speaking, personal communique to and from the *Viper* was not permitted. This was supposed to be a secret mission, after all. And if Jad knew what Karim suspected he did, that'd leave the young officer open to blackmail, the go-to tactic of the noble types.

"You all right there, sir?"

Karim lifted his head to his newly appointed steward: Jamal Bitar, the same that had served Malouf. Though not mandated to serve Karim, who was merely the acting captain, the young, wide-eyed Bitar had remained a vigilant servant to him ever since the end of the battle. Karim got the distinct impression the steward wanted to be as far away from Malouf as possible, even if it meant bending protocol to do it.

"Everything's fine," Karim said as he shook Jad's comments from his mind. "Anything to report?"

The overzealous steward gave him an exaggerated salute. Karim could never recall him being so animated with Malouf. "Nothing, sir. We're still a day's journey from the capital."

"Very well." Karim nodded, then ordered, "No disturbances. I have business to attend to."

Bitar pushed open Karim's door, leading a hand into the cramped room. It was too bad Malouf was being tended to in his quarters, as it would have been nice to have some leg room while being acting captain.

Karim waited for the door to close behind him before he crossed to the chest at the end of the room. His movements were almost mechanical as he opened the chest and stuffed his latest earnings into a hidden slot along its side.

With a heavy sigh, Karim looked deeper into the hidden slot to the letter that lay within. Several thoughts were on his mind: Did he have to? Had he not sent enough to his father already? His old man must have sent Issa a letter of her own. That must've been why she brought him up the day before. And knowing Issa, she would have sent what she could afford, even more than that, more likely. Karim inhaled deeply, he couldn't leave it all to her...

Reluctantly, Karim stood and moved to peer over the letter once more:

My son,

I'm sorry to trouble you again like this. I hope you know I wouldn't if I saw any other way.

Collector Vaziri returned. He's asking—insisting—that we pay double this coming moon, and he wants our share ready by next sundown. I know you're away someplace, and I know you can't say where, but please; if you can, our people need your help.

If this letter fails to reach you in time, I will figure something out. Maybe it's time we speak to those guardians. Two of them, young ones, showed up a few weeks back. I know you think them radicals, and maybe they are, but we have to do something if we don't get the monarchy's coin. I don't want to start a fight, but if Vaziri does, we'll give him one.

Ogó'ala be with you.

— Your Father

Karim had crossed out the last lines in frustration the previous night. He wished his old man would drop the "Old Ways" crap, at least with him. His father knew very well how little he cared for it. Besides, the letter alone was enough to land Karim in trouble, without adding mention of Ogó'ala and fanatic guardians on top of it.

His father's fears were well founded though. This "Collector Vaziri" had been hounding the inhabitants of Karim's old district for moons now, and with each cycle that passed he demanded more and more.

Karim's father had mentioned nothing about defenses or Guardians of Àyá before, however. It was starting to sound like the tensions between the empire and the old local tribes were turning hot all over again. That was the last thing Karim needed right now.

Fidgeting with his hands, he finally pulled out a fresh piece of parchment and set his pen to work:

Baba,
    I have received word of your plight. These coins should keep that tax collector away until my return. I have a lot to tell you.
    — Your Son, Karim

Karim lifted the parchment to his viewport, the light from outside making the material glow and slightly translucent. For a moment, he mused if his letter was perhaps too brief. But he didn't have much more to say, and nothing in particular came to him. He could only hope that Nabila could get the coin to his father before the deadline arrived. The *Viper* wouldn't return until the next morning, maybe even late afternoon, and Karim wouldn't be able to see to his father until late the next day after debriefing.

Deciding he was finished, he pulled from his hidden stash and poured a fair amount of coin into a small purse. When he couldn't fit any more inside, he tied off the top, then turned to the door to speak to his steward outside. "Can you send for Nabila if she's able? I need to hasten something to the capital."

"Right away, sir." Before the end of his words, Bitar was

already trotting down the corridor with a hurried skip. It had not been lost on Karim how well received he was after taking over. He almost pitied the crew more than he did himself. Once they returned home, things would unfortunately return to the way they were before.

As he waited, Karim's thoughts turned to his family once more. With the thrill of the chase and the buildup of the Kidogon pirate operation, he had pushed all thoughts of family to the back of his mind. He found himself a little uncomfortable that now, with time freely available, he was no more eager to think on those he had left behind in al-Anim than he had been before.

It wasn't that he didn't care about his family, or that he didn't want to spend more time with them. He did. However, the navy had given him so many opportunities, so many experiences, he didn't want to give that up, and his family wasn't as supportive of his long-term plans as they could be.

A knock at the door shook him from his reverie.

"Come in," Karim said, adjusting his uniform.

Through the threshold stepped Nabila, the sunlight through his viewport reflecting in her golden eyes. Karim gestured to her wounds, which had been mended. "It looks like you're doing better."

"Your surgeon is the best I've seen on an imperial ship," she said. Her voice was softer than usual.

"Well, this is a very special ship."

Nabila smiled, tilting her head to one side. "You need me to take another letter?"

"If it wouldn't be too much trouble. It's an emergency and—"

"I'm the fastest shifter you have. I know, I know. You

only want me for my wings." She smirked and rested a casual hand on her hip.

Karim always felt small pangs of guilt when he asked favors of Nabila. Her attraction to him had been very obvious from the start, and though he had been clear that he would not reciprocate—she was his subordinate, and he felt nothing in return anyway—he still needed her for his personal messages. Nabila's infatuation proved useful with that. He couldn't trust anyone on this ship but Issa, after all, and Issa couldn't sprout wings.

"It's not much." Karim ignored her twinkling eyes. He could easily see how their honey color could ensnare most men. Issa had told him once that his own reluctance had been what piqued the shifter's interest in the first place. He tried to soften the brush-off with a smile. "Just something that needs to be sent to the capital. Something that needs to get there faster than any of the others can manage. It's right there on the desk… if you're up for it."

"Of course I'm up for it." She swayed over and swept the letter from the tabletop. "Who do you take me for?"

Karim's eyes shifted to his desk. He needed to write a second letter, but Nabila leaned against the parchment on his desk as though something was *actually* about to happen between them. Eventually, however, she relented, and stepped away from the worktop with a coy sigh. Karim tried to squeeze by her, catching against her closer than he intended. He hoped she wouldn't assume anything more than the innocent accident it was.

"Don't let me disturb you from your work," Nabila said as her arms shrunk to wings. "Take my clothes back to communications, will you?"

For a moment her loose wrappings seemed to hang, suspended in the air, before falling from her gull form. She flew to the viewport and tapped on the window, an indication she needed to be let out. Karim shook his head and had to suppress the urge to snicker as he stood to open the viewport. She looked up at him, waiting.

"Thanks again, this means a lot." Karim swung the hinge wide.

Nabila gave a small squawk, which he took to mean "anytime," before flying off into the clouds.

Karim dipped down and gathered her clothes—more like rags, really. A scent of jasmine hung in the air. It reminded Karim of the flowers his father used to grow back home. He and Nabila had had idle conversations about the slums they both came from, but he couldn't recall ever mentioning his father's garden. Karim tried to ignore the fact that the aroma was likely meant for his benefit. She was definitely hoping for more of a send-off than what she had gotten this time.

Curiosity led his nose deeper into the fabric. Just as he took a second whiff, a knock on the door made him jump. Muffled voices rumbled on the other side—bickering, by the sounds of it. Karim listened for a moment but couldn't make out the tones.

"Chief Officer!" came a familiar voice.

Issa?

Karim marched forward while Issa's voice shouted through the door. "Can you please just get out of the way, kid?"

Karim swung the door open to the sight of Bitar blocking the threshold, the young man's tense frame screaming total defiance.

"Apologies, sir." The steward whipped his head to Karim as he held his arms out, blocking Issa on both sides. "I told the gunnery chief you weren't to be disturbed—"

"And I told you this is serious," Issa spat.

Karim raised his hands. "Both of you calm down." He rested a gentle grip on Bitar's shoulder, leaning his head close to him with a light voice. "Thank you, Bitar, but if Chief Akif ever needs to see me, you let her in right away."

"Um... of course, sir. My apologies, sir." Bitar turned on the spot with a crisp salute as he gave a nervous sidelong glance to Issa. "My mistake, ma'am."

Karim smiled to him before turning to Issa. She seemed out of breath, her skin blemishing almost as red as her under tunic. "What is it, Officer?"

"It's the sea speaker, Chief," she said. "There's a problem."

CHAPTER 22
KARIM

"Not strictly a problem, per se, Chief Akif," Surgeon Abadi explained a few moments later. Karim and Issa arrived at the storeroom serving as a makeshift brig and infirmary both, as Abadi rubbed his hands in a patched cloth. "Not right away, at any rate. As long as he gets the proper care, he has some life in him."

"I see," Karim said, then glanced over Abadi's shoulder to the closed door. "I thought stoneskin meant he's marked for death."

Abadi pressed a rust-covered rod into a tall bucket. Its red-hot tip released a burst of steam that rose quickly from the iron container. Had he used the heated slab against the pirate? Even as the steam slithered up quick and wide, neither of the mystguards who stood next to the surgeon moved at all, their eyes fixed on the wall opposite their station and their faces appearing as stone statues.

Abadi adjusted the monocle at his eye. "Not too many survive the touch of Gods' Glass. This one must have timed it perfectly. The stone starts at his left hand, the initial infection perhaps even originating from the tip of his forefinger."

Karim had heard of the rare disease before. But most who contracted it died within hours, their final moments filled with fever and madness both. According to the stories, at least.

"But his mind... has his mind been compromised?" Issa asked, giving voice to Karim's thoughts.

"Oh, no." Abadi took the monocle from his eye and dropped it into his robe's pocket. "He will have his mind until the end. The stone will crawl through his body until it is all that remains. When it has no more surface skin to cover, it will attack the muscles and, eventually, the mind. Painful business in the end. Very painful."

Karim swallowed hard. It had taken them moons to find this lone pirate, and all that searching had been for nothing. Now he understood what those marks on his face were. It hadn't been a bad burn or rough scabbing after all.

"So he's only got... what?" Karim asked. "A day? A week at most?"

"I can't say how long it'll be, at least until we get back to the capital. My instruments on this ship are limited, of course. But if you want an educated guess, I wouldn't worry. He should have the better part of a year."

Karim let out a sigh of relief, exchanging a look with Issa.

"But his condition will quickly worsen if we strain his body at all." Abadi lifted his rod once more, then bent down to pick up the bucket. "I would advise against the more... aggressive methods of questioning."

Karim rubbed his hands behind his back, a nervous tick he thought he'd done away with.

"What about stonesbane?" Issa asked, tapping a hand

against Karim's fingers. He stopped fidgeting. "It's supposed to be a cure for his infection, right?"

"It's a tricky business, that concoction," Abadi said with sigh. "And it's not a cure. It merely delays the inevitable. But if one is skilled enough, they can sustain one's life indefinitely… in theory. There are rumors that the golden lord's own personal guard and court have been afflicted for years now. So long as one has the resources, one could live a full life with the disease. After all, the stoneskin essentially serves as, well, extraordinarily tough skin until it takes the mind."

The old man pulled an assortment of beads from his pocket and fit them around his wrist, each representing a different discipline mastered by the surgeon. "I've only mixed the potion once during my time in the academy years ago, and it wasn't very good. It's easy enough to brew, but it's very hard to draw enough potency for long-lasting impact. Only a *true* master alchemist can stretch it any more than a week or two…"

"And are you not a master alchemist?" Karim questioned, hoping he didn't appear desperate.

Abadi shrugged. "I dabble…" Karim and Issa traded skeptical looks. Abadi noticed and scoffed. "I hold the official title of an alchemist, but my specialties lie elsewhere. Ever since the empire regulated our mystic population and the tools they use, the stonesbane potion went out of style. Precious few specialize enough to brew the potion to absolute potency. I'm afraid I'm just not one of them, talented though I may be."

A chill ran through Karim's chest. *So the pirate is as good as dead, then.*

"There is an alchemist in Vaaj who may be of help," Abadi said as though he could read Karim's thoughts. "Al-

Dima is her name. But getting her assistance will be more than a little difficult, especially these days with the expansion to the Eastern—"

"We have the key to a mountain of skyglass sitting right behind that door." Karim did his best not to raise his voice as he pointed over Abadi's shoulder. "Surely that's enough to warrant her aid."

Abadi raised an eyebrow, disregarding Karim's near outburst. "It's not up to me, sir. It'll need to be taken up with someone above my pay grade. I can send out the request, however, if you wish it. We studied together briefly."

Karim couldn't seem to catch a break. Ever since they'd set sails to the clouds there seemed to be one problem after another. The closer he came to achieving some semblance of success or good fortune, the more hurdles appeared to block his path.

"May I see him?" Karim asked after a short pause.

Abadi tilted his head. "You are the acting captain, yes?"

"I am..." Karim said, trailing.

"Then I don't see why my opinion matters. He's in no immediate danger, after all." Abadi pivoted on his heel with a nod to the doorway.

One of the sindisi guards moved to unlock and open the door. Then he turned back to Karim to await confirmation, swift and professional as always.

"Go on." Issa motioned to the storeroom, her fierce eyes looking grim. "I'll be here if you need anything."

Karim nodded before stepping toward the door, the sindisi swinging it open before him.

The room was dimly lit with only a few lanterns set along the wall that flared against the outlines of bundled ropes and sealed barrels. A musty odor wafted from the cramped room. Karim couldn't see the pirate at first, though the man's bald head was outlined subtly with an orange rim light.

Karim picked up the lantern nearest to him and stepped slowly toward the pirate. In the faint light, it looked as though Abadi had stripped the pirate down to his undergarments. Once he was a step away, Karim hovered the lantern over the man's bare chest and legs. Stone covered half of the man's body, the worst of it along his fingers and left arm. Near the underside of his wrist was a scar—rather, a tattoo—depicting a swirl. Karim thought he recognized the symbol, but he couldn't be sure. Oddly, most of the disease seemed unconnected and in patches.

"Show me your back," Karim ordered, but the pirate wasn't responsive. "Please," he added. There was no need to set the man on edge straight from the start. "I need to see the extent of your condition."

The man was slow to move, but he eventually stretched out to show his back. His body looked as though it might have once been brawny. There were still faint marks of muscle that had since been replaced by the stark outline of his rib cage. Along his back and side were more gray spots, like a leopard with rocks tarred to its hide.

Karim was no expert when it came to the malady—or any, for that matter—but he couldn't help thinking Abadi's assessment was a touch optimistic. The man looked as though he'd be dead in weeks if all these craggy blemishes came together to consume his skin.

Karim let out a small sigh as he touched one of the spots. "How long do you have?"

"Not as long as I had before," the pirate said darkly.

Karim hadn't expected so deep a voice. Now that the man was relatively free from exhaustion his speech sounded full and broad, yet calming at the same time, and his island accent was smooth and delicate. Karim retracted his hand from the spot at the man's rib. It felt harder than simple rock, like nothing could cut through it.

"It ain't contagious," the pirate said, a smirk in his tone.

"I'm aware." But Karim took no step forward. For the first time, he made proper eye contact with the man. Despite his condition he seemed perfectly at ease. Karim had seen such eyes before. They belonged to men who knew when it was all over. Somehow the pirate's expression shook something within him. Sure, the pirate was only an asset, but he was still a man marked for death. "I never got your name..."

"Jelani," he said as he settled his back against a bundle of ropes. A sturdy link of chains bound his hands and ankles.

Karim moved his fingers toward the chains to loosen them. "Are you in pain?"

"No, the opposite. Ever since I got this." He lifted his scaled hand. "Ain't got no pain to feel. And anytime I take a beating... instead of bruisin' I get these damn welts." He moved to show the right side of his face, where the stone lined from brow to chin. "Got these off the back of a fireball."

Karim couldn't pull his eyes from the man's collage of deep brown and graying skin. He laid his lantern next to the pirate and sat alongside him with a sigh. "The disease grows swiftly, does it not?"

"If I don't take the right potions, yes. Your brewmaster say he knows someone though…"

"So he says," Karim replied.

He trusted Abadi. How could he not when he spent moons watching the surgeon turn out miracle after miracle? But the man said it himself: stoneskin was not one of his strengths. With things so tenuous regarding the skyglass' location, the entire weight of their mission might rest on Karim's healthy dose of doubt.

Taking a deep breath, Karim settled his nerves. He knew they were the cause of the stress riddling his veins.

A silence fell between the pirate and Karim for the briefest of moments. Neither man seemed to know how to fill the stillness, least of all Karim. He hadn't realized how comfortable he was in the silence until the man called Jelani spoke again.

"How many of my crew do you have?"

"You know I can't tell you that," Karim answered.

"Just got to know if you have a certain woman. She got short hair, and skin like mine."

"She's infected too?"

"Nah, nothin' like that. She just… ah, forget about it. Your brig is too small. I would have—" He stopped himself and turned his head away.

Karim thought back to the prisoners they had captured. He couldn't remember anyone by that description, save for the woman whose throat had been slit before she'd been peppered with arrows. But the man wouldn't be asking about her. He saw what had happened.

"You needn't worry about her, or anyone else for that matter," Karim assured him. "We aren't savages."

In truth, Karim favored a more liberal view on what constituted prisoners of war than his immediate superiors. These may be pirates, but they were Kidogon pirates under the protection of Golden Lord Zuberi. They weren't Vaaji, and they weren't stateless either. That put them well within their rights under the *Jultian Accords*, as far as it concerned him.

"But if you want help with *that*," Karim pointed to Jelani's crusty hand, "you're going to need to help us."

"You don't call what you did to that woman savagery?" Jelani questioned flatly, pointedly disregarding Karim's remark.

"That was self-defense. And if I've heard it correctly, most of you islanders think us no more than lyricists. Savagery hardly lines up with our reputation for being poets and philosophers…"

"Times change. And small dogs got the most to prove." Jelani gave him a short shrug. "You gonna have a hard time gettin' anything out of me, either way. Don't matter how mean you may or may not be, ain't nothin' you can do to get me to talkin'."

The man was right. The other prisoners were safe, Karim spoke the truth in that—as long as the decision remained in his hands—but Jelani… Jelani had information the empire needed. If Karim thought for one moment torture would help pry the skyglass' location from the pirate, he wouldn't hesitate to use the method. But against someone who felt no pain at all? The tactic would be useless. Karim didn't have to threaten violence to get what he wanted, however. He just had to get the man talking, get him comfortable.

"You shouldn't believe everything you hear about my people. We have a lot of enemies, and enemies tend to favor the more damning tellings." Karim cleared his throat. "This disease, it's caused by Gods' Glass, is it not?"

"That's right." Jelani flexed his fingers, the rocks between his webbing scraping against one another.

"That's how your people were able to attack us that day," Karim said.

It had been a mystery none of the captains could figure out at the time. The people of Kidogo had no real defenses against the Vaaji fleet, save for their lowly tide lord's then-feeble flotilla, yet their mystics had somehow been able to stir a power greater than even the old legends spoke of: a kubahari who scholars thought long dead, a remnant of the Lost City. To call something like that, Gods' Glass would have been the only feasible way to do it, to empower their summoning, despite its risks.

"So that was *your* fleet?" Jelani asked flatly.

"Not my fleet exactly. But yes, I was there."

"Well congratulations, then."

"Congratulations?"

"Seems you been promoted." Jelani nodded to the door. "The way you walked in here, the way you ordered those guards outside—"

"No, I'm not the captain," Karim said. "Just a…" He let his words trail off in the air. What was he really? When Malouf returned to full health would Karim even want to stay on? It didn't matter right now, at least. The pirate seemed to be comfortable enough to engage in conversation. Maybe now was the time to get to the point. "If you are infected by the Gods' Glass, then you truly are one of the mystics we are looking for." Karim shifted his shoulders to the pirate. "Where is it?"

"'You know I can't tell you that,'" Jelani said, echoing Karim's earlier statement.

Karim fought an open scoff down to a mere smirk. *Damn pirate.*

The dark man had even managed a passable Vaaji accent in imitation of Karim. He couldn't be sure in the dim light, but it looked as though the pirate was smiling before he spoke again, "So, seeing as torture is off the table—"

"There are other ways to get you to talk," Karim spoke sharply. "Some might even have you *wishing* you could feel the physical pains." There had to be at least one telepath stationed at al-Anim. The pirate couldn't hope to withhold information from a mind reader.

"Good luck with that." Jelani rubbed his forehead with his bound hands casually. "I reckon most my crew is dead or escaped. Best thing for me to do now is die, I guess. I'll be long gone before you get what you want from me."

Karim clenched his jaw and stood from his seated position. Breaking this one would take more time than a single conversation. Taking another glance at the man's wrist, Karim reexamined the tattoo engraved there. That spiral design looked familiar, something from a long time ago...

The symbol of Àyá?

Karim chewed the fresh thought over as he moved to the door. If the symbolism there meant what it usually did, then he had one last piece to play in this game. Looking over his shoulder to make sure Jelani's eyes were on him, he kissed his hand and placed it on the side of the doorway. "Until next time, pirate."

Karim stepped through the door methodically, slowly.

One, two, three...

"You Jo'baran?" Jelani asked with a poorly hidden touch of curiosity lining his words. If there was one thing Karim knew about the followers of the Old Way, they were always looking for fellow devotees. Such a simple gesture was all it took to capture the pirate's attention.

Perfect, Karim thought as he turned, brow lifted in staged confusion. "Excuse me?"

"You just offered grace to Deh'ala, no?" Jelani leaned forward keenly as Karim blinked twice with parted lips, the sculpted face of surprise. "I thought the Vaaji were students of al-Qiba?"

"They—we are," Karim faux stuttered. "What do you know of Jo'bara?"

224

"It is my life." Jelani dipped his head, gesturing his bound hands as though to bow.

Karim hummed through pursed lips and smiled inwardly. Here laid the path he needed to get into this man. "A priest and a pirate? Bit of a contradiction, don't you think?"

"Desperate times." Jelani lifted his craggy hand again. "Desperate measures."

"Sindisi Abbas, inform the helmsman to set a course for Kidogo," Karim commanded a few moments later.

Abbas gave him a short nod and marched off toward the bridge.

Issa turned to watch him go as she crossed her arms and canted her head in confusion. "I thought we were going back home?"

"You didn't see that pirate," Karim answered. "He's not got long left to live. And... I think I can break him. With your help."

CHAPTER 23
ZALA

WHEN THE FIRST DAY PASSED NO ONE EXPECTED TO SEE anything. Mantu and Sniffs tried their best to save the tree, but once they finally cut it down, it splintered into an ashen waste along the beach. While the burning tree had kept them warm during the night, they went unrescued and, thanks to Zala, had no other means to get off the rocky isle.

Mantu never made good on his promise to beat her for her mistake — more likely due to tiredness than mercy.

The next day passed slowly as they fed on the crabs and fish they caught along the shore. Though they kept their bellies full, they had no fresh water to wet their cracking lips. The rum helped dull their thirst for a while, but it left them more drained than refreshed soon after, and the hangovers were brutal. None were worse than Fon's.

"There's a reason I never drink," she said, clutching at the sides of her temple. Zala laid the aziza on her lap and undid Fon's tight braids — they were half undone as it was anyway.

"These are too tight," Zala said. "I can't say this will get rid of your headache, but it should help some."

Fon didn't fuss as Zala carefully worked her fingers through the knotted hair, being careful around Fon's sunburnt ears.

For hours the sun seemed to beat down on the group without mercy. For most of the day, they had used the large rocks for shade. But now, with the sun straight up in the sky, there was no place for shelter. Zala would have dipped back into the ocean again, but her skin was already pruned and the water was only mildly cooler anyway.

"Oh, what I would give for an elemental right now…" Zala croaked through a dry throat.

A dark shadow passed at her side as Shomari used his cloak to cover her and Fon.

"Not all elementals can manifest drinking water, you know," he explained.

"Liya told me she could pull the salt from seawater, though," Zala said, thankful for the shade. Even Fon's own breathing seemed to eased against Zala's thigh.

Shomari scoffed. "She talked a big game. She could barely raise even a single wave."

"Hey!" Fon said irritably as she lifted her head with a start. Zala threw up her hands as Fon's customary glare shot toward Shomari. "Be respectful of the dead. We may be joining them soon."

Shomari shrugged. "I'm just saying there's more to it than havin' the power."

Fon didn't seem to hear him, her eyes cast out beyond the ocean's horizon. "I don't want to die here." Zala wasn't sure she had heard the aziza right at first—Fon wasn't one to lose sight of hope. "Not like this."

Shomari bent a knee and lowered to Fon's face in Zala's

lap. "You will not be dying here, Little Flutter. We will survive this. Trust me, a pakka is knowing these things."

Zala looked away from the two, thoughts turning painfully to Jelani while the cat comforted the aziza. Her eyes darted around for any distraction they could find, and as if on cue, she saw it: a mere dot cresting the horizon.

A ship!

They were rescued—or so Zala desperately hoped. The next few minutes would reveal the ship as a friend or foe, and their chances were far from good.

None of the Great Nations were friends to pirates, but if the ship turned out to be one helming from one of the royal navies, then Zala thought they could play the role of merchants well enough—though it'd be difficult explaining the gravesites, and the loot that had washed ashore.

If the ship was one of the rival pirate companies, things could be just as bad. Not counting one of their own from Kidogo, a merchant ship would be their best bet. Though there was always the risk a merchant could recognize Zala and the crew from a previous boarding, and they could hardly be expected to extend warm welcomes if they did.

"My coin's on them being Ya-Seti," Sniffs snorted when he made his first sighting.

Ode leaned on one leg—his other had started to turn green like his arm. "I'll take that bet. I say it's the Vaaji again."

"No, it can't be. The Vaaji don't have sails like that," Mantu said, crossing his arms.

"How would you know?" The old man licked his chapped lips. "It's too far off."

"Mind if I get in on the bet?" Zala asked. She was alone in her meager chuckle.

When the ship grew large enough to be seen clearly, a

shudder forced its way down Zala's spine. The flag above the approaching vessel was black, which meant pirates. Shomari shared a narrowed pair of yellow eyes with Zala and his paws curled around his rapier hilt. Hopefully, the pakka wouldn't have to put his swordplay to use. Even with his extraordinary skill, he was too tired to take on an entire ship, regardless of the crew.

And the ship looked large enough to be carrying a big one.

"We're saved!" shouted Fon, wrapping her tiny arms around Zala's neck. The aziza seemed like the only one who was excited, save Zala who's previous hope had quickly turned dark.

"We don't know that yet." Mantu stepped forward. "Could be the Tango Raiders or the Ajowan Poachers."

"It's the *Redtide*," Ode added darkly. "Meroé Rovers."

Sniffs gasped. "No... you don't think it's really them crazy dikala, do you?"

"Black flag. Narrow hull. Kubahari horns lodged into their bowsprit." Ode squinted his eyes. "She can *only* be the *Tide*. Unless someone else took the ship as their own. Seems doubtful."

Sniffs turned to Mantu anxiously. "Them rovers shouldn't recognize you, Mantu. Your beard covers your markings."

"Let's hope so." For the first time in days, Mantu looked fearful.

Zala remembered why Mantu had left his beard so unkempt now. It wasn't entirely out of laziness—it was to cover up the Aktahrian tattoos that decorated his cheeks and just under his chin. In the academies, Zala had learned that some soldiers had applied tattoos to connect with their telepathic generals. But she didn't think Mantu was so highly ranked. Hadn't he just been a deckhand with Kobi? Or had he claimed himself a captain?

"Who are the Meroé Rovers?" Zala whispered to Shomari.

"In short? Enemies of Aktah. They started out as archers and were said to be zebra riders before they took to the seas. They generally focus on the Aktahrian noble ships, military too. I've even heard them targeting common folk. Of course, they're not opposed to the occasional easy picking on the side." Shomari gave Mantu a sidelong glance.

Zala looked to the large man as well, whose crossed arms looked like constricted chains across his chest. "And Mantu used to be a soldier for Aktah, right?"

"I believe so."

"Perfect." Zala stood up, smiling.

Shomari tilted his head. "How's that perfect?"

"Give it a minute. You'll see," she mumbled. Then, turning a louder voice to Mantu, she said, "When they get here, they'll ask who's in charge. If it's you, Mantu, there'll be a lot of eyes on you. Eyes you probably don't want."

Mantu clenched his jaw.

"You all right, Captain," Sniffs reassured him. "I can barely see your markings."

"But if they're looking close enough, anyone could see his tattoos peeking at the top of his beard," Zala added slyly.

"Enough," Mantu grunted. "Duma, you will be the acting captain when they come."

"Who's Duma?" Shomari whispered behind Zala.

"That's Sniffs' real name," Fon mumbled with warning eyes.

"Oh," Shomari said.

"I-I don't know 'bout that, Mantu." Sniffs shook his

hands in front of his face. "I don't know nothin' about being no captain. Them pirates not gonna believe me."

"It's not that difficult," Mantu said in irritation. "Just stand there and tell them what happened to us."

Zala stepped in front of Sniffs with her hands on her hips. "Quick, why are we stranded?"

"Um... um... we was attacked," Sniffs stammered.

"Why are you so nervous? Do you have something to hide?" Zala stepped closer to the giant, and in that moment her words seemed larger than his bulk.

"Nah, nah, nothin' like that—"

"Who are these people with you? Are they your crew?"

"No—I mean... Yes, ma'am, yes... them is my crew." Sniffs' every word grew more incoherent.

"Did you capture anyone?" Zala continued, refusing to let up. She tried her best not to look to Fon or Shomari, who were surely holding back grins at the outrageous sight: a small woman talking down a goliath of a man. "Are these all your people?"

"Yes."

"How about that one with the beard? He looks a bit different. How long has he been with your crew?"

"Him... he is... he's..."

"Shomari, bring that one to me. I want to see what he's hiding under all that mess."

Shomari smiled as he trotted over to Mantu, but the very temporary captain stopped him with an outstretched hand. "Don't you dare lay a finger on me, cat. Okay... okay, Zala. I get where you're going with this. What does it matter? Our story is whatever we want it to be. Our captain could have been killed and Duma is the next in command. Even if he doesn't have the experience, that's the point, isn't it?"

"But you want someone who won't draw unnecessary attention," Zala started. "My husband's a navigator, remember? He spent loads of time with Kobi. I know the way he talks; I know the terminology."

"She does do a good impression of Captain Kobi," Fon added with a wry grin.

"Make me the captain and you can hide between the rest of us. Sniffs—I mean Duma—is nearly a giant, everyone looks at him half the time. It helps we've got an aziza and a pakka. They're more common in the isles, but they always draw eyes. Ode's got an infected leg. And I have half an ear left. If anything, you are the most plain of us here. Mantu, if you introduce yourself as our captain… well, it's your life you'd be bartering with and—"

"Okay, your point's made, chana." Mantu's face twisted with disgust. Finally, he recognized the corner he was in.

"I need to hear the words, Mantu." Zala crossed her arms. "We all do."

Mantu took a deep breath. It was a while before he spoke again, as though the words pained him beyond reason. "You are the *acting* captain now."

"Official proclamation of the code, please." Zala tilted her head. "So no one is confused, of course."

"By the right of Yem, Zala of Kidogo, you are now acting captain of the fallen *Titan*." Each word seemed as though they were being pulled from Mantu's throat. "Just remember, Zala, the best lies have truth laced in them. Don't go runnin' your mouth too much."

"A captain without a ship. Is that a first?" Shomari asked.

"No," Fon answered. "A few years back Captain Sofala took on the crew of *Moyo* without a ship. Same sort of circumstance, except they were stranded on a prison ship."

"All right, enough with the history lesson." Ode spat up bloody phlegm. "They'll be on us soon enough. Are you ready, *Captain* Zala?"

The title took Zala aback at first, but she relaxed her shoulders before anyone could see the change in her face.

"Yes," Zala said. "Everyone just… follow my lead."

Mantu shook his head. "I'm gonna die here today, ain't I."

CHAPTER 24
ZALA

WHEN THE PIRATE SHIP FINALLY CAST ANCHOR, ZALA waved her hand in the golden lord salute—pointing at her ear with thumb and little finger outstretched. All pirates, at least the decent ones, knew the signal.

When the first rowboat reached the shore, its leader returned the salute, gesturing for peace. She was tall and thin, mostly at the neck which was covered in a spiraling tattoo. Her skin was darker than midnight, and her hair was matted in locs. Her voice came out in a thick, husky rasp, mouth working around a curved, wooden pipe pressed between her lips. The scent on the air was of strong Vaaji hash as she spoke her greeting through purple smoke. *"Weiya, awei."*

Zala's heart rose when she recognized the words of the Ya-Seti. At least she could communicate with the captain. Mero-Set was the third language she had learned after Julti and the Mother Tongue, and easily among those in which she was most proficient.

"Yawei, ʝita," Zala responded warily, offering a quick bow

of respect as she waved a hand to her chest in a friendly Ya-Seti gesture. Then she realized she may have overdone it. Only the Ya-Seti nobles used elaborate gestures paired with their words when speaking. And whoever this woman was set the tone of the conversation by way of a puff of purple smoke from her pipe—the most *informal* sort of greeting.

Zala didn't recognize the leader or the other members of her mostly female shore party, who were all wearing a trim of red on black. Unlike other crews, their outfits distinctly matched, looking more like naval uniforms than pirate garb. Their postures, too, spoke of naval discipline not often seen among even Golden Lord Zuberi's own. Mantu seemed to recognize her well enough. He kept shifting his weight from left to right while digging his feet slowly into the sands.

The crew members stepped from their boat and moved to flank Zala's own. Each woman carried distinct-looking recurve bows, the favored weapons of the Ya-Seti. Zala knew too well how deadly they could be in the right hands—she still missed her own. Mantu and Sniffs had likely lost hers when the Vaaji attacked. She couldn't blame them entirely though. If she had still had her favorite bow, she probably would have lost it in the battle as well, just as Sniffs had lost his signature axes.

A thick tension hung in the air as the rovers stomped through the sands, eyes concentrated in small slits. Most of the women had arrows already nocked, arms tense and ready for the draw, though they pointed their aim toward the ground.

Zala could only hope that Mantu kept his wits about him. Their own crew would have done the same thing if *they* had come upon a random group on a deserted island.

Once the archers encircled Zala and her crew, another

one of them—perhaps the leader's second—gave the dark woman a nod.

The captain let out a second puff of smoke and continued to speak in Mero-Set. *"What happened to you lot?"*

"The Vaaji happened," Zala answered in the Ya-Seti Tongue, trying her best not to side-eye the new pirates at her sides. *"Have you seen that new ship of theirs?"* She stepped in front of the captain, who was craning her head in examination of the sunburnt and drained crew.

The leader turned her attention back to Zala. *"No, the seas have been clear. There was a storm headed south and west though."*

"This new ship of theirs doesn't travel by sea," Zala said. *"It's a flying ship. A sky ship."*

Her words were met with a wave of raised eyebrows throughout the landing party.

"It's true," Fon said meekly in the Mother Tongue. She had come a long way in understanding Mero-Set since Zala had started teaching her, but still had a way to go before she was truly comfortable with the words.

"*You* may fly, little one," the captain replied, yielding to the Mother Tongue with perfect enunciation. "But ships do not."

"They *do* have one," Zala said. "I don't know how… but we're telling it true."

The woman's eyes inspected Zala. The rest of her crew examined Zala's like they were crazy. "How long have you been out here?"

Zala understood what the question really meant. Their captain was wondering if they were mad with thirst, simply delirious from days alone with nothing to drink. Zala played along.

"We're coming up on our sixth day this afternoon." She

put her hand to her head and drooped her eyes subtly. "We ran out of water on our third."

The leader hummed under her teeth. "Who is captain here?"

"Well..." Zala trailed off, she had to sell the lie by sounding uncertain. "I suppose it's me now... Our captain died in the attack."

"Were you first mate, then?"

"No, I wasn't. I..." Zala bit her lip as her attention was pulled to one of the other pirates who was getting too close. The woman was crouched down to the ground, almost like she was about to sniff it, her long hair of locs sweeping along the sands.

"She was our navigator," Shomari stepped in, putting himself between the one circling closer to Zala's side.

"A pakka and an aziza together..." The captain took a long drag from her pipe. "Haven't seen that kind of pair in some time."

The slightest of sighs came at Zala's side, and she knew without looking that Fon was rolling her eyes at the idea of she and Shomari being "that kind of pair."

Good, Zala thought. *Keep your eyes on them and not on Mantu.*

"There was that pakka back on Kidogo," one of the pirates closest to Shomari said, looking the pakka up and down with a spear clenched between her hands. "That brown one, remember? He wouldn't leave Iokaja alone."

"Ah, yes," the captain said. "They've a certain taste for aziza, don't they?"

Zala's lips parted in surprise. "You've come from Kidogo?"

"We have. We were there not five or six nights past, in fact, though we didn't stay long. There was talk of a few there plagued with the stone. Couldn't have them infecting my crew—"

"The disease doesn't work like that," Zala said quickly, sounding a bit too defensive. "You can only get it from Gods' Glass."

She bit down on her tongue when she saw the change in the captain's eyes at being interrupted. It didn't really matter how ignorant this captain was; all that mattered was that Zala got her and her group onto the ship safely. But she had dealt with this since Jelani had contracted the disease, and it still ate at her insides.

"Yeah, that's what the scholars say," the captain replied dismissively. "But I'm not gonna take the chance, not with my crew's lives at stake."

"They're clean," a pirate spoke behind her.

Zala turned her head to the voice. She hadn't noticed the captain's second who was patting down the others. She lingered far too long when she got to Mantu and Sniffs. The captain nodded in response and stepped from the rowboat, leaving a lone crew member on guard at its side, one of the few men.

"Wait, Captain," the second said as she started to pat Zala down. It wasn't long before her hands crossed along a pair of objects at Zala's waistband. "What are these?" She pulled free the songstone and Gods' Glass Zala had.

"Objects given to me by my husband," Zala said. "I'd prefer to keep them."

"You a mystic?" the captain asked as she approached.

"I'm not. But he is."

"Then you won't be needing this," the captain's second said as she took the Gods' Glass and stuffed it into a pouch at her belt. "What's this other one?"

"A songstone. Something I can hear his voice by. Well…

just one song. That, I'd *really* like to keep, if that's okay with your captain."

It looked like the woman had other ideas, and her hand was already hovering near another open pouch at her waist, but her captain's voice stopped her. "No, Lishan. Let her keep that one."

"Are you sure, Captain?"

"I'm sure."

Reluctantly, the woman stuffed the stone back into Zala's hand and shuffled off to start patting down Fon.

"Marjani," the captain said. "Have you picked up anything else?"

Zala turned to the woman who had looked like she wanted to take a whiff of the sands before. She was a small woman, not unlike Zala, just as bony and narrow, though her face was stretched and her locs were nearly as long as she was tall. Each time she shifted in the sands her blue, white, and silver beads interwoven with cowry shells along her hair clacked together.

"*Theirs are the only tracks for days, Captain*," she replied in Mero-Set. The captain's eyes darted to Mantu far too often for Zala's liking.

I need to keep her eyes on me.

Zala bowed her head. "I didn't catch your name, Captain…"

"Nubia." The woman didn't turn her gaze. "Captain Nubia of the Meroé Rovers."

"I'm Zala. Formerly of the Titans."

Nubia whipped her head to Zala. "The Titans? Captain Kobi's Titans?" Her sword hand drifted to the hilt at her belt; the archers pulled back on their bowstrings. "Is he on this isle?"

"He was hit by one of them Vaaji fireballs," Ode spoke

up. His green leg was still shaking under his weight. Zala frowned. It was going to have to be amputated. No healer could do anything for it now.

Zala turned back to Nubia and pointed to her own raw left ear and nodded. "I was right next to the captain when it happened. I was lucky; he was not."

"Lishan. Marjani," Nubia said flatly to the woman who had been checking the men's pockets and, what Zala now assumed was a pather—a mystic who could read the history of objects and the esoteric echoes they left behind.

In an instant, the women clicked their tongues and snapped their fingers. Two more archers came to their side and they moved to sweep along the beach, crouch-walking as they rose their bows high.

"You don't trust my word?" Zala asked, stealing a glance toward Mantu, who had started to sweat. The man was fixing to run at any moment.

Hold fast, you fool. Where are you going to escape to?

"I've just met you, chana." Nubia smirked, pulling her pipe from her mouth. "You know how this works."

Zala stood her ground. The other women would find nothing. There was nothing *to* find, right? But if they were this keen to catch Kobi when Zala had already claimed him dead, perhaps Mantu's fears were more than just paranoia.

A few moments later, the four women returned from their search empty-handed. The one named Lishan sent a nod her captain's way. "They're alone, Captain. No one else here."

Zala turned back to Nubia. "I told you, didn't I?"

The captain shot a sharp glance back. "And I told *you* that you should know how this works."

Nubia's crew traded nervous looks amongst themselves, a fresh tension settling on the group's shoulders. Zala could see it in their faces plain as day. Their captain was not to be trifled with. Out the corner of her eye, she saw Shomari's paws twitching at his side. If this came to a fight, could he pull them through? He hadn't had anything to drink in days...

Zala reminded herself that she was unarmed — Mantu had seen to that straight away. She wondered for a moment if she could make use of the sand at her feet, but even if she managed to blind Nubia — a miracle unto itself — she wouldn't even get a step toward the captain, not under the gaze of Ya-Seti markswomen. Perhaps Fon could fly — no, she was still grounded with her injury.

Even if all of that hadn't been true, how was she supposed to relay any plan of attack with so many eyes on her? Fighting was *not* an option here. She forced her attention back to the woman before her, who puffed a ring of smoke to the side, eyes fixed on Zala's own.

The captain took the pipe from her mouth once more, silence hanging thick in the air before —

"Pfft, you've got spirit, girl," Nubia said. The unvoiced sighs of relief through the group was palpable. Even the archers seemed to ease the tension in their bowstrings as they recognized their captain's amusement. Nubia jerked her head to the horizon in question. "Where were you lot headed?"

"To..." Zala hadn't thought of that part yet. But there was only one place a person would go if they were tracking any kind of Vaaji ship. "To al-Anim. I have a contact there who has information on their shipping schedules." Zala tried not to let the relief show as she voiced the lie. "Golden Lord Zuberi would pay top coin for it."

Nubia pursed her lips through the last puff of her pipe. Her eyes were slits, expectant.

Zala forced her voice down an octave, emulating the late Ajola as best she could. "I will gladly tell you more about it…" Zala glanced between Nubia's fierce eyes and the guarded expressions of her crew. "*If* you'd be kind enough to bring my crew and I aboard your ship." She stood still as she could with her arms planted behind her back.

Nubia handed her pipe to one of her crew before she replied, "You're in luck. As it happens we're headed to al-Anim ourselves. We might be inclined to help you on your way for… seventy-five percent of your profits."

"Seventy-five percent?" Zala did her best to feign outrage at the insult. In the back of her mind, she was already feeling the stress of how to get out of the lie she had put herself in, but one thing at a time...

"Seventy-five percent. More than fair considering we're saving your stranded asses." Nubia turned her head to Lishan, who was a step behind her.

"More than fair, ma'am." Lishan's expression and tone was a challenge as she waited on Zala's objection.

But Zala refused to give her the satisfaction; she'd got what she wanted, anyway. "Deal."

She stole a glance at the archers still hanging at the group's sides, their stoic expressions impossible to read. She fought back the shiver from her spine. Showing fear would do none of them any good—her crew was counting on her. She could only hope that Mantu was keeping his eyes low and his beard covered. His death would be their own. Shomari made it clear the rovers played by the rules of guilt by association.

"Well then, it's settled." Nubia clapped her hands together, rubbing them. "Let's get your crew on board, *Captain* Zala. I warn you though, we won't have slackers aboard the *Redtide*. There'll be no need to pledge yourselves to her, but we expect you to pull your weight until we get to al-Anim."

ZALA HADN'T REALIZED HOW DIRTY KOBI HAD KEPT HIS ship until she set foot on the *Redtide*. In the few hours she spent on the frigate, she had organized the storeroom's loot by the value of treasure, stitched the sails, swabbed the deck twice, and performed other menial duties that brought forth sores to her palms.

Cleaning the deck had been her primary task. The first round was to wash up blood left over from an Aktahrian prisoner Nubia's crew had captured a week prior. Apparently, they had strung him up by his thumbs until his skin cracked and bled. Mantu had looked as though he'd be sick when he saw the pools of blood surrounding pieces of loose skin atop the deck, so Zala had volunteered for the task. The second washing had been to take care of bird shit, which had been more to Zala—and Mantu's—liking.

"Hey, you kinda look like an Aktahrian," one of the pirates had said when Mantu finished swabbing his portion of the quarter deck.

"Get that all the time," he had replied. His voice was divorced of all the conceit it usually had and he kept his eyes low and deferential. "But close though. My parents are from Asiya Bay."

The answer seemed satisfactory to the pirate, and he continued on his way.

Zala decided that the Ya-Seti crew were more than normal pirates. She had heard rumors before about their immaculate harshness and cruelty. But seeing it firsthand was a different thing.

Zala came to realize that so long as one was loyal to them, or at the very least stayed out of their way, they took no issue. And from what she knew, they didn't serve the golden lord directly, more interested in taking down Aktahrian soldiers, no matter if they were currently enlisted or not.

The one thing Zala didn't have an issue with were the crew's sea shanties. They were less sing-song and more rough, grittier—or at least that was the best way Zala could think of it. It sounded more like poetry than a ballad, less lyrical and more a spoken word:

Of the arrow, by the bow, for the Kor
We break our vows for the shore
Our generals ask, "Do you love your country?"
We puff our chests and tell it bluntly.

The Kor claims love for his country.
Yet still, those on the borders go hungry.
He says he'll fight the raiders all.
Instead, his treaties stand them tall.

The Kor says a lot but brings naught
In a simmering pot spilling rot.
The Captain's shown our day will come.
She fights the outlaws, the filth and scum.

So hide behind your walls and your suits of golden
plate.
Your words will not protect you when we at your
gate.

"These bitches are radicals," Mantu whispered to Sniffs as he shook his head. "We gotta get up outta here."

Zala sat stitching a patch of sails as she overheard their conversation.

"Did you hear that last song? Gods, who *don't* they hate? They even want their own king dead..." Mantu twisted the sopping rag in his hands, draining it in a splash over the deck at his knees. He glanced about nervously and bowed his head low to Sniffs as he scrubbed beside him. "That captain knows me. I know she does. I remember her from that battle at Nene Kato."

"She barely looked at you." Sniffs rubbed Mantu's shoulder gently.

Mantu didn't seem to notice the contact. "That's what she wants me to think."

"I don't know, Mantu. If she knew who you used to work for you'd be dead already, ya?"

"Maybe the rovers have grown wiser. They might be playing the long con, giving us up to the Vaaji for ransom." Mantu splashed his rag into his bucket again. "If it wasn't for these damn markings, my Asiya Bay story would hold."

"And what kind of ransom would *you* fetch?" Zala cut in with a snort. The two looked up in shock and outrage.

"I'll have you know I'm wanted in all the port cities of the Esterlands, *including* al-Anim," Mantu shot back.

Zala tilted her head skeptically. "First I'm hearing of it."

"Whatever." Mantu waved his rag dismissively. "Soon as we hit the shoreline, me and Duma gonna make a break for it."

"Relax." Zala's voice cut in a sharp whisper as one of the crew, a young girl with thin hair, passed by. She gave the little girl a short nod, waiting for her to pass out of earshot before continuing. "They don't expect a thing. Nubia said she'd give us safe passage so long as I point her to al-Anim's 'schedules.' We'll be free to go after that. Then I—we—can find Jelani."

"Yeah, 'bout that," Sniffs said as he scrubbed away the last grime from his section. "What was that shit you was going on about at the beach? Ain't no schedules. I ain't never heard Captain Kobi talkin' 'bout it none."

"She was frontin', Duma. It was a way for us to get on this ship." Mantu couldn't help smiling. Where everyone else on the crew found Sniffs to be irritatingly dimwitted, Mantu somehow found it charming. "Listen, Zala, you don't know this dikala like I do. There's a reason I've been in this game so long. You just know things…"

"Well, as your *captain*," Zala reminded him, "I'm ordering you to calm your damn nerves. Don't do anything rash. Keep your head down and do your work. We're only on this ship for another day or so."

"*Acting* captain." Mantu jabbed his brush at Zala, soap flecking off with every word. "By *my* say so. Don't go forgettin' that, chana." Another of the *Redtide* crew came passing by. Mantu gave her a short smirk, then cast his eyes down to his work. Without looking up he spoke again. "If anything fishy happens, we're out of here. With or without the crew."

"That's right," Sniffs chimed in with a whisper.

"Why are you so quick to give up on your own crew? Some of them could have survived." Zala touched the song-stone at her waist without realizing she had reached for it. "We'll need you and Sniffs' help if we're to find them."

Mantu lifted his chin. "I know good and well you ain't referrin' to the crew of the *Titan*."

"I am. You knew those men and women. Jelani was close to you."

"Jelani's long gone—" Sniffs started to say, but Mantu shot a sharp look his way, shaking his head.

"We don't know that." Zala stuck a vicious finger out at Sniffs while she ground her teeth in anger. *How dare he say Jelani's gone?* None of them could know that. She turned her dangerous look to Mantu. "You don't know that…"

"Duma is right." Mantu leaned close to Zala, returning her pointed stare with his own. "We've got to make sure *we* can survive before we go and worry about anyone else. I got enough on my plate with Nubia lurking around before I can even *start* to think on Jelani, no matter how close I was to the man. Like I said, once we hit that port, we're out of here. It's time to find a new crew."

Zala recoiled at Mantu's words. "How close you *are* with him."

Mantu turned back to his work. "Right…"

Zala kept her gaze fixed on Mantu, but the burly man gave no quarter, simply carrying on with his washing. For a moment she thought about pressing the issue, but she knew she'd only end up making a scene that none of them needed right now.

Mantu's paranoia—at least regarding the rovers—wasn't entirely unfounded, as she had come to find out firsthand since coming aboard. Any unnecessary eyes on him would not get her to Jelani any sooner. And it wouldn't do to have Mantu feeling defensive toward her either. When they got to al-Anim, she'd need all the help she could get.

"Look, you know I'm pretty good with a plan," she said after a while. Mantu eyes spoke disbelief. "Not with the palm tree, I'll admit that one. But *I* saved Kobi. If Jelani hadn't kept him alive, and if I didn't trap those Vaaji attacking him, he'd be dead. You know that. And that time at Ajowan—"

247

"That wasn't you," Mantu said sharply.

"It was… Jelani told me to keep quiet about it because of Kobi's pride."

Mantu's eyes changed. Perhaps it was recognition, though more likely it was doubt. Zala couldn't tell. "So what? You're good at coming up with plans *some* of the time. What good will that do us now?"

"You're still a pirate, aren't you?"

"For life."

Zala looked over her shoulder. Nubia's crew had their attention fixed on other tasks, cannon cleaning, deck scrubbing, and wrangling ropes among other duties. When she was sure she could not be overhead, she leaned in close to Mantu and Sniffs. It was a long shot, but it was the only thing she could think of that would keep the men with her while she searched for her husband.

"Nubia said she saw a storm heading south, right?" Zala asked. Mantu nodded. "What if I can get us that sky ship?"

CHAPTER 25
KARIM

Save for the scratching of Karim's reed pen against parchment, the war room was silent and empty besides himself and Issa. He couldn't keep his hand from shaking. It wasn't from nerves or anxiety, but because it felt like his fingers just couldn't sketch fast enough. Issa watched him intently, sitting just to his right as he finished his last line swoop.

"You know what that symbol is." Karim pointed down at the fresh ink. It wasn't a question. If *he* recognized it, she would too.

Issa pulled the sheet closer to her and rose an eyebrow at the dark spiral etched into the paper's center.

"This is the mark of an *oni'baro*," she began, bending her nose closer. "Yep, that's the symbol of—"

"A Jo'baran priest, right?" Karim felt the widening of his eyes, the excitement building in the pit of his stomach. Finally, he was making progress.

"Yes," she replied softly. "Why are you asking?"

Karim jabbed a finger at his drawing. "That pirate is

marked with this symbol. I reckoned he was some high priest or some such, I just couldn't remember the name. Before I left the room I kissed the door like Baba does all the time, and the pirate took the bait, hard. He thought he caught me slipping up, thought he found another one like him. So, I was thinking you—"

"You shouldn't do that, Karim." Issa's voice came with a sliver of indignation. "You shouldn't play fast and loose with the Old Way."

"Or what? If I speak ill of Eke's name my lilies shall wilt?" Karim wanted to take the harsh words back as soon as he said them. He wasn't thinking, just reacting. Years of old dogma had long killed his patience for the Way's followers. But winning a religious debate with Issa at that moment wasn't the point.

He sighed. "We can't hold to a moral compass that prevents us from completing our mission."

"I thought we already completed it. The *Viper* works— she passed with flying colors, if you'll excuse the pun—*and* we secured one of their sea speakers. I don't remember the brief saying anything about going back to Kidogo."

"You and I both know the empire rewards initiative. Back at the academy who were the ones top of the class? Who were the ones promoted? The ones who had a bit of initiative, that went the extra league. Just imagine if we came back home with a successful testing of the airship, the sea speaker, *and* a report of a captured Kidogo coast." Karim stood up for emphasis—Issa had been sighing heavily between his every breath, just waiting to interject. Karim pointed to the floor below. "That pirate is the key to Kidogo's skyglass. And he's on borrowed time. I can break him!"

"But the doc said he'd be okay—"

"Abadi couldn't give a straight answer about his timeline. He doesn't know much more than we do." Karim took up a chair closer to Issa, scooting it near enough so she could really see the earnestness in his eyes. "We don't even know what kind of treatment the pirate was using before we found him."

"Probably stonesbane like Abadi said."

Karim shook his head. "Not necessarily. You know as well as I do that there's another salve out there he could have used. And you know what happens when it stops working."

Issa pinched the edge of her brow, her boot tapping against the table leg in a steady beat. Her silence was answer enough for Karim. She knew what he was getting at. It was she who had brought up the idea of stonesbane, after all. But she must have known that if the pirate was taking the more common salve for the stoneskin malady then there was a heavy price attached. Issa stood up from her chair and moved to the back of the room. The inclined window cast her as a silhouette against the bright cloud astern.

"If it's foolsbane," Karim said, still sitting. "If he was using the salve and not taking the potion, then his infection will spread, and rapidly. We have no idea how long he'd been using it prior. The longer the use, the more the suppression, the fiercer the stone will fight back and fester through his body."

Karim let the silence settle as he watched for Issa's reaction. Her shadowed figure still kept rubbing at the bridge of her nose.

Karim continued, "You didn't see him. His back, his body, there was so much."

He knew she'd come to reason. It was just a matter of time. But he thought better of his original idea—he wouldn't try to bring her in on the religious angle. Perhaps there was another way to earn her help.

A knock came at the door. "Acting Captain, I have a report." It was the muffled voice of Steward Bitar.

"Enter," Karim said.

The door swung open to reveal the straight-backed steward. "Sir, due to the damage to our sails, it will be four days before we arrive at Kidogo."

"Four days?" Karim shifted in his chair with alarm. "It only took us a day and a half to get to the Ibabi Isles."

"Yes, sir... When we were operating at full sails."

"Do we not have a spare set stored aboard?"

"Unfortunately not, sir. As a prototype, she's built too small for that sort of *luxury*." The steward rolled his eyes at what Karim assumed was the lack of foresight from the designers. Karim had always figured the man to be the fastidious type. "We were only meant for a short trip. Boatswain Handal says he made note to Malouf before we left that we might've needed them, but the captain said—"

"Say no more." Karim lifted a hand and leaned his head back with a sigh. It was just another of Malouf's blunders, another oversight Karim didn't want to go over.

"Is there nothing else that we can do?" Issa asked, her voice returned to its usual sharpness.

"Ma'am." Bitar bowed with a formal salute. "I've been told that, skyglass aside, there's nothing that can be done for our speed without a resupply."

"How much sooner will we arrive if we kick up the glass?" Karim asked.

"That's not my area, sir, so I'd have to check with the engineers. But if previous discussions track… it'll probably cut our travel time by half."

"Order it," Issa said, walking forward along the long

table. Bitar gave a slight look to Karim, who nodded affirmation.

"Right away." The young man bowed again. "Acting Captain." A nod for Issa. "Gunner Chief."

"Acting Chief Officer," Karim corrected, giving Issa a sidelong glance. She returned the gesture with a slight nod, though her knitted brow betrayed her surprise.

After the steward closed the door, Karim turned to Issa as she asked, "'Acting Chief Officer?'"

"Malouf's been out almost a full day. I need someone I can trust. Who else would it be?" Issa looked unconvinced. Karim pressed on, turning back to their previous matter. "So you agree with me? We should go to Kidogo?"

She pulled up a chair in answer and sat down. Her brow furrowed as she interlocked her fingers and focused in on the different maps strewn about the table. "What does he want?"

"What does who want?"

"Your pirate. What's he looking for out of all this?"

Karim stroked the edge of his beard line. His first thought was that the pirate would likely want a lifetime supply of stonesbane. But he couldn't give the man that, not when the surgeon said it was so difficult to brew. It would have to be something else.

"Come on," Issa said. "You spent almost half an hour with the man. What does he want?"

Karim threw his hands up in forfeit. "I don't know… probably a crate-load of stonesbane. But that's not an option for us, is it?"

"Maybe it's just that easy. Let's offer him some, see what happens."

"And if he demands we provide it first? Or isn't interested at all?"

"Well, if he goes that route, *you* have to remind him of all the people who would lose him. He's an oni'baro. Trust me, there are plenty of people depending on him, wherever he's from. Do you know if he has any family?" Karim could see Issa tilting her head out the corner of his eye as he mulled it over. "A partner?" she added.

"A woman…" Karim's response was barely above a whisper, as though the thought had barely escaped the recesses of his mind. "He asked about a woman."

Issa brightened and her smile was radiant against her sun-baked skin. "Well, now we're getting somewhere."

CHAPTER 26
KARIM

Two days later, Karim stood at the *Viper's* bow to await the pirate's arrival on the weather deck. His casual lean against the bowsprit railing was more theatre than anything else.

He wasn't sure how to best settle his nerves as he stared out toward the clouds circling around the *Viper*. Every so often the exhaust fumes that had served as their false storm parted to show a sliver of an island below. Karim looked down on it, trying to make out a beach or mountain ridge, wondering where the coveted entrance to the skyglass cavern was hidden from him.

He would have loved nothing more than to take Hajjar or Damji or any of the other elementals down there to start pulling rock from the earth piece by piece until they found what the empire desired. But the island was protected in more ways than one, and if they took that more direct route, the pirate lords would be on them long before they made any real progress. Forget about securing the cove on top of it all.

The *Viper* continued its slow rotation, fog clouds encircling it, Karim's thoughts turned as dark as their false storm. He cursed the shamans of old for their meddling and their protections around the island. It was just one more obstacle thrown in his path.

The clink of chains dragging against wood brought Karim's attention behind him. He was met with the image of his pirate prisoner shuffling his way along the deck, a pair of mystguards at each of his arms and a bag over his head.

After the sindisi took their last stride atop the final step to the bow deck, they pulled the sack from the pirate's head. The man squinted his eyes against the bright light. Despite his haggard breaths, his tattered clothing, his ruined, stony arms, and all the rest, his head was held high, his expression ever-stoic as he locked eyes with Karim. It was difficult to judge the pirate's mood, Karim had come to realize. Too difficult.

In the pair of days it had taken for them to arrive above the island of Kidogo, he had visited the man who called himself Jelani each night before he took his rest. The first night, Karim had checked to see if he was right about the use of salve. He half expected to see the man covered in fresh blight as it fought to take back hold of what was lost. But the pirate looked just as he had before—which meant that he had been taking true stonesbane, not one of its imitators.

On the second night, Karim thought he had caught the pirate singing to himself, which was confirmed by Sindisi Abbas when they exchanged looks before Karim was let in. When the door cracked open Jelani stopped singing immediately and pretended to snore instead. And again, Karim saw no noticeable difference in his stony skin.

Now, with the man standing just before him, he was

certain that Surgeon Abadi was correct in his original assessment. Perhaps the pirate *did* have the better part of a year after all. But they were here and there was no going back now—not by any route Karim would accept entertaining, at any rate.

He would have the information he needed. The pirate would bend to him no matter what had to be done. The moment Malouf woke up it would be a return to business as usual. Karim would be back to second string and any chance of true progress would be lost to him. He would not allow that to happen. If he could just manage to crack the problem of the island and break this pirate, the grand admiral would have no choice but to acknowledge his worth to the empire. To make him a proper captain.

He'd long since deserved a ship of his own.

"Where do you want him, sir?" grunted Sindisi Abbas when they had finally brought the prisoner before him.

Karim gestured an open palm to his left. "Just here will be fine."

The mystguards set the pirate firmly down at Karim's side, but they did not move to step away.

"No need to stand so close." Karim smiled. "I'd like to speak with our guest alone, if you don't mind."

"He might jump, sir," the younger, leaner Sindisi al-Fasi said firmly. "I would not have us stray far."

Karim hummed under his teeth then turned to the dark man on his knees beside him. "Tell me, pirate. Are you suicidal?"

Jelani didn't stir and instead looked straight out into the fog and clouds billowing against the high-winds.

"Al-Fasi," Karim said. "Turn his wrists over."

With more force than was likely necessarily, the young sindisi clutched Jelani's wrist and forced them over to show crusty skin that looked like it was swallowing the faint, dark mark of a spiral.

"The pirate might not be so..." Karim pursed his lips. "*Chatty-chatty* as his people would say. But these marks tell us more than we need to know. You see, that black swirl just under his infection there is a mark of an oni'baro. Do you know what that is?"

Young al-Fasi shook his head, no hint of recognition under his dark eyes and furrowed brow. But his senior comrade answered for him, "The marking of the oni'baro."

Karim turned his look to Abbas. "And tell us, who are oni'baro?"

"They're highly respected individuals of the Heretic Faith," Abbas said as he stared straight at the pirate's cheek. "Some call them monks, others call them priests. They are neither. No better than blasphemers."

"But one vital piece of information that is quite beneficial to us," Karim finished for him, staring at the other side of the pirate's cheek. The man's face didn't as much as twitch. "One thing that all oni'baro swear to—"

"Is that we don't take our own lives," Jelani finished Karim's sentence with a slow turn of his head, their eyes meeting once more. His lips remained thin, but Karim could have sworn there was a bemused smile behind the look.

Karim dipped his head. "That's right." He turned to the mystguards. "So no, al-Fasi, I don't think we'll need to worry about that today, especially with our captive so capably restrained. I have no intention of relieving him of his bindings. But by all means, remain close by. I shall simply be speaking with Jelani here personally. If you'll excuse us."

Al-Fasi answered with a sharp bow, then turned on his

heel to guard the far side of the railing. Abbas mirrored his younger partner and took the opposite side of the deck.

Karim let the soft melodies of the wind fill the silence as he watched Jelani, waiting for him to divulge something by way of a move of his lips, a twitch in his ear, anything at all. There was nothing but that stone-face, that statue's glare. No, not a glare. Karim wouldn't ascribe the man's look to something so stern. There was life behind his eyes, there always was. But it was the life of a still pond with schools of flitting fish circling gently beneath its surface. There had to be a way to stir him, to disturb that pond of his.

Karim pointed over the railing to where the island of Kidogo was gradually revealing itself through the clouds. "You know what that is, don't you?"

Jelani lifted his chin and peered over before saying, "Look like a tract o' land surrounded by water."

Smart-ass, Karim thought to himself with a sigh.

"It's Kidogo," he said as evenly as possible. "It is your homeland. A land where people need an oni'baro like you." It was only for a moment, but for the first time he saw a crack in the man's brow, though the small dip was corrected almost as soon as it happened. "I remember that skirmish. I was there, you know. The ship I was stationed on was among the second line, which made me one of the lucky few, isn't that right? If the fighting had gone on any longer, if my ship had been called forward to the front, we would have been swallowed by the kubahari—it *was* a kubahari, correct?"

Jelani nodded slowly.

"I remember seeing all the people on the beach. They were other oni'baro, were they not? They must have been like your kin. Funny, a few days ago when we boarded your ship I only saw you afflicted. Were there others before?

259

Others who didn't make it as far as you?" A smirk curled across Karim's lips when he saw the pirate grinding his teeth. Interesting. *That* he could use. But it wasn't time for that yet.

Trailing a hand across Jelani's back with a gentle stroke, Karim continued softly, "Tell me, Jelani, what do you want?"

The pirate closed his eyes, drawing air through his nose with a measured breath. He swallowed hard before answering, "I'd like a nice warm bath, and maybe somethin' better than stale meat and bread harder than rock, ya?"

The smirk that had been forming into a full smile across Karim's mouth dropped swiftly to a frown. But, like the pirate, he knew he couldn't break face for long. With a deep breath of fresh ocean air, he held back the rising heat in his belly.

"I misspoke, I apologize. Jelani, what do you *need?*" Karim pointed to the stone spreading along the man's forearm. "I can help you with that, for instance."

"I already chatted with your surgeon. He made it known he ain't got the skill."

"Who said anything about Surgeon Abadi?" Karim leaned on the railing coolly. "I received word back from the capital this morning. There's an alchemist on the navy's payroll who knows the potion well. I'm told she's advanced her own mixture doses to the point of lasting three weeks at a time." It was a lie—there had been no such message. But Karim reckoned the woman Abadi had mentioned before would indeed come through. Besides, he might get lucky and learn what he needed with the promise of the supply alone.

"That's what you want, isn't it? That's why you've fallen from esteemed oni'baro priesthood to mere piracy. I know how expensive true alchemists can be." Another break flitted across the pirate's brow. "What if I had a sample of what you need on board, right now? Enough for you to sample *if* you cooperate."

Jelani turned to Karim, looking him full in the eyes as though to measure the truth in his words. "You have the bane on this ship?"

Karim traded a brief look with Sindisi Abbas, who had clearly caught onto the lie he was spinning. As Karim turned his gaze back on their prisoner, he thought he caught Jelani's eyes tracking the minute exchange, though it was too quick to tell.

"I do," Karim said, nodding. "The potion is yours. *If* you can give me what I want." Karim turned his face back to the pirate. "We can help each other, Jelani. Just tell me how to get into that cove. Tell me where the skyglass is, and I promise you, you'll never have to worry about this"—he tapped a single finger against the man's rock-solid arm —"ever again."

Jelani closed his eyes and lifted his chin up to the sky. There it was, the defeatist expression Karim had been looking for. He could feel his heart pounding against his chest, anticipation charing through his fingertips. The pirate was going to give up the information. Karim would secure the cove and return home with praise from the grand admiral, Emperor and Empress al-Nasir themselves, perhaps. There was no chance Malouf would keep his position now.

The light chuckle that vibrated through the pirate's chapped lips quelled Karim's optimism though.

"You ain't got no stonesbane on this ship," Jelani said at the end of his chuckling. "And no one to brew it properly, ya? I've barely been on the ship two days, maybe a touch more. Stonesbane takes at least three to brew. You almost had me there, kijana."

Karim started to work his mouth around another lie, another story ready to loose from his lips, but he stopped short. Lying to this man clearly wasn't going to work, not if he was just going to continue to do it off the cuff as he had been, and especially not if he had to keep exchanging glances with his guard. He gave Abbas a poignant look at the thought.

Karim sighed. "I'll be frank, then. I do not have the stonesbane available right now, but the moment we get back to al-Anim I can assure you'll have it."

The light that had crested the edge of Jelani's eyes darkened, and his voice came out earnest and stark. "Then put me back in my cage. You can wait for your answer 'til we back in your capital. And by then, though, my demands are gonna be more than just one bottle." He turned his voice over Karim's shoulder. "Sindisi Abbas, I think it's time for me to go back below."

Karim seethed and ground his teeth. "Do not presume to order my crew."

At the ship's edge he could see the sliver of Kidogo staring straight up at him. He knew exactly which cove needed to be searched, but it didn't matter if he didn't have the sea speaker to get him through the shaman's protections.

"Everything in order, sir?" Sindisi Abbas asked as he approached the pair. "Shall we return him below?"

"No," Karim blurted. "I have one more question for our guest." Jelani turned to Karim with a bored expression, as though expecting yet more empty lies. Instead, Karim asked him something he knew would halt the man. "Who's the woman you were asking about before?"

That brought the pirate up short. *Just as expected,* Karim thought with satisfaction. "There are people you left behind who wouldn't want to see you dead, am I right? I can ensure you make it back to them... to her.

"It's really very simple, Jelani. Just give us what we want. There have been others who've tried. The cove's seal is broken by... what?" Maybe he could catch one of the pirate's slip-ups as he ran through his theories. "Is it a code word?" Nothing. "Some ritual?" Still nothing. "We will find out eventually. We have our ways, no matter how slow-going. But if we find out how to break that seal on our own, there's nothing I can do for you. If you're the one who gives us the information, then you will survive, you understand? Your woman won't have to see you go mad with the stone. I've skimmed my surgeon's books, and I know how bad it can get. How men turn into beasts, how they rip apart anything they can get their hands on, any*one*. You don't want that. You don't —"

"Stop," Jelani whispered. Another look of sadness passed over his eyes for a moment. What was he thinking? What fueled the melancholy behind that gaze? "I meant what I say, kijana. Take me back, or kill me now."

"No, I don't think I will." Karim turned to Abbas. "Bring me our second prisoner."

"The traitor, sir?"

"Indeed. And bring Hajjar with you."

Abbas turned on his heel and followed his orders. Karim knew they would not be waiting long. Even if the ship hadn't been as small as she was, Abbas never gave his commanding officers the chance to grow impatient.

After a few moments of staring out at the clouds shifting around them, he turned his head to the pirate once more.

"You brought us to this moment, Jelani. It didn't have to come to this."

"Do what you gotta do, kijana," the pirate returned dismissively with a heavy shrug.

Not three minutes later, Abbas reappeared at the bow. The mystic, Hajjar, stood at his side and a thin young man, a pirate named Rishaad, hung limp between their grips.

Where Jelani might have had spots of rock where his brow and cheek once were, Rishaad was riddled with bruises of black and blue. It hadn't been difficult finding out everything they wanted to know about the boy: where his family hailed from in Vaaj, when he had abandoned his post near the al-Haru desert, and when he had joined with the pirates near Kidogo. The young man had cracked like an egg. It had been so easy, Karim had entertained the possibility that the boy was some sort of spy feeding them false stories. If he had served them any worthwhile information, Karim might have pursued the thought. Alas... if only this Jelani could be so forthcoming.

"Hajjar," Karim said. "Do you remember what I asked of you earlier today?"

The mystic stood straight. "Of course, sir."

"Do it now."

A liquid whip flashed in Hajjar's palm, and it shifted like a snake ready to strike. The mystic flung out his shoulder, and the tip of his water belt caught Rishaad by the ankle. Before the traitor knew what was happening he was flung bodily overboard with a scream that could only be loosed from someone in free fall.

The only thing holding the man up was a flimsy line of liquid.

At the other end of that lifeline was Hajjar's mystical clutch. With another deft motion, the mystic slammed his

264

water-filled palm into the ship's bowsprit, freezing it against the wooden slats. No sound of a splash below came, and the screaming from the traitor continued a beat longer than it should have.

Karim peered over to see Rishaad dangling from a very precarious cord of water. Jelani took a hasty look too, his mouth agape. There was no stopping the shock on the pirate's face. It had happened so fast, any man would have been caught off guard.

"Oh, sorry. Where are my manners?" Karim smacked his hand lightly against his forehead. "That was Rishaad. A traitor to the empire. Unlike you, he has very loose lips."

"Leave the boy out of this," Jelani said darkly.

Karim ignored him. "He told us all about your crew and how your woman made a play for captain."

"I say leave him be."

"He told us how you shared some of your stonesbane with other crew members. Very noble of you."

"Listen to me."

Karim pulled at Jelani's collar and brought the pirate in close. "No. You listen to *me*. It's clear you don't give a damn about your own well-being, but perhaps you're the type that's motivated by the pain of others." Karim nodded toward Hajjar. "Officer, tell me. How long can you keep up the frost?"

"My record's ten minutes, sir, but that was on a cold day." The young mystic looked up through the break of cloud and into an unusually warm winter sky, a meaningful tilt to his head. "On a nice day like this. Who can say?"

"You ain't gonna hurt him," the pirate said. "I know you ain't. Not like this."

Karim leaned in close, giving a moment of pause for effect. "Are you really willing to test that belief?"

"What is the meaning of this?" came a low and weathered voice from behind. Karim could hear the disappointed valleys creasing Vice Admiral Shamoun's forehead before he even turned to see.

Karim pivoted on his heel to find exactly the expression he had expected: Shamoun with one foot belowdecks and another stepping up toward them, pursed lips, knitted brow, and deep lines beneath his bald and dark scalp. His presence brought a silence with it, the kind of silence that came about when children were caught in a game they shouldn't have been playing. No one dared to speak as the vice admiral clenched and unclenched his fist, looking for his legs in his clumsy gait as he moved to the ship's portside railing for support.

He tipped his nose over the edge and hummed a curious note. "Interesting. I could have sworn al-Anim was bigger than this when we set off." A sage smile met his lips before he turned a dark look to the others. "Pray tell, which island is this?"

When no answer was forthcoming, Shamoun gave a resigned sigh, then turned toward Hajjar. "Officer Hajjar, lift up that prisoner and take him back to the brig. Sindisi Abbas, and you al-Fasi, return the sea speaker to his own holding as well, please."

"But, sir, we almost—" Karim interjected, but was immediately halted by Shamoun's commanding glare.

The old man turned the look onto the others. "Well, what are you waiting for?"

The dark glint in his eye had Hajjar retracting his water whip in seconds and lifting a very grateful Rishaad back over the railing while the mystguards collected Jelani.

"This isn't over," Karim muttered as Jelani passed, but the pirate gave no response. In just a few moments the deck

266

was cleared save for Shamoun and Karim. Only the subtle wisp of fabricated cloud floating about them betrayed the stillness.

Karim broke the silence first. "Sir, I was moments away from figuring out how to break open the cove."

"I've only been under with whatever medicine Surgeon Abadi had me on for two days. Tell me, what brought us so far off course? Before I was knocked out, I had the *distinct* impression we were to return to the capital."

"We were, sir, but then I realized the pirate had stone-skin, and—"

"The good surgeon also tells me that the pirate has plenty enough time before going critical. As long as we do not overexert him—or throw him overboard."

"Sir, I was merely using the traitor to—"

"Say you extracted the information you desire," Shamoun cut him off again. "What then? What was your next step?"

"Well… I intended to secure and hold the cove."

"And how well did that work for us *last* time?"

"But sir, the sea speakers are all gone. They can't call that ancient creature again."

"Be that as it may, the pirates' precious golden lord is onto us." Shamoun jabbed his head down below. "You see those little specks on the northeast corner of the island? Those are fortified ships sent directly to the tide lord of Kidogo. Do you know who holds that title now?"

Karim chewed on the thought before saying, "Tide Lord Ganaji, I believe."

"And do you know what her background is?"

"Our brief mentioned her heading the golden lord's guard."

Shamoun took a step toward Karim. "Up until a few

267

moons ago, yes. She was a personal guard to Zuberi himself. And when he caught wind of what happened on Kidogo— and that we were poking around without his knowledge— he promoted his top woman to defend it. This is no mere bandit isle, Karim."

Karim didn't answer. There wasn't much he could say.

The old man gave Karim a not-unkind look through his sternness. "Don't fall apart now, el-Sayyed. Your time is coming. You've done plenty enough on this trip to earn it, and if anyone disagrees on that, I'll see to it that they are swiftly corrected. But for now... let's go home."

CHAPTER 27
ZALA

ZALA DIDN'T KNOW EXACTLY HOW SHE'D EVER GET THAT sky ship, but she knew it had been the perfect thing to say to Mantu to keep his head on straight. If what he and the others thought was true and Jelani had been captured by the Vaaji, that was where her husband would be.

But the Vaaji would be long gone by now, back to any one of their sprawling port cities—and who knew where from there. The capital, al-Anim, was closest, and with the bulk of the Vaaji Navy based there or nearby, it made the most sense for a return point in her mind. But Vaaj was a large coastal country, so it would take many moons to scour its cities from south to north.

None of that ultimately mattered though, not when Zala's "crew" consisted of a sum total of six people—each loosely willing to take part in any plan she'd came up with. The women and men of the *Redtide* might have been able tip the scales some, but any sort of joint effort was unlikely at best. After all, the rovers had only allowed Zala and the others on board out of opportunism and greed, not loyalty or the kindness of their hearts.

The second morning on the ship saw yet more chores that needed completing: stitching of more sails, cleaning the cannons, and washing another pool of blood from the remains of another "interrogation" on the weather deck. By the time the sun fully broke the horizon, Zala's arms were aching and blisters lined her hands.

When the call for breakfast came, Zala was more than ready to eat. But as she stood in line to wait for her portion of bread and fish soup, she saw several of Nubia's crew whispering excitedly to one another. Some even hastily downed their bowls and shuffled to the ladders leading up above.

Before the third pair of pirates could jog past Zala, she stopped them with an outstretched hand. "What's going on? Is there another ship? Are we mustering?"

"*What? Oh, no,*" one of them said in Mero-Set. "*The first mate is fighting that pakka. They've been going at it for a few minutes now, apparently.*"

Zala's eyes shot wide. "What?"

"Hurry," the second pirate said to her friend. "We're going to miss the rest of it."

And they raced off with the others. Zala overheard the first one say she "had coin on the cat." Her response was met with a guffaw from her fellow as their feet disappeared above.

By the time Zala turned back to the galley it was nearly empty. What had happened? She'd expected trouble from Mantu or Sniffs, but not Shomari. It had barely been a full day and already her crew was picking fights?

Shaking herself from her thoughts, Zala dropped her empty bowl—which joined the others scattered about the floor—and rushed after the pirates. Sure enough, only halfway up the ladder she heard the clash of steel on steel mixed in with the whoops and hollers of an audience that had been thoroughly riled up.

Grab a sword, find Fon, make for a longboat—and hope we're close to land, Zala thought as she climbed the last rung of the ladder.

But when her head broke the plane between the galley and the weather deck she wasn't met with the image of a vicious battle. Hells, Shomari was grinning between blade strokes as he hopped from the deck to the ratlines and back again. Lishan, the first mate, kept jabbing at him with her spear, nearly tagging him at the end of each of his jumps.

Zala shouldered through the crowd surrounding the fight. There was no order to the chaos as the pirates haphazardly mobbed the pair, eyes desperately trying to track Shomari's acrobatic antics.

He's showing off. Zala would have smiled, if she wasn't so frustrated with the pakka.

One moment the masses gathered around the main deck, then—as Shomari grabbed a rope and flipped over yet another thrust from Lishan's spear—the sea of pirates rushed to the quarterdeck. And on and on the great sway of onlookers went, with only a few moments ever settled in a single location. As a gap emerged in the crowd after a particularly swift back and forth, Zala spotted Fon floating atop a set of crates.

"What does he think he's doing?" Zala asked harshly as though Fon had something do with it.

"He's been at it all morning," Fon shouted over the swordplay. "He's been sparring anyone with the spine to try him. Says he'd *'be paying ten gold apiece'* to anyone who could disarm him. This big guy showed up first. He didn't last two strokes. Then there was this lady who was almost as acrobatic as he was. She lasted a little longer. Oh! Then there was this other aziza, she was an elemental, and—"

"And he thought this was a good idea why?"

The group shifted once more as the fight moved from the quarter deck back to the main deck again. Zala almost got trampled before Old Man Ode pulled her up by the shoulder.

"That cat's crazy, ain't he?" He smiled widely while limping back to watch the bout with a surprisingly enthusiastic *whoop*. It was good to see his new pegleg was at least functional.

Fon landed at Zala's side. "I don't think he was thinking about if it was a good idea or not. He said something about being bored and wanting to..." She placed a finger to her lip. "'*Make sure my sword hand stays loose*' was the phrase he used, I think." She shrugged. "You know how he gets. He always has to test his skill against everyone he meets."

"He never challenged me," Zala said, not *quite* letting the pout seep into her voice.

A burst of laughter leapt from Fon's lips before she could cover it with her hands. "Sorry, sorry. But come on, we've all seen the way you fight."

Zala scowled as Shomari scurried to all fours in an attempt to sweep at Lishan's leg. Somehow the woman evaded his strike, lifting her heel up and away to kick at the passing pakka. The impact sent shudders down Zala's spine and Shomari let out a cat's cry.

It was the first time she had ever seen Shomari take a hit.

She wasn't sure if she should feel worried that he wasn't as untouchable as she had always thought, or elated that he'd finally tasted a slice of humble pie. The rovers' cheers came so loud Zala thought her eardrums would burst.

Covering her ears, she turned to Fon. "What happened to Mantu and Sniffs? They didn't go running off and do something stupid too, did they?"

"Well, that depends…" Fon said meekly. "Do you consider taking in bets something stupid?"

Zala twisted her fingertips into the sides of her temple. She couldn't begin to understand how Kobi had managed his crew. Maybe he had only allowed them to run as wild and free as they had out of pure necessity to keep himself sane. If it was true, she didn't blame him one bit.

When she looked up again, Shomari feinted a move right and then jumped atop the shaft of Lishan's spear. In what seemed like the same motion his back paws drove into her wrist, forcing her to drop her weapon and withdraw the saber at her side.

This time a distinct round of applause coupled with guttural laughter came from the right. Mantu held a clenched fist high in the air, spit casting off from his mouth as he roared, Sniffs mimicking him at his side. Amazing how only two men could match the enthusiastic clamor of an entire pirate crowd.

"Well, at least they're a bit more at ease," Zala said almost to herself.

"I ain't never seen Lishan take so long to bring someone down," a long-faced pirate near Zala said to one of her companions. She recognized the woman from that day on the beach, the mystic pather, though today her hair was decorated with red and yellow beads instead of blue and white.

"We've never seen Shomari fight someone this long either," Fon called over to the pair. Zala shot eyebrows at her diminutive friend. "Oh, sorry." Fon turned to Zala. "This is Marjani. Marjani this is Zala." Zala gave Fon a look. "I mean—*Captain* Zala."

"Ahoy there, Zala," the woman called Marjani said, dipping her head in a low bow, her locs nearly sweeping the deck. A slight shiver drove through Zala's veins at the sound of the woman's accent. She couldn't be sure with so few words from the woman, but she had a hunch Marjani was from Jultia, Zala's own homeland. Then she remembered that Marjani had been speaking Mero-Set to her crew on the beach, not the Mother Tongue.

"Good afternoon," Zala said, steeping her words further in her isle accent.

"I told you the Will of the Gods always catches up to a cheater," said a round-faced man who stood just at Marjani's shoulder. Zala had no idea how she had missed him. His skin was a shade or two lighter than anyone else on the deck, made yet more stark by his curly, jet black hair that hung over his eyes.

The woman sucked her teeth. "She's not cheating. The Gods blessed her with short-sight and she uses it well."

No wonder she's lasting so long against him, Zala thought. Facing up against the reflexes of a pakka was far more feasible when one could see literal seconds into the future.

"Don't worry." Fon smiled. "We always say Shomari cheats by being born a pakka."

The fight finally settled in the center of the ship, both fighters showing their fatigue as their cuts came less sharp and their dodges appeared more sluggish. Though Shomari still looked a bit dazed and uncharacteristically shaky on his feet—clearly still reeling from the hit he took—it was also clear that Lishan was the worse off of the two.

Or at least, that's what it seemed like on the surface.

274

Her exposed arms were turning purple where Shomari had landed hits with his blunted sword, and blood started to stream from her nose and down her chin. Another cut higher on her eye was running so freely it trickled down her cheek and onto the deck below.

Despite the blood and bruises, her expression didn't change. Zala knew that look, the expression of someone who was used to taking a beating. For someone with her talents to carry such a fierce resolve, she must have seen some real combat in her time. The woman's lips were flat and unmoving, and her stare never wavered. Her braids danced at the edges of her eyes as she swayed.

She was not someone Zala ever wanted to fight.

Lishan wasn't looking Shomari in the eye, and wasn't trying to intimidate him either. Her gaze seemed to hover somewhere around the pakka's middle with utter concentration, a fighter's stare. She was dueling the weapon, not the pakka.

For a brief moment Zala wondered how Shomari was faring as he circled the woman wearily. Jelani had always said that those who weren't used to getting hit always had a hard time coming back after taking a real "pop."

Zala was still struggling to decide which of the two was more likely to win when Nubia came storming through the crowd.

"*Lishan, what are you doing?*" Nubia demanded in Mero-Set. Only some of the crew seemed to understand her words, Lishan clearly one of them. The rest looked clueless. "*Put down that saber.*"

Without a second's hesitation, not even a scowl or readied excuse, Lishan dropped her blade to the deck. She twisted on her heel and faced her captain, back straight, and hands tucked neatly behind her back before saying a curt, "Yes, ma'am."

Nubia traced her eyes over the rest of her crew as though daring them to say anything about her cutting in their fun. Not a single one of them even met her gaze.

But Shomari wasn't one of her crew.

"This little contest is my fault, ma'am," he said gently. "I might have let things get a little — "

"I didn't ask you a damn thing, cat," Nubia said sharply. Zala thought she heard a gentle purr come out from under Shomari's maw.

Nubia gave another look around the crowd, her eyes settling on Mantu and Sniffs—who looked like they were more interested in a trio of seagulls passing by. Then her glare hovered to where Zala stood. And it took Zala a moment too long to realize she had been staring back.

"I don't know how things were run on your ship," Nubia said. "But here, all sparring finishes when first blood is drawn." She turned her voice to the larger group. "As all my crew should very well know."

Judging by the shame crossing all their faces this didn't seem to be news to them. They had been too caught up in the thrill of such a close match—Zala couldn't really blame them. If there had suddenly been a new contender for Shomari back when they were with the *Titan*... Well, they'd have been no better in their excitement, no matter the ship's rules. Not that it would ever happen. Kobi had no such regulations for first blood.

In fact, during Zala's first week on the crew she had seen a man bludgeoned to death for some trivial dispute about a spilt cup of palm wine. In the end, Kobi lost both involved: the man who had been beaten down and the one who had done the beating who had dropped dead later that

276

night. The healer had said he'd taken too many blows to the head.

"Lishan," Nubia commanded. "To my quarters."

Again, with a soldier's swift obedience, Lishan set off past her captain and down into the lower decks. Before Nubia followed, she surveyed the pirates once more. "The rest of you, get this shit cleaned up." She stuck her serpent-shaped pipe into her mouth, inhaled, and then allowed two streams of purple smoke to escape from her nostrils. "*Now.*"

Dozens of feet scampered across the wood as the crew set to work putting everything back in order. Seemingly satisfied, Nubia stepped down the stairs to deal with Lishan.

"Don't look so frightened." Marjani gave Zala a swift pat on the back. "She only got like that 'cause it was Lishan. If it was any of the others, she wouldn't have went all military captain on us. She's just afraid her favorite mighta gotten hurt."

"I could have done without the death stare," Zala said, feeling a shiver down her spine.

"Oh, that woulda still been there. That's, like, her signature move. She don't like none of us gettin' roughed up outside of raids, especially us mystics. She woulda just left off the speechin' a bit."

"You heard her, a bout ends when first blood is drawn!" Mantu shouted from the top of a barrel. "The way I reckon it... that means my boy Shomari won!"

Shomari pulled Mantu down from the barrel. "No, no, Mantu. Bet's off."

"*Your* bets might be off." Mantu smacked Shomari's hand away from him then shouted, "But I had some good wagers with a few of these fine people here."

Zala wondered where all Mantu's fear and paranoia had

run off to. Only days ago he had been talking about abandoning ship, and now he was trying to scrape in extra coin without a care in the world.

That's why he's a pirate, Zala supposed.

The pursuit of gold and silver beat out his better judgement. Fortunately, Shomari seemed to be winding him down, offering up the coin from his own earlier bets to quiet his complaints. But when the pakka caught her eye, Zala gave him a look that said, "We'll talk about this later."

With all the excitement dying back down, Zala's hunger announced itself once more with a large rumble from her belly.

"Yeah, we could eat too," the man, who Zala assumed was Marjani's friend or lover laughed from her side.

"Ekko's always ready to eat." Marjani smiled, rubbing the man's belly. "Mind if we join you in some fresh fish slop?"

Zala caught the automatic "no" already rolling off her tongue, rethinking her response. Her mind went back to Siya, to Ajola, Rishaad, and all the others she had never gotten to know because she didn't give herself the chance. But once they reached al-Anim their lie about the schedules would be revealed, so they would have to abandon Nubia's crew and lose themselves among the city's streets to stand even a hope of survival. But something in Zala's mind told her it wouldn't hurt getting to know these two.

Kobi's ship had seen plenty of seams within the crew's dynamic, and Zala had been too slow to part them because she refused to interact with them personally. Every crew had fissures. If at any point their trip to al-Anim ran aground, perhaps it was best to have a few friends on her side, or at least some who would be sympathetic toward her and her friends. It might give them a better chance to get out alive.

Besides, Fon had already come to know them, it seemed, and she was an excellent judge of character. As Zala peered at the aziza, her friend looked up with raised eyebrows and a shrug.

"Hells, why not," Zala answered with a smile.

CHAPTER 28
ZALA

POCKETS OF GUARDED FERVOR PEPPERED THE MESS HALL. Though the captain had made her displeasure very clear, the collection of pirates in their corners couldn't help but discuss the great fight between woman and pakka. Between chugs of rum or slurps of soup, Zala listened as each crew member recounted their own version of the bout, each one more exuberant than the last.

"Did you see when the cat used the ratlines to flip overhead?" came a husky voice from a dark corner.

Another voice, much lighter, answered from beneath the light of a lantern. "He didn't have shit on Lishan. It was like she fought with the eight arms of an octopus. I ain't never seen her move so fast." Zala had to turn to listen to this quiet voice, her charred ear was still hard of hearing despite the ship surgeon's best efforts.

"Shit!"—this exclamation came long and stretched —"Not even the fight between Lekkun and Balo in the pits was half as good."

"You think there'll be a rematch?"

"No chance. Cap'n was pissed. Maybe when we get back from al-Anim we can convince Lishan and the cat to enter the pentagon arena. There's still time yet until the new year."

At first Zala had tried to ignore the conversations sprouting up like a chorus of morning seals. Marjani was in the middle of a very funny story about how she and Ekko had first met on the docks of Pyrus while Ekko had been making a run from the city guard. To keep her ears from the rest of the room's less interesting rambling, Zala asked, "Oh? What did you steal, then?"

"Nothin' at all, I swear it." Ekko threw his hands up in mock innocence. "Well, I suppose *technically* I swindled that one old woman in a game of shells—you know, the one with three cups. But I don't count that. Old lady had the quickest eye I've ever seen."

"He used an illusion to make it seem like the cup she chose was empty," Marjani finished for him, a wry smile on her lips.

Fon dropped her bowl on the table in exaggerated shock. "How could you trick an elder like that?"

"Hey, it all balanced out. Later on I found out that she was a mystic herself. Some old Ya-Seti archer with eagle's eye. So she was cheatin' too. Besides, that was ages ago. I'm all grown up since then."

"If two years counts as 'ages,'" Marjani mocked.

Ekko waved a huffy hand. "All in the eye, Jani, all in the eye."

"So when did you enter the picture?" Zala asked Marjani.

"Right." Marjani perked up, throwing her long hair over her shoulder. "So, Nubia had me and some of the others followin' a lead down on the docks when this old hag starts to shouting. *'Thief! Filthy little thief.'* Oh man, if you had heard her voice you would've snapped your ears with clams."

Ekko gave a disgusted start. "The worst."

"So, of course, who am I gonna believe in this situation?"

"The 'little old hag,'" Zala answered.

"I had no choice. So I tracked Ekko through the streets, and I found him hidin' in the shitter of this old bath house. He gets to talkin' real fast and explains everything—"

"And then she says there might be a place for me on Nubia's ship," Ekko finished on cue like they had told the story dozens of times before.

"Just like that?" Zala said through a gulp of soup and raised eyebrows. "You believed him?"

"As if. But an illusionist is hard to come by, and I needed to earn some favor from Nubia that week."

"She still won't admit it was my charm that won her over."

Marjani slapped Ekko across the shoulder. "Pfft. You wish."

Zala smiled. "You two remind me a lot of Shomari and F—" Fon gave her own slap to Zala across the knee.

"Oh, hey!" Ekko said, gazing over Zala's shoulder. "Looks like Iokaja is doing okay after all."

Zala turned to the largest aziza she'd ever seen walk up from an entrance way she knew to lead to the infirmary. The aziza was barely over five feet, but by her people's standards she was practically a giant. She looked almost nothing like Fon, too. She had the alabaster skin of an albino, red-spotted freckles stretching from ear-to-ear over the bridge of her nose. Her eyes were a slate gray instead of the forest green usual among her kind, and her head was shaved bare

—save for the barest stubble of red hair. And unlike Fon, she did not share in any forehead tattoo. Instead, her face was decorated with a nose ring.

Just as Zala turned to Fon to point the other aziza out, her friend dropped her spoon into her bowl with a loud *clunk*.

"It was so nice sharing this meal with you," Fon said quickly as she pushed back her seat, her spritely wings lifting her smoothly from her chair.

Zala put a hand to the aziza's wrist, leaned in close, and muttered, "What's wrong?"

"Not to say anything against other aziza," Fon murmured. "But they tend to ask a lot of questions of me."

Zala scoffed as Fon tried to subtly pull away. "That's it? You're just being shy."

"*Pẹlẹ o, lejò,*" came a deep voice from behind in what sounded like the Faerie Tongue. Zala had trained in the language during her days back home in Jultia. She turned to see the aziza standing behind them.

"*Bawo, òrẹ́,*" Zala replied cordially.

Fon, who had still been trying to pull herself free, turned to Zala with a sharp look. "What? You never told me you spoke *Zizah'r*."

Zala shrugged. "You always spoke in the Mother Tongue. I was taught it's rude to assume someone else's language."

"You speak it well, human." The aziza Iokaja took a seat next to Ekko, quickly stealing his half-left bowl of soup.

"Been meanin' to ask," Marjani said through a bite of bread. "How many tongues *do* you know?"

"Me?" Zala glanced at Fon, starting to appreciate what she had meant about being asked too many questions. Before now the conversation topics had been relatively broad, save for Marjani's story of how she and Ekko had met. "Oh, well, you know, you pick stuff up here and there when you spend so much time on the isles. So many different folks moving through."

"Right, but you speak most of them real good. Formal-like, I mean." Marjani dipped her bread into her soup thoughtlessly. "How about Julti? Do you know that one?"

Again, Zala slipped back into a heavier accent to cover her homeland tongue. "I've caught a little bit of that. But I'll butcher it if I try."

"You're not fooling anyone with that accent, chana. Not me, anyway." Now Zala could *really* sympathize with her aziza friend as she shifted uncomfortably in her seat. Marjani just smiled, while Ekko and Iokaja sat forward intently. Did they really have to press in so close? An awkward quiet settled between them, one that Zala wished she could fill without revealing anything too much one way or another.

When she didn't answer, Marjani relented. "S'okay. We all got secrets on this ship. We ain't gonna try and pry nothin' from you."

Zala nodded, raising her eyes back up from where they had fallen to the table. Fon spoke up then. "So, how did you all get in with Nubia?"

"Well, I wasn't so fond of the captain at first," Ekko started. "It didn't help that Marjani here basically stole me away from my comfortable life of small cons. Getting on the ship and hearing how the one thing she pretty much cared about was killing some 'Captain Kobi' took some getting used to. But she liked me well enough—more than enough. Cap'n likes us mystics, ain't that right, Jani?"

"Damn straight. She treats us well." Marjani lifted a cup, a gesture mirrored by her fellows, who struck wood together over the table, causing rum to slosh over the oak finish.

Zala rested her elbows on the table and said, "I've been meaning to ask. That is… if you don't mind. What are your Blessings? I mean, Ekko, you're an illusionist, right?"

Ekko gave her a nod of affirmation, and Marjani thumbed to herself, saying, "I'm just a pather. Not much use during raids, but when we're in cities tryin' to track this person or that I get to dust off the old tricks I learned from the academies."

Zala looked at her with new eyes. So she had been brought up in Jultia as well? Maybe they had already crossed paths without realizing it. But no, couldn't be. Marjani was at least a generation or two older than she was.

"That's how we found you at that isle, by the way. I tracked some wreckage out at sea to your group," Marjani said. Then she nodded to her tall aziza companion through another sip of her rum. "Iokaja here has all the usual aziza qualities: flight, essence sense, self-healing, you know. But she's also got elemental parents. Human ones."

"I'm not so good with the aziza side of things," Iokaja admitted. "I'm only a quarter-breed. Nubia fancies me mostly on the back of my elementalism. What about you? Um…"

"Fon," Zala's friend said through a stilted smile.

Iokaja didn't seem to notice. "You look about half, right? Your mother or father?"

Zala tilted her head. "Father? I thought all aziza were female?"

"Yes and no," Fon said. "It's complicated." She turned to Iokaja. "And yeah, it was my mother. You?"

"Aziza grandmother," she said. "But I never grew up

285

with my clan in Kunda—neither did my grandmother, as far as I know. Probably why my sensing is so weak."

And why she's so tall, Zala thought.

"Oh, I'm naturally bad with it too," Fon admitted. "But there are some exercises I learned over the years that could help. If we ever get the chance between chores, I can show them to you."

Iokaja's freckles lifted around her cheeks in a smile. "That'd be great, thanks."

And to think Fon didn't want to speak with her at all.

Of all the pirates Zala had met, Fon was easily the friendliest. Making conversation, and friends, was as natural to her as flight.

"It's really Ekko here who's the most impressive of us, though," Iokaja went on. "If it weren't for Lishan he'd probably be Captain Nubia's favorite."

"Oh yeah? Why's that?" Zala asked.

Ekko was slow to speak, his bashfulness apparent beneath very rosy cheeks.

"He's too modest," Marjani spoke for him. "And a little shy." She nudged him with her shoulder. "But he's Twice Blessed. He's not just a half-way illusionist. He's a *sonamancer* as well, a *true* illusionist: sound and sight."

Zala and Fon's eyes went wide in shock, but Ekko seemed a bit uncomfortable.

"I wouldn't presume to call myself a *true* illusionist," he corrected. "A sonamancer, sure. I can keep sounds contained pretty well. But I ain't got the talent for making proper illusions of people or anything. I can only do items, locations, that sort of thing. You know, make the ship disappear if we need to make a getaway or something like that... and even that I can't do for long."

Marjani turned to Zala with a look. "See what I'm saying? Modest as *Zothina* Herself."

"I've been pledged to about a dozen different ships with twice as many captains," Iokaja said. "None of them treated the mystics and wageni nearly as well as the captain does."

Zala looked around to all the other crew members, realizing how well fed they appeared. So unlike Kobi's own crew.

"When's the last time you lost someone?" she asked.

Ekko pursed his lips. "Maybe… one moon back? We had some bad information on that one though. And none of our mystics died."

"How many are lost in a year?" Fon ask.

Iokaja answered, "Maybe a little over a score."

"*What!?*" Zala's voice came out louder than she'd intended. A few heads in the dark corner lifted in interest. Zala gave an apologetic wince to quell any concerns before lowering her voice again. "Kobi lost that many in a *week*. Starting to wish I had signed on here from the start."

"Well, Cap'n does take some getting used to," Ekko confessed. "And we don't always agree with the way she likes to get things done. But she respects the vote. And her heart's in the right place. All of us have a story about Captain Nubia, especially her original crew from Ya-Set. The only time I might be at odds with her is when she rants on about the Aktahrians. They're not all bad like she says."

"Aha! Jultia!" Marjani said suddenly in Zala's direction. "You're from Jultia, aren't you? Where about? Awassa? Dawaf? No wait, you're one of them noble types from Nali-bela, right? That's why you're so well spoken."

Zala stiffened at the naming of that last city; she hoped Marjani didn't notice. Her shaky voice, however, was no help as she uttered a stammering, "W-what?"

"That's where you're from, isn't it? You sound like 'em when you end your words sometimes. I've been trying to figure it out."

"I thought you said you weren't going to pry."

"Guessin' don't count," Marjani said with a throwaway gesture. "I was just curious. I don't care *why* you're hiding it; I just wanted to know what you was actually hidin'. No need to get jumpy."

Iokaja frowned through her last gulp of rum. "You know, I hope you're not like this when you have your one-to-one with Nubia."

"What one-to-one?" Zala faltered, almost too afraid to ask.

The *Redtide* trio looked to each other with cheeky smiles that started another strain in Zala's neck. What were they getting at?

Ekko, running his hand through his thick black curls said, "I guess Nubia was busy with that Aktahrian yesterday, and then with that fight with the pakka... but she'll send for you soon. Just you wait."

CHAPTER 29
ZALA

IT WAS MIDDAY WHEN CAPTAIN NUBIA CALLED ZALA TO her quarters.

The room was small and dimly lit. No luxuries adorned the walls, just a simple desk strewn with scrolls and maps and an odd set of skulls set next to a trio of candles. Zala didn't have to guess who those skulls belonged to. Neither did Mantu, who met her eyes knowingly just before he left his very own one-to-one session.

The fact that the Aktahrian was still alive was a good sign, but his paling skin told her he was only just. At least now he'd be sobered up from his previous delusions of a good bet, his paranoia renewed as he, Zala assumed, went back to the comfort of the dark and secluded crew quarters down below.

Breathing deeply through her nose, Zala took a seat along the opposite side of Nubia. She tried her best not to observe the room too closely, not wanting to seem rude. The one item in the captain's quarters that didn't make Zala's skin crawl was the recurved Ya-Seti bow that hung above the viewport. Perhaps it was a good thing Mantu and Sniffs had lost the one they took from her. The bow that hung as display looked almost exactly like the one Zala had once possessed. Who knows what Nubia or the others would have thought if they had seen her slinging their nation's signature bow on her back. After all, she had pulled it from the dead hands of a Ya-Seti archer.

"Captain Zala, thank you so much for joining me," Nubia said kindly. Her lips pressed around a stick of more Vaaji hash, which filled the room with a musky odor. The scent was mixed with streaks of steam cast off from a cooked puffer fish. And next to her plate sat a fluffy stack of folded *injera*. "Would you care to join me over a mid-day meal?"

"Of course." Zala took a seat across from Nubia, her stomach growling. The fish soup she had shared with Fon and the others was good, but it had done little to satiate the hunger she had worked up in the morning. "It's been a while since I've had injera with a meal."

"It's one of Jultia's better contributions to Esowon," Nubia said. "Especially when we've spent so much time at sea…" Zala nodded through a mouthful of injera-wrapped fish. "Tell me, Captain Zala, where do you come from?"

"Kidogo," Zala said once she had freed her mouth of food.

Nubia pulled her pipe from her mouth, then pointed it at Zala. "Not your crew. I mean where are *you* from?"

Zala stopped chewing. Was this a trick? Zala thought back on Mantu's advice from before. It was easier to lie when there was a hint of truth in her words.

"I grew up in Jultia," Zala confessed. Was her accent that obvious?

"Is that why you voice the Mother Tongue so well? You speak it better than you let on."

Zala didn't know where the conversation was going, but it felt an awful lot like a trap. "I don't know what you mean."

"You try to hide it, especially among your crew," Nubia said. "You use their words, yet not like a native. You shouldn't hide your intellect, chana."

That was easy for Nubia to say. Zala couldn't help but be well spoken—it was the way she was raised, though she hadn't had any say in that matter. But she didn't like being the black sheep within the group. She needed to fit in somehow.

"What brought you into the pirate life?" Nubia asked casually.

Zala bit down on her first response. She didn't think she'd need to divulge the full truth about Jelani, at least not now. "This line of work earns coin fast."

"It also earns one a quick death." Nubia pulled a strip of fish meat from the bone. "Something tells me you didn't have to be in this life. I thought the citizens of Jultia were fanatics for that place, and they don't exactly struggle like those on the isles."

"It's not all it's cracked up to be," Zala said, pushing down old memories.

"Fair enough." Nubia chewed down on her first bite of food. "We don't have to open old wounds. I would, however, like to know how you came to be in Kobi's crew. I'm sure you know we have little love for his people…"

"Trust me, I didn't like the man either."

"You don't have to convince me." Nubia smiled. "We don't attack those merely by association, despite the rumors. But before Kobi turned away from the Aktahrian Navy and into this life of piracy—or excuse me, 'aggressive entrepreneurship,' as Golden Lord Zuberi would have us call it—he made himself one of our primary targets. We've been hunting for him for years."

"But the golden lord says we aren't allowed to attack one another if we want his protection from the other nations." Zala held her hands together tightly. This was quickly beginning to sound like an interrogation.

"I don't associate with Lord Zuberi directly." Nubia sat back in her chair, her tone dark. "We like to think ourselves true rogues of the Sapphire Seas."

Where is all this leading? Zala adjusted herself in her chair, gripping the underside of its seat.

"How much did you know about Kobi?" Nubia asked after a short pause.

"He was… a hardass." Zala chose her words carefully.

"Yes, I've heard that about him," Nubia mused. "What I meant is if you knew about what he did *before* he became a pirate." Zala shook her head. "You are familiar with the war between Aktah and Ya-Set a few years back, right?"

"Of course," Zala said. "*The War of Red Dunes*. I used to overhear the scholars talking about it all the time. I remember when the Jultian King had thoughts of lending assistance to Ya-Set. The people didn't want it though, least of all my instructors—parents, I mean."

"I don't blame them. It wasn't your people's fight." Nubia sat up from her chair. She lifted one of the skulls from her desk as she put out the flame in her pipe. "But Aktah was vicious. Did you know they killed more commoners than soldiers?"

"I've… heard the stories."

"It didn't matter if we were farmers or merchants," the woman said. "If we were Ya-Seti, we were dead. Aktah broke all the rules of war, all common decency, even after the accords." Nubia's gaze drifted, and for a moment she seemed to be elsewhere entirely. Long seconds passed, tension hanging in the air before she drew a deep breath and continued. "Kobi was no better. I was already captain when we first met on the battlefield. I can still see that great big gut of his." She turned her dark eyes back on Zala, like a panther ready to pounce.

Zala withdrew from her stare, breaking the uncomfortable eye contact.

"He still had it." Zala tried her best for a smile. Was that even the expression she should be going for? Nubia had her on edge. "The crew used to wonder how he ever found a shirt that fit..." she said awkwardly, awaiting Nubia's response. The captain's narrowed eyes softened slightly at their edges.

"The second time we met he attacked my home village without mercy. They were a peaceful people, no threat to them. There wasn't even any military thinking behind it, just senseless slaughter." Nubia clenched the skull in her hand.

"Wait, I remember that story." Zala straightened in her seat. "That's the reason Kobi left their navy. He didn't agree with their methods. He—"

"Believed whatever helped him sleep at night, I'm sure. Well, trust me, I was there. I *heard* the way he ordered his crew."

"That's just the way he talks—talked," Zala defended, despite her better judgment. "He was always demanding, but—"

"Are you calling me a liar?" Nubia pressed her face close to Zala's. Zala fought a gulp as she heard the skull start to crack in the captain's grip.

Her voice caught in her throat before she could speak

again, her heart seeming to skip a dozen beats at a time. "Of course not. Kobi was a… despicable man." She had never defended Kobi before, and she had no earthly idea why she was trying now of all times.

"I'm sorry." Nubia took a step back from Zala, her grip loosening on the skull. "You're not the one I'm angry with. Tell me," She took a seat and settled her shoulders back into its silky cushions, "how did he die? Did he suffer?"

"He took a fireball to the face, so I assume his death was instant. But, you know… I've never died before." Zala shrugged with a half-smile. She needed to stop doing that—smirks and grins were not the way to handle someone like Nubia. But it couldn't be helped either way. Her nerves were getting the better of her.

The captain sucked her teeth, and turned back to the porthole. Zala gave a quick glance to the room's exits. She felt cornered by Nubia's questioning. She hadn't yet been threatened directly, but she still felt one wrong word away from seeing how Nubia had earned her notorious reputation. The rest of her crew might have had stories of her nobility, but so far all Zala could gather from her was that she had a malice that was very touch and go.

It was unlikely Zala would need one but, in her books, an escape route was never a bad idea. But the only exits she could see were the porthole Nubia herself had turned to gaze out of, or the door she had come through when she entered, where a guard was still posted outside. The only two weapons in the room were Nubia's sword, which swayed from the scabbard wrapped at her waist, and the bow that hung just above her head.

Zala took in a breath, shaking her head. Perhaps she was just being paranoid.

"Well, good riddance, I suppose." Nubia's flared nostrils

eased. "He burned my people, and it was fire that took him in the end. There's an elegance to that. It was the Will of the Gods. I can accept that." Zala relaxed her shoulders, though her hands still dug into the bottom of her seat. "But I'm sure some of his crew still followed him, even as he abandoned their navy."

"You'd still pursue them even when their captain is dead?" Zala had a sliver of hope that the news of Kobi's death would be enough for Nubia. As she thought on it a little longer she realized it was a foolish belief.

"They are just as guilty of the war crimes he committed. Just because they were ordered does not absolve them of fault." Nubia's eyes became slits as she tilted her head. "Were there any more of his crew from Aktah with him that you came across?"

Zala suppressed another gulp as nervous heat stung her ears. She had hoped to avoid this subject. Though perhaps overly cautious, Mantu kept himself hidden well—save for the bets surrounding Shomari. Besides that, he never left his sleeping quarters if he didn't have to, and he had requested work where he and Sniffs could be left in isolation. Plus, Fon and Shomari had kept most of the crew's attention, which meant the collective paid the other human crew members no mind. But someone had to be watching Mantu closely—at the very least to make sure they weren't casing the *Redtide's* cargo.

Had Nubia sussed Mantu out and was looking for Zala to confirm her suspicions? Could Zala betray Mantu? He wasn't exactly loyal to her and he had probably wanted her dead only a few days ago.

No, that couldn't be it. If the captain thought Mantu her enemy, she would have had his beard shaved to check for his tattoos, and this conversation wouldn't be happening.

Nubia knew that the Vaaji had shipwrecked them, and al-Anim was the nearest city. If anyone survived from their crew, the captain must have only wanted to know if she might find some former Aktahrian naval officers running around the port city.

"There were a few men from Aktah," Zala confessed. "I'm not sure if they were formerly of that navy or not. None of them survived as far as I know. And if they did, I'm sure you'll bring swift justice to them." Nubia eyed Zala a long time before she turned back to the porthole.

Zala held in a breath tight against her chest. *Was that believable enough?*

"So these shipping routes in al-Anim," Nubia said calmly. Zala let out a breath. The act of holding it in and quietly letting it out over and over again was becoming stressful. "Do you know where it's located exactly?"

"Not precisely, but I know it's deep in the port city," Zala assured her. "I have a contact on Shroud Street who'll help us." In truth, it was Zala's hope that she could lose Nubia and her crew within the thick crowds that often gathered there.

"I suppose we'll find out soon enough." Nubia thumbed a hand toward the windowpane. "That's the last of the Ibabi Isles. It'll only be another half-day now." Outside, Zala could see the impressions of a small island passing by.

She had nearly made it from a desolate island to the Vaaji capital with whatever stroke of luck she had been bestowed with. Call it the Will of the Gods or whatever it was. Jelani had to be close, but where would the Vaaji keep their sky ship? Certainly not at the seaport itself. More likely it was stationed deeper in the capital somewhere.

For now, Zala had to figure out how to slip the *Redtide* and her crew without Nubia noticing. Once they realized there were no shipping routes to barter with, it'd be the end of Zala and her little crew.

The room darkened for a moment, as though a lantern had flickered out and died, but the sudden shroud came from outside. Odd. There hadn't been much of any clouds dotting the sky when she had been up on deck.

The door behind Zala swung open to reveal Lishan, now back in undamaged black and red garb, face cuts sealed, and all traces of blood wiped away. "Captain, situation above deck."

"What is it?" Nubia asked as she pulled a dagger from beneath a map on her desk. Zala hadn't even considered something could be hidden there.

"Strange storm brewing up above. We might need to take another route."

"A storm?" Zala asked. "On a day like—"

Her heart plummeted.

There was no way. It couldn't be true. They would have been back in al-Anim days ago. They *should* have been.

Disregarding courtesy, Zala shunted her chair back with a grating of wood and rushed to the single porthole in the room. As she peered through, her breath caught in her throat. It wasn't a storm cloud. It was dark and thick, but there was a subtle cyan hue pulsating beneath the cloud bank, and it pointed out in the distinct yet lumpy shape of an arrowhead.

Most of all, it wasn't following the wind.

"What in Yem's name are you doing, *Captain*?" Nubia asked with a face of stern chastisement.

Zala turned to face them both, captain and first mate. It was the first time she had seen the captain's mask slip, her brow arching like hills. Her second shared the same expression. It didn't matter if they didn't believe her now.

What mattered was getting onto that sky ship.

"I know you won't believe me, Captain." She swallowed hard. "You didn't before on the beach, at least. But there's something I have to tell you. And we're going to have to act *right now*."

CHAPTER 30
ZALA

"Captain, you can't really believe this shit, can you?" Lishan asked with an exasperated gesture Zala's way.

"I'm sorry I lied about the schedules," Zala said quickly, very much aware of how utterly cornered she was if things turned south. "It was the only way you'd let us on board and take us to al-Anim."

"Captain, she's just covering her ass! You can't be — "

Nubia silenced her first mate with a single glance and a flick of her pipe.

In all the time it had taken for Zala to hurriedly recant her story, Nubia hadn't moved an inch. The captain sat quiet and unmoving. She hadn't even taken a drag from her hash pipe for the last several minutes, and the room, for once, was free of the hanging purple plume.

Zala looked over her shoulder to the dark cloud falling back outside. It was already barely a quarter-league away, even as the *Redtide* pushed onward. Waiting wouldn't help anyone here.

Zala stepped forward. "The longer we wait, the more likely they'll get away. *Please* believe me, the Vaaji have a sky—"

"Besides giving your word, what can you do to convince me?" Nubia finally asked.

"If I was going to lie to you, why would *this* be the lie I chose? Don't you see that cloud?" Zala pointed through the porthole.

Even as she spoke she couldn't decide how she might convince the woman. She could understand how they couldn't see the subtle change in hue—hells, if she hadn't been so close to the damn sky ship that day, she wouldn't have known what to look for either. It didn't help at all that they were going so much faster than the cloud bank too, the tell-tale clues of the hidden ship diminishing with every passing moment.

"I know you can barely see it from here," Zala went on. "But just look at the shape of its end. What kind of cloud have you seen that drifts like that?"

Neither party looked convinced, Lishan with a slitted glare and Nubia with her usual passive facade. Then an idea struck Zala. "Fon. Fon will tell you!"

"Who's Fon?" Nubia questioned, turning to Lishan.

"It's our aziza," Zala answered before the first mate could butt in again.

An inquisitive look stretched across Nubia's brow as she rolled her pipe around her knuckles. "And what can she do to prove what you say?"

"Because aziza can see the essence of living creatures," Lishan answered with a frown.

Or something like that. Zala would have smiled if this were any other circumstance.

"And how is it we can trust what your aziza might say?" Lishan asked, then scowled. "You've already lied through your teeth."

Zala noticed that the first mate's hand had never left the hilt at her side. It seemed like every time Zala spoke the woman's grip tightened all the fiercer, veins lining blue along the back of her hand.

"Why would I confess something like this?" Zala seethed. She clenched her own fists in front of her face in frustration. These fools had to understand. And now. "We're, what, a half day from al-Anim? Maybe less. My crew and I could have kept quiet and given you the slip with none of you the wiser." Zala ignored Lishan's scoff. "And then we could have gone around looking for the bloody sky ship ourselves."

"So why tell the captain now?" Lishan pressed on. "What's changed?"

"Because a few days ago I didn't have a clue how I was going to find the thing. And now it's there. *Right there*. The damn thing is ready for the taking!"

"Say I do believe you," Nubia said as she rose from her seat. She strode to stand in front of Zala, towering over her. The captain's eyes flitted to the porthole at their side. "If I help you take it... I'm supposed to just hand it to you?"

"I could give a shit about it. If we capture it, it's yours. You didn't see how it ripped through us. No vessel I've seen could ever hope to take it head on. But I've seen it in action, and it hasn't marked us yet. We can make the most of this. Together, Captain, we've got a shot. And just think, if *you* bring this thing down, can take it over, the golden lord would grant you anything you asked."

Zala stared up into Nubia's dark eyes, looking for

anything that might reveal she had convinced the woman. There was the smallest twitch above the captain's cheek where two silver piercings dotted her skin. Zala couldn't tell if the expression was the start of a smile or a grimace. But there was nothing else she could do now, there was no other play to make. Honesty was the only path she could take here, no matter how treacherous it might be. It was her only hope back to Jelani.

Nubia would either believe her... or kill her on the spot.

"We should throw them overboard, Captain." Lishan decided. "The whole lot of them."

Nubia lifted a hand and Zala felt a chill slither down her spine.

"Fine, then," the captain said. Zala turned a glance to Lishan who was halfway to unsheathing her saber. But Nubia stopped the woman with her free hand, the other pressing her pipe between her lips once more. For the first time Zala was thankful for the smoke that billowed in her face as Nubia said, "Let's go talk to your aziza. Last I checked, we had one of our own on board as well."

AFTER A TENSE WALK THROUGH THE SHIP AND UP THE ladder to the top deck, Zala, Nubia, and Lishan found both aziza atop the forecastle. Each winged woman was in identical poses only an aziza's grace could manage, twisted into impossible contortions. Atop the deck their silhouettes laid flat against the midday blue.

"Be sure to breathe through your nose and out your mouth when you transition from Illopa's curled cradle into Ugara's broad stance," Fon was saying to a struggling

Iokaja, who was trying to stand from her elaborate prone position.

The taller of the aziza held her stance solid for a moment —far longer than Zala could have ever managed—before toppling over. With a short laugh that spoke more of wounded pride than humor, Iokaja said, "It's impossible to make that switch. My arms are too wide and lanky."

"You'll get it." Fon offered Iokaja a hand up. "It's all in your core. Master that and the rest comes easy, including your sensing abilities."

"Sorry to interrupt," Nubia said as they reached the pair. "But we need your wings."

"Another scouting assignment, Captain?" Iokaja stood straight, her wings flapping in anticipation.

"Of a kind, yes."

Zala threw a glance over her shoulder. The sky ship's cloud was nearly lost to the horizon. She twisted again, squaring herself to her friend. "Fon, it's back. *They're* back."

A new light shone in Fon's eye, an earnest look that rarely crossed her usually joyful face. Before responding, she turned her chin to the skies, causing her already large eyes to go wider. "Where? I don't see anything."

Nubia pursed her lips at Fon's response and turned to Zala. "So you're not lying, then."

Lishan stepped between them. "We still should have the aziza check it out."

"Check what out, Captain?" Iokaja looked from first mate to captain, her brow furrowed.

Zala tapped Fon on the shoulder and pointed to the stern of the ship. When Fon's eyes went from orbs to determined slits, Zala knew the aziza had seen the odd cloud.

Fon lifted determined eyes to Zala and asked, "What do you need us to do?"

As they waited for the aziza to do their work in the skies, a gathering amassed below on the main deck. Rumblings of sky ships and Vaaji drifted along the afternoon winds, growing louder with each new group to lift their heads above deck and see what all the fuss was about.

Zala didn't pay any of them mind as she stood above them on the ship's sterncastle alongside Nubia and Lishan. All of their chins lifted to the sky. The strange cloud that Zala knew to be the sky ship seemed to mock her in its graceful flight. It must have been nice being way up there, away from the dangers a ship like the *Redtide* could loose.

She wondered where they might have kept Jelani. Could he see her? Sense her near? They probably left him in some dark, dank brig with no sunlight.

She clutched at the songstone tucked in the pocket of her waistband once more, but didn't remove her intense gaze from the sky ship's artificial haze. Her eyes were watering from the strain; she hadn't even blinked since they had moved to the ship's stern.

"What's taking them so long?" Lishan asked impatiently.

Zala stewed. "Fon's got a bad wing, give her time."

Nubia seemed to be taking the situation seriously now, and judging by the first mate's darting eyes, Lishan had picked up on it too. Zala could see the tension starting to creep onto both pirates' faces and the way they paced.

Lishan leaned in to mutter something in her captain's ear, but a slight shake of the head was all the response she got. They continued to wait.

Finally, two dots in the sky materialized through the cloud break. Before long they had reformed into the shapes of two aziza floating through the air.

Iokaja was the first to land with their news. "She speaks the truth, Captain. There *is* something living up there. Several somethings."

"You see? We have to move. Now," Zala demanded.

"Very well." Nubia turned to Lishan. "The cannons aren't going to be worth a damn. Are the twins up for a fight right now?"

"They're still down below—they've not come up from their cabin since the last raid. Last time it took them a week's meditation to recover," Lishan said as she peeked over the sterncastle's railing to search for them among the growing crowd.

Nubia shielded her eyes from the sun while staring up at their target. "They don't seem to be moving too fast." She turned back to Zala. "Why's that?"

Zala was about to open her mouth, but then another voice came from behind to say, "Because I cut their sails." It was Shomari. He shouldered through what was now a crowd of at least thirty. When he reached the top step of the sterncastle, he and Lishan gave each other considered nods —a fighter's respect.

"If they're lacking in replacements, they're left with whatever magicks are holding them up," he said.

"How do you know they need sails?" Lishan asked with a sideways frown.

"They have them, don't they?" Shomari shrugged. "Oh, my apologies, you've never seen the thing. Doesn't look much different from an ordinary ship, 'cept that it, you know, flies."

"Our real problem is nothing on this ship can touch them," Zala weighed in. "Trust me, we tried, and you found us stranded on the Ibabi Isles days later." She shook her head, then nodded her chin up to the cloud in the sky.

"They're too high up and it's not a normal ship. We can't fight it like one."

"Then what do you suggest?" Nubia asked.

Zala didn't have an answer. She had been trying to work something out in her head for several minutes. Her effort leading up to now had been spent trying to convince them of the threat, but she never really considered what it'd take to *actually* attack the thing. But she couldn't just stand there and offer nothing, not after all the damned effort getting them to this point.

"Zala," Fon said meekly at Iokaja's side while she rubbed the back of her shoulder. The flight must have strained her still-healing wing. "What about Ekko?"

"What about hi—" Zala started, and then she understood what Fon was getting at. "Ah, that could work perfectly. But not without…" Her mind was already racing with the possibilities as she rushed to portside for a better look at the skies between their own sails.

Yes! There are enough clouds ahead of it, she thought. *It could work…*

Still looking out into the ocean with her hands raised to measure the distance, she asked, "Besides Iokaja, do you have any other strong elementals on your crew? You mentioned something about twins. The more the better."

"I've a handful decent enough at what they do," came Nubia's voice. The question was plain in her statement.

"Then that's it." Zala spun on her heel, anticipation welling up in her chest and shaking through her fingertips. "That's what we'll do."

Lishan cleared her throat doubtfully. "Apologies. And excuse me for not being telepathic. But what exactly is 'it'?"

"I don't think this has ever been done before," Zala said,

raising her voice so the rest of the *Redtide* crew could hear. They were already eavesdropping anyway, so she may as well make a show of it. "But if it does work... we'll become the most notorious pirates in history!"

CHAPTER 31
KARIM

FOR THE DOZENTH TIME IN THE LAST HOUR, STEAM whistled and snaked through pipes and funnels straight into Karim's face. This time, however, he anticipated the whine that bellowed from the pistons and wheels. He pulled his loose headwrap around his mouth and held his breath until the latest pipe-burst finished its screaming episode.

The brass container holding the skyglass within the *Viper's* engine room was difficult equipment to work with at the best of times, and at the moment it was being pushed to the limits of its endurance.

Karim turned at the sound of a hacking cough from below. "We've gone through all the reserves, sir," Engineer al-Kindi said through his last cough as he finished patching one of the first pipes to burst. "The skystone is meant for lift, not thrust. We're putting too much strain on her! I've spoken to the damned Malouf family about how we can squeeze more efficiency—"

"Just by having a better quality of brass," Al-Kindi's

second, Amir, finished for him in rote imitation. "But to do that we'll have to sacrifice intake —"

Karim lifted a frustrated hand and halted Amir's response. He'd already spent an hour listening to their ranting. His visit was supposed to have been a brief check-in, but when shit had hit the winds he had been pulled into the chaos with all the rest. Not that he minded: Karim had always preferred this kind of practical work.

"It's fine, it's fine," Karim said. "The fault is mine. I shouldn't have had us fly to Kidogo with half a ship in the first place. And using the spin to cloak our flight in the exhaust isn't helping with the strain either. What's the time difference if we use this last piece of glass to its core?"

Al-Kindi's second said, "Without it we'll take more than a day to get back to the capital. With, maybe half that."

"I think the crew is ready to get back home," Karim replied. "And there's nothing between us and al-Anim now. So I say we use it."

Al-Kindi grumbled again. "I told those damn engineers we should have stocked more sails. But oh no!" He threw his hands in the air. "Captain Malouf needed extra space for his private study. '*What's the point of extra sails when we've the skyglass,*' he said. '*It's a waste,*' he said. I'll tell him where he can find his waste..."

Karim cloaked his laughter beneath a faux cough. Al-Kindi's Malouf impression was far too good.

"Well," he said. "I wouldn't call us *sitting* ducks exactly, just very slow ones. I'm sure the yardhands back home will get an earful from you."

"You can bet your ass they will. The next time we're sent out I'm stuffing extra sails into Malouf's bookshelves myself if I have to." Al-Kindi tilted his head with a raised eyebrow before adding, "Uh... *sir.*"

Karim smiled the engineer's worry away. At least, he hoped he did. He'd take the man's informal bluster over the upper-deck officers' ass-kissing any day.

A voice bellowed from the pipe strapped up near the entrance door below. It sounded like Communications Officer Tahan. "Acting Captain, are you still with Chief al-Kindi?"

The lead engineer stomped over to answer the call, but Karim halted him. "Don't worry, I've got it."

He left the latest pipe he had been tending to alone and walked down the spiral staircase to the first level. He passed Amir, who at that moment had been plugging two cracks in his own console's piping, gloved hands stretched wide as though desperately holding a sinking ship afloat. Karim gave him an encouraging pat on the back before leaning his mouth close to the funnel that would reach the bridge.

"Officer Tahan, this is el-Sayyed," he said. "Go ahead."

"Requesting your presence on the undercarriage, sir. We have a sighting."

THE VIEW THROUGH KARIM'S TELESCOPE WAS MORE THAN a little troubling. Perhaps a league away, just ahead of the *Viper*, was what looked to be a frigate or perhaps a carrack. It was hard to tell which class exactly with all the clouds obstructing his view. He'd have told the engineers to ease on the exhaust, but that would have exposed them. There was only the thin line of natural clouds ahead.

"Sir, I took a look myself when there was a clearer break," Officer Ahmad said. "She's flying merchant colors from Ya-Set. I don't think we have to worry overmuch."

A sliver broke through the haze. But even with the

slightly more open view Karim couldn't pinpoint the ship's make.

Still looking through his scope, he asked, "Have they altered their course in any way since you spotted them?"

"No, sir. They've maintained their south and east passage with no deviation. Looks like they're headed to al-Anim too."

"And how many ships pass through this lane typically, would you say?"

"Not too many, sir. In truth, it's an uncommon path. Looks like they came through from the Ibabi Isles. Unusual, but it does happen from time to time. Why? What are you thinking, sir?"

"Could be nothing." Karim handed the brass telescope back to Ahmad. "But better safe than sorry. Order the bridge to follow the natural winds instead. We're going against them right now, so anyone looking up here may take notice of us."

"Right away, sir." Ahmad collapsed the telescope, stuffed it into his belt, and made his way up the sole ladder leading to the rest of the ship.

Karim turned his gaze back out to the airship's bow. Besides himself, there were a handful of others on the undercarriage. They had been on cleaning duties when he came down, most of them scrubbing down the cannons or wiping down the jutted platforms.

A moment passed and a slight lurch shifted Karim's weight to one side. He grabbed the nearby railing for balance just as a red tunic caught the corner of his eye. He turned to the approaching acting chief officer.

"What's going on now?" Issa asked.

"Probably nothing," he said flatly, but something faint nagged at the back of his mind. "I thought going this way would keep us out of the eye of the merchant lanes, but it seems we have one bearing in on us from the central Ibabi cluster."

Issa squinted through the wisps of fog. "You think they might be pirates?"

"Could be. But they're just as likely to be merchants late for a shipment, and they're braving the more treacherous route. Still, it warrants caution."

"Malouf's not going to like it."

Karim squared to Issa so swiftly he nearly lost his balance. "Malouf's awake?"

That was the last thing he needed right now if the situation was indeed more than delayed merchants.

"Only a few moments ago," Issa said. The concern etched on her face telegraphed that Karim must have had one of his fixed stares. "He asked when we'd return to the capital."

"Is he taking command again?"

"Not yet… Doc has him on rest, seeing as it should be smooth sailing from here."

Almost on cue, Dahlia Fahyad with her jewels and gold-laced robes came clinking down from above deck. She nearly slipped on her hems as she climbed down the last ladder rung.

"What's this I hear about us taking yet another half day to get back home?" she asked in a shrill voice.

Karim lifted his hands kindly, though such prudence was more often than not the farthest thing from his mind when he spoke with this woman.

"Just a precaution," he assured her. "We've a ship below that might have spotted us."

Fahyad stretched out her hands in question, making the cuffs of her robes jingle like a fortune teller's bangle. "So what? We're up here and they're down there. Why do we need to reroute because of them?"

"The grand admiral made it clear he didn't want us seen," Karim said as mundanely as he could. "That's why we set out during the eleventh moon's gloom. But right now we are finding cloud cover very sparse. And if we continue with our current path, it is likely someone on that ship might take notice of our artificial veil."

"Well you wait until the captain hears about this," Fahyad huffed. "It's preposterous."

"For the time being, until our captain is back on his feet, *I* am your acting captain. And it is my responsibility to keep us safe."

Despite her flaring nostrils, Karim kept his voice even. "Don't worry. It's probably nothing."

CHAPTER 32
ZALA

NUBIA PRESSED HER HAND INTO HER HEAD. "OKAY, SAY that one more time. You want us to what?"

The whole of the *Redtide* crew had congregated atop the weather deck by the time Zala had gone through her plan twice. Nubia wanted to hear it again—mostly from what Zala assumed was disbelief—not misunderstanding. It wasn't a good sign.

"If your illusionist is as good as you say," Zala said. "We could trick the Vaaji into thinking we're still headed off into the horizon. To them, it'll look like they are still in the sky while we use your elementals to push on the winds and force the sky ship down to us where we can board them. Then from there... business as usual."

Nubia pinched the side of her brow in thought. "Ekko is good, but he's not *that* good. And I've got four elementals besides Iokaja, though they'll need time before they can get something that big pushed down."

"This will never work," Lishan interjected. "There's too much risk. And we can't even see the thing on top of it all."

Zala bit at her lip. It was true. She was asking for the impossible here. The illusionist and the elementals would never be able to bring the ship down before tiring out. They wouldn't get within a league of it before their plot was uncovered. And, just like a few days ago, they'd simply expose themselves and get blown out the water.

Tapping her hands together, searching for the rhythm that often brought her best ideas to mind, she eyed Lishan. "My glass. The Gods' Glass you took off me on the beach. Did you store it somewhere?"

Lishan crossed her arms. "I know you're not suggesting our mystics use it?"

"It's the only way to make this work."

"Maybe you don't know, but bad shit happens when mystics overuse the glass. What I took from you was barely the size of a plum."

Zala narrowed her eyes. "I know all too well."

"Oh yeah, how's that?"

Zala didn't even consider her next words before she spoke them, too fed up with Lishan and all of her needless rebuttals. "Because my husband has stoneskin."

Silence ensued.

Out of the corner of her eye, Zala could see Fon and Shomari shift uncomfortably. It was out now. There was no going back, so she went onward.

"And my husband is on that ship. The Vaaji took him from me, took him from us." She gestured to her friends. In the crowd she could see the baggy eyes of Old Man Ode near one of the longboats, and Mantu and Sniffs were alongside one of the cannons. "That's why I'm doing this pirating shit to begin with."

She let that hang a moment, hoping the honesty of it lent her some credit in the eyes of the crowd. "And my husband is an oni'baro. He told me how he and his fellow priests used their a'bara to call the kubahari to them that day. I *know* you've all heard the story. That was him, and that was *his* fellowship, his people. The glass they used was the size of a large melon—that much between *twenty* of them. What we need to do isn't nearly as grand. We'd only require five mystics, including Ekko."

Zala waited for Nubia's response, but again it was Lishan who spoke instead. "We can't force our mystics to do this for you. You're asking them to gamble with their lives."

Zala ignored the woman and locked her gaze with Nubia, who still looked undecided between her pursed lips and knitted brow. "I understand you barely know me. Truly, I get it. But I ask you, I beg you to help me."

Finally, Nubia met Zala's gaze properly. Again, it was that same look between a smile and grimace.

"They may volunteer if they wish," she said, "but it's up to them."

"That's fair." Zala swallowed hard, then turned to the watching crew. "I haven't been able to speak with most of you personally." She realized now that she didn't even know which of them she needed to campaign to, save for Iokaja, who stood on the sterncastle alongside her, and perhaps Ekko, whose pale face stuck out in the crowd, and Marjani just next to him. "You don't know me, and I don't know you. But I can assure you that my heart is true. I ask a lot, but if we work together—"

"Wait, something's wrong," Fon said, pointing to the sky as her eyes glowed white.

"She's right," Iokaja confirmed. Her own eyes were a milky shade as well. "That flying ship of yours is moving."

"What?" Zala asked as she turned away from the crowd to take a look for herself. When she caught sight of the distinct cloud she could see it rotating to its rear and moving in line with the wind.

"Do you think they're onto us?" Fon asked.

"No. They're just playing it safe and trying to keep out of view." Zala swallowed hard. She sounded false even to her one good ear.

It was one thing attacking an unsuspecting ship. But one on high alert? That was an entirely different scenario, an entirely different ask.

Zala could already see the doubt pressing in on Nubia's features. If Zala lost *her* confidence, she could kiss any hope of rallying the *Redtide's* crew goodbye.

"Captain," Zala murmured as she moved closer to Nubia. "You know this doesn't just benefit me. Think of what you could do with that ship in your hands. We all know the old stories: the dragons, the rocs, and the kongamatos. Whole empires ruled on the backs of those beasts. Whoever controls something like this, whoever controls the skies, will dominate like our ancestors did before. That's the kind of vessel you need if you want to get any *real* kind of vengeance against the Aktahrians."

She hoped Mantu would forgive her. With her voice so low he wasn't going to hear her, but the guilt hurt all the same.

"These tiny coastal raids you've been doing for years can't have amounted to much." Zala knew she was treading rough waters here, but it was all she had. Nubia was likely a breath away from retracting any semblance of support she might have flirted with before. "Imagine having the might of a roc to wreak havoc on a city like Khopesh, or Pyrus. You can't do that with sea vessels, but with that thing..."

Nubia was as unreadable as ever. What did her damned face mean? It was irritatingly flat and stoic.

After a moment, however, the captain's expression turned and began darkening. Zala feared the coming answer, the coming denial. Her hands fidgeted at her sides.

Then a voice rang out from somewhere in the crowd. "I'll fight at your side, Captain Zala." She turned to see Ekko pushing forward to the front of the gathered crew. Iokaja's pledge came second. "And I."

"You know I've got you, chana," purred Shomari.

Fon grabbed at her wrist with a wide smile. "You don't even have to ask."

"Well if this fool is going," Marjani sauntered up to Ekko's side, "you'll have me as well."

More pockets of support trickled among the crew members, building out like a ripple set by the single stone that Ekko had thrown. Soon, it was a clear majority in favor of a raid. But it wasn't Zala they had put faith in. She could see it in how they all came forward in their pairs and trios. It was their interpersonal relationships with one another that brought them to the line. One agreement followed another, and on and on it went. But there were two Zala had hoped for, who did not step forward.

As the sea of pirates moved up, Mantu and Sniffs seem to recede back into the shadows of the sails that snapped above.

Another silence came then, and everyone turned to Nubia. The captain took the sterncastle's railing in hand and leaned forward with the slightest hint of a smirk. "It seems decided, then. Crew, make ready for boarding!"

"STOP FOLLOWING ME, ZALA," MANTU SAID AS ZALA sidestepped yet another hammock to get to the retreating man. Sniffs stood just at his side.

After Nubia had disbanded the crew for preparations, the pair of men were first to rush belowdecks instead of to the armory, where everyone else was quickly heading. Zala wouldn't have even seen them if she hadn't instantly started searching, knowing they would turn tail.

"Come on, you know we'll need your help," she said.

"Not my problem," Mantu answered, dipping his head low to avoid the next room's doorframe. "You might have convinced those fools, but I ain't got no interest takin' on a fight like that."

"You seemed fine enough when I said I'd take it for us a few days ago."

"That was when I thought it'd be on the ground somewhere in al-Anim." Zala nearly walked straight into his chest as he spun on his heel with an outstretched finger. "I ain't think we'd be tryin' for it out in open sea like damn fools. Been there, done that. Unlike you, I *learn* my lessons. I lost nearly my whole crew last time." His sidelong glance pointed to Sniffs. "I ain't willin' to lose any more."

"What are you so afraid of?" She pointed out a porthole to where the sky ship was already slowly descending, pushed down by the subtle winds of the elementals. At their current rate it would take less than an hour until the enemy was in range. "We have surprise this time. And a good plan. They won't be expecting an illusionist's cloak, or mystics strong enough to get the thing down in the first place. If it's their advantage in the air you're worried about, they won't have it for much longer."

"That's if everything goes *exactly* according to plan." Mantu shook his head as he plopped down into a hammock in the darkest corner of the room. "And it's not just that. You weren't there when they boarded us the last time. They ain't like no Vaaji Navy scrubs I ever saw. They was organized. Don't go lookin' at me like that, you know what I mean. I mean more… put together than their usual deal. This is an elite unit we—you—are goin' up against."

Zala crossed her arms, putting on her most disappointed expression. But Mantu was unfazed. Sniffs, however, was uncharacteristically quiet and still as a shadow. Since the start of Zala's pestering he hadn't been parroting Mantu the way he so often had before.

"Elite unit or not," Zala said, "we've got the *Redtide* at our side. You know how vicious Nubia's crew is. Look at how Lishan took on Shomari. We'd be fighting with *both* of them at our backs."

Mantu threw his hands back behind his head casually. "Look, I wish you the best. Yem's Blessings and may Ugara's Spear guide you and all that, truly. But I ain't fightin' alongside these crazy people. It's bad enough we been on the ship as long as we have. No one's noticed me yet, I'll give you that for your last plan's credit. But the moment they realize who I once fought for, their song's tune'll turn. It'll be one of their arrows straight into my chest if I'm *lucky*. Or did you forget about the kijana who was strung up by his thumbs?"

Again, Zala waited for the "yeah, yeah" or "that's right" from Sniffs, but it never came. The large man had been looking down, though his gaze wasn't fixed on the wood below his feet. Not exactly. Zala could tell his eyes were avoiding something, hovering at the edges, and the clenched jaw beneath his cheek looked like he was chewing at whatever was troubling him.

"What about you, Duma?" Zala questioned. "Are you going to hang back too?"

For the first time he looked up, but not at Mantu or Zala. His nose turned to the barrels ahead of him.

Clearing his nose, he said, "I mean... it like what Mantu say."

"Fine, then. Just sit here like cowards." Zala stormed off.

She didn't need them. Like she'd said, they had Shomari and Lishan. That pair alone was enough to take on a score of soldiers.

But after she took her initial steps away she thought back to what Mantu had said. It was true she was already unconscious when the Vaaji had boarded Mantu's ship. She didn't have a clue what they were capable of head-to-head. But, if everything happened the way she wanted it to that wouldn't matter. No matter how well prepared the enemy were, no matter what advantage they had, they were going to lose.

Zala was halfway across the room back to the ladder when a meaty hand gripped her shoulder. She turned to see Sniffs with an inquisitive wrinkle along his forehead. Clearing his throat, he said in a murmur, "I know what it feel like."

"What are you talking about?" Zala asked as she peered through the gap of his bulging bicep through his akimbo stance. Mantu looked ready to take a nap.

"Jelani. I know how you's feelin' 'bout him." Sniffs took a glance over his shoulder, his voice still low. "Back at Ajowan I weren't sure if Mantu made it out of them raids. It was torture to know if he was dead or not."

"I remember that," Zala said, reflecting back on the pair of days many of the crew had been thought to be lost to that seedy island. She recalled how Sniffs had dragged his feet, and how he had spent barely a moment away from the crow's nest until his beloved was found. She could never forget how Sniffs had beamed when he'd seen Mantu who had been a little bruised and bloody as he came hobbling out of that isle's dark jungle.

"I know Mantu and me give you a hard time," Sniffs went on. "But I get it. Mantu ain't right on this one. I'd do anything for him. Like you for Jelani."

Without warning, tears stung Zala's eyes. Out of anyone on the crew, she'd never expect it to be Sniffs who'd have such a heart. Maybe that was what Mantu was drawn to. She had just never seen it firsthand before.

"You don't have to do this for me," she said. "You can stay with Mantu. Keep him safe from Nubia's crew like he'd want."

Sniffs shook his head. "I ain't doin' it for you. I'm doin' it for your bond with your man. Somethin' like that is sacred. It's the purest gift Illopa can give us."

Zala couldn't help it then, and the first of her tears rolled free down both her cheeks. "Thank you."

Sniffs smiled before turning to the back of the room. "I'm goin' with them."

Mantu shot up from his lounged position. "Like hells you are."

"Don't worry," Zala said. "I'll keep him safe for you."

"With those scrawny little arms?"

Zala had a retort in waiting, but another voice from behind undercut it. It was one of Nubia's deckhands. "Cap'n Zala, Cap'n Nubia wants you above deck to lead your crew at portside. That flying ship is nearly halfway down. Are they ready?"

Zala looked up to Sniffs, who flung up the hand signal

for the *Titan*. She returned the gesture, a circle around her eye that said, "good looking out." The silent exchange brought a shocked grimace from Mantu's face.

Turning to the *Redtide* crew member, Zala nodded. "Let's get us a sky ship."

CHAPTER 33
KARIM

THE *VIPER* WAS FINALLY APPROACHING THE FIRST OF THE natural clouds when Ahmad came back down with his report.

"I instructed the helm as you said, sir." He nodded to Karim. "We're keeping to natural winds. Priestess Fahyad tried to order us to stay the course, but I told her she..." he trailed off, then gulped.

"Go on..." Issa encouraged, amusement twinkling in her eye. She held no love for Dahlia Fahyad either.

"I told her she's not the acting captain and she got... heated with me. I believe she said something about me knowing 'Shati'ala's rage.'"

Issa shook her head. "Don't worry about her. She gives al-Qiba a bad name all on her own."

"What's this about the priestess?" Hajjar called from one of the cannon platforms. "Oh come on, Ahmad. You have to know by this point she's all bark."

"She reminds me of my mother," he said, paling.

Hajjar chuckled. "Remind me to skip your dinner parties back home, will you?"

Karim didn't share in their little side conversation or humor, his eyes never wavering from the still unidentified ship on the horizon. "Ahmad, pass me that spyglass again."

When he felt the cool metal on his hands he lifted the instrument to his eye to confirm that the ship had yet to cross the horizon line ahead.

"What's wrong?" Issa asked at his side.

Karim hummed under his teeth. "How long would you say it would take for a ship like that to edge over the horizon?"

Issa shrugged. "A half-hour, maybe a little more. The winds are low right now, so it could take a while."

Something nagged at the back of Karim's mind as he continued to watch the ship. For the life of him it looked like the vessel on the water had decided to match speeds with the Viper.

He shared a curious look with Issa.

"Do you think they saw us, then?" Ahmad suggested, peering over Karim's shoulder.

"Perhaps, but—" Karim came up short as he felt ocean mist dotting his lips. How was that possible? They were at least half a league in the sky, so how could ocean air be touching at his mouth and between the scar that ran through it?

He turned to Issa as he wiped moisture from his mouth. "Do you feel that?"

Issa copied his gesture and dew came away from her chin. She looked to her hands in question. "Salt water. Cloud mist is far more fresh."

Karim's heart jolted as revelation dawned on him, and

his voice came cold and chilling. "We're not in the air anymore."

"What?" Issa asked, uncertainty in her worried eyes.

Karim raised the telescope once more to watch the ship on the horizon. Now that he was looking for it, something did look off. The flag should have been flapping from east to west—instead, it drifted north to south.

Karim whipped his head around from where the three of them stood at the stern and down toward the bow. What he saw made his stomach lurch.

"Gunner, behind you!" he shouted.

But it was too late. Before the officer could even react, a sword drove through his back and out his chest. When his corpse dropped, Karim could see a half-dozen pirates climbing up the longboat davits, seemingly stepping into being from thin air.

"An illusion well?" Issa suggested as she drew her sword from her scabbard, already rushing forward to meet the pirates.

"They *did* see us," Karim seethed through gritted teeth as he mimicked Issa's move, only a pace behind her. "Battle stations! Protect the bridge! Protect the bridge!" Karim rushed over to the communication tube near the middle of the platform as Ahmad pushed forward with buckler and saber. "Al-Kindi, use glass at full," he bellowed. "We need to get in the air."

"Sir, it's our last reserves," came the man's muffled voice in return.

"We're being boarded. Use it at full thrust to the sky. Do it now!"

Karim turned just as the airship jostled underfoot. And as they moved up, the illusion well that had been cast around them fell away. Right along the portside, the very ship they had expected to see cresting the horizon was riding the steady waves alongside them, cannons bared like the fangs of some great water demon.

The *Viper* ascended quickly. As they rose, Karim could see the ruby red writing of *Redtide* along the enemy ship's hull. His heart leapt into his mouth when he caught sight of dozens of pirates attempting to board. The airship pulled up farther and farther into the sky and a few of the climbing pirates fell back in the ocean or onto their ship's deck. Those already on board at the far end of the bow were making short work of gunners who were fatally slow to react.

Hajjar ran ahead of Karim and stood his ground by the deck ladder, throwing up an ice wall to halt the pirates' progress on the platform. Just as soon as the wall rose, however, it rapidly began to melt.

"Damnit," Karim cursed. "They have elementals."

Karim pressed forward, but Issa caught him at the shoulder. "What are you doing?"

"Helping the others!"

"You need to secure the bridge." Issa turned her head down the platform and cupped her hand over her mouth. "Hajjar, climb!"

"But the others will have no chance!" Karim said.

"They're trained for this. They know how to make a tactical retreat. Come on. We don't have the time. You too, Ahmad, move it, move it. Don't be a hero."

Issa pulled Karim behind her by the wrist, running to join Hajjar at the ladder to the upper decks.

"Climb, el-Sayyed, you stubborn ass!" Issa said. "We've got to go."

Karim looked to the carnage on the platform as the last of the ice wall melted away. How had this happened? And what were they going to do to stop it?

His moment of hesitation was met with a slap to the back of the head, and Issa shoved him against the ladder sharply. He darted up as fast as he could, clearing the top and pushing into the tight corridor above. Issa soon joined him, and as she unlatched the ladder door from the wall catch at their side, Karim reached down to Ahmad.

But just as he grabbed the young man's wrist, the tight grip that took hold of his own went immediately limp. Karim watched in horror as a spear tip skewered the man's throat clean through. A geyser of blood poured from his mouth.

The officer was dead before he fell.

Issa pulled Karim back and slammed the hatch door down with a bang. Hajjar, not missing a beat, shot his hand down, frost expelling from his fingertips like a miniature snowstorm. The edges of the hatch froze over in an instant.

"That should give us enough time to get to the bridge at least," he said, wiping sweat from his brow.

Karim stood shocked for a moment. He fought to drive out the image of Ahmad being run through, but he wasn't winning.

There'll be time for mourning later, he tried to convince himself.

"Good," he answered Hajjar, trying his best not to let his voice crack. "Officer Akif and I will head there now. I want you back in the engine room to protect al-Kindi, you hear me?"

Hajjar snapped a salute at his chest with a quick "right away, sir" before turning on his heel and sprinting down the corridor.

As the mystic hustled away, a door swung inward to reveal the head of a frightened Steward Bitar. "Can we please have a proper guard take my place?"

"Not now," Karim said. "We need them protecting the bridge and the engine room."

"Is it not over yet?"

"Not quite," came Issa's answer. "Stay in the brig and keep it locked down."

Bitar saluted sheepishly and ducked back into the doorway. Karim and Issa headed off in the opposite direction, and as they dashed around the tight corners of the ship, Issa asked the obvious question to Karim. "How did they—"

"I've no idea," he replied. "Let's just secure the bridge and figure out the how of it all later."

CHAPTER 34
ZALA

"JUMP, JUMP!" ZALA HEARD FROM BEHIND AS SHE CLUNG to the side of the sky ship's railings. She hadn't expected it to take flight again so quickly.

"Jump, you damn fool. Get up here!" the baritone voice came again.

Zala threw her chin over her shoulder to see Sniffs with an outstretched hand. Mere feet below, Mantu was moving to leap from the *Redtide* to the quickly ascending sky ship. Zala was surprised to see him on the deck at all after their previous conversation. But she was none too shocked to see his feet hesitating on the deck. And the longer he took to think, the more impossible his odds became.

Zala saw his fall before he even leapt. In truth, it was a fair jump. The man got nearly four paces high in the air, and he *did* manage to hook a finger against the bottom of the sky ship's undercarriage. But he couldn't hold on long enough for Sniffs to grab him, and he slipped, falling into the ocean with a splash.

Sniffs bent his knees, ready to jump back down. But

they were too high now as he, like Mantu, took his time to think on it.

"Don't you dare, Sniffs," Zala shouted from the side. "A jump from this height might not kill you, but it'll hurt real bad. I've seen how you dive. Climb up. We'll get him after we take the ship."

Sniffs gave her a nod and scaled the side. Zala followed suit, edging over the railing behind Fon and Shomari. Ahead, Iokaja and a second elemental, one of the twins, were working their way through an ice wall blocking their path. A trio of Vaaji corpses laid lifeless feet from Zala.

"*Climb, el-Sayyed, you stubborn ass!*" she heard a woman shout in High Vaaji from somewhere ahead. "*We've got to go.*"

Through the faint reflection of the ice wall turning into slush, Zala could see three figures: one on a central ladder, the other at its foot, and a Vaaji officer with a saber and small shield in defense of them both. When the last of the crystals diminished, Lishan was the first forward. The young Vaaji officer had turned his back to them as the ice wall came down, making a move to climb the ladder. He only got three rungs up before Lishan's spear drove through his neck in a shower of blood.

Was this the elite force Mantu had spoken of? This was going to be too easy. Granted, the plan hadn't started off as perfectly as Zala would have liked it to. She hadn't expected the Vaaji to lift their sky ship so suddenly, but just as she thought, the Vaaji hadn't—at least up to this point— suspected they were being pulled down at all.

The ship was as good as theirs.

Just a few moments more and Zala would be back with Jelani. Anticipation welled in her stomach as she thought of his deep brown eyes and the touch of his fingertips, no matter how jagged and ruined they were now. She already had a few ideas where the Vaaji might keep their prisoners, now that she had a measure of the ship's design.

I'm coming, I'm here.

Zala took a quick headcount of the crew who had made it aboard. There were a little under two dozen of them: the two aziza, Shomari, Sniffs, Ekko, Lishan, Captain Nubia, and a handful of other members of the *Tide* she hadn't yet learned the names of.

Seeing that their numbers weren't as large as she first assumed, reality set in for Zala, and she wondered if they could pull it off with so few of them.

Despite the slight stumble at the start, the rest of the crew were in good spirits. They slapped each other's backs in jubilation, making comments of how easy it was to secure the ship's undercarriage, and how the handful of Vaaji they'd fought seemed green at best.

The platform was nothing like anything Zala had seen before, a thin line of metal grating intersecting with even smaller platforms that jutted out from the center. At either end, longboats hung from davits. Some platforms led to mini-cannons on loose swivel-heads instead of fixed points like regular ones. Others led to nothing but a semi-circle guardrail big enough for two. That must've been where the elementals stood, the same ones who had hurled fireballs that first time the pirates and Vaaji met.

Peering over one of these platform railings, Ekko gulped. "Did I ever mention I was afraid of heights?" He turned with a bright smile, seemingly expecting someone to be there to share in his light chuckling, but there was no one at his side. He jerked his head from left to right, then back down to the *Redtide*, which was quickly receding farther and farther below. His eyes were dower. "Damn. Marjani didn't make it on..."

"Mantu neither," Sniffs said as he collapsed onto the platform with a heavy thud.

"It's okay," Zala assured them both. "We'll pick them both up once we make this thing ours. Keep your heads."

"This shit is iced pretty good," Iokaja voiced from the foot of the ladder as she stuck her hand against the hatch leading above. "At least one of these dikala is half-decent at their job."

Nubia lifted her chin, her usual flat expression etched on her face devoid of excitement and discouragement both.

Business as usual, Zala mused.

"Can you blast through the hatch?" Nubia asked.

Iokaja gave her a short nod. "Yes, ma'am. Just gonna be a moment is all. The dikala used some concentrated magic. Brilliant use of his a'bara, really. But he's only buying time."

"We should have the aziza secure the weather deck before we get up there," Lishan suggested to her captain as she wiped blood from her spear tip.

Nubia nodded. "Agreed. Anya, give Fon your crossbow. Iokaja, switch out with Sura."

A mousy girl no more than sixteen handed her weapon to Fon. The aziza turned the crossbow in her hand comfortably.

"Oh, it's been too long since I've had one of these," Fon said.

Iokaja got off the ladder in trade with the second elemental on the boarding crew. The robust woman named Sura put her hand to the frost above and started heating it with the tips of her fingers. Her twin sister must've not made it on board either.

Two elementals, an illusionist, a woman with short-sight, and the greatest pakka swordsman I know. That should be plenty, Zala tried to reassure herself.

As shavings of the wood came down around Sura's hands, the two aziza met at the platform's center. They gave each other curt nods, then flew, Fon to portside, Iokaja to starboard. A few moments later a pair of Vaaji archers came hurtling down the sides of the sky ship and straight below into the clouds beneath them all. Their screams seemed to go on forever.

"The future mother of my children, ladies and gentlemen," Shomari purred.

Oh, right, and two aziza. We're good.

Nubia turned to the limited crew as her elemental continued to work above. "Once that hatch is open, we want control of the helm. We need to get to their weather deck as fast as possible. Once we have the bridge secure, we can get this thing directed back to the sea, where the rest of the crew can board. That's priority number one, people. Captain Zala, I'll take Lishan, Duma, and this half of the crew here up to the top." She gestured to the group pressed against each other on the left side of the platform. "You'll take your pakka, Ekko, and the rest." She held an open hand to the group on the right. "*You* make sure to secure belowdecks for any stragglers. Keep those Vaaji off our backs. Agreed?"

"Agreed." Zala nodded as the hatch fell away between Sura's heated hands.

"Then let's go already, before they pin us down here!" Sura said, pulling herself up through the hatchway and into the ship.

Nubia lifted her sword overhead and was second up the ladder. "You heard her, Rovers. Let's move!"

A coolness came to Zala's middle. She thought it was the wind at first, but the clouds were surprisingly calm even this high in the sky. She would have sworn she heard a whisper atop the air currents, a song that drifted to her ears with the voice of…

She gasped and her hand flew to her belt strap as pirate after pirate rushed past her to make their way up the ladder. She fumbled with the sack tied to her waist sash. The object there slipped in her fingers twice. Then her fidgeting hands, finally, settled enough to clutch the songstone secured there. It glowed bright and orange in her hand.

The voice that came from it was unmistakable.

CHAPTER 35
JELANI

THE SCREAMS COULD BELONG TO NO ELSE, NO OTHER group. Pirates were on board. By the Great Mother and Her oceans, pirates were on board.

"Help! I'm in here!" Jelani bellowed as he shifted against his restraints. He tugged against the chains holding him to the wall of his too-small room, but there was no give.

It was one thing to stay calm and composed when he had no hope of rescue, but having the potential for a real chance at escape so close at hand was another thing entirely. He wasn't just going to sit idly and pass it up.

Jelani stared hungrily at the door across from him, merely a pair of paces away—less than that. Kicking out his foot, he could *just* make contact, but not nearly enough to crack or break it. If he could just use his stoned hand to smash against the door, maybe he could get out.

After that bald commander—or admiral, or whoever he was—had broken up the impromptu interrogation a few days back, Jelani had been separated from the others in the brig. His room wasn't much of an upgrade though, just as cramped as his cell even if it *did* come with a proper cot and pillow.

After his dozenth heave and tug, his chains ringing like tambourines, he stopped and asked himself the question: what kind of pirates did he know that rode the sky? Only a week ago the idea of a sky ship—airship, as the Vaaji called it—was complete fantasy to him. There was no way there were already others... Then, an idea struck him.

He touched his ear to the floorboard beneath him and reached out with the a'bara he so often used when he spoke to the sea. The sounds of battle had stopped, replaced by a crew speaking to one another. A crew making a plan. The voices came unclear—tones instead of distinct words. But one voice made his heart stop. A woman's voice.

He pressed his ear into the ground until he couldn't push any farther. He needed to hear the voice again. He needed to be sure.

Then it came once more. It might have been muffled and faint, but there was no denying it... It was Zala. He'd recognize that fiery tone anywhere, one that could burn through wood and stone alike.

Gods... he thought with a gasp.

She was alive; she was trying to rescue him. No one else would ever be so foolhardy as to try and take down this airship a second time. That was his Zala though, through and through. He almost didn't recognize the smile crawling across his lips.

He twisted his head to and fro. He had no idea where exactly he was on the ship, or how to even make his presence known. His eyes fell upon the oak cup and bowl his captors had given him only hours before. He kicked it and it clattered against the wall. Even if someone was listening for it, it wouldn't have turned a single head.

Letting out a heavy sigh and rolling his eyes at himself in frustration, he turned back to the door and shouted again. Louder. It was probably just as pointless, but what else could he do? He didn't know where in the ship he was, and without pressing his ear to the ground and using his mystic ability for tones, he couldn't hear much of anything either.

Why did the battle stop? Jelani thought. *Ugara, give me a sign.*

Perhaps he was speaking to the wrong God. He couldn't decide which one could help him now. Not here. Not while he was stuck in the sky with no way to speak to the sea.

The sea and sky... that's it!

Jelani pounded his chained fist into his forehead as his mind shot back to the one item Zala never parted with, the one connection he still had with her. How could he be so dim? How could he forget after all this time that he could communicate with her, even if it was only with a single song.

Without another thought, Jelani closed his eyes and began to sing the hymn he knew would reach the songstone he'd given Zala:

> *Everywhere that I be, everything that I see*
> *Your spirit's surrounding me, like Mother's*
> > *undying sea*
> *Anywhere that I fly, anywhere way up high*
> *I feel your uplifting cry, like Father's immortal sky*
> *Take me away and I'll fall in the Mother's Grace*
> *Father will be protecting me, with your energy*
> *You always stay like the clouds and the waves,*
> > *so blue*
> *By sea and by sky I will stay with you, always be*
> > *near to you*

As the last of his song slipped from his lips he stayed quiet, listening...

There was nothing. Nothing at all. The fighting must have met an impasse, or else somebody had won. Whether the victors were his captors or saviors, he couldn't be sure.

All he could do now was wait.

CHAPTER 36
ZALA

ZALA PRESSED THE SONGSTONE TO HER EAR. THOUGH THE voice in it came light and jagged, perhaps from the stone's disuse or Jelani's cracked and dry voice, its owner was clear.

"Zala, the enemy are up here, not down there," came Shomari's voice from the hatchway above.

He held out a furry, padded hand to her. She took it and lifted herself up into the tight corridor with the pakka's help. Though narrow to the point of cramped, it was one of the most beautiful pieces of architecture Zala had ever seen. The hall was made of fine oak and polished to a gleaming finish. Each stretch of wall was covered in elegant flags and tapestries, all the deep, rich of Vaaji colors with their star-and-sword symbol at each decoration's center.

Had she not known this to be a military vessel she would have thought it some noble's personal leisure skiff.

"Captain Nubia's unit is already off." Shomari gestured to the far hall that curved up into a ladderway. "Shall we take the other side?"

"No," Zala answered, perhaps a bit too quickly. "We need to make our way to the brig. It's got to be on this deck somewhere."

One of the crew members Nubia assigned to Zala spoke up. "But the captain said we need to watch their backs for stragglers."

Zala was already geared for her answer, her half-truth. "And we're gonna need all the support we can get. If it takes your captain too long to control the helm and get it back down to the *Redtide*, we'll need the prisoners' aid. The brig will have our crew there." She turned to Shomari. "Right?"

The pakka shrugged. "Perhaps. I was a fair bit away when the Vaaji boarded so I'm not sure how many they took. But I do know they captured more than just Jelani."

That was enough for Zala. "Everyone, let's spread out," she ordered. "The faster we find their brig, the faster Nubia gets *proper* support." The words came out of her mouth so fast that even she believed they were the truth. "You lot here, take that corridor to the left. Ekko, you and those behind you, to the right. Shomari, on me."

"And where do we meet when we've completed our search?" Ekko asked, already turned toward his assigned corner.

"Right here at the hatchway," Zala said. "Don't be longer than a few minutes."

"Aye, aye," he said with a salute and trotted off with his band of pirates.

Zala clutched at Shomari's wrist and pulled him to the nearest door. Her voice came low. "Can you get this door open for me?"

"You think it leads to the brig?"

"Yes."

"Then why didn't you keep the others around?"

"We don't have time for questions—from *them*, I mean," she added quickly, not wanting to give the wrong impression to her pakka friend.

Shomari shrugged and dropped to one knee while pulling out a set of pins from his belt. It took less than a dozen heartbeats for him to get the door open.

As the wood pushed inward it revealed a tight entranceway with two small desks set at either side of a door. And pressed against the door was a cowering soldier who held his saber close to his chest. The steel rattled against the metal fastenings of his armor so rapidly it sounded almost like music.

Zala held out a friendly hand. "I'm not here to hurt you, Vaaji. I just need your keys. Give them to me." Before Zala could end her last word, the officer was already throwing down both key and saber.

"'Scholars and poets' to the last, it seems," Shomari purred out the side of his mouth.

Zala would have smiled at the cat's comment, but her focus was only for the keys. She kicked the officer's sword aside and away, then grabbed the ring of keys on the floor. When she moved forward to the door, the young Vaaji flinched.

Zala scoffed. "I told you I wasn't going to hurt you. Step away from the door and—"

She lifted her hand as the young man jolted to the right. At first she feared a surprise attack, but he was diving for cover behind the desk—and he caught his hand on its edge. It sounded like he might have broken his wrist bone.

"Oh, my word. I meant what I said, kijana!" Zala sighed while the young man moaned on the floor. She moved round the desk and picked up the keys at his feet, nodding to Shomari. "Watch him, will you?"

"Will he be wanting a hug?"

Giving the pakka a half-smirk, Zala drove the first set of keys into the brig's door. Her heart was in her throat. Jelani was just behind this door; she would be with him soon. Had she not been caught up so intently by the thought of finally embracing him once again, of hearing his voice in the flesh, she would have already asked the obvious question. "Uh, which key is it?"

"Silver one," the officer said. "Shape of a roc holding a *grootslang*."

"The hells is a grootslang?" Shomari asked.

"Giant half elephant, half monstrous water snake," Zala explained.

"Ah, I see why you'd shorten that," Shomari said. "You hairless think of everything." He put an arm around the whimpering officer. "And I like this one. If only everyone we met could be as helpful as he is. What's your name, Vaaji?"

"B-Bitar, sir. Steward Bitar."

"And he calls me sir! Oh, Zala, can I keep him?" Shomari batted his nonexistent lashes Zala's way—probably not entirely joking.

Again Zala ignored the pair as she found the key described, then pressed it quickly into its slot. The door creaked open and a set of barred holdings revealed themselves. The room smelled of trapped sweat and what Zala hoped wasn't blood. It was dark, lit only by a single lantern at its end, which flickered shadowy edges of the bars along the walls.

"Jelani," she said into the darkness. "Jelani? It's Zala."

A few figures stirred, some coming to grab at their bars. "Zala? Zala from the *Titan*?"

She recognized that drone of a voice. "Rishaad? Is that you?"

"A-am I dreamin'?"

"No, you're not." Zala rushed to his cell to get a better look at him. The boy was bruised, each of the black and blue welts about his brow and cheeks lined by dried blood and healing wounds. "Where's Jelani?"

"H-he... I don't know."

"Was he here? Is he on this ship?"

"Y-yes. They had him." Zala gave him a look. "They *have* him."

She pressed her nose between the bars. "Where, Rishaad? Where?"

"They moved him somewhere else. I ain't knowin' where."

Zala clutched the bars so harshly she nearly made her palm bleed. Seething, she ripped her hands away—a bit of skin coming loose against the rough bar—and stomped back into the entranceway.

"Get the other prisoners out." She flung the keys to Shomari, who caught them effortlessly with a single finger. "I've got to find Jelani."

"What about the others? We're supposed to meet them at the hatch."

"I won't be long, trust me."

The cat gave her a look. "And if you are?"

She halted. "Then lead them. Clear out any stragglers like Nubia said. You're our best fighter—yes, including Lishan."

"If something goes wrong and I'm stuck having to come up with a new plan, I'm holding *you* responsible. The Gods didn't bless me with brawn *and* brains."

"Look at him." Zala pointed to the steward at his feet. He was paler than the clouds themselves. "If this is all the Vaaji have, you'll be fine."

Shomari gave Zala an apprehensive salute as she shuf-fled passed the pair and into the corridor. With a light hum he said, "Aye, aye, Cap'n."

CHAPTER 37
KARIM

When Karim ordered the securing of the bridge, he hadn't expected half the ship to come huddling into the room. The space was meant to hold a dozen at *most*, not the near score lining its edges.

Everyone was working on top of each other, and Karim barely had the space to breathe between orders. There was nowhere else to go though, nowhere that didn't have pirates closing in.

The bastards would be on them any minute.

"They've breached the weather deck!" came one cry from somewhere on his left.

"We've pirates pounding at the engine room's first-level door!" came another to the right.

"What in Shati's name is that?" came the last from—who knew where.

Karim twisted to the viewport, where a pirate hung from above. She was dipping her head low outside the glass. Her voice came muffled as she shouted, "Captain, their helm's right here! They've got the bloody helm at the bow of the—"

The elemental mystic on the bridge, Damji, shot his hand out, and a sudden torrent of air blasted the pirate off the glass and into the clouds. The woman didn't even have time to scream. Damji might not have been as powerful as his comrade Hajjar, but he had "one hell of a right whoosh," as Issa had taken to calling it.

"Good shot, Damji," Karim said as the flags by the wall at the elemental's side fell still once more behind him. "Keep them off our backs."

"Aye, sir, I'll put some fear in their hearts!"

As his younger officer said it, an idea sprung to Karim's mind. "In fact, Damji, let's have you over here. Come. Right here next to the helm with me. Kill any pirate that dares to come close. And you two." He turned to the other pair of elementals at the back of the bridge, who were pressed between a bowman and Ifran the cook. "Go with your sindisi, take port and starboard. If any more try to come down the sides, you end them."

They saluted in unison and answered with a sharp, "Aye, aye, Captain."

Issa's murmur came to his ear. "You thinking of trapping them on the weather deck?"

"I am," was his answer.

"What about the stern of the ship? Malouf's balcony is pretty exposed."

Karim snapped his fingers and directed his voice to communications. "Message down to the engine room. Have Hajjar move up to the captain's quarters instead. Sindisi Abbas can hold the room."

"On it, sir," came Officer Tahan's answer. Even among the dense crowd her voice carried over them all.

"And we'll need to chain the hatch to the upper deck. Once they realize we're pinning them in, they'll try and climb back down. You, Officer." He pointed to one of the juniors he knew to be a fair swordsman. "Take a pair of your best and make it happen."

"Right away, sir." The man sped off, tapping two at the shoulder to come along.

"I will go with them," Shamoun said as he unsheathed the saber from his belt and followed along.

Karim shook his head. "Sir, you should stay on the bridge where it's safe. You've only just recovered from your injuries yesterday."

"Yes, and I recovered to be of some use, not simply stand here and watch," the elder grunted.

Karim knew better than to argue with the vice admiral, especially now in the heat of battle. Without a word, he nodded in affirmation—not that Shamoun was looking for permission. The old man was already halfway out the door.

Each time a new group set out, Dahlia Fahyad opened the bridge door and closed it straight away. She clutched a set of beads in her hand and whispered into them, and a light shimmer seemed to envelop the door to seal it shut. Her shoddy religious advice aside, she was a fair enchantress. Karim never would have thought they'd be making use of her skills like this, though.

In short order, the room was back to its intended capacity, at least for now. When Karim gave his next order, he could actually see his communications officer. "Tahan, get me a report on the engine room."

"Calling now, sir."

"We've got enough air between us and that bastard ship now. Ask Al-Kindi how long it'll take if we keep at full speed back to the capital."

348

Tahan made her message, and a short moment later her answer came. "He says we'll be back in half a day at capacity, sir."

Not nearly fast enough.

Garnering any support from the port city was out of the question. They were alone in the skies.

"He says if we keep at current levels," Tahan continued, "he can't promise the engine will hold together under the stress—or the *Viper* herself, for that matter."

"We've no choice but to clear the ship, then, officer-to-pirate. Send out new orders to whoever's still able to engage. We can't hide out anymore." It had been Karim's plan to keep as many of his crew safe as possible. But now with the pirates seeming like they had an upper hand, he couldn't afford potentially losing the ship. The admiralty would never have it. And neither would he. Not on his watch.

Just then, a new message came through loud enough for all to hear. "Supply room to bridge! Supply room to bridge!"

Almost everyone turned their heads to the call, waiting for the follow up.

It didn't come.

After a long—painfully long—moment, a quiet rasp came from the pipe. Karim looked to Officer Tahan for clarification.

"Sea speaker, sir." The officer frowned deeply. The bridge was dead quiet. No one moved as they waited for Tahan's next response. "That's all I got."

Karim's throat went dry, his mind racing. He looked to Issa, who stood with one hand on the helm. The worry was plain on her face. They both knew what this meant. The pirates weren't just here to take the ship—they might not have even cared for it at all. They wanted to steal the pirate from them, the one Karim now knew was the key to it all.

Well, if they wanted him, he wasn't going to make it easy. A sliver of fear sat in his heart though. Did they already have him? How much of the crew quarters had they cleared already? And what of the brig? His thoughts flashed to Steward Bitar.

Shit…

He twisted back to Tahan. "Do we have a count of how many pirates made it on board?"

"There's been so many different reports," she replied. Her voice was on the edge of quivering, but she steadied it under her professional front. "It could be as little as a dozen, and no more than two, if I guess it right. I really can't be sure, sir, with so many incoming—"

Karim leaned in close, holding her shoulder firm. "Can I trust the bridge to you? Damji will keep the pirates away, and it'll take a long while for even the *Redtide's* crew to get through the priestess' enchantments."

"Of course, sir." Her voice very nearly cracked this time. Then she straightened up, her voice coming more firm. "Yes, sir. I will."

"Good, good," Karim said, then he turned his head to the rest of the bridge. There were only nine remaining now. "I will join Shamoun in clearing out the corridors of these scum. Tahan will have the bridge while I am away."

"Aye, Cap'n," came the chorus of voices.

"And I'm coming with you," Issa said. Karim didn't give her any push back at all.

As the pair of them moved to the bridge door, Fahyad gave him the first nod of respect he'd ever received from the woman. "Clean our ship of this filth, el-Sayyed."

"I will, Priestess."

The door opened to the cacophony of metal on metal, grunts and heaves echoing down the tight halls. With a deep breath, Karim drew his saber — Issa his mirror at his side — and they set out down the narrow paths before them.

Jogging, Karim spoke over his shoulder. "We'll need to move that pirate somewhere more secure. The brig is likely compromised. I wouldn't be surprised if the captives have already made it out and joined the boarders."

"So where can we take him? Back to the bridge?"

Karim shook his head. "We won't be able to double back in time, not in all this. They'll cut us off. We'll need somewhere else — " He faltered. The answer was obvious. "Malouf's quarters. Hajjar is already on his way there. And that damned door of his could halt a siege. We can't let them have that pirate, Issa — not at any cost."

As they rounded their second corner they were met with their first obstacle: a pair of pirates, one pulling out a long knife while the other withdrew an axe from the chest of one of Issa's own. The gunnery officer fell back lifeless and the pirates rose to their feet, just beside the ladderway leading down to the supply deck.

Karim's military training sprung forth faster than his thoughts could, and he charged forward without realizing what he was doing. He had hoped to take the bastards unprepared, but the first pirate was no green deckhand. The lean woman was ready, giving parry and pushing Karim's saber harmlessly aside. A sweeping sidestep and an upturn of his saber blocked the second pirate. Karim had barely raised his weapon in time to defend the attack. The tip of his saber caught the the wall, slicing wood.

The space was too narrow, *dangerously* too narrow.

Any time Karim tried a swing or slash he hit the ceiling or the walls, and his speed suffered for it. When he switched to thrusts, the only attack viable to him, he became far too predictable. Issa tried her best to support him with short thrusts from her daggers, but the two of them just got in each other's way. They had never fought together like this. There was no training regime that prepared them for a bout amidst such tight confines.

The pirates, however, were clearly used to cramped spaces—fighting in alleys or amid smaller ships was their bread and butter.

Before long, a kick from the first pirate sent Karim's saber flying to the ground. The second pirate followed the side kick with a frontward one, sinking her boot deep into Karim's abdomen.

Karim fell back quick and hard with a thud that rocked the corridor floor. All the wind was knocked out of him; he was helpless, a guppy ready to be swallowed whole by two vicious predators.

Issa sprang ahead, and her red under-tunic flared. Her push forward was only a feint though, a bait for the first pirate to thrust for and stumble forward off balance. Issa checked the pirate's wrist and blade with her own dagger, holding both firm as she came overhead with her second weapon.

The dagger cleaved. Blood splattered.

Issa's blade was lodged firmly in the top of the first pirate's head.

She tried to pull the blade free, but it wouldn't budge. Fear sliced through Karim, he couldn't get up, his chest too tight, the pain too much.

The second pirate cried out and raised her axe above her head. Issa let go of the unmoving dagger and let the corpse drop to her side. But she left herself open. The second pirate's axe came arcing downward fast. Karim threw out his leg and caught her at the knee. She buckled. To Issa's credit, she didn't miss a beat, dodging to one side and throwing her dagger out in one motion.

It landed straight into the second pirate's shoulder, and she fell back. More blood painted the walls.

"You son of a bitch!" the pirate cried out, struggling next to her dead comrade.

"Daughter," Issa corrected the pirate as she took up Karim's fallen saber and finished the job.

Retrieving her dagger from the pirate's shoulder, Issa spun her weapon in hand and said, "You might be a better swordsman than me, el-Sayyed." She stuck out her hand. "But you chose the wrong weapon for the job. Again."

"So did you," Karim huffed painfully. "You should have... used that first pirate as... a body shield. You left yourself open... but thanks," Karim grunted as she lifted him up. It felt like his chest had caved in. More than his ego would be bruised come next morning—provided they lived that long.

"Can I borrow that?" He gestured down to the dagger protruding from the first pirate's head.

"Please do," Issa said. "Where's your janbiya?"

Karim tugged the dagger free and wiped it on his tunic. "Left it in my room. Like a fool, I didn't think I'd be needing it..."

"Come on." Issa trotted over the corpses. "Our pirate's just around the corner."

A short walk and over three bodies later—one pirate and two of their own—they found themselves at their prisoner's special quarters. Karim jostled for his keys and set the right one to the hole. The door swung open and, by Shati'ala's Will, the pirate was still there. Shackled to the

353

back of the room, Jelani almost looked as though he was expecting someone else.

"What?" Karim dipped his head. "Not the face you thought you'd see?"

Jelani didn't respond, his lips pressed flat together per the usual. Karim nodded to Issa and she stepped into the room, giving the threshold a swift kiss as she passed. She grabbed the bag that hung near the door and threw it over the pirate's head.

"I told my captain this space might've been too small for a man your size," she said, leaning in close to the bag. "So we thought we should relocate you somewhere with a bit more leg room." She took up his chains and dragged him along.

Karim followed behind, keeping the pirate between himself and Issa as they made their way to the upper deck and Malouf's quarters. The corridors stunk of musty sweat mixed with the coppery tinge of blood. Down by the corner, Karim could hear a new fight breaking out, a cry and grunt rebounding off the walls. They didn't have time to check which group held the advantage. Now that they had the pirate in hand, they needed to secure him above all else. Then, and only then, would they give their support.

And Karim was keen to give it.

After climbing the final stairs and into the last hall leading to Malouf's grand double-doors, Karim finally let go of the tightness in his throat. He pounded on the door and bellowed, "Captain Malouf! Open up. It's Chief Officer el-Sayyed." He was surprised how much he hated the sound of his old moniker. He had outgrown it in the past few days. "It's me and Officer Akif."

"Hah! You think me a fool?" came the man's shrill voice.

"You failed at the balcony, so you thought you'd try the front door instead?"

"What? Sir, it's me!"

"Perhaps. With a pirate's knife at your back, no doubt! I swear, if you try coming in here, I've got a crossbow bolt with your name on it." Karim heard a strain in the man's voice like he was on the losing end of a pulled drawstring. A light chuckle came from under the bag. Karim gave Jelani a sharp smack across the stomach, then shook his aching fingers. He'd forgotten the stone was on the man's abdomen as well.

Another voice from within came then. "Sir, it's really them. We should open the door."

"No, you fool of a child. They'll slit our throats."

"Put that away, will you?" Karim could tell now this was Hajjar's voice. "You're gonna hurt yourself, sir."

Issa stepped forward and pressed her lips against the door to say, "Captain, you've Hajjar in there with you, don't you?"

"H-how would you know that? W-who's voice is that?" Malouf questioned in a stammer.

"It's Gunner Chief Akif. And I know because I was there on the bridge when el-Sayyed gave the order for Hajjar to come support you. Please, you have to let us in."

A short pause came, though Karim would have thought it a lifetime. He expected to hear the turning of a key and the creaking of a door opening. Instead, he was met with a sharp and piercing, "Trick! It's a trick! Step away or I'll have my elemental here fry you with a hellstorm."

Karim groaned and pounded on the door once more. "We have to secure the sea speaker. We have the damned pirate with us right now. Open. This. Door." He waited a moment. "That's an order!"

"You can't order me, el-Sayyed. I am able-bodied. I take back claim of the *Viper*."

"On Shati'ala," Karim spat. "I swear I will—"

"Don't move, Vaaji!" a female voice came from behind. "You've nowhere to run."

Karim and Issa shared in a grunt as they spun on their heels, weapons raised for the fight. Yet the hall was empty, save for the patterned red-and-black rug and the tapestries along the wall.

There was no one there.

CHAPTER 38
ZALA

ZALA TRIED TO SHOUT "DON'T YOU DARE MOVE," BUT somehow, her voice was gone. Even as the two Vaaji clutching Jelani turned to look, they didn't actually see her but... through her in a strange way.

Whatever the reason, they couldn't see or hear her, and she didn't take long to capitalize on the advantage. Even as she took two strides toward them, sword raised overhead, they still did not react. Three steps from them she brought her sword down, but then was halted by a hand at her wrist, a second around her mouth.

A trap?

Zala started to thrash against whoever held her, kicking the walls and screaming shouts that never came. "Take it easy, Captain Zala. It's hard enough keeping up this illusion as it is."

Zala settled and mouthed the name "Ekko," but still nothing came out.

"I'll give you your voice back once we get away," he

said. "That pakka of yours is plenty mad, I can tell you. Asked me to bring you back immediately."

She spoke again, tried to explain that the man with the bag over his head was her husband. It would only take a moment. If he could hear her, he'd understand.

As Ekko pulled her back, the male officer, or whoever he was, stepped forward with a cautious hand outstretched, his ear leading his light shuffle. The port windows at his sides shone bright against the old scar across his lip.

The man mouthed something, though Zala couldn't hear him; it was like there was a wall that blocked all sound between him and her. Ekko was powerful, but inelegant with his casting, it seemed. The woman next to the man had Jelani in chains. She answered something, something muffled. Zala could have sworn she heard or at least read "I heard it too" from her lips. But she couldn't be sure as Ekko forced her down the stairs and away from the love of her life.

She jostled in his grip again, but he was too strong. They rounded a corner and she bit down on his hand.

"Aw, damnit." Ekko winced. "What was that for?"

With Ekko clutching his hand and distracted, Zala bounded forward and around the corner again. As she turned the bend, however, a gust of wind threw her bodily against the wall. Her head smacked violently against wood and a knot swelled. She rubbed at it instinctively as she looked back up.

A young Vaaji officer with thick eyebrows and a mole over his lip stepped down the stairs, his hands rotating around a vortex of wind. Though muted and faint, Zala thought she could hear him speaking through Ekko's illusion.

"Corridor... clear," he said. "Don't… see any…"

That male officer joined him at his side, dagger in hand. "Illusionist... here. I know... Keep... wind... drive back... even... can't... see them."

"Captain Zala, we have to go." Ekko came to her side and pulled her away. The wind spiraling down the hall blew his thick curls back around his ears.

Zala followed him reluctantly and they turned a corner away from the howling gusts and gales. She could feel the moment her voice returned to her, like pinched fingers had let loose of her throat.

"What was the bite for?" Ekko asked as he descended a ladder to the supply deck. Judging from the clashing of steel on steel, there was a battle down there too. A vicious one.

"My husband," she croaked. Her voice still felt husky from all of the silent screams. She didn't move to follow. "That man was my husband. He was so close."

Ekko looked up to her. "How can you know? There was a bag —"

"That man, that captain, whoever! He mentioned a sea speaker." She stared down the hall, where she could still hear the wind's call. "And I'd know him anywhere. I need to go back."

"And face off against that elemental on your own?" Ekko looked between her and the path below with wide eyes. "That's suicide."

"I'm this close; I can't just give up. I promised him I never would."

"This ain't givin' up, Captain. It's survivin'."

"No." Zala took a step back in the direction they came. The mystic came around the bend though, followed by another of his comrades, the one with the scar across his lip. He still rotated his hands like before, sustaining his tiny hurricane before him. Instinctively, Zala dipped low and raised her sword.

"He can't see you. I'm still throwing the illusion that way," Ekko said from below. "Come on. Your people need you, Zala. *Your* people. Fon and that pakka are holding off the exit for us, but they can't hold it long. Your friend's already lost her wing…"

That halted her. "What?"

"Fon. She needs you."

But Jelani needed her too.

She stood there, stock still, thought rooting her to the floor. She was stuck in indecision. This was why she didn't make friends, didn't make connections. This pirate shit was supposed to be temporary, just a single moon's endeavor— two at most. She couldn't even remember when they had started now, exactly. She had told herself, promised herself never to be in the position she had fallen into now. There was just no choice when it came between husband and friend. But Fon was different; Shomari was different, even Ekko was different. They put their trust in her and now they were suffering for it.

"Zala!" Ekko snapped, tugging at her leg. "I can't hold the image for long. Let's go."

Forgive me, Jelani, she thought as she stared down the hall, where the winds picked up with stronger force, the mystic shuffling cautiously forward. His gales were just starting to tickle the tip of her nose.

She turned and nodded to Ekko, then stepped onto the ladder to follow him down. Her hands quivered as she gripped the rungs. Her decision was made, but she didn't feel any better for it.

The moment she landed in the supply room, the clash of battle grew louder. Some of the cries—most of them—were familiar to her. Shomari's pant, Fon's moan. She had heard them pushed to the brink before; and their voices were telling her they were being pushed hard.

"Just through this door, follow me," Ekko said. Zala only now saw the sweat soaking through his loose shirt sticking against his pale skin. His magic was draining him terribly.

Shouldering against the supply room door, they came out at the end of a long and narrow hall, the same they had started in when they came up from the undercarriage and platform. At the corridor's center, where Zala had told them all to meet up—stars, she didn't know how long ago—stood Shomari, Fon, Iokaja, Lishan, and Rishaad.

There was no sign of Nubia or Sniffs.

Around them lay the dead, pirates and soldiers both, so thick there were parts of the cramped hall nearly filled to the brim with bodies. The fighting pirates were pinned on both sides at the center of the hall, struggling back to back with barely enough space to defend themselves.

Zala clamped down on the worry that threatened to grip her as she wondered where Nubia, Sniffs, and the others were.

They'll be here soon, she convinced herself.

Ekko raced forward with an axe at his side. The first officer he engaged was too slow to turn, and Ekko caught him in the back with his sharp weapon. Blood came away through the exposed portion of the Vaaji's padded armor.

"I've got her!" Ekko shouted. "She's fine!"

"Good, I can be killing her myself!" came Shomari's voice through a labored thrust of his rapier. Zala knew she'd be getting an earful for leaving him alone—especially as lead.

Coming to Ekko's support, Zala drove her sword

forward into the next officer, feeling that bone and sinew through the stab that always unsettled her so. She watched as Fon tried for a one-wing flutter to avoid a blade thrust, but her awkward half-wing—barely still attached—couldn't get her over. The enemy's blade caught her on the arm, and she tumbled back against the ceiling and the far wall.

"Flutter!" Shomari called out, reaching out for her but just missing. His second cry, one of pure terror, haunted Zala. "Fon!"

Shomari sprang up and rushed along the wall, but there was far too little space for him to maneuver.

Zala saw it before it happened. One of the older and darker officers, a bald man without the usual Vaaji beard, was tracking the pakka like a hawk. Shomari only made it three steps along his wall-run before the tip of the officer's blade caught him across his ankle and he fell in a huddle of the Vaaji. Zala lost sight of him in the masses.

Not Shomari! she thought in horror as she tried to push forward, but there were simply too many bodies in the way, too many fighting officers to get through. There was nothing she could do as she watched the officers at the far end stab down where Shomari had fallen.

"Iokaja, catch!" Ekko shouted as he threw a marbled ball her way. She caught it and, in an instant, her eyes blazed white. It took Zala a moment to realize the object was Gods' Glass. No wonder Ekko had been able to hold that illusion so long and so well.

Zala took a breath and blinked as several whips of wind blew past and around her. She couldn't hear anything. Her eardrums felt compressed like she stood in the middle of a monsoon.

Lifting her head with great effort, she could see Iokaja with hands lifted toward either end of the hall. Everyone, like Zala, was pinned down within their own personal cyclones. In all there were a dozen, friend and foe, who could not move a muscle against the manifested winds.

Zala had seen mystics work with Gods' Glass before, had seen how it made their eyes glow as bright as the stars with the energy of a'bara. But this was different. Iokaja was reaching into a deep well of magic, the deepest form of her a'bara. Her eyes weren't just bright, they radiated in pulsing waves. Perhaps it was because her skin was so pale, or maybe it was the contrast of her freckles and red-stubbled hair, but her skin seemed to glow and the pattern in her wings looked to shimmer.

A God among mortals, Zala thought, the name of the object in the aziza's hand suddenly took on new meaning.

Gritting her jaw, Iokaja grunted, "Get. To. The. Fucking. Hatch."

The swirling air around Zala seemed to open to the touch, giving her a path to step out and walk free. She turned her head to Ekko, who pressed forward as well, his mouth agape, just as in awe as she was. It was one thing to hold down twelve people separately; it was entirely something else to have enough control to then free a careful few from that hold. Zala's gaze shifted to the Gods' Glass in Iokaja's hand, no more than the size of a grape. She knew all too well what would happen if the aziza used the glass to its limit.

"Go!" Iokaja groaned again.

Ekko was the first to drop down the hatchway, followed by a bloody Lishan, who shot Zala a wicked scowl as she went. Zala waited to see Rishaad lift up next at the far end, hopefully Fon or Shomari straight after.

No one moved.

Zala's heart didn't pound against her chest as she

expected it to; instead, there was nothing but an empty stomach, a dry mouth, and a numbness that made her sick. She couldn't believe it. No... she had to see for herself.

Stepping over bodies and slipping through the officers still caught in their mystical seals—one of them even reaching for Zala's shoulder in extreme slow-motion—she made her way to the other end of the hall.

"Can't. Hold. Long," Iokaja said.

Zala put a hand to the aziza's shoulder. "Can you make a path to them... please?"

The strain lining Iokaja's brow said "no," but the slight drop in her eyes told Zala the aziza would do it.

"Stand. There." The white-eyed mystic flitted a look to the hall's far end. Zala made her move and watched as bodies pushed down and away, seemingly of their own accord.

As the dead and living untangled, they revealed more crumbled bodies on the ground around pools of blood. Only one of them breathed out. Gasping, Rishaad said, "Quick, help me pull some of these bodies off. Fon and Shomari aren't moving—they can't breathe—"

Zala didn't listen to the rest of what he said. She rushed to his side, where a red cloak lay exposed to the air. It was redder than it should have been. Shomari was littered with stab wounds, and slick blood matted his black fur, fur that did not rise with the rhythm of breath. But when Zala set her hand just beneath his maw she felt gentle but staggered air brushing against her palm.

"Thank the moons," she breathed low.

She turned to the back wall where Fon had landed, but there was only one body there, a Vaaji officer whose back was raked through by claw and bite marks.

Even while stabbed to near-death, the pakka had protected her to the last.

Rishaad pulled the officer away and Fon, like Shomari, was a bloody mess. She was breathing normally, however, and despite being free of stab wounds, her eyes were unmoving in what must've been shock.

"Fon..." Zala trailed off, relief snatching away the tightness in her chest. In its place, though, it left a pulsating, nagging guilt.

A cold flash surrounded them then, a bright light that glazed the blood-stained walls with a silver hue for an instant. Zala turned to see that Iokaja had given in at last. Her eyes were back to their normal slate, and her once glowing skin was back to its normal alabaster. And, thankfully, her hands were free of stoneskin, the Gods' Glass still intact. At her back was an ice wall, not much different from the one they were met with when they had first boarded.

Iokaja fell to her knees just as Ekko climbed back up to poke his head through the hatchway. The soldiers started pounding against the ice. Each time one of them struck with the blunt end of their daggers or saber hilts, Zala could see the impressions of their fists. Then a voice called them back.

"Stand away, stand away!" it said. It sounded like the man from before—the one with the scar. "I've Hajjar and Damji here. They'll get it down."

"Well, shit," Ekko said. "What we gonna do now?"

Everyone turned to Zala. Ekko, Iokaja, Rishaad, and even Fon had cast her eyes to her captain. And though Zala probably imagined it, she could have sworn she heard a light purr beneath her.

She wracked her brain for what they could do, but she was drawing blanks. They couldn't push forward, couldn't take control of the helm as Nubia had tried to do.

And Sniffs is with Nubia... Zala thought. *Focus, Zee. Focus.*

The only way was down, but that only got them one platform lower. Where were they supposed to go from there? Any way she sliced it, they were trapped.

Zala watched as everyone looked at her, watched as the ice wall began to melt. It was like the one with the scar had read her thoughts as his muffled voice came through the ice, "It's over, pirates. It's all over."

Zala had failed them. She had brought them all here. She was the one who had gone off looking for Jelani on her own when she should have stayed with the group. But it was only a moment, one damned moment! She hadn't thought it would cost them this. It had been so easy to board, after all. How had the Vaaji turned the tides so quickly?

She sat there toiling with what she could have done better. Perhaps she should have left Shomari straight away —maybe she could have found Jelani sooner. Or perhaps she should have gone with Ekko when he grabbed her. Or maybe she shouldn't have left them alone at all. Then she could have led them like she was supposed to, secured the ship, and *then* have Jelani back in her arms.

Now, Shomari was as good as dead. Fon's wing was coming away at her shoulder. And Zala had no clue if Sniffs, Nubia, or any of the others were alive or dead. It was either give themselves up and let themselves be captured, or fling themselves over the platform below and hope the Gods she didn't care for would carry them to safety. Iokaja was the only one who could make it away with her wings; none of the rest of them could fly.

Then it hit her suddenly. "The longboats!"

Iokaja seemed to know where she was going with this. "Maybe. There's still some Gods' Glass left."

"What?" Rishaad asked at Zala's side. "What does that mean?"

"No time, help me get them up," Zala said, gesturing to Fon and Shomari. "Here, help me."

A renewed spirit had Zala's hands working fast. It took only a moment for Rishaad, Iokaja, and Ekko to help her along, though it was difficult to pull Shomari up without hurting him, and the cat howled all the while.

"What in Yem's name is taking you lot so long?" came Lishan's voice from below.

Ekko handed her Fon and said, "Help her down. We're getting out of here."

"Wha — How?" she asked incredulously.

No one answered her, too busy getting Shomari down through the hatchway. Before long, they were all through save for Zala, who watched the last of the ice wall turn from a solid block to a translucent sleet. Through it she could barely make out the man who stood on the other side: a turban atop his head, a golden cap with a jewel holding it down. She couldn't see his features though, not through the blur.

"Run all you want, pirate," he said in the Mother Tongue, sneering. "You've nowhere to go."

Zala threw up the first pirate sign she had ever learned, and it wasn't a polite one. She didn't much care if the exact message was received or not, but by the distorted curve of that scarred mouth, the officer probably got the gist.

She dropped down the hatchway, forgoing the ladder for a straight jump, and rushed to join the others climbing aboard the nearest longboat. As she pressed herself between Rishaad and Fon — who had Shomari's head in her lap, the cat opened his eyes, just a hint, and stammered out, "W-was... was it worth it... chana?"

Shame weighed against Zala's heart and she didn't answer him, instead turning to Lishan's questioning face.

"So? What's going on?" the *Redtide's* second asked skeptically. Beside her, Rishaad didn't have to say a thing. His raised eyebrows were question enough.

"We're gonna drop," Zala said, withdrawing her dagger. Iokaja did the same.

"Drop?" Rishaad coughed through his disbelief. "Drop!" He didn't seem to have the words beyond the single exclamation.

Zala ignored him. "Now, Iokaja. Hold on, everyone!"

Woman and aziza both looked to each other in shared terror.

"We sure about this?" Iokaja asked.

"No," was Zala's answer. "On my cannon count. One."

Lishan stood up. "Wait, wait, wait, you're not going to—"

Iokaja took a deep breath. "Two."

"What do I even hold on to!" came Rishaad's panicked call.

Zala's muscles tensed. "Three."

As one, they slashed their daggers through the ropes holding the longboat up. In the next instant they were hurtling down fast, faster than Zala had expected. She felt her stomach in her throat.

Iokaja flung out her arms to slow and balance their descent with the air, but her natural a'bara couldn't hold. Zala clutched against the side of the boat, watching as the ocean below came racing toward them. They were going to break against the water. And it was going to hurt. Bad.

"The glass!" Zala howled against the rushing wind. "The glass!"

"No! There's too little!" Ekko warned in a roar as Rishaad screamed at his ear.

But Iokaja didn't listen. She pulled the glass from her waistband and her eyes flared white once more. Their descent slowed, but not nearly quick enough. They might survive, but they were going to be battered and —

"Brace yourselves!" Zala bellowed just as the longboat dipped bow-first into the waves.

A splash and then a horrible splintering sound came. Zala's head snapped back as she plunged into ice-cold water. But the rush of the ocean, like always, soothed her. For a single moment, however brief, the world stood still. Her worries were gone, the pain in her heart subsided, and she was just... okay. She was alive. Even as the fragments and wreckage descended about her.

Then the ocean, in its cruel way, spat her back out and shot her up to its surface, where reality set back in. But at least now it was a reality she could cope with. Almost.

Everyone had found their own piece of wreckage: Lishan clinging to a plank, Ekko and Rishaad sharing the remains of the stern, Fon and Shomari holding onto each other — though the water around them was thick with red.

Iokaja, however, was beyond fatigue. She was slipping off the debris she clung to, and Zala saw a sight she had never wanted to see again. Laced between a single freckled hand, cracks of jagged rock were snaking along the aziza's arm, all the way from fingertip to shoulder.

Stoneskin. The blight of Gods' Glass.

And in that moment, Zala understood it, understood how her husband could have put himself in the position to contract the disease. She had heard the story, thought she had comprehended it then. But seeing it before her, a mere breaststroke away, and knowing the sacrifice Iokaja had made to give them a fighting chance, Zala couldn't help but get teary-eyed.

The aziza hadn't even needed to help. At any time she could have flown off and let them plummet to their deaths without her. The sorrow Zala felt couldn't be described in a single word. Part guilt, shame, remorse, gratitude, none of it was enough. It all rolled up into one crushing pain.

But they were alive. She clung to that. It was the only thing she could feel that didn't make her want to dip her head low in the water and never come back up again.

A horn bellowed from the side. In the distance, the *Redtide* approached, its bowsprit silhouetted against the late afternoon blue. Zala turned up her chin while shivering against the cold of the ocean. Up above and between the clouds, the sky ship drifted away.

And with it, Jelani.

CHAPTER 39
KARIM

"They should have used the gliders," Issa said at Karim's side as they watched the *Redtide* pull away to the west, where the sun had began its descent.

Karim withdrew from the railing and stomped down the platform. "They probably would have if they knew we even had them."

"Will we pursue?"

"No," he said, though the answer galled him. "The *Viper* is already hanging by a thread. We need to get back home."

Whatever the reason, whether it be clean waters or clear skies, the sunsets over the Sapphire Seas were always a beautiful and gentle tangerine bordering on bright salmon. It was far more pleasing than in al-Anim, where sunsets were dusty and drab most of the time. And just then they were graced with one of the most beautiful sunsets Karim had ever seen. Yet he cared nothing for the picture ahead of him; he loathed it, even. How could such a majestic place be ruled and controlled by vile pirates? How could such a picture show itself in light of the dead who lay among him?

As he approached the ladder leading back into the ship, he stopped at Ahmad's corpse. The blood around the young officer's neck was dry now, caked within the metal grating where he laid. Karim knelt down to touch his cheek, feel the bristle of what had been his attempt at a beard. A twitch came to Karim's lips as he thought back to how the other crew members teased the boy about it growing out in patches. The deck officer had tried so many tricks to get it to grow: brushing it thrice a day, drinking more water than he should, using oils from seedy merchants, and eating a stricter diet.

And it was all for naught.

A sniffle came at Karim's elbow as Issa said, "His sister is a few moons out from the academy. She always said she wanted to serve on a ship with him."

"And now she never will," Karim snarled. He shot up to his feet, sniffing back a reaction he refused to let loose. Taking up the ladder — still slick with shaves of ice water — he started his climb.

On the next level, the carnage was worse. The dead lined the walls, packed against their edges. Surgeon Abadi and a few junior officers helped tend to the injured who could not be readily moved. And just near the brig, where a pool of blood sat thick and wide, Steward Bitar was being attended to by Officer Tahan. As Issa made her own way up through the hatchway at his back, Tahan looked up with red eyes.

"Is it true about Ahmad?" she asked as she rubbed dawa root into Bitar's wrists. She was doing a brilliant job of holding back her tears, professional to the end. "Is he really..."

Karim couldn't bring himself to nod an affirmation. It made it too real.

"Yes," Issa said, answering for him. "He's gone."

The confirmation brought a clenched fist from Karim and he punched the wall nearest him, painting his hand red from the blood spread against it. "This is my fault, all of it!"

In an instant, Issa was at his shoulder. She whispered in his ears, "Come, don't let the crew see you like this." Karim didn't budge. "Please, Karim. Let's go to the navigation room to discuss—"

"What's there to discuss?" he bellowed, but bit back the rest of the tirade he wanted to shout. His voice had drawn the heads of the caretakers and injured both. Issa dragged him away, and he let her. He knew he shouldn't have raised his voice when others were mending. They were stressed enough as it was.

The journey to the navigation room was a blur to him as Issa led him by the wrist. Level after level passed them by, every corner revealing more bodies added to the dead. It was all just blood-spattered walls, and the stink of turning wounds.

Conscious thought didn't return to him until Issa slammed the door to the navigation room and twisted on him with a pointed finger. "What in Ogó'ala's name was that?"

"So many are dead," Karim breathed as his back fell heavy against one of the hung maps. "Do we even know the count? What is it?" He looked up to the ceiling for answers. "Gunner Hadi was first. Then the others on the platform. Deck Officer Ahmad just after that. We couldn't save that junior in the hall. I couldn't even begin to count the dead from the supply hall—"

"Look at those you've *saved*, Karim." Issa stood in front of him, her eyes just as red as Tahan's had been. "Vice Admiral Shamoun. Officer Tahan. Mystic Hajjar and

Damji. Sindisi Abbas. Captain Malouf." Karim scoffed. "Me, Karim. You saved *me*."

Despite those last words, Karim couldn't stop shaking his head. He refused to hear it. "None of that matters, Issa."

"It does. If Malouf was at our head, we'd all be dead or captured now. He never would have even caught that illusion well we were in. Gods, not even I did until you saw through. Think how close we were to the pirate's first kill!"

Karim turned away from her and paced to the far end of the room. But that loathsome, dazzling sunset was waiting to mock him at the window once more. He turned again to see Issa and fumed. He had nowhere to go.

Gritting his teeth, he said, "Had Malouf been at our head, we would have never gone back to Kidogo as I said. He'd have gone straight to al-Anim to gloat."

"Karim…" Issa's voice had a deep sense of tenderness now, like a mother to a child. He hated it. Even as she approached him again, he gave her a sharp look that rooted her to the rug beneath her. "Karim, you thought you could get more information, that you could secure the cove. We *both* thought that pirate was as good as dead. And while I'll admit I didn't like your plan at first, you need to give yourself *some* credit here."

"You don't get it. 'We thought' and 'we could have' won't cut it with the grand admiral, certainly not the emperor or empress. I'm done, Issa. Finished. Forget me being a *captain*. I'll be lucky enough to stay on as a *grunt*. Mark my words here and now. If by some miracle they do keep me on, I will *never* fail like that again."

Issa's eyes seemed on the edge of hurt. Karim must have been piercing her with a look far more severe than he intended, but he meant what he said. He couldn't allow something like this to ever happen again.

A silence hung between them for a long moment with only the slight sway of the ship and the shifting of pens and parchment on the table to fill it. A shadow passed through the room. Karim didn't need to turn to know the sun had dipped below the horizon.

Quietly, gracefully, Issa went to each lantern and filled them with lights, likely a gesture to stave off the unusual awkwardness between them more than anything else.

The room wasn't nearly dark yet.

Once she finished with the last one she turned her chin over her shoulder to look at him. "Maybe that's not so bad."

"What are you talking about?" Karim answered dully, as he plopped into a seat at the table.

"We're no longer required to serve the military. We always said we'd leave once our mandate was filled — "

"Don't start with all that." Karim massaged the center of his forehead while speaking into the table. "Not right now."

"I'm only saying that we can leave whenever we — "

The door burst open. Karim and Issa both had their daggers in hand before realizing the trio at the door was Vice Admiral Shamoun, Sindisi Abbas, and a dark woman Karim assumed was one of the pirates between them.

"Congratulations, *Captain* Karim," Shamoun said, beaming. Karim had never seen him in such bright spirits before.

"Please, sir... I'm the acting captain — chief officer, really."

"I think we can drop the technicalities for now, el-Sayyed," Abbas said. "Look who you've brought in."

The vice admiral and mystguard tossed the pirate down in front of him. The woman whipped her head to him with a positively hateful glare. Two piercings were lodged below her right eye, matted locs came down over her face, and spiraling tattoos snaked around her neck.

"May I introduce to you the most infamous pirate of the Sapphire Seas." Shamoun didn't hide the pride in his voice at all. "Captain Nubia of the Meroé Rovers. Now a prisoner of the Vaaji Empire."

CHAPTER 40
ZALA

ZALA WIPED THE SWEAT FROM HER BROW FOR THE dozenth time that hour. She sat at a bubbling cauldron brimmed with the scent of mazomba scales. It filled her very small room in the Seaborne Inn with a particularly pungent odor.

It had been the last day of three she spent brewing her stonesbane concoction, the worst day of them all. The first two days were bad as well, though less smelly. The issue then wasn't the stench but her poor aptitude for potion making as she awkwardly went along trying her best not to botch the cook, leaving the room a mess.

On the second day she had to cover a burnt piece of floorboard the brew had frothed over onto with a threadbare rug. The moment the rug touched the heated elixir it too burnt and Zala franticly stomped it out before the whole room went up in flames. It took Zala an hour to finally accept the dark mark next to the bottom of the window would never come out.

Ultimately, though, her cook was a relative success. And

377

by her own estimation, the potion—when done—would last at least three days, maybe four.

It was the least she could do for Iokaja.

A knock came at her door and she dashed to answer it. She opened it to Fon, who held a slimy eyeball between her palms, green coloring the aziza's cheeks as she stifled a belch.

"Get in, get in," Zala beckoned her into the room.

"Hey, hey!" an old and shrill voice called out down the hall. "Is that number-four with that smell? You know the chambermaids say it's against the rules to brew potions in here!"

"*Keeba yuh mout, an mind yuh owna, dikala,*" Zala shouted back in Pakwan. She knew the old man was from Imtubo and wouldn't understand her.

"What did you say to me?" She could almost hear his knees cracking as he came down the hall. "Just wait until I get over there. You damn whores and your love potions… every damn time I get a room here!"

Zala slammed the door and turned to Fon. "Don't worry, it'll take him a half-hour before he comes knocking. Thanks for picking this up." She reached out her hand to Fon.

"It's okay, I can do it." Fon strutted to the side table that had served as a prep station for Zala's work. "That old brewmaster told me how."

Fon set the moist eye on the table and moved to cut into it with a knife.

Zala sucked her teeth. "Of course the fool told you to cut it. Give it here." She wiggled her hands for the knife and Fon, red around her pointed ears, gave it up.

"The brewmaster's great and all, but he, like most, doesn't know the first thing about stonesbane." Zala took the flat of her dagger and smashed the tokoloshe eye into a

378

wooden cup. "Cutting it doesn't get nearly enough juices out of the eye. It's the difference between making the potion effective for a few days rather than a few hours. The eye work is the only part I can squeeze so much time out of. To do the rest right you need far more training than I've ever gotten before." She turned to glance over her shoulder at the aziza. "How's your wing healing?"

Fon tried to flutter her right wing, but it only lifted half its usual span. "Well, at least I still have one, right?"

"And Shomari? Brewmaster's taking care of him like I told him to, ya?"

"Oh yes, he's healing fine. Though…" Fon's eyes went downcast.

"What?" Zala asked as she added the juices and the tokoloshe's eye to the frothing cauldron. "What is it?"

"Well… he only teased me twice while we were chatting. His banter's not been up to scratch since… you know."

A lump welled in Zala's throat. She hadn't been able to look anyone in the eye since they had returned to Kidogo, least of all Shomari, who she suspected had never been so close to death's doorstep.

"He'll bounce back," she decided to say, though she wasn't entirely sure of it. Shomari's somber eyes, his curled-back ears, the way he jittered at the tiniest of sounds… she had never expected to see him that way.

"Right, right," Fon mumbled, just as unconvinced. "What do they say about pakka? Nine lives, ya?"

"And that was his first," Zala answered.

With that, Fon perked up. "That's a good one. I'll tell him that next time I see him. That'll cheer him up. Do you mind if we practice it some? I don't want to mess up the delivery."

"It's only one line, Fon," Zala said, smiling back.

"Yeah, I know, I know, but you know I'd fumble something as simple as a Mero-Set greeting."

"Right," Zala said through a giggle. She was amazed she could still do that. It felt wrong that she could, like she shouldn't have been allowed to at all.

From the side, she heard the cauldron sloshing over and some of the potion brewing within spilled out. The liquid hit the floor with a splatter akin to blood, and the sizzling of the cooled-down froth brought with it the images of steaming ice.

And just like that, she was back on the sky ship.

She couldn't help but see the cracks of Iokaja's stone-infested arm, Shomari's body riddled with stab wounds, and all the others who had perished because of her mistake. Her selfishness. Most of all, though, the image that shrouded darkest in her mind were Mantu's eyes.

When the *Redtide* had picked them up, she hadn't even been able to tell the pirate if his lover was alive or dead. In sharing with him her uncertainty, she had expected a strike or tirade, and she would have been deserving of both. Instead, a single tear streamed down the man's cheek and he left her without a word to go about his business on the ship until their return to port.

As though reading her thoughts, Fon asked, "Have you seen Mantu since we got back?"

Zala took a deep breath, and a well of tears she thought had long drained, renewed in her eyes. Her voice hitched as she answered, "Yeah, yesterday afternoon when I traded for the mazomba scales. He's still looking for a crew, but no one is taking him on."

"Did you tell him about the *Redtide* heading back out tomorrow?"

"No." Zala slumped on the bed. She found no comfort in

its stiff foundation of straw. "No, I couldn't talk to him. You saw the way he was when we got back. The man's broken."

Fon sat next to her, resting her four fingers gently against Zala's knee. "I think it's been enough time. And we'll need him if we're really going out to al-Anim. The rovers lost a lot of their best fighters on that sky ship."

"I know, I know," Zala said, almost to herself. Then it all came rushing to her again. The hurts from that wretched day burst all as one in her chest. Fon took her in an embrace, quelling the shakes.

"It's all my fault, Fon."

"Don't say that."

"It is. What in the hells was I thinking going off like that, putting you all in danger? Your wing, Sniffs, Shomari. How can any of you forgive me when I failed you?"

Fon let Zala cry for a moment, and then for several more. Even the potion seemed to calm in the wake of her outpour of grief and heartache.

"And that's not the worst of it," Zala said after her last tear. She picked up the ladle resting at the cauldron's edge and stirred to stop her trembling hand.

"Part of me thinks I made the wrong decision in the end, that I should have gone after Jelani even though—" Her voice caught in her throat again. "Does that make me a bad person? How can I be a good wife when I turned away from him? How can I be a good friend, and then turn away from you?"

"The Gods put us through these trials," Fon breathed lightly. "I don't know why. And I can't imagine being in the position that you were. You have my heart for that, you hear me?" She took Zala's face in her hands. "You hear me?"

Zala nodded through a frown and Fon took her into

another hug. The aziza's skin was so warm, impossibly warm, like the sun's own rays rested beneath her skin.

"Come on, I want to show you something," Fon said, guiding Zala to the small slit of a window at the room's side. "Look just there."

The aziza pointed up to the moons in the sky, though they were smudged by the pane in need of a wash. Each moon was nearly full, peeking through the clouds. "Just as Yem and Àyá's moons go through their cycles, so too do we. Zee, you didn't come this far just to stop now. New beginnings mean new chances. As her friend, all I can ask of Zala is for her to be better than she was yesterday. If she can promise me that, that's all that matters to me. And she was already pretty good these last few days." Fon nodded to the brew bubbling softly behind them. She smiled softly at Zala from the reflection in the window pane.

Zala didn't turn back to her friend, still gazing up at the moons that were indeed cresting the edge of a new cycle, as she was on the crest of her own. Could she do it, she asked herself. Could she set the wrong right? Deep within her a voice told her that she could not, but another — Fon's voice — told her otherwise. And like the sun's warmth trapped within the aziza's tiny frame, like everything she touched, Zala felt the words fill her, felt them fight off the ice threatening to envelop her heart.

Wiping her face free of tears, she settled her breath back to a steady pace. Then she turned to Fon to look within those hazel orbs with all truth in her next words. "Thank you, Fon. Under the light of Yemàyá, I promise you."

A smile creased the aziza's mouth. "Good, I'll hold you to it. Now, get ready. We set out for al-Anim at dawn."

Zala, Karim, & Jelani

A NOTE FROM THE AUTHOR

Thank you for reading my sophomore novel.

Originally, I outlined and wrote the story as a duology between Zala and Karim. But when I started drafting it, it was apparent that their stories were far too connected to divide them into two separate stories.

And *then* I realized their large tale couldn't be told succinctly in one book, so I decided to give their story more breathing room in an entire trilogy. In fact, many of Nubia's crew (Ekko, Marjani, and Iokaja) were late additions that I'm delighted are in the story and part of this world now.

I hope you enjoyed the story. I initially wanted to finish it within six months, but, in the end, it took two years and it was well worth the wait (at least for me).

If you enjoyed *By Sea & Sky*, please leave a review on your favorite retailer or social media (and don't forget to tag me).

THE CHRONICLES CONTINUE

A pirate crew in shambles. A military officer on the rise.
And a city of ruin and silk.

Zala wants nothing more than to free Jelani from the clutches of the empire. But Karim must extract information from her husband at all cost.

If either of them fails, it would be the end of them — Zala's life bond, and Karim's military career.

But little do either of them know… there's another plot brewing behind their backs.

And it involves a certain airship.

Delve into this pirate fantasy inspired by the West Indies, The Swahili Coast, and Arabia, where Zala and Karim will face off against callous marauders and loathsome imperials.

Visit antoinebandele.com to learn more about this story.

ALSO BY ANTOINE BANDELE

AN ESOWON STORY

The Man With No Name

The Kishi

Demons, Monks, and Lovers

Stoneskin

By Sea & Sky

TJ YOUNG & THE ORISHAS

The Gatekeeper's Staff

CHRONICLES OF UNDERREALM

The Legend of Cabrus

ABOUT THE AUTHOR

Antoine lives in Los Angeles, CA with his girlfriend.
He is a YouTuber, producing work for his own channel and
others, such as JustKiddingFilms, Fanalysis, and more.
Whenever he has the time, he's writing books inspired by
African folklore, mythology, and history.

antoinebandele.com

GLOSSARY

Terms and Locations from Esowon

- **A'bara:** The word for "magic" in the Old Tongue.
- **Ajowan:** The southern most island of the Sapphire Isles.
- **Akeem:** One of the Great Cities which holds one of the most sacred religious sites.
- **Aktah:** One of the Great Nations, just north of Ya-Seti. Known for its ancient history and large pyramids.
- **al-Anim:** The capital of Vaaj.
- **al-Qiba:** The monotheistic religion of Vaaj. It holds Shati'ala, the Goddess of Free Will and Magic, as its Supreme One.
- **Andala:** One of the Great Nations north of the Midland Seas.
- **Asiya Bay:** The inlet sea between the borders of Aktah to the west, and Vaaj to the east.
- **Awassa:** A small coastal city in Jultia.

- **Àyá:** The Goddess of the Rivers and the Little Moon.
- **Aziza:** A fae species originating from the jungles of Kunda, though many half-breed offspring can be found throughout Esowon.
- **Chana:** Slang used for female pirates of the Sapphire Isles.
- **Dawa:** A common root used as an all-purpose healing salve and poultice.
- **Dawaf:** A forest city of Jultia.
- **Deh'ala:** The God of Gates and Thresholds.
- **Dikala:** An insulting word used mostly among the peoples of the Sapphire Isles and the Esterlands.
- **Golah:** The former empire which stretched from Bajok in the south to Imtubo in the north.
- **Golden Lord:** The ruler of the Pirate Nation of the Sapphire Isles.
- **Grootslang:** A creature known colloquially as an elephant snake residing in large caves near the Fog Lands, though scholars have spotted them within Kunda Jungle as well.
- **Ibabi Isles:** A collection of uninhabited islands north of the Sapphire Isles and south of Asiya Bay.
- **Illopa:** The Goddess of Love.
- **Impundulu:** One mystical bird native to the Fog Lands at the southern tip of Esowon. Their wings and talons are said to summon thunder and lightning which make the Fog Lands uninhabitable. Legend states these creatures were the direct creation of the God of Lightning and Storms, M'Bani.

- **Imtubo:** One of the Great Cities which holds three of the most prestigious academies in literature and arts, science and mathematics, and theology.
- **Injera:** A spongy flatbread from Jultia which serves as a replacement to utensils. It is foundational to all Jultian meals.
- **Janbiya:** A curved dagger used by the people of Vaaj, both military officers and common folk.
- **Jo'bara:** The Old Way. An old religion that gives praise to all the old gods without putting any one above another.
- **Julti:** The language and tongue of Jultia.
- **Jultia:** One of the Great Nations, just south of Ya-Seti. Known for its unique religious fervor and sweeping palaces. Some claim it to be a pioneer of Esowon's future infrastructure.
- **Jultia Accords:** The treaty to end the Red Dunes War. Brokered by Jultia, a neutral nation between the fighting Aktahrian and Ya-Seti Nations at the time. Though the treaty was drafted specifically for those two nations, its terms of peace and war conduct extended to the entire Esowon Esterlands.
- **Khopesh:** The military capital of Aktah. Also the favored sidearm weapon of the Aktahrian military.
- **Kidogo:** The northern most island of the Sapphire Isles.
- **Kijana:** Slang used for male pirates of the Sapphire Isles.
- **Kongamato:** A flying creature with leathery skin, bat-like wings, and beak filled with razor-sharp

teeth. Also known as a "boat-breaker" among the
river people near Kunda Jungle.

- **Kor:** The primary ruler of Ya-Set.
- **Kor'de:** Spouse to the ruler of Ya-Set.
- **Kubahari:** A giant sea creature of legend. One of
  the most ancient beings of Esowon noted for
  their large and magical twin-horns.
- **Kunda:** The largest unbroken rainforest in the
  world. Home to many of the ancient creatures
  and mystical beasts of the Old Times.
- **Mazomba:** A giant fish of mystery whose scales
  can often be found near the Ibabi Isles.
- **Mero-Set:** The language and tongue of Ya-Set. It
  is unique in that its formal speech and dialect is
  paired with many hand gestures.
- **Nene Kato:** A small fishing village on the
  northern coast of Ya-Set.
- **Ogó'ala:** The Supreme God. Also known as the
  King God.
- **Oni'baro:** Religious devotees and leaders of the
  old spirit-religion, Jo'bara.
- **Pakka:** Cat-men from the forests of Daji and the
  jungle of Kunda, though their kind can be found
  all throughout Esowon.
- **Pakwan:** The language and tongue of the
  Southern Sapphire Isles.
- **Pyrus:** The commercial capital of Aktah.
- **Sapphire Isles:** Seven Islands that cut between
  the nations of Aktah, Ya-Seti, Jultia, to the west,
  and Vaaj, to the east.
- **Shati'ala:** The Goddess of Free Will and Magic.
- **Sindisi:** The military title given to the

mystguards of Vaaj. They are tasked with the protection of the nation's active-combat mystics.

- **Sonamancer:** A mystic who can manipulate and alter sound waves.
- **Tarha:** A tight headwrap typically worn by Vaaji females.
- **Tokoloshe:** A gremlin creature from the swamps of the Kunda Jungles and its outskirts. Child-size bodies, gauged eyes, and a hole in their heads. Though originating from Kunda, these mischievous bunch of creatures can often be found wreaking havoc on local villages.
- **Ugara:** The God of War.
- **Ula:** The Goddess of the Cosmos and Foretelling.
- **Wageni:** A non-human.
- **Ya-Set:** One of the Great Nations. Known for their skilled archers and lavish palaces.
- **Yem:** The Goddess of the Oceans and the Big Moon.
- **Yemàyá:** The Twin Goddesses of the Oceans, Rivers, and Moons. Also an expression used at the turn of the new moons.
- **Vaaj:** One of the Great Nations, just east of the Sapphire Isles.
- **Zanziwala:** Also knows as the "Big Isle." This island is the central location of the Sapphire Isles and the hub of all commercial activity in the Sapphire Seas. Home to the golden lord and his wealthy merchant court.
- **Zothina:** The Goddess of Modesty.
- **Zizah'r:** The native language and tongue of the aziza.

Printed in Great Britain
by Amazon